THE PROGRAM

THE PROGRAM

SUZANNE YOUNG

SIMON PULSE
New York London Toronto Sydney New Delhi

SIMON PULSE

An imprint of Simon & Schuster Children's Publishing Division

1230 Avenue of the Americas, New York, NY 10020

First Simon Pulse hardcover edition April 2013

Copyright © 2013 by Suzanne Young

Case photograph of couple copyright © 2013 by Michael Frost

Case background photographs copyright © by Thinkstock

All rights reserved, including the right of reproduction in whole or in part in any form.

SIMON PULSE and colophon are registered trademarks of Simon & Schuster, Inc.

For information about special discounts for bulk purchases,

please contact Simon & Schuster Special Sales at

1-866-506-1949 or business@simonandschuster.com.

The Simon & Schuster Speakers Bureau can bring authors to your

live event. For more information or to book an event contact

the Simon & Schuster Speakers Bureau at 1-866-248-3049 or visit

our website at www.simonspeakers.com.

Designed by Mike Rosamilia

The text of this book was set in Adobe Garamond Pro.

Manufactured in the United States of America

2 4 6 8 10 9 7 5 3 1

Library of Congress Cataloging-in-Publication Data

Young, Suzanne.

The Program / by Suzanne Young. — 1st Simon Pulse hardcover ed.

p. cm.

Summary: When suicide becomes a worldwide epidemic, the only known cure

is The Program, a treatment in which painful memories are erased,

a fate worse than death to seventeen-year-old Sloane, who knows that

The Program will steal memories of her dead brother and boyfriend.

ISBN 978-1-4424-4580-2 (alk. paper)

[1. Suicide—Fiction. 2. Brainwashing—Fiction. 3. Memory—Fiction.

4. Love—Fiction. 5. Science fiction.] I. Title.

PZ7.Y887Pr 2013   [Fic]—dc23   2012004197

ISBN 978-1-4424-4582-6 (eBook)

For Lynny and Rich,
who have always been there for me

And in loving memory of my grandmother
Josephine Parzych

THE PROGRAM

PART I
UNCOMFORTABLY NUMB

CHAPTER ONE

THE AIR IN THE ROOM TASTES STERILE. THE LINGERING scent of bleach is mixing with the fresh white paint on the walls, and I wish my teacher would open the window to let in a breeze. But we're on the third floor so the pane is sealed shut—just in case anyone gets the urge to jump.

I'm still staring at the paper on my desk when Kendra Phillips turns around in her seat, looking me over with her purple contacts. "You're not done yet?"

I glance past her to make sure Mrs. Portman is distracted at the front of the room, and then I smile. "It's far too early in the morning to properly psychoanalyze myself," I whisper. "I'd almost rather learn about science."

"Maybe a coffee spiked with QuikDeath would help you focus on the pain."

My expression falters; just the mention of the poison enough to send my heart racing. I hold Kendra's empty stare—a deadness behind it that even purple contacts can't disguise. Her eyes are ringed with heavy circles from lack of sleep, and her face has thinned sharply. She's exactly the kind of person who can get me in trouble, and yet I can't look away.

I've known Kendra for years, but we're not really friends, especially now. Not when she's been acting depressed for close to a month. I try to avoid her, but today there's something desperate about her that I can't ignore. Something about the way her body seems to tremble even though she's sitting still.

"God, don't look so serious," she says, lifting one bony shoulder. "I'm just kidding, Sloane. Oh, and hey," she adds as if just remembering the real reason she turned to me in the first place. "Guess who I saw last night at the Wellness Center? Lacey Klamath."

She leans forward as she tells me, but I'm struck silent. I had no idea that Lacey was back.

Just then the door opens with a loud click. I glance toward the front of the classroom and freeze, my breath catching in my throat. The day has just become significantly worse.

Two handlers with crisp white jackets and comb-smoothed hair stand in the doorway, their expressionless faces traveling over us as they seek someone out. When they start forward, I begin to wilt.

Kendra spins around in her seat, her back rigid and straight.

SUZANNE YOUNG

"Not me," she murmurs, her hands clasped tightly in front of her like she's praying. "Please, not me."

From her podium, Mrs. Portman begins her lesson as if there's no interruption. As if people in white coats *should* be waltzing in during her speech on the kinetic theory of matter. It's the second time the handlers have interrupted class this week.

The men separate to opposite sides of the classroom, their shoes tapping on the linoleum floor as they come closer. I look away, opting to watch the leaves fall from the trees outside the window instead. It's October, but the summer has bled into fall, bathing us all in unexpected Oregon sunshine. I wish I could be anywhere else right now.

The footsteps stop, but I don't acknowledge them. I can smell the handlers near me—antiseptic, like rubbing alcohol and Band-Aids. I don't dare move.

"Kendra Phillips," a voice says gently. "Can you please come with us?"

I hold back the sound that's trying to escape from behind my lips, a combination of relief and sympathy. I refuse to look at Kendra, terrified that the handlers will notice me. *Please don't notice me.*

"No," Kendra says to them, her voice choked off. "I'm not sick."

"Ms. Phillips," the voice says again, and this time I have to look. The dark-haired handler leans to take Kendra by the elbow, guiding her from the chair. Kendra immediately lashes out, yanking her arm from his grasp as she tries to clamor over her desk.

Both men descend on her as Kendra thrashes and screams. She's barely five feet, but she's fighting hard—harder than the others. I feel the tension rolling off the rest of the class, all of us hoping for a quick resolution. Hoping that we'll make it another day without getting flagged.

"I'm not sick!" Kendra yells, breaking from their hold once again.

Mrs. Portman finally stops her lesson as she looks on with a pained expression. The calm she tries to exude is fraying at the edges. Next to me a girl starts crying and I want to tell her to shut up, but I don't want to attract attention. She'll have to fend for herself.

The dark-haired handler wraps his arms around Kendra's waist, lifting her off the floor as she kicks her legs out. A string of obscenities tears from her mouth as saliva leaks from the corners. Her face is red and wild, and all at once I think she's sicker than we ever imagined. That the real Kendra is no longer in there, and maybe hasn't been since her sister died.

My eyes well up at the thought, but I push it down. Down deep where I can keep all my feelings until later when there's no one watching me.

The handler puts his palm over Kendra's mouth, muffling her sounds as he whispers soothing things into her ear, continuing to work her bucking body toward the door. The other handler dashes ahead to hold it open.

Just then the man holding Kendra screams out and drops her, shaking his hand as if she bit him. Kendra jumps up to run and the handler lunges for her, his closed fist connecting with her face. The shot sends her into Mrs. Portman's podium before knocking her to the ground. The teacher gasps as Kendra flops in front of her, but Mrs. Portman only backs away.

Kendra's top lip is split wide open and leaking blood all over her gray sweater and the white floor. She barely has time to process what happened when the handler grabs her by the ankle and begins to drag her—caveman style—toward the exit. Kendra screams and begs. She tries to hold on to anything within her reach, but instead she's leaving a trail of blood along the floor.

When they finally get to the doorway, she raises her purple eyes in my direction, reaching out a reddened hand to me. "Sloane!" she screams. And I stop breathing.

The handler pauses, glancing over his shoulder at me. I've never seen him here before today, but something about the way he's watching me now makes my skin crawl, and I look down.

I don't lift my head again until I hear the door shut. Kendra's shouts are promptly cut off in the hallway, and I wonder momentarily if she was Tasered or injected with a sedative. Either way, I'm glad it's over.

Around the room, there are several sniffles, but it's mostly silent. Blood still covers the front of the room in streaks of crimson.

"Sloane?" the teacher asks, startling me. "I haven't gotten

your daily assessment yet." Mrs. Portman starts toward the closet where she keeps the bucket and mop, and other than the high lilt of her voice, she has no noticeable reaction to Kendra being dragged from our class.

I swallow hard and apologize, moving to take my pencil from my backpack. As my teacher sloshes the bleach on the floor, choking us with the smell once again, I begin to shade in the appropriate ovals.

In the past day have you felt lonely or overwhelmed?

I stare down at the bright white paper, the same one that waits at our desk every morning. I want to crumple it into a ball and throw it across the room, scream for people to acknowledge what just happened to Kendra. Instead I take a deep breath and answer.

NO.

This isn't true—we all feel lonely and overwhelmed. Sometimes I'm not sure there's another way to feel. But I know the routine. I know what a wrong answer can do. Next question.

I fill in the rest of the ovals, pausing when I get to the last one, just like I do every time. *Has anyone close to you ever committed suicide?*

YES.

Marking that answer day after day nearly destroys me. But it's the one question where I have to tell the truth. Because they already know the answer.

After signing my name at the bottom, I grab my paper with a shaky hand and walk up to Mrs. Portman's desk, standing in the wet area where Kendra's blood used to be. I try not to look down as I wait for my teacher to put away the cleaning products.

"Sorry," I tell her again when she comes to take the sheet from me. I notice a small smudge of blood on her pale pink shirtsleeve, but don't mention it.

She looks over my answers, and then nods, filing the paper in the attendance folder. I hurry back to my seat, listening to the tense silence. I wait for the sound of the door, the approaching footsteps. But after a long minute, my teacher clears her throat and goes back to her lesson on friction. Relieved, I close my eyes.

Teen suicide was declared a national epidemic—killing one in three teens—nearly four years ago. It always existed before that, but seemingly overnight handfuls of my peers were jumping off buildings, slitting their wrists—most without any known reason. Strangely enough, the rate of incidence among adults stayed about the same, adding to the mystery.

When the deaths first started increasing, there were all sorts of rumors. From defective childhood vaccines to pesticides in our food—people grasped for any excuse. The leading view says that the oversupply of antidepressants changed the chemical makeup of our generation, making us more susceptible to depression.

I don't know what I believe anymore, and really, I try not to think about it. But the psychologists say that suicide is a *behavioral contagion*. It's the old adage "If all your friends jumped off a bridge, would you, too?" Apparently the answer is yes.

To fight the outbreak, our school district implemented the pilot run of The Program—a new philosophy in prevention. Among the five schools, students are monitored for changes in mood or behavior, flagged if a threat is determined. Anyone exhibiting suicidal tendencies is no longer referred to a psychologist. Instead, the handlers are called.

And then they come and take you.

Kendra Phillips will be gone for at least six weeks—six weeks spent in a facility where The Program will mess with her mind, take her memories. She'll be force-fed pills and therapy until she doesn't even know who she is anymore. After that they'll ship her off to a small private school until graduation. A school designated for other returners, other empty souls.

Like Lacey.

My phone vibrates in my pocket and I let out a held breath. I don't have to check to know what it means—James wants to meet. It's the push I need to get through the rest of the period, the fact that he's waiting for me. The fact that he's *always* waiting for me.

As we file out of the classroom forty minutes later, I notice the dark-haired handler in the hallway, watching us. He seems to take extra time on me, but I try hard not to notice. Instead I keep my head down and walk quickly toward the gymnasium to find James.

I check over my shoulder to make sure no one is following me before turning down the stark white corridor with the metal double doors. It's nearly impossible to trust anyone not to report you for suspicious behavior. Not even our parents—especially not our parents.

It was Lacey's father who called The Program to tell them that she was unwell. So now James, Miller, and I do everything we can to keep up the front at home. Smiles and small talk equal well-balanced and healthy. I wouldn't dare show my parents anything else. Not now.

But once I turn eighteen, The Program loses its hold on me. I won't be a minor so they can no longer force me into treatment. Although my risk doesn't technically lower, The Program is bound to the laws of the land. I'll be an adult, and as an adult it's my God-given right to off myself if I so please.

Unless the epidemic gets worse. Then who knows what they'll do.

When I get to the gymnasium doors, I push on the cold metal bar and slip inside. It's been years since this part of the building was used. The Program cut athletics immediately after taking over, claiming it added too much competitive stress to our fragile student population. Now this space is used for storage—unused desks piled in the corner, stacks of unneeded textbooks.

"Anyone see you?"

I jump and look at James as he stands in the cramped space underneath the folded bleachers. Our space. The emotionless armor I've been wearing weakens.

"No," I whisper. James holds out his hand to me and I meet

him in the shadows, pressing myself close to him. "It's not a good day," I murmur against his mouth.

"It rarely is."

James and I have been together for over two years—since I was fifteen. But I've known him my entire life. He'd been best friends with my brother, Brady, before he killed himself.

I choke on the memory, like I'm drowning in it. I pull from James and bang the back of my head on the corner of the wooden bleacher above us. Wincing, I touch my scalp, but don't cry. I wouldn't dare cry at school.

"Let me see," James says, reaching to rub his fingers over the spot. "You were probably protected by all this hair." He grins and lets his hand glide into my dark curls, resting it protectively on the back of my neck. When I don't return his smile, he pulls me closer. "Come here," he whispers, sounding exhausted as he puts his arms around me.

I hug him, letting the images of Brady fade from my head, along with the picture of Lacey being dragged from her house by handlers. I slide my hand under the sleeve of James's T-shirt and onto his bicep where his tattoos are.

The Program makes us anonymous, strips us of our right to mourn—because if we do, we can get flagged for appearing depressed. So James has found another way. On his right arm he's keeping a list in permanent ink of those we've lost. Starting with Brady.

"I'm having bad thoughts," I tell him.

"Then stop thinking," he says simply.

SUZANNE YOUNG

"They took Kendra last period. It was horrible. And Lacey—"

"Stop thinking," James says again, a little more forcefully.

I look up at him, the heaviness still in my chest as I meet his eyes. It's hard to tell in the shadows, but James's eyes are light blue, the sort of crystal blue that can make anyone stop with just a glance. He's stunning that way.

"Kiss me instead," he murmurs. I lean forward to press my lips to his, letting him have me in a way that only he can. A moment filled with sadness and hope. A bond of secrets and promises of forever.

It's been two years since my brother died. Practically overnight, our lives were changed. We don't know why Brady killed himself, why he abandoned us. But then again, no one knows what's causing the epidemic—not even The Program.

Above us the bell for class rings, but neither James nor I react. Instead James's tongue touches mine and he pulls me closer, deepening our kiss. Although dating is allowed, we try to keep our relationship low-key at school, at least when we can. The Program claims that forming healthy bonds keeps us emotionally strong, but then again, if it all goes horribly wrong, they can just make us forget. The Program can erase anything.

"I swiped my dad's car keys," James whispers between my lips. "What do you say we go skinny-dipping in the river after school?"

"How about you get naked and I'll just watch?"

"Works for me."

I laugh, and James gives me one more squeeze before taking his arms from around me. He pretends to fix my hair, really just messing it up more. "Better get to class," he says finally. "And tell Miller he's invited to watch me swim naked too."

I back away, first kissing my fingers and then holding them up in a wave. James smiles.

He always knows what to say to me. How to make me feel normal. I'm pretty sure I wouldn't have survived Brady's death without him. If fact, I know I wouldn't have.

After all, suicide is contagious.

CHAPTER TWO

WHEN I WALK INTO ECONOMICS, I TELL MY TEACHER that therapy ran late, taking out one of the fake passes that me, James, and Miller made weeks ago. Since The Program started monitoring our school, I've found that my boyfriend is not only a talented liar but also a master of forgery. A handy skill to have as of late.

Mr. Rocco only glances at the pass before motioning me toward the back. It's the fifth time I've been late this month, but luckily no one ever questions me. I've learned how to appear well. And in their eyes, talking to a professional is a sign that I'm trying to stay healthy.

"Hey, gorgeous," Miller says when I sit down. "You and James have a good *therapy* session?" He's sitting in the desk next to mine, staring into his lap as the teacher turns to write on the dry-erase board.

Miller and I have been friends since the beginning of last year, sharing most of our classes together. He's tall and wide, and I imagine if our high school had a football team, he'd be their star athlete.

"Yep," I respond. "Think we really had a breakthrough this time."

"I bet."

He smiles but doesn't look over. Instead he continues to doodle in a notepad that he's got stashed under the desk. My heart thuds in my chest at what I have to say next.

"Lacey's back," I say quietly.

Miller scratches his pen harder into the paper. "Where'd you hear that?" I try not to react as the color drains from his face.

"Kendra Phillips told me before they came and . . ." I lower my voice. *"Took her."*

Miller finally looks sideways at me, obviously hearing about Kendra for the first time. His brown eyes narrow, maybe deciding if he truly believes that Lacey could be home. But then he just nods and goes back to his notepad. Never saying a word.

His silence nearly breaks me, and I spread my fingers out on the cool desktop, trying to keep my emotions in check. I stare down at my fingers, at the plastic heart-shaped ring there. James had given it to me the first time he kissed me—a few months before my brother died. Lacey and Miller always joked

SUZANNE YOUNG

that this ring was the closest I'd ever come to getting a real diamond from him. Then James would laugh, saying that he knew what I *really* wanted and it didn't sparkle.

It was a different time then—a time when we all thought we'd make it. I close my eyes to keep from crying.

"I think . . ." Miller pauses, like he's not sure he wants to say it. When I turn to him he bites on his lip. "I think I'm going to go to Sumpter to see her."

"Miller—" I start, but he waves me away.

"I have to know if she remembers me, Sloane. I won't be able to think of anything else until I know."

I watch him for a long moment, see the pain behind his eyes. There's nothing I can say that will change his mind. Not when he loves her so much. "Be careful" is all I can utter.

"I will."

My fear is strong enough to choke me. I worry that Miller will get caught at the alternative school and be flagged in the process. We're expected to keep our distance from the returners unless the time is monitored at the Wellness Center, at least for a while. If we're caught interfering with their recovery, we can get flagged or even arrested. And none of us wants to be sent away to become comfortably numb.

Miller is quiet through the rest of class, but when the bell rings, he gives me a nod. It might be dangerous for him to approach Lacey at this point, but if she was herself she'd want him to try. "See you at lunch," he says, touching my shoulder before walking toward the door.

"See you then," I respond, and quickly pull out my phone. I text James. MILLER'S GOT A STUPID PLAN.

I wait, still in my seat as the classroom filters out around me. When a message pops up on the screen, I feel my chest tighten.

SO DO I.

PLEASE DON'T, I type. I'm terrified that my boyfriend and my best friend will get flagged, and I'll be left all alone in this barren place. This barren world.

But all I get back is: I LOVE YOU, SLOANE.

James and I watch as Miller waits in the lunch line, his movements slow and lethargic. He hasn't been the same since I told him about Lacey, and I hate myself for it. I should have let James break the news.

At the start of lunch, James and Miller decide that after classes we'll go to Sumpter High—the school for returners—and wait for Lacey to walk out. There's no way Miller would get more than a few words in at the Wellness Center, not when handlers will be guarding Lacey for three more weeks. Miller is hoping that, in the parking lot of Sumpter (with the proper diversion), he can get Lacey alone long enough to remind her of who he is. He thinks he can get her back.

James is next to me with his head on his folded arms as they rest on the lunch table. He's trying to look casual, but his eyes are trained on Miller. "At Sumpter, you and I are going to create a distraction," James says in my direction.

"And if it doesn't work?"

His mouth turns up, his eyes flicking from the line to mine. "I can be distracting, don't you think?"

"James, I miss her too. But I don't want anything to—"

He reaches out his hand to clasp mine. "I know the risk, but what if she's still in there somehow? Miller has to try, Sloane. I would do it for you."

"And I would for you," I answer automatically. But James's face clouds over.

"Don't say that," he snaps. "Don't even think it." He lets go of my hand. "I'll kill myself before they ever take me into The Program."

Tears burn my eyes because I know it's not an idle threat. It's a real possibility. James doesn't try to console me this time, there's no point. He can't promise me he won't kill himself. No one can.

Six weeks ago, after they took Lacey, I had to fight hard to keep from slipping into the depression that seems to be always waiting. The depression that tells me I'll never make it. That it'd be easier to just let go. James convinced me and Miller that Lacey was gone forever, as if she was dead, and told us to mourn—privately. But now she's back and I'm not sure how to feel anymore.

James doesn't speak again until Miller drops down in the seat, the food on his tray jumping as he does. The room around us buzzes, but it's quieter than usual. Word of Kendra's *transfer* has put everyone on edge.

I notice the dark-haired handler standing by the exit door, not trying to disguise how he's watching me. I lower my eyes to my half-eaten hamburger. Kendra called to me as she was being dragged out. She made him notice me. I can't tell James.

Just then James rests his chin on my shoulder as his fingers touch mine. "I'm sorry," he murmurs. "I'm a dick, and I'm sorry."

I look sideways at him, his blond hair curling at the ends near his neck, his blue eyes wide as he stares at me. "I don't want anything to happen to you," I say quietly, hoping Miller won't hear me and think of Lacey.

James moves to put his arms around my waist to turn me toward him before pressing his forehead to mine, ignoring the fact that everyone can see us. His breath is warm across my lips. "I don't want anything to happen to me either. But I'll keep us safe."

I close my eyes, letting the heat of his body compensate for the cold fear in my chest. "Promise?"

It takes him so long to answer that I give up and let in the dark thoughts once again. The idea that James can be ripped from me at any moment, or that I can get sent away to be changed forever.

But suddenly James buries his face in my hair as he hugs me to him. I stop worrying about the people around us, or even about Miller. I need to hear it. James knows I need to hear it. So then to my absolute relief his mouth is next to my ear and he whispers, "I promise."

*   *   *

Sumpter High looms in front of us, looking more like a hospital that an educational facility. The stone facade is washed in white and the large rectangular windows are most certainly sealed. There's a circular drop-off area near the front, but Miller and I are sitting in the cab of his truck in the back parking lot, staring ahead in silence.

James plans to meet us here after he puts in an appearance at his last class, but Miller and I had study hall, so we took off early with one of the fake passes. There are only ten more minutes until Sumpter lets out, and the anxiety at seeing Lacey again is growing, both in me and in Miller. I turn to look sideways at him.

Miller's hat is pulled low, shading his eyes. Even though the ignition is off, his knuckles are white as they wrap around the steering wheel. All at once I'm scared of what he'll do and how he'll keep it under control. We shouldn't be here.

"Is there even a real plan?" I ask. "James wouldn't tell me anything."

Miller doesn't seem to hear me as he gazes out the windshield. "Did you know that Lacey was a natural blond?" he asks, sounding far away. "She always had that red dye in her hair and I figured it was brown underneath, but it wasn't. I saw it in an old picture of her once. I'm a jerk for not knowing, right? I should have known."

I've been friends with Lacey since elementary school, so I can remember when she had yellow pigtails. It's such a small thing for Miller to feel bad about, but I can tell that he does. As if knowing this detail could have saved her from The Program.

"She loved you," I whisper, even though it's almost cruel to say now. "It was all real."

Miller smiles to himself, but it's pained. "If you can't remember, it didn't happen. And since she won't . . ." He trails off, staring once again at the large building.

I think about the Lacey we knew before she was taken. Her bright, bloodred hair and black, tight dresses. She was a force of nature. She was a presence. Leading up to The Program she'd been acting differently, and yet, none of us said anything about it—maybe hoping it would go away. We all failed her.

The handlers had been waiting at Lacey's house the night they came to take her to The Program. We were dropping her off, and I can still remember James joking about the unfamiliar car in her driveway, saying that it was pretty late for her parents to have friends over—maybe they were swingers. Lacey smiled but didn't laugh. I just thought she was tired. I should have asked if she was okay.

But I didn't. She gave Miller a quick kiss and climbed out, walking to her house. She'd barely gotten inside when we heard her scream. We all rushed to get out of the car, when her front door opened.

It's a sight I'll never get out of my head. On either side of her were the men in white coats holding her as she thrashed around, screaming that she'd kill them. She managed to get loose and tried crawling back into the house, calling for her mother as the handlers dragged her out. Tears streaked mascara down her cheeks, and she begged for them to let her go.

Miller started toward the house, but James grabbed him, wrapping his arm around his neck to hold him. "It's too late," James whispered. I looked back at him fiercely then, but I saw the devastation on his face. The fear. James met my eyes only to tell me to get in the car.

James pushed Miller and me into the backseat and then got behind the wheel, pulling away quickly. Miller was clutching my shirt, ripping it at the collar as we drove past. And the last thing we saw was Lacey getting Tasered by a handler, flopping to the floor like a dying fish.

I reach now for Miller, trying to pry his fingers off the steering wheel. When I finally do, he turns to me. "Do you think there's a chance, Sloane?" he asks almost desperately. "Do you think there's any chance she remembers me?"

The question chokes me, and I press my lips together to keep myself from crying. There is no chance—The Program is thorough. The Program works. But I can't bear to tell him that, so I shrug. "You never know," I say, fighting the feeling of loss. "And if not, you can always reintroduce yourself when her aftercare is over. Start again."

Once she's healed, Lacey's allowed to carry on with her life without interference—at least that's what The Program brochures have told us. But I've never seen a returner go back to their old life. Or even want to. Whole sections of their lives have been erased; past relationships mean nothing to them. In fact, I think the past might even scare them.

Miller sneers at the thought of this new Lacey, the hollowed-out one. He wants her to remember him, what they built together. Both Miller and James think The Program is a fate worse than death.

Lacey had thought the same. The reason her own parents turned her in was that they found a bottle of QuikDeath in her room. She'd been planning to kill herself and had bought the drug from some burnout after school. Miller hated himself for not knowing. James and I often wondered if he would have killed himself with her.

When Lacey was sent away, Miller broke into her bedroom because he knew he'd be erased from her life—that we all would be. But when he got there, her pictures were gone, and so was her clothing and personal items. The Program had wiped the space clean. All Miller had was a notepad that Lacey had left behind in his truck. He kept it, hoping it held some small piece of her.

We sat by the river one afternoon and looked through Lacey's handwriting, laughing where she drew pictures of our teachers in the margins. But soon, the notepad changed. The math problems dissolved into black spirals scratched into the paper with pen. Her mind was infected, and it was apparent through the pages how quickly the depression had taken hold. It'd only been about two weeks.

I hate The Program and what it does to us, but I also know

that I don't want to die. I don't want any of us to. Despite everything, our school district has the highest survival rate in the country. So in some sick and twisted way . . . I guess The Program works. Even if the result is a life half lived.

James pulls up beside my window in his father's beat-up Honda. He smiles when he sees me, but it's too wide, too normal. He nods at Miller.

"Your boyfriend looks worried," Miller mumbles as we watch James pull ahead to park. "That's never a good sign. James never worries about anything."

I don't answer because I know it's not true. But I'm the only one who gets to see that side of James. Otherwise he's our rock. Our steady.

Miller opens the door and climbs out, leaving me sitting for a moment in the warming sun that's filtering through the windshield. Outside, a bell rings, signaling the end of the returners' day, and I swallow hard.

I open the passenger door and walk toward where James and Miller are talking, and I glance over my shoulder at the school as a few students and handlers begin making their way to the parking lot. Sumpter is small, with about two hundred students altogether. But that number grows every week, with five schools filtering kids through The Program. And since doctors claim a fresh returner's brain is like Swiss cheese, with holes where memories used to be, patients need continued aftercare in a safe environment. Now returners stay here until graduation, which makes me doubt their "life without interference" claim.

Back when the treatments first started, returners were sent into the general population to start over. But after they started having meltdowns—like total brain-function-drooling-on-themselves meltdowns from the overstimulation—they opened Sumpter and assigned them a temporary babysitter with a white coat and a Taser.

Even so, handlers aren't the only thing to fear. Fresh returners are a threat in themselves. In their confusion, they might inadvertently turn you in for harassing them, getting you sent away. So no one goes near them.

At least, not until now.

The minute I reach the guys, James smiles at me reassuringly. It's time. Miller lowers his baseball cap and puts his phone to his ear as he wanders away, pretending to talk. My heart pounds in my chest as people walk past us. I used to know some of them.

Other than at Sumpter, returners aren't seen around town much. Our community opened a Wellness Center a few months ago in order to create a "safe environment" for returners and normals to interact. It's The Program's belief that assimilation is the key to a full recovery—only it has to be on their terms, like watching us closely at a rec center that's really just an extension of treatment. But while all students in the district are forced to complete three credit hours a semester there, most of the returners *want* to go. Obviously they don't know any better.

James forges passes and skips the Wellness Center, calling it all Program propaganda—a science fair with returners as the

SUZANNE YOUNG

main exhibit. Really, I think the Wellness Center was set up to prove that returners aren't freaks. That they can blend with society post-treatment. But no amount of commercials showing kids with smiling faces playing foosball is going to ease our fears.

I haven't completed any of my Wellness credits for this semester yet, but from what I've heard, returners go to the center with their handlers. That alone highlights how different they are. They've been reset—both emotionally and socially.

James must sense my anxiety because his fingers find mine and intertwine for a second before he lets me go. "Whatever happens," he says, "just play along."

"Not reassuring."

"We're going to pretend to be on a field trip."

I raise my eyes to his. "Seriously?"

"Well, I'd let you slap me in a jealous rage to get attention, but that sort of hostile behavior is frowned upon."

"James, I still don't—"

"What are you two doing here?" a deep voice cuts in. I jump, but James is collected as he turns sideways to the handler glaring at us. Several returners stop, noticing us. Their eyes are wide and curious—innocent expressions that makes me feel sorry for them. Dana Sanders stands in the background, not remembering that she dated my brother for over a year.

I keep my mouth shut and let James do the talking.

"School project," he says smoothly, reaching into his pocket. "Dr. Ryerson said that we could monitor the parking lot to see how well-adjusted the returners are. He's really proud of the strides The Program has made in behavior modification." James takes out a paper, signed by "Dr. Ryerson," who I'm sure not only doesn't exist, but is also untraceable.

The handler looks over the note as my pulse continues to pound in my ears. Behind the guy's shoulder I finally see her, and every one of my muscles tenses.

Lacey Klamath—my best friend other than James and Miller—is walking across the parking lot with textbooks pressed to her chest. Her hair is now pale blond and tied up in a high ponytail. She wears jeans and ballet flats with a short-sleeved cardigan buttoned at the waist. She looks so completely different that I'm ready to scream. That's . . . that's not my friend.

"We only need a few minutes," James says. "Maybe a few interviews?"

I feel a touch on my arm and swing my gaze to James as he smiles at me, as if I'm part of this conversation. "So," he continues to the handler, "do you mind if we hang around for a bit?" James sounds like the most stable person in the world, but his fingernails are digging into the underside of my arm, and I know he's seen Lacey too.

"No," the handler says, shaking his head. "You can speak with them at the Wellness Center. This is a private school, and any official statements should come from—"

I glance past him again and see Miller. He's walking directly toward Lacey, and when he stops in front of her, I hold my breath. Her head snaps up as he says something.

SUZANNE YOUNG

"I'm going to have to ask you to leave," the handler says to James and me. "Now." He then takes out his radio, and calls in a code I don't understand.

"What if we don't talk to them?" I ask quickly, trying to buy us another minute. A second handler crosses the lot, and I'm afraid he's going for Lacey and Miller, but instead he notices us and changes direction. We're out of place here, and I think suddenly that this risk is too big.

"No," the handler says. "And I'm not going to ask you to leave again."

Fear spikes through me because I don't know what to do next. Just then Miller pushes through the crowd, his face down-turned. "Let's go," he says to me and James as he continues his path toward his truck.

"Who is that?" the handler calls, pointing toward Miller's back.

"He's our ride," James says, and takes my hand. "Well, thanks for your help." He backs us away, nodding to the handlers. We turn, our steps fast but not too fast. When we're almost to the truck, James tilts his head toward mine. "Don't look back at them," he says. "Never look back."

Miller's waiting at his truck, his hat pulled low to protect his face. He doesn't want to be recognized as Lacey's ex-boyfriend. We're not sure if the handlers guarding the returners are privy to that sort of information, and it's best not to take the chance. I hope they don't know who we are.

The parking lot starts to empty, and the handler that was

talking to us is gone, but I see the other one with Lacey. He holds the door as she climbs into the passenger seat of a car, then he slams it shut and eyes us suspiciously as he walks around.

Behind the window, Lacey's eyes find us, staring blankly. The handler asks her something when he gets in the car, and she pauses for a minute before shaking her head.

I look away then, feeling broken. Lacey doesn't know us. Not even me.

None of us speak as her car pulls away, the new Lacey leaving us behind on the asphalt. When she's gone, Miller leans against the hood of his truck with an unreadable expression.

"Well?" James asks.

Miller lifts his head, his brown eyes glassy. "Nothing," he answers. "She remembers absolutely nothing."

James swallows hard. "I'm sorry," he says. "I thought that maybe—"

Miller exhales. "You know what, man, I really don't want to talk about it right now."

James nods as they stand there impassively, but I can't take the quiet and step between them. I don't want to give up on Lacey, but I feel lost. Lost and helpless. "And now?" I ask Miller.

"Now," he says, leveling his stare on me. "Now we go swimming and pretend that today never happened."

"I don't think—"

"I'm going to run home and get my trunks," Miller interrupts, turning away. "I'll see you guys at the river."

James darts a panicked look in my direction as if telling me not to leave Miller alone. I'm not sure I can handle anymore today, but as Miller rounds the truck, I call to him. "Wait," I say. "I'll keep you company, and James can meet us there."

"More time for me to undress," James says, taunting us. "Maybe I'll even find someone else to rub lotion on my back."

"Good luck with that." Miller laughs and climbs into the driver's seat. I look back at James one last time, and he gives me his signature smile, wide and cocky. But it's not real. Sometimes I think it's never real.

James is the best at hiding the pain, disguising the feelings. He knows what it takes to stay out of The Program. He'll keep us safe.

He promised.

CHAPTER THREE

"YOU'RE WEARING FAR TOO MANY CLOTHES," JAMES calls from the river as he swims toward me. I'm sitting in the grass, the glittering sun making James's eyes that clear blue. They stop me from saying something smartass back. They're gorgeous and arresting, and I love the way he looks at me.

As if reading my thoughts he stands up in the water, shaking out his hair. "You should come in," he tells me. He's not naked. Completely. He's wearing black boxer briefs that hang low. I grin, watching the water drip down his skin as he walks my way.

"Dude, put on some clothes," Miller says as he appears over the hill. He's wearing his swimsuit, two towels over his shoulder. He throws one at James.

James shoots me another glance and winks, as if telling

me I missed out on a great opportunity. He's probably right. Not that I would have gone swimming. I don't even know how.

James wipes his hair with the blue-striped towel. "Sorry if my physique is intimidating you," he says to Miller. "I didn't have time to go to my house."

"Or you're avoiding it because you stole your dad's car," Miller adds.

James smiles. "Something like that."

"Does anybody have food?" I ask, leaning back on my elbows. I squint my eyes against the sun as I look over my shoulder at Miller. His face is still pale, and I know he must be thinking of Lacey. She used to come swimming with us too. She used to be one of us.

"Energy bar?" He fishes in his pocket and then tosses one to me. I look down at it and groan.

"I hate peanut butter."

Miller shakes his head. "Sorry I didn't have time to bake you a lasagna, princess. Next time I'll be more considerate."

"Good to hear."

James lays his towel on the grass next to me and then stretches out on his stomach, watching me open the wrapper. "I like peanut butter," he says nonchalantly. I laugh and hand the PowerBar over to him. Before he bites into it, he narrows his eyes and nods his chin to me.

"What?" I ask.

"Give me a kiss," he whispers.

"No." Just a few feet away Miller is stretching and putting down his own towel, getting ready for a swim.

Yes, James mouths.

I shake my head, not wanting to make Miller uncomfortable. Before it wouldn't have mattered. He and Lacey sometimes spent the first half of our swim dates back at the car. But now it seems wrong to kiss in front of him. Salt in an open wound.

James's eyebrows knit together as he seems to realize it too. He lays his cheek on his folded arms and watches me solemnly. I reach to stroke my fingers down his shoulder, over the names on his arm: Brady. Hannah. Andrew. Bethany. Trish.

And they're just the ones who died. The list doesn't include the ones who were taken away by The Program. It doesn't even include Lacey.

"Is the water cold?" Miller asks, staring at the river.

"Hell yeah," James responds, not looking away from my eyes. "Feels good though."

Miller nods, then walks to the water. Once he's wading out, I lower myself down to rest my cheek on James's arm, my face close to his. My heart is aching. My confidence is worn thin.

"Tell me it will be okay," I say seriously.

He doesn't hesitate. "Everything will be okay, Sloane. Everything will be fine." He puts no emotion behind his words, but I can believe him. He's never given up on me.

So I lean in and kiss him.

There is a splash behind us, and we both look at the water. I hold my breath as the river seems to swallow the ripple, smoothing it down with the slow current. James sits up next to me, staring at the water. And it isn't until Miller breaks the surface again, yelling about how cold it is, that we ease back down. Grateful that he came up for air at all.

When we leave, I drive home with James, my head resting against the window as I watch the road. He's taking the long way, the route that winds through the farms and hills. It's beautiful and peaceful, and for a minute you can almost believe we live in a beautiful and peaceful world.

"Do you think Lacey will come back to us eventually?" I ask.

"Yes." James reaches to turn on the radio, flipping through the stations until he finds some horrible pop song with a catchy hook. "Want to go somewhere this weekend?" he asks, pretending that I never mentioned our friend. "I'm thinking of camping on the coast."

I look sideways at him. "Don't do that," I say. "Don't change the subject."

James doesn't turn to me, but his jaw tightens. "You know I have to," he murmurs.

"I *want* to talk about it."

He pauses, and then begins again quietly. "I'm going to borrow Miller's tent because it's nicer, but he said he doesn't want to come. I don't know, maybe that's a good thing. We can be all romantic." He tries to smile but won't meet my glare.

"I miss her," I say, my face stinging with the start of a cry.

James blinks quickly, as if holding back tears. "I'll even buy that disgusting sausage stuff you like. What's it called?"

"Kielbasa."

"Nasty. I'll grill kielbasa and we'll roast marshmallows. If you're good I'll even bring chocolate and graham crackers."

"I can't do this," I whisper, feeling like I might shatter into a million sharp and jagged pieces. "It hurts too much. I can't hold it in, James."

He winces at my words, and then presses on the brake, guiding the car to the side of a deserted stretch of road. I'm already falling apart as he stops and unbuckles his seat belt. He grabs me roughly and pulls me into him, pressing me against his chest as his hand knots in my hair.

"Do it," he says, his voice cracking.

And so I cry. I sob into his T-shirt, cursing The Program. The world. I yell for Brady and my friends, calling them cowards for leaving us. I don't understand why they'd do this to us, ruining our lives by taking their own. I scream until the words are no longer recognizable, only sounds choked with emotion. Indescribable loss.

And after twenty minutes of this, I'm so exhausted that I just whimper, still clinging to James's wet shirt. His arms never falter around me. He never interrupts. When I'm finally quiet, he leans down to kiss the top of my head.

"Better?" he asks softly.

I nod and start to straighten, my face feeling swollen. When

I'm sitting up, he pulls his T-shirt over his head, then clenches it in his hand to wipe my tears and runny nose. His blue eyes look me over as he fixes my hair and makes sure there's no smeared mascara. He puts me back together just like he always has.

When he's done, he tosses his T-shirt into the backseat. He glances down at the steering wheel and takes a deep breath. I take one too.

"It's going to be okay, Sloane."

I nod.

"Say it."

"It's going to be okay," I repeat, staring back at him. He smiles, reaching out to take my hand before kissing it.

"We will get through this," he adds, but he's turned back to the road, and it sounds more like he's trying to convince himself than me.

When we're driving again, I check my reflection to see how bad the damage is. My eyes are red-rimmed, but not terrible. We'll need to drive around for a little longer, at least until the blotchiness fades. I can't let my parents see me cry.

"James Murphy," I say, watching the sun fade below the horizon. "I love you madly."

"I know you do," he answers seriously. "And that's why I won't let anything happen to you. It's me and you, Sloane. Just us. Forever just us."

My mother is waiting on the front porch when James pulls his father's car to the curb. She exhales, her hand on her chest as if she thought I was dead because I'm over two hours late and I didn't call. I don't want to get out and face her.

"You've got this," James says, sounding light. "Tell her that I tried to teach you to swim at the river today. She'll appreciate that."

"Yeah? Can I tell her how you tried to get me naked in the backseat of this car before leaving, too?"

He shrugs. "If she's that curious."

I laugh and then lean over to kiss him quickly on the lips. I've never learned how to swim. It's not because of my crushing fear—which I have now—but because when we were younger my brother took lessons while I studied ballet. And the more time passed, the more afraid I became of ever getting in the water. Now I wish I'd learned with Brady. I might have saved him.

I pull back from James, sadness settling on my skin as he looks me over. "Good night, Sloane," he whispers.

I nod, missing him already, and then climb out of the car.

"Why doesn't James have a shirt on?" is the first thing out of my mother's mouth. I hold back my smile.

"He was teaching me how to swim," I say as I step up onto the porch, keeping my face down.

"Oh, that's good, I guess," she says, as if conceding. "But I was worried, honey. The school called and said you left early for therapy, but then when you didn't get home on time . . ."

I want to tell her to stop worrying about me because The Program already watches us closely enough. I want to tell her that this pressure is going to kill me. But lashing out will only make things worse, so instead I smile brightly.

"Sorry I didn't call," I say. "When James picked me up from therapy we decided to go to the river. It's such a beautiful day."

My mother glances up at the sky as if confirming this, and then she touches protectively at my arm. "You're right," she says. "And I'm glad you're enjoying yourself, Sloane. It's nice to be happy." Her expression darkens. "It's just that after your brother . . . What if you—" She pauses, choking on her own words.

"Everything will be okay, Mom," I answer, the words robotic in my mouth from the number of times I've said them to her. The number of times James has told them to me. "Everything will be just fine." And then I open the door and go inside.

CHAPTER FOUR

"SO HOW WAS SCHOOL?" MY FATHER ASKS AS I STAB my pork chop while we sit at the dinner table. I look up, used to this conversation. My parents' expressions are so worn, and yet they stare at me like I'm their last hope for survival.

"Good."

My mother smiles, giving my father a reassured side-glance. Normally, from here our topic would switch to the latest news: how the Northwest has the highest suicide rate in the nation. Could it be because of the rain? That the incidence of suicide is spreading to other developed countries and they're paying close attention to The Program, hoping to adopt one of their own. And my favorite, how a scientist or doctor has claimed to have found a cure—propaganda by the drug companies who have lost revenue from the banning of antidepressants.

But tonight I'm too lonely to hold up my part of the conversation. The way Lacey returned, washed out like that—it makes me hate life. And it makes me miss her even more.

Before she was dating Miller, Lacey used to go out with jerkoffs. She said bad boy was her favorite flavor. They were always older, too old to go to The Program. I can remember a guy in particular, Drake. He was twenty and drove a Camaro. We were sixteen. Lacey showed up at my house one night wearing sunglasses, and I knew something was wrong. We went quickly to my room before my mom could see her. When she took off the glasses, I saw she had a black eye, cuts up and down her arm. She said Drake had pushed her out of the passenger door—while the car was still moving.

Looking back now, seeing how she cried because she didn't want her parents to find out, I wonder what else Lacey hid from people. How much I really knew her. We decided that she couldn't cover the marks so we staged her falling off my front porch, calling my parents out to see her injured, setting up the alibi. She never told anyone else about Drake—although I told James and he beat the hell out of him.

I lied for Lacey then, just as I lied to myself as she got infected. Maybe if I were a better friend I could have kept her out of The Program. Maybe we're all sick.

"You're not eating," my mother says, interrupting my thoughts. "Everything all right?"

I look up, startled. "Lacey came back today," I say, my voice wavering. My father's eyes flash with worry, and for a second

I think that they understand. That I can tell them the truth about The Program—how it brings us back empty.

"Really?" My mother sounds nothing short of gleeful. "Well now, see. That wasn't very long."

I have a gut check and look back down at my plate, the pork chop slaughtered around the bone, the applesauce bleeding into everything. "It was six weeks," I murmur.

"Exactly," my mother answers. "Went by faster than you thought."

I remind myself of the parental outreach The Program uses—weekly support groups for parents of dead teens, access to the latest advances in their methods. It's like The Program learned to get to us through our home lives. I think they can get to us anywhere.

"And how did she look?" my mother asks. "Did you see her at the Wellness Center?"

My fingernails are digging into my jeans, into the skin underneath. "Yes," I lie. "And she's blond again. She's . . . completely different."

"I bet she looks beautiful," my mother says. "The returners always look so healthy, don't they, Don?"

My father doesn't respond, but I feel him watching me. I wonder if he's gauging my reaction, mentally going through the "Is your child depressed?" checklist The Program provided them. I'm not sure I have the strength to put on the mask, but I look up anyway. And smile.

"She does look great," I reply. "Hopefully she'll be able to hang out again soon."

SUZANNE YOUNG

"Just give her time to heal," my mother says, grinning at me like she's proud. "Thank God for The Program. It's saving so many lives."

My stomach lurches and I stand up quickly, not wanting to cry when I've made it this far into the conversation. "I'll do the dishes tonight," I say, grabbing my plate. "After that I've got a ton of homework."

I rush from the room, getting into the kitchen just as the tears start to sting my eyes. I need to do something before I break into sobs in front of them. There is a pamphlet for The Program sitting next to our phone in the living room—something every parent received when our high school became part of the experiment. But to me that paper is like a threat, always reminding me of the next step if I slip up. So I don't slip up. Ever.

I look around the kitchen and my gaze rests on the gas stove. Walking over, I turn it on—the flames catching life in shades of blue and orange. I'm going to die if I don't cry right now. The sorrow is going to rip through my chest and kill me.

But instead, I turn over my arm, the tender part exposed, and stick it into the fire. The burn is immediate and I scream out in pain, backing away as I cover the area automatically with my hand. My entire body reacts, as if all of me is on fire.

I decide that I like it. I like the pain and distraction.

Tears stream down my face even though the emotional release feels good, and I drop onto the tile floor. My parents rush in, and the minute they do I hold up my arm, the blistered area bright red against my skin. "I got burned," I sob. "I leaned against the stove to grab the pan and the burner must have turned on."

My mother gasps and runs to turn off the burner. "Donald," she says. "I told you to put the pots in the sink."

He apologizes and kneels down next to me. "Let me see, sweetheart." And they fuss, letting me cry as long as I want because they think I was accidentally injured. They have no idea that I'm really crying for Lacey. For Brady. And most of all, for myself.

James sighs. "You shouldn't have started in the car." His voice is concerned on the other end of the phone as I hold it to my ear. I'm curled up in bed, my arm bandaged and Tylenol PM making me sleepy. "That's the problem, Sloane. Once you start, you might not be able to stop." He pauses. "I shouldn't have let you cry."

"I just had to mourn a little," I say. "Not all of us can get tattoos."

"This isn't about me. Now how bad is the burn?" he asks.

"Blistered."

"Goddamn it." There's a rustling, and I imagine him roughly rubbing his face. "I'm coming over."

"No," I say. "It's late. I'm going to fall asleep soon anyway. You can be sweet to me tomorrow."

"I'm going to kick your ass tomorrow."

I smile. "Really? You really think so?"

"Go to bed, Sloane." He doesn't sound nearly as amused as he normally would. "I'll be there early to pick you up. And please," James says, "don't do anything else stupid tonight."

I swallow hard, too exhausted to cry anymore, and agree. After I hang up, I pull the comforter over my head. I think about my brother in my last moments of consciousness—guilt heavy in my chest. Sometimes it hurts so much that I pretend he never existed at all, as if that can make me okay. But then I remember his smile, his jokes, his . . . life. And I understand what my parents have lost and why they're so concerned about me. I ask myself if I'd be different if I were them, but I don't know the answer.

I feel a light touch on my cheek, and my eyes flutter open. James looks down at me as he stands next to my bed, his face worried. "We're going to be late for school," he says. "Your mom finally sent me up here to get you."

I feel confused and glance at the clock, seeing that it's past eight. I get up on my elbows and look around the room, disoriented. When I do, James moves to sit on the edge of my bed. "Let me see your arm," he says, taking it before I can agree.

He peels back the bandage and I wince. "I'm really unhappy with you right now," he says, not looking at me, just examining my burn. "I like your skin better without the scars." His eyes meet mine, and then he leans down to kiss just above the tender spot on my arm. He climbs onto the bed and gets under the sheets next to me, not caring that my parents are downstairs and could come up at any second.

"I know it's not easy," he whispers, his breath warm as his lips touch my ear. "But we have to push through." He picks up one of my curls and twists it around his finger, wrapping and unwrapping. "Every morning I think this will be it, the day I get sick. The day the handlers will flag me, take me. And I don't want to get out of bed. But I do. Because I can't leave you here alone."

At the thought of losing him, I reach out to take his hand, squeezing my fingers between his.

"We have to fake it to make it," he says, sounding bitter. "And I don't make it without you, baby. Brady told us to take care of each other, and I'm not going to let him down again."

"I'm tired of faking it."

"So am I." He breathes. "So am I."

He pulls our held hands to his mouth and kisses mine. Then he turns and puts his lips on my neck. "Let's ditch," he murmurs between kisses. "We'll say you have an appointment and go to the river, lie around in the sun all day."

I smile. "Didn't we do that yesterday?"

"Yes. But I could use another day off." He takes my thigh and pulls it over his, leaning in to kiss my collarbone.

"Stop," I say, but it's halfhearted. Truth is, I could use the heat that James gives me. But before we get too far, he sighs and pulls away.

"You're right. I really shouldn't take advantage of you when you're injured." He sits up, pulling back the cover and exposing my pajamas. "Wear a skirt maybe," he says. "Staring at your legs always puts me in a better mood." He flashes that broad smile as he stands. He goes to my door and pauses, his facade nearly crumbling. But without looking back, he nods and then goes downstairs.

CHAPTER FIVE

WHEN WE PULL INTO THE PARKING LOT, I GO TO climb out of the car when James catches my hand. "Hey," he says seriously. "I have to tell you something before we go in."

My heart skips a beat. "What?"

"I didn't want to say anything when we were at your house, but Miller broke into Lacey's bedroom last night, hoping to talk to her. He thinks he might get flagged today. I'll let him tell you the rest. But he's okay. He's alive."

I lower my head and try to catch my breath, taking my hand from James's before resting it on the dashboard to steady myself. "He's okay?" I ask, looking sideways at him. He nods, but there's something in his expression that keeps me from feeling relieved.

"Do *you* think they're coming for him?" I ask.

"I hope not."

I close my eyes and throw my head back against the seat. "Why did he do that?" I moan. "Why didn't he just wait?"

"I don't know," James says. "But I think we should take off early today, maybe after lunch. We need to keep a lower profile around here."

"Says the guy who faked a school project at Sumpter."

"That was different. I was trying to help Miller."

"It was dumb," I say. "We have to do better. It's our fault if they take him."

"I know that," James snaps. "Don't you think I know that?"

We stare at each other, his features taking on a wild edge. James feels responsible for my brother's death. For my safety, and Miller's safety. It's just how he is. And sometimes I'm stupid enough to believe that he can really keep us safe.

"I know everything you think," I murmur, despair settling in my chest.

James's expression softens. "Come here," he says. At first I don't move, the impending threat on Miller making the space in the car, in the world, suffocatingly small. "Sloane, I need you," James adds, his voice thick.

And when I hear his plea, I push aside everything else. I lean into him, digging my nails into his back as I clutch him to me. He flinches, and then squeezes me tighter. The minute I turn eighteen, James and I are going to leave town—start over someplace else. But we can't go yet. They'll find us, issue an Amber Alert as a way to track us down. We'd never get away. No one has ever gotten away before.

We stay close until James's hand slides onto my bare thigh just below the hem of my skirt, his breathing deepening. "My lips are tired of talking," he whispers next to my ear. "Now kiss me and make me forget," he says.

I pull back to see the sadness in James's eyes, the mix of desire there. And so I whisper that I love him, then climb onto his lap and kiss him, as if it's the last one we'll ever have.

In economics class, I stare at Miller as he sits next to me with his head lowered, drawing in the notepad he has under his desk. I'm checking his mannerisms to see if there's anything that can get him flagged. He seems fine.

"Well?" I whisper as the teacher starts walking around to hand back quizzes. "What happened at Lacey's?"

Miller pauses in his sketching. "I slipped in through her window after her parents were asleep. I tried to tell her that I wasn't going to hurt her, but she started crying." He shakes his head. "She thought I was there to kill her or something. Who knows what The Program has told her about me."

I put my hand on my forehead, leaning my elbow on my desk. This is a major disaster. This is enough to get him taken away for sure. "Did she call for her parents?"

"No," Miller says. "She told me to get out—even after I tried to explain who I was, she told me to get out." His tone is flat. "I guess I was hoping that on some level she could still love me." He looks over, his eyes glassy. "Do you think she could?"

"Yes," I say, "I do. But Miller, you could have been arrested. Sent away. And then what? What would I do without you?"

"I had to try. You wouldn't give up on James."

I pause. "No. I wouldn't." He nods, looking sorry that he made the comparison, and goes back to his notepad. "Are you going to keep trying?" I ask.

"No point," he answers. "She's not the same person. I don't even think she'd fall for me again."

I blink back warm tears. "I'm sorry."

"I know," he says. "I have to move on, right? At least that's what my mom tells me." Miller's mom was never crazy about Lacey in the first place. She hoped her son would end up with someone more on the cheerful side. But in our lives, there isn't all that much to be peppy about anymore. And those that are have usually gone through The Program.

"Miller, you don't—"

"Sloane Barstow?" Mr. Rocco calls, and then glares me into silence. Miller's head is down as he continues to doodle in his notepad under the desk, but I'm relieved that he isn't planning anything crazy. If we can just keep it together through this latest threat, we'll survive. And maybe in a few months, when her monitoring is over, we can convince Lacey to hang out with us again.

"James and I are leaving after lunch," I whisper when I'm sure the teacher isn't looking. "You in?"

"Hell yes. You think I'm here to learn?"

I smile. Miller sounds like himself for the first time today.

Just before I text James to tell him it's on, I glance once more at Miller, catching what he's drawing in his notepad. A large, black spiral, taking over the entire page. I turn toward the front, pretending not to notice. In my pocket, my phone vibrates.

I covertly slide it out and check the message. KEEP MILLER CLOSE. EXTRA HANDLERS ON CAMPUS.

"Miller," I whisper. "James says there are more handlers today. Do you think they're here for you?"

Miller licks at his bottom lip, as if considering, then he nods. "Could be. Let's leave before lunch then," he says. "We'll go to my house."

I agree and text James, glad to leave. The last thing I want is to see my best friend get taken away. Again.

I sit next to Miller on his flower-patterned couch as James is in the kitchen rummaging through the refrigerator. Miller chews on his thumbnail, and when he moves to the next finger, I see that they're all bitten painfully short, bleeding under the slivers of the nail still there. I reach out and smack his hand away from his face and he rests it in his lap.

"Saw her on the way to school today," Miller says, staring out the picture window across from us.

"Lacey?"

"Yeah. Drove by Sumpter and saw her in the lot, talking to Evan Freeman. She . . . was laughing." He begins biting on his nail again, but I don't stop him. Instead I lean my head on Miller's shoulder and stare out the window with him.

Returners aren't allowed to get too close to people for a few months after coming back, but they are allowed to make a few friends—especially if they're also successful graduates of The Program. I guess the handlers figure that if they're both scrubbed clean, they can't be bad influences on each other. Before Miller, Lacey actually went on a few dates with Evan Freeman. She said he used too much tongue.

And now, the fact that Lacey was talking to him—laughing— all while not realizing that she already knows him, makes me sick. It's so disturbing that I can barely handle it.

"What do you think they did to her in there?" I mumble, not sure I really want the answer.

"They dissected her," Miller responds, spitting out a bit of nail. "They opened up her head and took out the pieces, putting them back together as a happy-face puzzle. It's like she's not even real anymore."

"We don't know that," I say. "She could still be the same on the inside. She just doesn't remember."

"And if she never does?" He turns to me, a tear spilling over onto his cheek. "Do you really think anything can ever be the same again? She's empty, Sloane. She's the walking dead now."

I don't want to believe that. I've seen returners for nearly two years, and although I've never had more than a standing-next-to-me-in-line-at-the-mall conversation, I'm sure they're still people. Just . . . shinier, as if everything is great. They've been brainwashed or something. But they're not empty. They can't be.

"It would have been better if she had died," Miller whispers. I sit up and glare at him.

"Don't say that," I say. "She's *not* dead. And in time we'll try again. She may not know you, Miller. But her heart will."

He shakes his head, not meeting my eyes. "No. I give up. I'm letting her go just like the psychologist said I should."

After The Program took her, they sentenced me, James, and Miller to two weeks of daily intensive therapy—therapy beyond the usual assessments. They asked for details, things they could use in her treatment. But really I think they were trying to see if we were infected too. Luckily we weren't.

I want to tell Miller not to move on, to wait it out and try to win her again. But in a way, I know he's right. The way Lacey looked, how she acted. She's not the same. And she probably never will be.

I remember the first time Miller met Lacey. I'd brought him to our table, hoping to introduce them, but Lacey was in the lunch line arguing with the lady at the register. Lacey was wearing this ridiculous black-and-white-striped dress that made her look like Beetlejuice, but Miller got this puppy-dog expression on his face. He leaned in and told me and James that she was exactly the kind of girl he was looking for—the kind who would piss off his mother.

I shoved his shoulder, but James laughed from across the table. "Don't do it, man," James told him with a smirk. "She's like a black widow. She eats dudes like you for breakfast."

And Miller just smiled as if the idea fascinated him. Lacey

wasn't so easy to convince. But when they finally got together, they were happy. They were so happy.

"I'm sorry, Miller," I say in a low voice. He nods and then turns suddenly to hug me. I rest my hand on the back of his neck as he squeezes me so tight I can barely breathe. I don't tell him it'll be okay because I don't know if I can hope that it's true.

Just then James walks into the living room, biting into an apple. He looks at us, tilting his head as if assessing the situation. He takes another bite and walks over, leaning down to put his arms around both of us. "Can I have some love too?" he asks in the stupid way he does when he's trying to make sure we're not getting too sad. He's trying to distract us. He kisses loudly at Miller's cheek, and I laugh, pushing him away.

James straightens, but Miller just stands and doesn't say anything. James's expression falters and he shoots me a warning look, as if telling me I shouldn't have let Miller break down like that. I shrug because I didn't mean to.

Glancing around the room to figure out what to do next, James walks to the fireplace mantel and picks up the latest family photo. "Man," he says, looking at Miller. "Your mom is smokin' hot in this picture."

"Go to hell," Miller says, biting his thumbnail again as he hovers in the doorway. They have this same conversation every time James sees Miller's mom, who is indeed very pretty. She's single, raising Miller by herself. She has blond hair and wears short skirts, and has a possible crush on my obnoxious boyfriend who she says is going to be a "heartbreaker" when he gets older. Uh, yeah. Not if I can help it.

"I'm just saying," James adds, walking back over to the couch and dropping down next to me. "If I didn't have this one"—he hikes his thumb at me—"I might be your new stepdad."

I laugh, slapping his thigh. "Hey!"

James winks at me and turns back to Miller. "I can teach you how to play catch in the backyard, okay, slugger?"

"Fine by me," Miller says, his normally amused expression at the joke gone. "I'll take Sloane in exchange. I need a new girlfriend anyway."

Both James and I pause in our laughing, Miller adding a new twist to the routine. Only . . . he doesn't say it like he's joking. He glares at James, at me, and then turns away. "I'm going to make a sandwich," he adds, and heads into the kitchen.

James's mouth opens slightly as he stares after Miller, a bit of pink high on his cheeks. "I think he was serious," he says, sounding confused. "Why would he say something like that?" James glances at me, his brow furrowed. "Does he like you?"

I shake my head, my stomach knotting. "No," I say honestly. And the reason it's so alarming is that we know it's out of character, that it's a break in Miller's personality. It's a sign we were taught to watch out for. "Should we talk to him about it?" I ask.

James puts his hand over his mouth, rubbing it as he thinks. "No," he says finally. "I don't want to upset him any more." We're quiet for a long minute, the sound of the refrigerator opening and closing in the background. James looks at me. "And by the way, you're not allowed to hook up with Miller."

"Shut up."

"I'll make you a deal. You don't hook up with him, and I won't hook up with his mom."

"James!" I go to hit him again, but he captures my hand and then pulls me onto his lap, making it impossible for me to get up. James is so good at making everything normal that I start laughing, trying to twist out of his grip. When Miller walks back in, a sandwich in his hand, he pauses in the doorway—no emotion on his face.

I stop squirming, but James doesn't let me go. He nods his chin at Miller. "We're clear that Sloane's mine, right?" he asks, not sounding combative, just curious. "That I love her and won't let her go, not even to you. You know that?" I wonder what happened to the "let's not upset him" argument.

Miller takes a bite of his turkey on rye and shrugs. "Maybe," he says. "But we all know that things change. Whether we want them to or not." And without betraying any emotion, Miller backs off and leaves, walking slowly up the stairs to his room.

James releases me and I sit next to him, stunned. Miller doesn't have feelings for me, I know that. He's just acting out. We've seen it before, how someone will piss off their friends or start sleeping around when depression takes hold. My brother acted out, but we denied it. We pretended not to see it. With that thought I turn to James, my face tight with worry. "Should I—"

"No," James says, holding up his hand. "I will." He kisses

the top of my head before walking to the stairs that lead to Miller's room. He's going to try a peer intervention, something we've been taught since the seventh grade. "This might take a while," he says to me.

I nod, and then watch as James goes up to try to bring Miller back.

In Miller's small, rooster-themed kitchen, I make some chicken noodle soup and eat it with crackers before washing out the pot. When I get tired of waiting, I move to sit on the stairs, listening for any sounds above as I rest my head against the wall.

It's forty-five minutes later when James appears on the landing. He smiles at me, a look that's to tell me everything worked out. Miller walks past him, and I back up into the foyer and watch him as he comes to pause in front of me.

"James says you'd never go for me because he's a better kisser than I am," Miller starts. "I told him we should put it to the test, and he punched me in the gut so hard I almost puked."

I dart an alarmed look at my boyfriend and he shrugs.

"It's okay," Miller says, touching my arm. "I deserved it. I was being a dick, and I'm sorry." His mouth quirks up in a smile. "I'm not really attracted to you, Sloane. I hope you're not too disappointed."

I roll my eyes and look back at James as he drops slowly down each stair. "Did you really hit him?"

"That's my idea of intervention. Worked, right?"

James is always thinking like that, that if he can distract

us long enough we'll forget how messed up everything is. He's right. It does work. But will it always? Will he always be able to make us laugh through our tears? I stare at him then, knowing how much I depend on him, on how he makes me feel. His smile fades as if he's reading the serious expression on my face. Rather than make a joke, he looks at the wooden floor.

"Do you guys want to watch a movie?" Miller asks, sounding more alive than he has all day. "My mom won't be back until four."

"Your mom—" James begins.

"Shut up," Miller and I say at the same time. James chuckles, finally glancing up, looking flawlessly charming. All is well. All is . . . normal.

We go into the living room, wasting an afternoon as if it were any other. But I can't help stealing looks out the window, constantly checking for the men in white coats.

CHAPTER SIX

FOR THE NEXT TWO DAYS, MILLER IS HIMSELF—OR A close enough version of himself. When he's not drawing in his notepad, he's staring out the window during class. Lacey must not have turned him in because the handlers haven't approached him yet. But there is one handler still hanging around, the creepy dark-haired one who side-eyes me. I don't mention him to James or Miller, worried they'll start a fight and get into trouble. Instead, I just avoid his gaze, trying not to get too freaked out.

"Miller," James asks as we walk out on Friday. "Are you sure you don't want to come camping? It'll be nice out there—quiet."

"Naw, man," Miller answers, taking his baseball cap out of his backpack and adjusting the brim. "I'm just gonna chill at home, play some video games. Maybe stop by the Wellness Center."

"You should come," I say. "You're going to be lonely."

Miller looks at me as he puts his hat on, a smile on his face. "It's one night, Sloane. It'll be fine. Besides, I already know how camping goes with you two." He motions between James and me. "And no offense, but I'm not really in the mood for your public displays of affection."

James laughs and moves to put his arms around my waist from behind, resting his chin on the top of my head. "Not true," he says. "We always wait until you're asleep."

I laugh and push him off me. But Miller still doesn't agree to join us, promising that he will next week. I don't want to leave him behind, but I don't think I can stay in town, either. I like being out in the woods. I like pretending that there's no Program.

And so we say good-bye to Miller and climb into James's dad's car, heading for the coast.

When we were younger, Brady and I would go camping together. My brother was an expert outdoorsman, so our parents let us go when I was just twelve and he was thirteen, although they'd come and check on us a few times. And when I was fifteen, they finally let us go on our own, as long as James was there too.

That first night, as I sat next to the fire pit, I watched James put the tent together while Brady was across the site, chopping wood. James had just turned sixteen, and his blond hair had grown out so that he had to swipe at it with the back of his hand. He was such a boy, shirtless and sweating, muscles already cording on his tall frame. And at one point, he looked sideways at me, almost startled to see me sitting there, staring at him.

Then his mouth spread into a grin. "You checking me out, Sloane?"

My face must have gone completely red because he apologized immediately, but I had already gotten up to walk to the spot that overlooked the ocean, unable to answer. He was right. I had been checking him out. It had never occurred to me before that moment that I thought of James as anything more than a friend, my *brother's* friend. I even had a boyfriend, Liam. Sure, I didn't much like him, just one of those "we have classes together so let's go out" type of relationships. But still, Lacey told me it'd be weird if I said no to Liam. I hadn't even let him hold my hand in the two months we were together—and believe me, that counted as pretty weird in everyone's book. And yet, there I was checking out James Murphy.

I sat on the sand embankment and bent my knees, resting my elbows on them. James had lots of girlfriends, never any serious. And now that I thought about it, James dating other girls twisted my stomach. I groaned out loud, wondering how I could have let myself be so stupid.

"God, Sloane" I heard. "I was only kidding."

I straightened my back, unable to turn to face James. But I knew him, and there was no way he'd leave me without finding out what was going on. Then, sure enough, he was standing over me. "You okay?" he asked. His voice held no hint as to what he was thinking; whether he was embarrassed for me, whether he had even noticed that he was right about the way I'd been looking at him.

I nodded, but he just chuckled. He tossed a tent pole on the sand in front of us and dropped down next me, bumping me as he did. James was big, and I fell to my side, catching myself with my hands. Normally I would have pushed him back, but I didn't want to touch him. I wanted to figure out how to make my feelings go away. Me, James, and Brady were a team. I didn't want to mess it up.

"Holy hell," he said, sounding amused. "You really were checking me out."

"I wasn't," I said quickly, turning to him. But it was too late. James read the truth all over my face. His easy smile slid away from his lips.

"Sloane," he whined my name. "You don't get to do that. This can't . . . We can't . . ." He stopped, his beautiful eyes holding nothing but pity for me. So I did the only thing I could. I punched him in the chest, making him gasp, and got up and walked away.

And here we are, over two years later. Once again I'm watching James build a tent, but this time my brother's dead. James's hair isn't in his eyes, but he brushes at his forehead absently anyway. At one point, he looks sideways at me, but he doesn't smile like he did that day. Instead his eyes are weary from putting up the tent by himself. He presses his lips together in an "I miss him too" sort of expression and I look away.

The team broke up, but it wasn't me who did it. It was Brady.

The fire crackles, the heat licking out toward my boots. The sun set a few hours ago, but neither of us said much throughout the day. It was nice that we didn't have to.

James taps my leg with a thin stick and I take it from him, looking next to me. "Marshmallow?" he asks, holding one out between his thumb and finger. I watch as the amber light plays off his features: his strong jaw, his golden hair. I smile.

"You're beautiful," I say.

"I look good naked too," he adds. "You didn't mention that."

"I forgot."

"You forgot?" He pretends to be offended, and then takes a bite out of the marshmallow before tossing the rest into the fire. James immediately drops out of his chair, crawling over to mine and grabbing me, pulling me down into the dirt with him.

"James . . . ," I start to say, laughing. But his lips are on mine, tasting sticky and sweet. He lays me back, his knee nudging my legs apart as he starts kissing my neck. "James," I murmur again, only this time it's with longing.

I love this—this moment. Because as we roll on the ground, the fire burning hot as James peels off my clothes, I can block out everything else. I can focus on how good I feel right now. I can pretend that there is nothing else but us.

And when we're done and James is panting next me, proud of himself as he should be, I stare at the stars in the sky. I lie there for a long time as James pulls his T-shirt back over his head, collecting the wrapper to toss out. When he comes back, he gets down next to me, moving my head onto his lap as we watch the sky together.

"Brady's a star up there," he says, "in some distant place where he doesn't hurt." James's voice cracks and he stops talking.

He sniffles, the tears rolling down his cheeks. He always lets his guard down enough to talk in moments like this—the only time his feelings are so raw he can't hide them.

"He loved you," I say, curling up against him. "No matter what he did, you were the best thing in his life."

James looks down at me, wiping his tears. "You were." He stares at me in a way that reminds me that he's only human. That he's as fragile as I am.

"I was just his sister. You were more than a brother. You were his other half."

"Then I sucked at it," James says. "Because Brady's dead. And I'm still here."

I sit up then, turning James's face to mine. "You're here for *me*. I wouldn't have survived without you, and I couldn't now. We're in this together, James. Don't forget that."

He exhales heavily and shakes his head, as if trying to clear it. I know that telling him I need him, that I can't live without him, snaps him out of the depression. It always has.

And when he's more himself, I kiss him again, before taking his hand and bringing him into the tent to sleep.

"We should really camp more often," James says as we're driving down the freeway. I smile and look sideways at him.

"It was fun."

"And I think your memory is fully restored now." He grins.

"Yes, James. It is soundly intact and filled only with images of your naked torso."

He raises one eyebrow. "Just my torso?"

"Oh my God, shut up."

"Don't be shy. I'm an amazing specimen." James is still grinning ear to ear when my phone vibrates in the pocket of my jeans. I take it out, glancing at the number.

"It's Miller," I say, and then click it on. "Hey."

"Sloane?" Miller sounds like he's been crying and sickness washes over me. I reach out and grab James's arm.

"What's wrong? What happened?" I say into the phone. My heart is racing in my chest.

"They're coming for me," he whimpers. "The Program is coming for me."

No. "Miller, where are you?" I shoot a look at James, and he's alternating between facing me and facing the road. His speed creeps up past eighty as we race toward town.

"I'm home," he whispers, sounding desperate. "But it's too late. I had to see her again."

"Put it on speaker," James says, his knuckles white on the steering wheel. I hit the button, and Miller's sobbing immediately fills the space in the car. I nearly crumble, but I hold up the phone, keeping back my own tears.

In life, I don't really get to see people cry—not anymore. James does every so often, but it's rare. And other than that, it's only when someone has cracked that they'll let someone see. I never once saw my brother cry, and I was with him when he died.

"Miller," James calls out. "Don't do anything stupid, man. We're on our way."

"I just can't . . . ," Miller mumbles. "I can't do it anymore. I followed Lacey to the Wellness Center and I tried to kiss her, to remind her. But she slapped me and reported me before I took off. My mom let it slip tonight that The Program is coming. They're coming right now. But I won't wait for them. I won't let them take me."

"Miller!" James shouts so loud I flinch. "What do you have?" Tears start streaming down James's cheeks and he presses down on the accelerator, sending us over a hundred miles an hour.

"QuikDeath," Miller mumbles. "I wish Lacey would have told me and we could have gone together. She wouldn't have gotten hollowed out. We'd be together."

"You can't be together if you're dead," James says. He punches his fist hard on the steering wheel, and I'm crying, looking for James to fix this. To stop it. "Miller," he says. "Don't do this, man. Please?"

Miller sniffles. "It's too late," he says, sounding far away. "I took it ten minutes ago. But I couldn't leave without saying good-bye." He pauses. "I love you, guys." Then the phone goes dead.

I gag, the emotion too strong for me to contain, and James slams on the brakes, guiding us to the shoulder. He grabs the phone from where it fell on the seat, immediately dialing 911.

He's covering his face, his body racking in sobs. "My friend," he yells into the phone. "He took QuikDeath. . . ."

I think I pass out then, because I don't hear anything else.

CHAPTER SEVEN

THE AMBULANCE IS GONE BY THE TIME WE GET TO Miller's house. There's no flurry of activity or sirens, so we know it's too late. We sit for a long time, staring at his white house with its black shutters. James doesn't hold my hand, and I don't reach for his. We're just quiet.

The sun sets behind the house and the living room light switches on. We can see Miller's mother in the picture window, curled up on the couch. There's another woman with her, talking and wandering around. James and I have been in houses after a death before, and it's not a good place to be—not when we're already so compromised.

"Miller was going to be eighteen in three months," James says, his voice strangled, but he doesn't bother to clear his throat. "He wouldn't have been scared of The Program anymore. He wouldn't have done this."

It's a question we often ask ourselves: Would we commit suicide without The Program, or does it help drive us there?

"I guess it doesn't matter now," I say, chills running over me as I continue to stare at Miller's house. My Miller—my friend. The first day I met him he was playing with the Bunsen burner and my homework caught on fire. Instead of yelling and dropping it, he grabbed my Diet Coke and doused it. Then he looked over and asked if he could buy me another one.

He came camping with us, he cut school with us, he loved us. He was such a good guy and he was such a good friend, and I just can't . . . I just can't . . .

"Sloane," James says, pulling my arm. But I'm rocking, banging my forehead against the window, trying to make the memories, the regret, the pain go away. I want to stop moaning because I don't even know what I'm saying. But I can't control myself. I can't control anything.

And just then James slaps me, hard. I gasp in a breath, snapped out of my hysteria as my cheek stings. Normally James would have talked me down, held me to him. But instead his eyes are swollen and red from crying. His skin is blotchy and wet. I've never seen him look like this, and I touch my face, still stunned.

James hitches in labored breaths, his body nearly convulsing with them. I've stopped crying, but my head throbs from where I was banging it on the glass. James still says nothing and then looks past me to Miller's house, just as the porch light clicks off.

He whimpers, and I reach for him but he backs against the car door.

Slowly, he pulls the driver's side handle and opens it, falling out onto the street. "What are you doing?" I manage to say. But he doesn't look at me as he scrambles up, staring at the house with horror on his face. And then James turns and starts running, his sandals clapping on the pavement. I push open my door and scream after him. "James!" I yell, but he's around the corner and out of my sight.

I can't move at first. I'm hyperaware of everything around me, the orange haze low in the sky from the sunset. The trees swaying in the wind. I think about going up to Miller's house and asking if I can lie in his bed for a while, feel close to him one last time. But that's the kind of thing that gets you flagged.

Miller. I'll never go with him to the river again. We'll never have lunch again. He'll never turn eighteen. Oh, God. Miller.

I blink, but no tears fall because my eyes are dried out and scratchy. I touch my cheek again where it still stings. It occurs to me that James didn't say anything—he didn't tell me I was being hysterical. He didn't hold me and tell me to cry it out. He didn't tell me it would be okay.

He didn't say anything.

Suddenly my heart explodes with worry. I clamor all the way out of the passenger seat and race around the car, getting in the other side and slamming it into drive. I need to find James. I grab my phone from the center console and call him, my fingers trembling over the numbers.

There's no answer until his voice mail picks up. "It's James. Talk to me, baby." I hang up and dial again, turning down the same street where I saw him running. It's empty, and then the streetlights turn on. Where is he? He needs to be okay. He needs to tell me I'm okay.

I press down on the accelerator, looking frantically around the streets. James's house is only a few blocks away, so he might be there. I hope he's there. I'm going to find him and I'm going to hold him.

The car tires bump the curb hard as I pull up to his house. I run, not even shutting the door, and race to his front porch. I rush inside and yell for him, but no one answers. His dad isn't home and I wonder what day it is, if he's on a date tonight.

"James?" I'm screaming. "James?"

Silence. I trip as I run up the stairs, banging my shin hard on the wood. I curse under my breath but scramble ahead. I have to find him.

I burst into his room, and the minute I do, I freeze.

My James is sitting on the floor near the window, shirtless, in jeans. He pauses and looks up at me, his eyes red and swollen, his mouth slack. I barely recognize him. I hitch in a breath as he lowers the pocketknife, blood running down his arm, pooling in his lap.

"I needed to add his name," he says, his voice thick. "I couldn't wait for ink."

I drop to my knees and begin crawling toward him, shocked, horrified, desperate. Miller's name is carved jaggedly into his flesh. Blood is everywhere.

James lets the knife fall to the carpet.

He blinks likes he's just noticing me. "Sloane," he says softly. "What are you doing here, baby?"

I reach for him and bring his head against my chest. His blood is warm as it runs over my hand. James lies there listlessly as if he's empty. As if he's dead, too. And I won't cry anymore today.

Because I know that James is now infected.

"It's going to be okay," I say, brushing back his sweaty blond hair. No emotion in my voice. Just the impossibility of it. "Everything is going to be okay, James."

Luckily the cuts aren't too deep, and I help James clean and cover them with a bandage and a long-sleeved shirt. I go through his dad's medications until I think I find something that will calm him down. I clean his room, trying to scrub the blood out of his carpet but then opting to cover it with a chair when I can't. I take the knife and throw it in the trash, considering hiding all the knives in the house, but I don't want his dad to be suspicious.

James stares up at the ceiling, shaking even under the covers. I get into bed next to him, glancing at the clock and knowing his dad will be home soon. I wrap myself around James and hold on tight. I wait until the pills take effect, and when he's asleep, I slip out. I hope that his father hasn't heard about Miller yet. I hope that he'll get home from his date and go to sleep, and then leave before James wakes up in the morning.

Then I'll come over and get James ready for school. He'll need time, need me to keep him normal, but then he'll be fine. James will be eighteen in five months, and then after that they can't take him away.

I'll keep him safe, just like he kept me safe after Brady died. Because that day at the river when my brother killed himself, I almost went with him.

CHAPTER EIGHT

MY BROTHER AND I WERE ONLY ELEVEN MONTHS apart, yet oddly enough, we never fought. Brady was my best friend, one of my only friends other than Lacey. And even though he had James, he never shut me out.

In the weeks before my brother died, James and I had been meeting secretly. When he'd stay over, he'd show up in my room at three in the morning, kissing me quietly while everyone slept. He'd leave notes under my pillow when I wasn't home. We'd become completely infatuated with one another.

We didn't tell Brady, not because we wanted to keep it secret, but because we didn't want it to be awkward. And if everyone knew about James and me, they wouldn't allow us constant access to each other—sleepovers, camping trips.

Brady had been seeing that girl Dana, but they broke up.

She told James that Brady was acting strange, that he was cold. James waved her off, but when he confronted my brother, Brady just said it wasn't a big deal. That she had bad breath anyway.

My brother had made it his personal mission to teach me how to swim, always going to our same place by the river. There isn't much of a current there, just a deep pool of water. But this one afternoon, he took me and James to a new spot.

"It's really beautiful there," he said as he drove. "It's perfect."

James snorted in the backseat. "Just so long as I get to see your sister in a bikini."

Brady smiled, his shadowed eyes glancing in the mirror, but he didn't tell him to shut up. Instead he kept driving, like he had all the time in the world. I looked back at James, but he just shrugged. I remember thinking that maybe we'd tell my brother that day, that maybe it was time for him to know about me and James. I even thought that maybe he knew about us, but James didn't think so. He said Brady was just stressed about finals.

We never got the chance to tell him.

I was in my bathing suit as Brady stood at the edge of the drop, looking down at the rushing water. A soft smile was on his lips.

"You can't swim in that!" James yelled to him as he laid out his towel far back in the grass. "We should have gone to our usual spot."

Brady looked over, the light reflecting off his black hair. The sun made his pale skin look sallow and shiny. "I didn't want to ruin it for you," my brother called.

James pulled his eyebrows together, and then laughed. "Ruin what for me?"

"The usual spot. I figured you'll still be able to go there after. Maybe you can teach Sloane how to finally swim." He darted his eyes to mine and smiled. "She might listen to you."

I paused then, and stared at him. "What are you—" Ice-cold pain ripped through my body when it hit me, when the moment actually became clear. At just about the exact same time, I saw James jump up from his towel.

My brother was poised on the end of a twenty-foot drop, and he bowed his head to me, his eyes glassy. The dark circles under them were navy blue. I hadn't seen it coming. I hadn't recognized the signs.

"Take care of each other," Brady whispered to me like it was a secret. And then he held his arms out at his sides and fell backward off the cliff.

My screams ripped through the afternoon air, and I looked back to see that James was still too far away. I didn't know how to swim, but I ran full force and dove in after him. The minute I smacked the water, cold rushed up my nose and I choked, flailing wildly. "Brady!" I tried to yell, but gulps of water kept entering my mouth.

There was another loud splash behind me, and I knew it was James. I don't even think he saw me as he swam past, just as good of a swimmer as Brady. A log was jutting out from the bank and I grabbed onto it, watching.

The current was so fast it was pulling my legs downriver

as my body clung to the wood. And then I saw Brady—he was floating, facedown. He wasn't swimming. I screamed again, pointing toward him as I watched his body slam into a rock, and then another. James's arms were furiously lapping over and over, but Brady was too far ahead.

I started to cry, sobs curling my body around the branch. When Brady's body slammed against another rock, it stayed there long enough for James to reach him. James banged against the boulder, crying out as he did, but he pulled Brady to shore and started giving him CPR.

He was frantic, pounding on his chest, breathing into his lungs. But I could see from where I was that even if Brady wasn't full of water, his neck was broken. His head hung oddly to the side; his eyes stared out at nothing.

My brother—my best friend—was dead.

Comforting numbness seemed to stretch over me then. James was crying, screaming for help. He stood up, his hand shielding the sun as he looked for me. And I let go of the branch, letting the icy water pull me under.

I tried to drown, and really, it wouldn't have been that hard. The current was strong enough to keep me under, and I hoped I would pass out, blocking the images of my dead brother's last stare. I knew I couldn't go on. I couldn't face my parents. My life.

But then James had his forearm around my neck, pulling me to the bank to lay me on my back. I was choking, vomiting even then. My ears were plugged but I could see James above me, tapping my cheeks to keep me awake. When I could keep my eyes open, he left, running to his towel where his phone was.

James saved me. But he couldn't save Brady—neither of us could. In the end we did just as my brother asked—we took care of one another. Sometimes the survivor's guilt was more than we could bear, a secret between us that we never let show. But we were all we had left.

As I sit in James's house Monday morning, watching as he slowly pushes his bandaged arm through a shirt I picked out, I think that it's always been him doing the work. James has been the constant. Now that part of him is broken, finally infected. And just like that day at the river, I want to let go and go under.

"I brought Pop-Tarts," I say, brushing his hair aside as he sits and stares out the window.

"When's the funeral?" he asks, his voice so low I can barely hear it.

I swallow hard. After I left James Saturday night, I pushed down every feeling I had, let myself become a machine, doing whatever's necessary to keep us alive. Together. When I got home, my parents told me that Miller's mom had called and spoken with them.

"They're not having a funeral," I say. "The Program thinks it might instigate more suicide, so just his mom is allowed to bury him." Miller's face, his smile, pops into my head, but I quickly lock it away. There is no time to mourn.

James presses his lips tight together as his eyes well up. "It was my fault," he says. "Just like Brady. I was too late. I should have never left him behind."

I wrap my arms around James. "Miller was sick, James. There was nothing we could do." He turns in my arms.

"And Brady? I was there and I couldn't save him."

My heart aches, but I can't let myself think about Brady today, not when we have to go to school. "I couldn't either. And what's done is done. You need to pull yourself together."

James reaches up to put his palm on my cheek, and I turn my face into it. "I can't," he murmurs.

I stare into his blue eyes, panicking, but I press my forehead against his. "I will save you this time," I whisper. "I will save us both."

James pulls me into a hug, burying his face in my neck, and I run my fingers down his back, trying to calm him. I've never felt strong, not when so many things in this world are out of my control. But now I have to be. Because I'm all we have.

CHAPTER NINE

In the past day have you felt lonely or overwhelmed?
NO.
Have there been any changes in your sleeping patterns?
NO. I haven't slept since Miller died.
Has anyone close to you ever committed suicide?
I fill in NO. I stare at the darkened oval, willing it to be true. Wishing that I could ever just fill in the goddamn NO! I blink back the tears that are starting, and I erase the mark, making sure no traces of it exist. And then, with coldness in my soul, I fill in YES.

After an hour of intensive therapy to deal with my "loss," I find James at my locker and walk him to his classroom, making sure he can pass for normal—at least for fifty minutes. When I get to economics, the first person I see is the handler, the dark-haired one who's always watching me.

Next to mine, Miller's desk is empty, and a deep hollow feeling opens in my chest. But in the corner, watching me with a soft smile on his lips—as if he's been waiting for me—is the handler.

My heart races as I sit, not looking back at him again. I wonder if I'm about to get flagged. Please, God. Don't let them take me.

When the bell rings, Mr. Rocco walks in and shoots an uneasy glance at Miller's desk and then at the handler before launching into his lesson. I clasp my hands under my desk, squeezing tightly to keep my composure. It's torture, trying to pay attention, trying to put up the appearance of wellness. I want my phone to vibrate so that I know James is okay too. But nothing happens.

Sweat has started to gather on my upper lip, and I feel like I can't take another moment of not knowing how James is when the bell finally rings. I jump and immediately stuff my book into my backpack, standing quickly as I head toward the door. Just then someone grabs my arm.

I swing around, startled, and am face-to-face with the handler. I suck in a breath, nearly falling over. It's happening. No. No. No. It's happening.

The handler lets go of my elbow and smiles sympathetically. "Sloane Barstow," he says, and his gravelly voice is like sandpaper on my soul. "I'm sorry for your loss. I just have a few questions for you if you don't mind." His eyes are wide and dark, his skin a deep olive. He's twenty, maybe younger, but I see no true compassion on his face. I see something else, something that makes my stomach knot. He *wants* to take me.

"I already had therapy today," I say, stepping back from him.

He laughs. "This isn't therapy. Follow me, please." He walks past me, and I'm struck again by the medicinal smell of the handlers. I wonder if he has drugs on him right now that could put me out, something they occasionally do when apprehending someone for The Program. Or he could use the Taser at his waist.

I feel for my phone in my pocket, but don't dare text James. I need him to stay calm. But then I wonder if they've gotten to him, too. I hope not. He's in no condition for an interview.

It happens, after a suicide. They send us all to counselors to make sure we're okay. Sometimes a few extras are sent in to interview those who aren't taking the loss well. But it's rarely a handler. It makes me uneasy that this is the same guy who's been watching me since taking Kendra. But I have no choice so I follow him toward the main office.

When we get there, a small room is ready for us. Two chairs face each other in the dim space. I gulp down my fear as I enter, hating the idea of being alone with this guy. But principals and teachers don't interfere with The Program. They look the other way when I enter.

"Please sit," the handler says, closing the door behind us and drawing the blinds. My fear is so strong, but I know I can't let it show. I take a deep breath and lower myself into the chair.

"This really isn't necessary," I say, trying to sound like a normal girl. "I hardly knew Miller."

The handler smiles at this, coming to sit across from me, the knees of his white pants almost touching mine. I try not to flinch away from him. "Really?" he asks, obviously knowing the answer. "Well, then how about Lacey Klamath? Or perhaps your brother? Were you close with them?"

I must visibly pale when he mentions Brady because he bows his head as if apologizing. "Miss Barstow, it has come to our attention that you are high-risk. You've suffered tremendous loss recently, so it's only my intention to evaluate you."

He's lying. He wants to flag me. They don't care about us, only the appearance that what they do works. I curl my toes hard in my shoes as the handler runs his eyes slowly over me. Goose bumps rise on my skin.

"Let's start with Miller. You were out of town when he terminated himself, correct?"

I hate him for making it sound clinical. "Yes."

"And Lacey was your best friend, but you were not aware of her condition before she was sent to The Program? You weren't trying to hide it from us?"

"No. I had no idea." And then I can sense what's coming.

"Are you hiding anything now?"

"No." I keep my face as calm as possible, meeting his eyes. I imagine that I'm a robot, void of feelings. Void of life.

"Do you have a boyfriend, Sloane?" The corner of his

mouth curves up when he asks, as if he's some guy I just met who's trying to flirt.

"Yes."

"James Murphy?"

Oh, God. "Mm-hmm."

"And how is he doing?"

"James is fine. He's strong."

"Are you strong?" he asks, tilting his head as he looks at me.

"Yes."

The handler nods then. "It's only our hope to keep you well, Sloane. You know that right?"

I don't respond, wondering what James will say under these questions. If they'll know from one look that he's sick.

"There is voluntary admittance into The Program if you start to feel overwhelmed. Or if you just need someone to talk to." He reaches out then and pats my thigh, a move that catches me off guard, and I jump.

The handler stands up and walks around my chair as if he's leaving. Instead he stops behind me, putting his hand on my shoulder. His fingers tighten on the muscle. "Have a good day, Sloane. Something tells me I'll be seeing you again soon."

And then he drops his arm and walks out, leaving me alone in the darkened room.

I practically run to lunch, terrified that James won't be there. I stop, swaying on my feet when I see him at our table, drinking from a carton of orange juice.

"You're okay," I say when I reach him, practically collapsing onto his lap as I hug myself to him. He doesn't hug me back, but he doesn't push me off, either. I press my face to his neck.

"Yeah," he says quietly. "I'm okay."

I pull back and look at his face, trying to gauge how damaged he is. His skin is pale and his mouth is sagging, like he's forgotten how to smile. I run my fingers over his cheek, and he closes his eyes when I do. "I was so worried," I whisper.

He doesn't move, and I hug him again, holding him tight like I want him to do for me, but he doesn't. After a while I let him go, and he starts to eat, taking small bites of his food. He stares across the cafeteria, but at no particular point. Just away.

"Has anyone interviewed you?" I ask.

He shakes his head no.

"They pulled me from class," I say.

James looks over at me. "What happened?"

"They asked about Miller. About you. . . ."

He doesn't react; instead he just turns back to his food. I miss him so much, even though he's right in front me. He's not the same. "No one's spoken to me," he says. "I haven't even seen any handlers today."

And although that should make me feel better, his statement only makes me more uneasy. Why did they pull me? Either I was the one being evaluated or they were collecting evidence on James. I'm not sure which it was.

"I want to get out of town," I say. "Do you think you can get away? I want to go camping again."

James chews slowly. "I can try."

The emptiness in his voice is killing me, and I'm not sure I can keep this up much longer. "Don't you want to go with me?" I ask, my voice small.

He nods. "Of course I do, baby."

I exhale, leaning to put my head on James's shoulder. Under the table, his hand finds mine and I feel better, like this small show of life can mean something. Movement in the corner catches my attention, and I dart my eyes over there, finding the handler watching me with a smile on his lips.

CHAPTER TEN

THE REST OF THE WEEK IS MORE OF THE SAME. I try to keep up the appearance of normal, especially when I feel *him* watching us. The handler is in my classes, the cafeteria, always staring. Always a smirk on his face. It's like he's willing me to mess up.

They don't pull James aside for an interview, and I wonder what it means. Did I seem more depressed to the handler? Have they already decided to take James?

When Friday comes, I practically drag James from the building, so relieved that I won't have to fake it through another day. But oddly enough, I don't think I want to cry either. I've almost convinced myself that Miller really wasn't our best friend. It's the only way I can deal.

I prepacked the car so we can head directly to the campsite.

James is silent in the passenger seat, staring out the window. My parents seemed a little wary about us going so soon after Miller, maybe even a little suspicious. They asked why James hasn't been by the house, and I told them he was studying—which is probably why they were suspicious in the first place. At James's house I've been a permanent fixture, whispering to him and pretending like we're being playful when his dad is around. Really I'm just telling him to hang on. I put him in his bed at night and tell him that I love him and that I won't let anything happen to him. He doesn't say it back. I'm scared that he never will again.

James sits, staring at the fire pit, while I put up the tent, grunting and scraping myself with the poles. I continue to look over at him, but he never looks back. When the camp is set up, I grab my sleeping bag from the car, feeling exhausted. I call to him, tossing the other bag in his direction.

"You can at least bring in your own sleeping bag," I say, trying to sound light. "You're making me do everything."

He doesn't respond, but he does get up, walking behind me to the tent. He climbs inside as we lay out our bags, his gaze a million miles away.

"Hey," I say, pausing in front of him to brush back his hair. "Do you want to lie down for a little bit?" His eyes meet mine, but only for a second, and then he nods and kneels down on his bag, spreading out on his back. I chew on my lip as I get down next to him, curling up against him the way he used to like. My thigh over his, my face at the crook of his neck.

I rest my hand on his chest and listen to him breathe. He doesn't touch me. "I miss you," I say quietly. "I'm so lonely without you, James. I'm trying to be strong, but I'm not sure how much I have left. You have to come back to me. I don't think I can get through this alone." My eyes well up, but James doesn't move. God, I just want him back. I want to hear his laugh, his sarcastic comments, his fake ego. "I love you," I whisper, and the tent is quiet.

I'm losing him, just like I lost the others. I sniffle back the start of tears and talk like he's there with me. "I won't let you go, you know?" I say. "I'm never going to just give up. So don't even think about getting another girlfriend." I smile, pretending he laughed. "I know things are bad right now, but they'll get better. You're not like Brady. You won't quit. You won't leave me on the side of a river wondering why. You're stronger than that. I know you are."

I slide my hand under his shirt, resting it over his heart. His skin is warm, familiar. The beating is slow.

"We should probably get that heart rate up," I say lightly. "You could use the exercise." I get up on my elbow, looking down into his beautiful face, his eyes fixed on a point beyond the tent that I can't see. "Hey," I whisper. When he slowly drags his gaze to mine, it's lost and unfocused.

James and I have a million shared memories, but somehow I know that talking about his little-league games or the time he sliced open his foot on a rock isn't going to snap him out of this. Instead I run my hand down his upper body and over his stomach, stopping when I get to the top of his jeans. And when I slip my hand inside them, his eyelids flutter and he takes a breath, but just a small one.

I think quickly, remembering that I don't have any condoms. I doubt James brought any, and neither of us, right mind or not, would ever take a chance. Not in this world. But I want him. I want him to forget how sad he is.

"I love you," I say, but James's eyes are shut. I lean down and kiss softly at his lips, nearly stopping when he doesn't respond. Then I kiss his neck, his chest. I undo his button as I kiss his stomach and then lower. And it isn't until I feel his hand in my hair and hear him murmur my name breathlessly that I know I have him back—even if only for a second.

"Do you want me to build a fire?" I ask. James is wrapped tightly around me, his cheek against the back of my neck.

"No," he says softly, holding me. "I just want to stay here with you."

I smile a little and realize it's the first real smile I've had since Miller died. The thought of him makes the happiness quickly fade. "Miller would want you to be okay," I whisper.

James swallows hard and his arms loosen from around me. "I'm not well, Sloane," James says. I turn and face him. His eyes are bloodshot, his chin growing stubbly.

"Don't say that," I tell him.

"I'm going to kill myself."

My entire chest seizes up, and I grab James hard, pulling him toward me. "Don't you dare!" I cry out. "I swear to God, James!" But I'm shaking so hard I'm not even sure he can understand my words. "Don't leave me," I sob. "Please don't leave me here alone. Please."

Slowly James puts his arms around me and guides me against his chest, brushing back my hair. "Sloane," he says. "I can't go into The Program. I don't want to forget you, forget Brady."

I pull back and look at him. "Do you think you'll remember if you're dead? You promised me, James. You promised forever." Tears roll down my cheeks, and I expect him to wipe them and tell me it's going to be okay.

Instead he tightens his arms, clinging to me silently as I rest beside him. But he didn't agree to not kill himself.

"Please hold on," I whisper. "Tell me you'll hold on."

His breath is warm against my skin. "I'll try."

We lie around in the tent until it's dark, leaving only to get energy bars and water, and then later to use the bathroom. I don't sleep all night, worried about what tomorrow will bring. Wondering if the old James will ever come back.

And when the sun rises again, I look over at him hopefully. He's on his back, staring into nothing, and I know that he's lost. And so am I.

CHAPTER ELEVEN

IT'S BEEN TWO WEEKS AND TWO DAYS SINCE MILLER died, but James is still not himself. I'm exhausted, keeping up our front, pretending to be okay. I do James's homework, ripping out his pages of black spirals and instead writing in math logarithms. I walk him to his classes, making sure he doesn't try to buy QuikDeath, always watching if anyone notices his change.

It's clear they do. Other students avert their eyes when we pass, not wanting to be associated with us for the risk of getting flagged. I know time is running out, and so I overcompensate even more. I get louder with my laughter. Kiss James passionately in the hallway—even though he doesn't respond. I'm starting to forget what he was like before. I'm starting to forget what we were like before.

Nearly a month after Miller's death, our classes change for

the semester. James ends up in my math class by some miracle—or maybe it's the fact that our student population continues to dwindle. There have been two suicides since Miller. I notice an increase in handlers, including the one who watches me.

And he's here now, standing at the door of our class with another handler, staring in. Next to me James sits, looking down at his desk. He hasn't taken out his notebook. He doesn't move.

"James," I whisper, hoping to not draw attention to us. "Please." But he doesn't respond.

There is a shuffling of feet, and I know it before I even look up, know it by the sound of gasps in the room. My eyes start to water, but I hold back the tears and watch my boyfriend. I know what's coming next.

"I love you," I murmur to James. "You'll come back to me." My words are barely a breath when the white coats come into my vision. Surrounding him. Grabbing him from his chair.

I almost vomit, but I grip my desktop and keep back my tears. Around me, the other students drop their heads, not wanting to betray their emotions. My James. My James.

The handlers are pulling him to the door, but James suddenly looks back at me, his blue eyes wide. He starts to fight, tearing from their grip. My face nearly breaks with a cry.

"Sloane!" he yells, falling to his knees as they hold him. "Wait," he says fiercely to them. But they're not listening. They're pulling him back, the one handler shooting me a glare, warning me to not respond.

I try to smile, anything to let James know that he'll survive this. And that I'll be here when he gets back. I kiss my fingers and hold them up in a wave. He stops, letting the handlers get ahold of him.

Then James closes his eyes, and lets them drag him to his feet and out the door.

When he's gone, several people look back at me. The teacher stares at me. Everyone is waiting to see my reaction, if I'll be next. If they'll come rushing in here any second. But I do nothing. Inside I'm dying, ripping apart and bleeding. I'm so far gone I'm not sure I can get back, but I open my notebook and poise my pencil over it, as if ready to write.

I keep my breaths measured, waiting. And then the teacher starts talking again, going on about the latest math concept. I hear the chairs squeak as the other students give her their attention.

I don't wipe my face as one tear, one I just couldn't hold back, hits my notebook with a quiet tap. I close my eyes.

James has always been terrible at math. Brady used to try to teach him, but it was no use. My boyfriend was completely helpless.

I remember once while they were doing homework, Brady called me into the kitchen. He and James were at the table, books spread out in front of them. It'd been a month since that first camping trip when James caught me staring. I'd spent every moment since then avoiding him. I tried to pretend that nothing had changed, even though I'd see him looking at me strangely, as if trying to figure out if he should talk to me or not. He did still talk, but I never met his eyes. I already felt stupid enough.

"Sloane," Brady called. "Check this out."

I walked into the kitchen, taking an uneasy glance at James as he sipped his soda, not acknowledging me. "What's up?" I asked my brother, nervousness in the pit of my stomach.

Brady pointed his finger to a problem on the page, a math formula with an example. "What's the answer?" Brady asked, grinning widely and looking over at James—who was continuing to not notice me.

I swallowed hard and then narrowed my eyes, computing the problem in my head. "X equals eight," I said. "Why?"

Brady laughed and James shook his head, a smile on his lips. James reached in his pocket and pulled out a five-dollar bill, slapping it on my brother's open book.

Brady picked up the money triumphantly. "Told you she was smarter than you."

"I never said she wasn't," James answered, finally darting a glance at me. "I already know your sister is smarter. She's prettier than me too, but I didn't bet on that. I just wanted you to call her in here so she'd look at me again. It was worth the five bucks."

Before I could even understand what he'd said, James was flipping though his book, the corner of his mouth turned up in a half grin. Brady handed me the five.

"You deserve this," he said, "for always putting up with his shit." Brady laughed it away as if James was just teasing me, and my face burned with embarrassment. Humiliation.

I crumpled up the money and tossed it at James, bouncing it off his cheek. He looked up, surprised, and Brady chuckled. "I don't want your money," I said, and turned to go up the stairs toward my room.

"Then what *do* you want, Sloane?" James called after me, sounding amused, as if daring me to answer. I paused at the stairs, but didn't turn around. And then I went to my room.

I know James won't come looking for me this time. Not like he did that day, apologizing. James is in The Program now. The James I know is gone.

"Sloane, honey?" I hear my mother say on the other side of my bedroom door. I lay listlessly on my bed, willing myself to answer her.

"Yeah?"

"It's time for dinner. Can you please come down? I've called three times already."

Had she? "Sure. Okay." I slowly stand, looking down at my clothes. I wish that there were bloodstains or tears, something to outwardly show how hurt I am. But instead it's just a pair of jeans and a pink T-shirt. Something so painfully average that it makes me hate myself. I head downstairs.

My parents sit at the dining room table, pleasant smiles plastered across their faces. I try to return a smile of my own, but I'm not sure I pull it off. My father's brow creases.

"I made your favorite," my mother says. "Spaghetti and meatballs."

I know the homemade sauce took her forever to make, so I say thank you. I take a seat and wonder what sort of pills I can find in the medicine cabinet, wondering if I can find something to help me sleep.

"James's father called," my mother says softly. "He told us James was sent to The Program today."

My stomach twists around her words, and I reach out to sip from my water. The ice cubes rattle in the glass as my hand shakes.

"He's going to be safe now," my mother adds. "We're all so grateful for The Program. We hadn't even known he was ill."

I'd known. But now I also know that he's gone, and when he comes back, I won't be a part of his life. He'll be wiped clean.

"Sloane," my father says in a low tone. "Your mother is talking to you."

I look up at him, the anger clearly on my face because he straightens in his chair. "What would you like me to say to that?" I ask, my voice barely controlled. "What is the appropriate response?"

"That you're happy that he's going to get better. That you're happy he won't harm himself."

"They took him," I snap. "They came into class and they dragged him out. There is nothing happy about this."

"Sloane," my mother says, sounding startled. "Did you

SUZANNE YOUNG

know he was sick? You didn't try to conceal it, did you? He could have . . ." She stops, looking horrified.

I can't believe they don't understand. I wonder if it's because adults would rather forget about their problems, the thought that ignorance is bliss. But The Program steals our memories. They reset our emotions so that we're brand-new, never having been hurt or heartbroken. But who are we without our pasts?

"James would have rather died than gone to The Program," I say, picking up my fork. "And now I know why."

My mother tosses her napkin onto the table. "He's going to get help, Sloane. Isn't that what matters? I wish we would have gotten to Brady in time."

I cry out, the rage inside me too much to contain. "Are you really that stupid?" I shout at her. "Do you really think Brady would have wanted his memory erased? Nobody wants this, Mom. No one wants to be numb. They're killing us!"

"No!" she yells back. "You're killing yourselves. They're saving you."

"By taking away everything that made my life worth living?"

"Is this just about James? Honey, I'm sure when he comes back—"

I throw my fork across the room, banging it off the wall. "It's not just James! They'll take out parts of *me*. Parts of Brady. I won't even know my friends. I won't remember why I love going to the river. . . . It's because that's where James first kissed me. Did you know that? That's where he first told me he loved me. And now they'll take that from him and he won't remember. He won't even know who he is."

"If it's meant to be, you'll find each other again."

I scoff. "I hate you," I say, tears streaming from my eyes.

I told my mother that once before, after my brother died. She threatened to send me to The Program and I never said it again. Now I stare at her, all my emotions spinning into a dark spiral.

"Actually, I take it back," I say to her, smiling sadly. "I hate myself more." And then I run for my mother's car in the garage, needing to get away. From her. And from everything.

CHAPTER TWELVE

I DRIVE THROUGH THE COUNTRY, THE LONG ROUTE
that James and I used to take. I don't turn on the radio; I don't
turn down the blasting heater. Instead I let sweat race down my
back. It's suffocating and thick in here, but I don't care. I slow
down when I get to the stretch of farm where there is nothing
but cows. Them and me.

When I'm on the side of the road, I put the car in park and
stare down at my hand. At the purple ring that James gave me.
It doesn't take long for me to dissolve into tears, screaming until
my voice breaks completely. I'm practically hyperventilating
when the thought hits me. When the clarity of it is too much
to resist. It's like a sudden calm, erasing my pain. It's peaceful-
ness. I wipe absently at my face and sit up straighter, shifting
the car into gear.

I know what to do. What James would have done if I'd let him. There's no way I can hide my despair. They'll come for me soon enough, if they're not planning to already. They'll take me away, mess with my mind, clear away my memories of James, Miller, and possibly even Brady. They'll take away everything that makes me me, and send me back clean. Empty.

I almost smile as I swing onto the road, driving too fast. Not caring if I crash. Almost hoping I do. But if I don't, it'll be okay.

Because I'm going to the river. I'm going for a swim.

I don't go to our usual spot. I go to where my brother died, and stand on the edge of the cliff, looking down at the rushing river water. It's barely after five, the sun's high above me, and I'm still in my perfectly normal clothes. In a way, I wish I'd worn something that meant more to me, like one of James's old sweaters, or Brady's T-shirts that we never got rid of.

I lift up my hand and look again at the purple heart ring. It seems like a lifetime ago that he gave it to me, and I realize it was. It was Miller's lifetime ago. I start to cry.

Bringing the ring to my lips, I kiss it, thinking of where James could be. We know nothing of The Program, what it really does to people. On the news a few months back, they did an investigative report, but the story was overshadowed by the rising number of deaths. Any small violations they found— overuse of pills, patients being tied down—were pushed aside and the focus was on the results. No one in The Program died.

SUZANNE YOUNG

They all went on to graduate, turn eighteen, disappear off the government radar.

I lower my arm and watch the strong current below me. The drop is nearly twenty feet. The river is deep enough here that I won't smack the bottom, but I will get pulled under. I will be swept away, just like Brady was that day. And like him, I won't fight it. I'll let the darkness take me.

Closing my eyes I silently apologize to my parents, to everyone I've let down. And then . . . I fall forward.

The wind rushes over my face and the feeling of dropping flutters my stomach and makes me gasp in a breath just as I hit the water. Sharp coldness envelops me and fills my mouth, and I swing out my arms as I'm plunged deeper, pushed forward. It's dark and icy and all at once I'm terrified—lashing out for something to grab onto. I fight to breathe, but take in a mouthful of water instead, gagging as my body convulses. *Oh, God. I'm drowning!* The pressure closes in on my chest, and I realize that I don't want to die. *I don't want to die here!*

Just then my body slams against a rock, hoisting me halfway out of the water. I hold on to it, vomiting up river until I'm sure I'll pass out and die anyway. My throat burns, my lungs ache. My arm is numb and I think it may be broken. I'm focused on trying to breathe, even though my throat feels too tight. My adrenaline is keeping me conscious, but beyond that is a fear I've never known. Vulnerability I've never felt—and never want to feel again. I start to whimper.

The river rushes by, my legs pulled downstream, but I hang

on, listening to the sound of my shallow breaths. My eyes feel swollen and raw, and I blink as I see the world around me. The green of the leaves, the gray of the rock, the glistening of the setting sun on the water.

I lay my head on my broken arm, my clothes stuck to me as I stare at my ring. I couldn't kill myself, couldn't let go like so many others had. I wonder if in their last moments they'd changed their minds, but there was no boulder to grab on to. I start to sob as I think about Brady and about how I should have gotten to him in the water sooner. Maybe he wanted to live. Maybe it's my fault that he didn't.

I cling to the rock, crying until the thoughts fade and my body's spent. When I feel empty, I gather my strength and climb across the boulder, dragging myself to the shore. My legs are so numb from the cold that I can barely feel them touch the ground. My arm starts to throb at my side, and one of my shoes is lost in the river. It's dark when I finally make it back to the car. I'd left my key in the ignition, and when I turn it, I crank the heat to slowly thaw underneath the warm air.

I stare through the windshield and think about how James will return from The Program. They might not let me near him for a while, but they will eventually. And James isn't like other people. He's smart. Resourceful. What if he doesn't get hollowed out? What if he comes back and remembers me? If it were me, if I'd been sent to The Program, I'd do everything I could to remember him. I'd find a way. I have to believe that James will too. I have to believe in him.

SUZANNE YOUNG

*　　*　　*

My father is sitting on the porch stairs when I pull the car into the driveway. He jumps up immediately, rushing toward me. I shut off the engine and wait until he wrenches open the door.

"Sloane!" he calls, and then stops when he sees me. "What happened?"

I slowly drag my eyes over to his. "I was trying to learn to swim," I say, and shrug. But when I do a sharp pain tears through my arm. I wince and look down at it.

"Are you hurt?" He leans in to touch me but I shrink away.

"Don't touch it," I say. "I think it's broken. The current was too strong and it—"

"Helen!" my father yells over his shoulder, calling to my mother. "Come on, sweetheart," he says to me, gently taking my uninjured elbow to help me out.

"Where were you?" My mother's voice is frantic as she jogs from the house, her skin pale in the light of the front porch. Her hands search me, brushing back my wet hair, looking at the cuts on my cheek.

"I was trying to swim," I say, and meet her tired eyes. "I know I've been horrible to you lately, and I thought maybe this could make up for it." My mother has always wanted me to learn how to swim, even though I was scared of the water. Once my brother was gone, I vowed never to learn. But I hope this lie makes her feel better. "I'm sorry," I add, lowering my head.

"Oh, Sloane," she says, hugging me. "You can't do things like this. I was so worried, I almost called the police to look for you."

I stiffen. "Did you?" I'm suddenly terrified that she used the number on the pamphlet next to the phone. That my own mother would turn me in.

"No," she says. "Your father said you'd be back. That you were just . . . venting." She pronounces the word as if she can't remember what it means. I shoot a look at my father, but he keeps his eyes downcast. I wonder exactly how much he knows about where I've been.

"It was an accident," I say to my mother, trying to sound as peaceful as possible. "I thought it'd be great to learn, something to surprise James with when he comes back. But then I got pulled downstream. I'll be more careful next time."

"We should probably get you to the emergency room for that arm," my father cuts in. My mother gives him an alarmed look, as if he's stealing me from her.

"It's okay," I tell her. "I know how much you hate hospitals." I smile then, trying to make her feel better. Or maybe I'm putting up the facade again: *I'm healthy, Mom. See?* The guilt from my outburst at dinner nags at me, the promise of James coming back strengthens me. I can make it through six weeks. James will be here and we'll be together. We'll beat The Program.

My mother hugs me again, and I wince at the pressure on my aching arm. "Sorry," she says. "I'm just so happy you're okay. I can't . . . I can't lose you, too."

Her words strike my heart and remind me of Brady, how she cried for weeks after he died. How my father would drink too much, and then they'd scream at each other. I'd tried to comfort my mother, until my own grief got the best of me. And then James became the only person I could trust to see that side of me.

"I'm okay, Mom," I say, sounding light, surprised how easily the lie comes out. "You don't have to worry about me."

She nods, clearly relieved, and I walk around the car as my father gets in the driver's seat. I raise my good arm and wave good-bye. Then I climb in and pull my seat belt tight. My father starts the car and backs us out of the driveway, smiling at my mother reassuringly as we pass her. But once we're in the street, he looks sideways at me.

"Sloane," he says, his voice low, "I know you weren't trying to swim. But what I need to know right now is if you're going to do it. If I have to call The Program to make sure your mother's last living child doesn't die."

"Dad—"

"Don't lie to me," he says, not angry. Just tired. "I just need the truth now. I don't think I can bear anything else."

"I won't hurt myself, Dad. I . . . couldn't."

He stares out at the road as we head toward the hospital. "Thank you."

And I watch my father, remembering how funny he used to be when Brady and I were kids. How he'd take my brother to R-rated films when he was in middle school, and me out for ice cream when I felt excluded. Now he looks older, wilted. The loss of my brother was too much for him, and sometimes I feel like he barely notices me at all anymore—except to make sure I'm still breathing.

When we get to the emergency room, I tell them the trying-to-swim story, staying mostly believable. I have a small, clean break, and they tell me I'm lucky. *Lucky.*

Once my cast is set, we leave the hospital to go back home, and my father is silent the entire way. I worry that he'll never speak to me again.

CHAPTER THIRTEEN

I WAIT. THE DAYS TICK BY AND I SIT ALONE AT LUNCH, watching the door, avoiding the gaze of the dark-haired handler. My arm is still in a cast, and I tell everyone it was an accident. They accept it with suspicious looks, but nothing more. After all, I'm smiling and looking pulled together. If I were sick, I couldn't do that. I'm fooling them.

I spend more time with my parents, nodding numbly when they talk about The Program or comment on the latest news story. Suicide has had a surge in London, and they've implemented their own version of The Program. So far it's been wildly successful, proving that America seems to have developed a treatment.

It makes me wonder about the future—the sort of people who will be walking around in twenty years. People who never experienced their teens because those memories were erased. Will they be naive? Empty?

I remind myself that James will be okay. He'll come back and be the same. I have to believe that.

After school, I decide to go to the Wellness Center to gain credits, prove a point. Being seen there will show how healthy I am. How involved I am in my own stability. But really, I'll be waiting for James, knowing he'll show up sooner or later.

The building is located within the middle of the city, a former YMCA. It's brick and old-looking, but the welcome sign is brightly colored, hinting at what's inside. The Program is proud of their returners, of their system that is starting to see increases in voluntary admittance. The Wellness Center is the perfect front.

Come see the results, come see how shiny and new you can become.

I stand out front, reluctant to go in. I'm afraid all these healthy people will see right through me, but I don't have anywhere else to go. I have to be strong.

"You need to sign in," the woman behind the desk tells me as I pause in the entry. Around her, the large open room is buzzing with activity, as if there's nothing outside these walls that could harm us. And the walls themselves are bright blue and green—loud and full of energy. I almost smile for real.

"Miss?" the lady asks, motioning toward the clipboard and the pen attached with yarn. "Sign in for credit."

I sign my name and address on the paper and then scan

the room. I recognize several faces—both returners and normal people. I don't know any of them that well, or at least, I don't until I see Lacey. She's on the couch playing video games with Evan Freeman. There is a handler in the corner, but he's not the dark-haired one I'm afraid of. He's blond, just standing there and watching Lacey silently.

I think about going over there, introducing myself, but something holds me back. In my head, I know that Lacey doesn't remember me, and yet, I hope that James will. So if I confirm that Lacey doesn't know me . . . what does that mean? I'm clinging to an unlikely expectation, but it's the only thing keeping me going. Every day I feel myself slip more and more, but I'm holding on. I'm holding on for James.

I wonder if Lacey even knows Miller is dead, if somewhere inside she misses him. Misses all of us. Can The Program take away our emotions, or do they always remain—only without a source?

On the other side of the room, a group of girls—including Kendra Phillips—are giggling and drinking Diet Cokes while sitting at a round table. I make my way over, casting another glance at the handler who seems to have noticed me, before sitting down with the girls.

They smile kindly, none of them remembering me as they keep talking, gossiping about boys, clothes, stuff that I can't even fathom caring about. But I've become a pretty good actress, so I laugh at the right moments, roll my eyes when it's needed. Inside, my heart hurts, but I cry only when I'm alone, on a long drive out in the country after leaving the center. No one is there to wipe my tears and tell me it'll be okay.

For three weeks I follow this pattern: Laugh, cry, laugh, cry. I've become numb, uncomfortably so. But it's the only way I can survive the time. When I finally get my cast off, I'm relieved as I stare down at my pale arm. James would have been so concerned if he'd seen me bandaged up the minute he got back. I hope he hurries.

The days tick slowly by.

I'm sitting at the table, painting my nails a horrid shade of pink as the girls talk about Evan Freeman—how he and Lacey are a thing. I don't react, pretending I don't know either of them. The door of the center opens, a soft jingle from the bells attached at the top.

I'm concentrating on painting the nail of my ring finger, gazing at the purple heart there. I'm about to move on to the next nail when I realize that the room has gone quiet. Finally. They've finally come for me.

Exhausted, I glance up, sure it's a handler to take me to The Program. But instead, the floor feels like it's dropped out from underneath me. There *are* handlers in their stiff white coats, but they're not alone. In between them, with a newly shaved head, is James. He's wearing a short-sleeved polo shirt, and I can see, even from here, the white marks on his arm. The tattoos have been removed, Miller's name stitched up.

James's eyes scan the room, curious but not intense. Not the way he usually looks at things. They don't even pause on me.

He's back. My James is back. This is the only reason I didn't die. This is the moment that kept me going.

James.

They walk him to a chair near the vending machines where a couple of guys sit, playing a game of cards. The handlers are letting James have his first bit of social interaction here at the Wellness Center where it can be monitored. He sits, not saying a word to the people at the table.

The handlers don't look at me, seemingly unaware of my and James's past. I wonder if that's true, or if they're trying not to draw his attention to me. Either way, I'm thankful that the dark-haired handler isn't here.

I run my eyes over my boyfriend's clothes. He looks smaller, as if he's lost weight while he was gone. I don't like that they took away his beautiful golden hair, but it'll grow back.

I ache to touch him.

I watch his slow movements, my heart pounding, adrenaline racing through my veins. The girls around me start talking again, but it's quieter, as if they can sense my change. I wait for the right moment to approach James. I won't let anyone keep him from me. I have to get close and make him see me. He'll be fine. He survived and now he's back. It's me and him forever.

Just then James pushes the cards away and stands, murmuring something to the handlers like he wants to leave. Panic explodes in my chest. He can't leave yet.

I jump up, nearly knocking over my soda as James turns to leave. He's flanked on either side by handlers as they head to the door, but I have to find a way to get his attention. If he can just see me, I know he'll remember. He'll ask if I'm checking him out. He'll laugh. He'll remember, I know it.

I think about what he would do if he were me. He'd be reckless. Sort of smartassish. I slide off my plastic purple ring and take aim. I wind up and shoot it, pegging James in the back of his shaved head. He stops, rubbing the spot. The handlers keep going, walking out the front door as the ring ricochets across the room, landing near the desk.

Slowly, James turns around, looking for whoever hit him. I'm in the middle of the room, not trying to hide the fact that it was me. His blue eyes glide over me, and I feel like he knows. I kiss my fingers and hold them up in a wave. Waiting.

James stares for a second and then rubs at his head again, as if it still stings. Then without smiling, without reacting at all, he turns and leaves the Wellness Center.

There's a knot in my stomach, one that's tightening. I hope that James will rush back in and acknowledge me, but when he doesn't, it's like my heart stops beating. Emptiness, deep and dark, swallows me whole. A tear slides down my cheek, but I don't bother wiping it. Why should I? Why should I even care?

When I take in a breath, it's a wheeze so filled with pain that the room goes silent. People turn to watch me as I stumble over to pick up my ring from the floor, so bright and hopeful on the linoleum tiles. The corner of the heart is chipped.

SUZANNE YOUNG

"Honey?" the woman behind the desk asks, the worry thick in her voice. I know I should pull myself together and answer. That I have to. But instead I walk out the door, wishing for the day to end.

The first time James kissed me we were at the river after my brother had bailed on us to go meet his girlfriend, Dana. James asked me to go with him anyway, and although I was nervous, I went. It'd been nearly three months since my feelings for him changed, since I'd noticed him.

I sat on a towel, skipping stones as James swam out to the small boat dock and did backflips into the water, the sun glistening off his skin. When he came back over to me, he was shivering. "Warm me up, Sloane," he said playfully, and got down on my towel, his dripping body cold.

"You're all wet." I laughed, trying to push him off as he tackled me.

"Now you are too." He used the bottom of my shirt to wipe his face, and I giggled, pulling it out of his hands. I was on my back and he hung above me, resting on an elbow, grinning down madly. "That's probably the closest you'll ever come to swimming," he said and shook his wet hair out, spraying me with droplets of water.

I held up my hands defensively, but when he stopped, his smile started to fade. He was watching me, almost curiously. I furrowed my brow. "What?" I asked.

"Would you let me kiss you?"

Tingles raced over my body and I felt my cheeks warm. I didn't know what to say . . . so I just nodded. James grinned, looking nervous. He leaned closer, stopping just when his lips touched mine. I was so scared of what would happen next. My first kiss.

"This is probably a big mistake," he murmured, and slid his hand into my hair, cupping the back of my neck.

"I know."

And then his lips pressed against mine, hot and soft. My arms wrapped around him and I pulled him down and he kissed me harder, his tongue touching mine. It was the most amazing feeling in the world, like an out-of-body experience. We kissed forever, or at least until the sun started to set.

When we finally stopped, James collapsed on his back, staring up at the sky. "Well, damn, Sloane."

I laughed, touching my lips with my finger. They felt swollen, but alive. Tingly. "That was fun," I managed to say.

James turned and looked over at me. "You know I'm never going to be able to *not* kiss you again, right?" he said. "For the rest of my life, every time I look at you, I'll have to kiss you."

I smiled. "The rest of our lives is a long time, James. I'm sure there will be other lips." The minute I said it, I hated the words. But James just slowly shook his head.

"Naw," he said, rolling to lean over me once again. "These are the only ones I'll ever want." And he kissed me again.

Maybe that's why I find myself at the river now, sitting on the bank watching the water. James had meant what he said, but that part of his life is over. Now he's someone else. Now my lips aren't his anymore.

He captured me that day. I'd liked him before, but after that, I couldn't go back to avoiding him. We spent every second we could together, even if no one knew. I wonder if things would have turned out differently if we'd told Brady. But then I wonder if my brother hung on as long as he did for us, to make sure we were okay.

It was two weeks after my brother died when James told me that he loved me. That he'd never leave me. That he would save us both. He promised.

He promised.

My parents ask about James, and I tell them he looks great. I smile. I joke that maybe he'll be good at math now. It's so fake that I see my mom and dad exchange a frightened glance, and then I excuse myself to my room. While I lie on my bed, I consider never leaving it again. But what good would that do? The handlers would just come and take me.

When I get up in the morning, I slip into a pair of jeans and a mismatched pair of socks. I don't bother brushing my teeth or combing my hair. I stare at the cereal in my bowl, not wanting to eat. Not wanting to feed this body. The idea of wasting away sounds so good that when my mother isn't looking I dump the food into the sink and leave the house.

I skip school. I can't even think about meeting with the therapist. Listen to the "good side" of The Program. Lie about how I feel about James being back. I won't go back to the Wellness Center again. I don't want to see James washed out. In a few weeks, he'll start talking, maybe even smile at someone. I wonder what I'll do if he gives another girl a plastic heart ring.

James doesn't know me, not even a flicker of recognition. It's like I never existed. We had so many secrets together and now they're just mine. The weight of them is too heavy for me to carry.

I park outside of a farm and take out a notebook, writing down my feelings. I have no one to tell anymore—not one person I can trust. I'm so alone it's like being dead but still conscious. In forty-five minutes, I've scribbled down so many words that they start to lose meaning.

Kiss, death, love, loss . . . the words are crashing into each other, and my tears soak the page. Then I give into the urge to cross off the words, pressing harder with each pass, making large circles. Soon I've gone through all the pages and I'm digging into the cardboard cover. I press so hard it's going through to my lap, scraping against my jeans. My skin. I press as hard as I can, and I whimper because it hurts. But I don't care. I can't care anymore.

I wish I were dead.

CHAPTER FOURTEEN

I'M CHEWING ON MY LIP AS I DRIVE, TEARING AT THE flesh, wincing when it burns. My lips are chapped from crying in my car day after day, but I don't care. My hair is knotted and uncombed, and again, I don't give a goddamn.

It's been four days since James came home. I sit through school but don't speak. Don't look up. My parents ask me questions that I answer vaguely. They're worried, but it doesn't matter. Nothing matters. Nothing ever did.

I drive by James's house sometimes. Once, I saw him through his living room window, staring out at nothing. I nearly went to the door, but I didn't know what to say. How do you tell someone that you're the love of their life if they don't know you? How could I survive his nonreaction?

When I pull up to my house after another bout of crying, I think about finally ending it. Stopping the fear and pain. I'm angry—angrier than I ever felt, but under that is a sadness I can barely comprehend.

I shut off the ignition and climb out of the car, walking lethargically up to the house. My hair is matted to my forehead, hanging partly in my eyes. I don't brush it back. I like it there because it helps me feel hidden. Like I could disappear.

I open the front door but the house is quiet. "I'm home," I say, but don't bother waiting for an answer. I start up the stairs toward my bedroom when I hear rustling.

"Sloane?" my mother calls, her voice sounding choked. I pause and turn to look at her. Her cardigan is wrapped tightly around her as she hugs herself, her brown eyes large and worried. For a minute I want to tell her that I'm okay, but I don't want to lie to her.

"I'm home," I repeat. I'm about to start up the stairs again, when my father emerges from the living room. His nose is red as if he's been crying.

"Honey," he says to me. "Come downstairs." His voice is soft, but different. Is that . . . Is that guilt?

My first thought is that James has killed himself. It's a mixture of devastation and relief. But then behind my father, the door opens. Two men, white coats, walk inside the entryway. My chest seizes.

"What are they doing here?" I ask, fear creeping over my skin. The handler with the dark hair is in my house. He's here for me.

My mother's lips quiver. "We were just so worried, Sloane. Since James came back, you haven't been the same. And after Brady, we couldn't take the chance. If you'd just—"

"What have you done?" I whisper.

My dad squeezes his eyes shut, and I can tell that he didn't want to do this. He didn't want to hand me over. I look at my mother again, hoping she can still stop it.

"What have you done, Mom?" But I'm so terrified that I can't breathe. The handlers walk through the entryway, stomping purposely toward the steps, toward me. With one last betrayed look to my parents, I tear up the stairs.

They can't take me. They can't take me.

I burst through my bedroom door and then slam it shut, locking it. I glance toward my window but worry I'd be too injured in the fall to get away. I look frantically around my room, at all the memories: the pictures of me and my brother. Of James. The handlers will take it all. They'll take everything.

Behind me someone jiggles the handle and then knocks. Bangs. I can't escape. And I can't bear the thought of losing everything. I can't let them have it.

I grab the picture of Brady and James off my mirror. In it, James is shirtless as usual and grinning widely, his arm over Brady's shoulders, the river behind them. My brother is midlaugh, as if James just said something really funny. I can't remember what it was.

The banging on my door gets louder and I hear my mother's

voice, pleading with me to open it. To not hurt myself.

I slip off my chipped purple ring, kissing it hard. *I love you, James*, I think. *Us forever, like you promised.*

I lift up my mattress, searching for the slit I'd made years ago when I was trying to hide notes from James. On the other side of the door, my mother announces to them that she's got the key. Just then I find the tear and slip the picture and the ring into it. Then I drop my mattress and cover it with the sheet. Once I'm gone, they'll sanitize my room, but they won't look there. I don't think they'll look there.

When I come back from The Program, I'll find it. And I'll find James and ask him about it. Maybe then we'll remember who we are. What we meant to each other.

I spy a pair of scissors on my dresser, surprised that I didn't notice them before. I consider fighting my way out. Stabbing the handlers—especially the one who has been after me from the beginning—and pushing past my parents. Refusing to let them take my life from me.

I grab the shears, clutching them in my fist.

There's a clicking sound and then the door swings open. My mother swallows hard when she sees the scissors in my hand. My father calls to me, sounding terrified.

I back toward the window. My face is hot and my mouth is wet. I think I'm drooling, overwhelmed with rage as I growl at them.

"Miss Barstow," the dark-haired handler says calmly as he enters. "Put the scissors down." He shoots a look to the other handler and they separate, each taking one side of the room to surround me.

"No." But my voice is like an animal's. My father starts to cry again and even though I'm angry, I can't hate him. Brady broke him. He can't go through it again.

"Miss Barstow," the handler repeats as he grabs for something at his waist. I suddenly realize he must have a Taser.

And I know it's over. This life, it's over. I meet my mother's eyes and force a bitter smile. "I'll never forgive you," I murmur. Then, just because this is my last moment of having a real emotion, I tighten my grip on my scissors. And I slash my wrist.

I fall back against the wall, the pain more immediate than I thought it would be. I close my eyes and feel hands grip me hard on my upper arms. A needle pierces my skin, and within seconds a wave rushes over me, crashing above my head and drowning me in sleep.

"Hello?"

I hear a voice, but I'm too tired to open my eyes all the way. I try again and fail. The voice laughs softly.

"Is there anybody in there?"

I feel a touch, a pinch in my arm, and then there's a rush of adrenaline. My eyes fly open and I take in a sudden breath. My arms are tight at my sides, as if tied down.

"Ah, there you are," the voice says. "Welcome to The Program."

PART II
THE PROGRAM

CHAPTER ONE

I SLOWLY LOOK TO MY SIDE, MY VISION A BIT BLURRY as I wake. Next to me, close, is the dark-haired handler. He smiles. "Worried I'd given you too much Thorazine. You've been out for hours." He reaches to brush my hair away from my face. I jump, turning my head violently away, repulsed.

"Don't touch me," I hiss. "Don't you dare touch me."

He laughs. "Miss Barstow, I know you're upset. I know you're unwell." He leans close, his voice a whisper in my ear. "But it's no excuse for bad manners."

I squeeze my eyes shut, thinking that maybe I should feel frightened, sad. But all I can feel is rage. They changed James. Lacey. They're going to change me.

"Now," the handler says, "I'm going to tell the doctor you're awake." He touches my hair again. "I'll be seeing you around, Sloane."

My stomach twists when he says my name. I try to turn my body away, but my hands are tied down with leather straps, buckled to the bed. As I move, my wrist hurts, and I remember how I cut myself in my room before they took me.

I clench my jaw tighter, listening to the sound of the handler's feet shuffling across the floor. When I hear the door close, I open my eyes and look around.

The room is white, just white. The walls are smooth and unmarked, and there is a chair next to my bed. Everything is clean and smells like rubbing alcohol. My heart pounds as I wait. I don't know what's going to happen to me. If it'll hurt when they get inside my head.

I lie back against the pillow, letting the sorrow seep in for a second. My parents betrayed me. I hate them, even though I know I shouldn't. They thought they were saving me, but instead they've condemned me to a half-lived life. I'm losing everything.

A tear tickles my cheek as it runs down, and I curse myself for not holding it in. I turn my head into my pillow to wipe it and then sniffle, staring at the ceiling. It's quiet—so quiet that the only sound is my breathing. I wonder if the silence alone can drive me mad.

The door opens with a quiet click. I freeze, not sure I want to look.

"Good evening," a deep voice says. It has the slightest hint of a British accent and it's calm. Almost inviting. I squeeze my eyes shut. "I'm Dr. Francis," he says, and I hear chair wheels squeak as he sits down.

I'm afraid to move, but when his warm hands touch my arm, I flinch. Then I realize he's undoing my wrist straps. I look suddenly to my side, where his fingers work to release me.

"I am sorry about this," he says as he unbuckles. "It's a precaution we have to take for all incoming patients."

"I don't want to be a patient," I reply.

Dr. Francis pauses, his green eyes searching my face as he studies me. His brown hair is clipped short and he's clean shaven. "Sloane," he says kindly. "I know you're scared, but we really only want to help. You don't see it, but you're sick. You even attempted suicide."

"No, I didn't. I just didn't want them to take me." I don't mention how I tried to drown in the river.

"We're not going to hurt you." He stands and walks around the bed, pausing at my other strap to undo it. "We're going to remove the sickness, Sloane. That's it."

"I've seen the returners," I tell him, narrowing my eyes. "I see exactly what you take."

When my hands are free, I sit up and rub my wrists, amazed at how much less vulnerable I feel now. But I'm in hospital scrubs, and I shiver, thinking that the dark-haired handler might have undressed me.

Dr. Francis pulls his eyebrows together with concern. "Everyone who comes into The Program is very unwell."

"That's not the point," I say. "We should have a choice."

"But how can a proper decision be made when the mind is clouded with disease? It's an infection, Sloane. A behavioral contagion. And we're the only cure." He pauses as if just realizing how cold he sounds. "I apologize," he says. "You should get settled first. I'll have the nurse come in to check on you." He nods to me before leaving the room.

I'm still shaking from the shot the handler gave me, but I can't help wonder if the doctor is right. Maybe I'm sick and don't realize it. I lie back in the bed, looking at the gauze wrapped around my wrist and remembering how desperate I felt.

But I can also remember the look on the handler's face when he came to get me—his predatory stare. He'd been waiting for that moment, waiting to get me here.

No. The Program isn't the cure. It's the end of me.

"And this is the leisure room," the nurse says, motioning ahead. She's grandmotherly, even wearing a knit sweater over her scrubs. But I think it's purposeful, that she's here to trick me somehow. I wrap my arms tighter around myself, my head still fuzzy, and shuffle behind her into the large room.

I'm dressed in lemon-yellow hospital scrubs with a matching robe, sunny slipper socks on my feet. I'd prefer something more depressing—maybe black, but I suppose that's why they picked yellow.

The leisure room doesn't look the least bit relaxing. Unlike the Wellness Center, this space has no color. It's stark white and bland, like a black-and-white movie with splashes of yellow. There are about twenty people in here. The Program takes patients between the ages of thirteen and seventeen, but most appear to be on the older side. There's no ping-pong table or chessboard. Instead there's a TV on one side with a couch in front of it. A few tables and chairs are poised near the windows—which I'm sure are sealed—looking over a lawn. There are a couple of computers with signs that read NO INTERNET ACCESS. The only thing that looks even slightly appealing is the game of cards going on at a table in the corner,

Three guys are sitting there, one chomping on a pretzel stick like it's a cigar. The way they interact—as if they're friends—floods me with a sudden longing for James and Brady. We used to play cards like that.

"Which facility is this?" I ask, feeling sick. There are three buildings that The Program uses. I wonder if this is the same one James was sent to.

"Springfield," she says. "Roseburg and Tigard are nearing full capacity. We can only handle forty patients at a time, so we're a tightly knit group here." She smiles and touches my shoulder. "We have about an hour before dinner. Why don't you try to make some friends?" she asks. "It's good for your recovery."

I throw her such a hateful glance that she backs up. *Friends?* They are about to erase my friends. With a nod, the nurse leaves me there, her grandmotherly facade falling away as she goes about her other duties.

I think then that maybe everything here is fake. They offer us a false sense of calm, but there is no such thing. This is The Program. I know how dangerous that is.

The guy across the room with the pretzel cigar laughs loudly, tossing down his cards. I'm so stunned to hear the laughter that I just stare, wondering how someone could laugh in a god-awful place like this.

Just then he glances over and notices me, his smile faltering a little. He tips his head in acknowledgment. I turn away.

I walk to the window and sit in the chair there, pulling my knees up to wrap my arms around them. How many people tried to jump out of these windows before they decided to seal them?

I've never been a fan of heights. Back when we were kids, my parents took us to an amusement park, and Brady convinced me to go on the Ferris wheel with him. I was probably eight or nine, and when we got to the very top, the cart stopped, frozen there. At first Brady joked around, rocking the cart back and forth. But he cut it out when I started crying.

"You must be afraid of heights, Sloane," he said, putting his arm protectively around me. "I'm sorry." He paused then, looking out over the park. "It's not good to have fears like this. It only makes it more likely that you'll die that way—a self-fulfilling prophecy."

I wiped at my face. "What?"

"I read it in a book once. So if you keep being afraid of heights, you'll probably die falling from something."

I grip the bar tightly, my breath starting to quicken. Brady chuckled.

"I don't mean today. I mean eventually. It's like the river, Sloane. You're afraid of swimming—so chances are, if you ever fall in, you'll probably drown. Your mind will make it happen."

I pause now, looking out on the lawn of The Program facility. I didn't drown in the river, even when I tried. But my brother did. Was it my fault because he knew I feared it?

"You look like somebody kicked your dog."

The voice startles me, and I look up to see the guy from the card table standing there. "What?" I ask, putting my feet on the floor.

"Yeah, you're right," he says. "They probably just erased its memory. Good point." He smiles. His dyed black hair is shaggy and long, sticking out in random directions, but not in an entirely bad way. The shadows are heavy under his eyes. On his neck, just below his jawline, is a jagged scar. I swallow hard and meet his dark eyes.

"Not really in the mood to joke around," I say. "Maybe another time." I turn toward the window, hoping he'll go away so I can retreat back into my memories. So that I can think of James.

"Okaaaaay," the guy says, taking a step back. "See you around then, sweetness." He shakes his head as he leaves, possibly surprised that I didn't want to chat. But I'm not going to do that here. I'm not interested in making friends. I'm interested in getting out.

CHAPTER TWO

IT'S EARLY WHEN THE NURSE COMES IN THE NEXT morning, the warm smile back on her face. I slept heavily, which I have no doubt is due to the medication they gave me before bed. "Time for you to meet your therapist, Dr. Warren," she says, taking my arm to help me out of bed. I feel groggy and sway on my feet for a second. "You'll really like her," she adds. "Fantastic doctor."

After a quick trip to the bathroom, I return, and the nurse gathers my hair into a ponytail. I don't stop her because it feels like sandbags are attached to my arms. She slides on my slipper socks and wraps my robe around me. "Okay, honey," she says. "Let's go. We don't want to be late."

I blink slowly and walk beside her as she leads me into the hallway. It's empty except for the dark-haired handler leaning against the wall, his arms crossed over his broad chest. He tilts his head down as I pass. "Good morning, Miss Barstow."

I don't respond, and instead tighten my grip on the nurse's arm. The handler is always there, always lurking. I'm afraid I'll never get away from him again.

"What time is it?" I ask the nurse, my voice raspy and thick with sleep.

"You have the first appointment of the day. Six a.m.," she responds.

I think that six in the morning is way too early to expect people to bare their soul, but maybe it's also a time when I'm more vulnerable. I clench my jaw, trying to fight back the fear as we pause in front of a wooden door. I don't know what's behind it. I don't know what they're going to do to me.

The nurse opens the door, and I hold my breath, waiting. She ushers me into a small office, clean and white. There's a comfortable-looking chair poised in front of a large wooden desk. The woman behind the desk rises and smiles at me.

"Good morning, Sloane," she says. Her voice is deep, authoritative and protective at the same time.

"Morning," I mumble, taken aback by how normal the room is. I'm not sure what I was expecting, but it definitely involved a much scarier scenario—electric-shock machines maybe.

"Thank you, Nurse Kell," Dr. Warren says to the nurse and then offers me a seat. As I collapse in the oversize maroon chair, I spy a glass of water on the good doctor's desk. Next to it is a bright-red pill. Doubt it's for her.

My eyes drift up to hers, and she presses her lips into a sympathetic smile. "You're angry," she says.

"You think?"

"Why?"

The question seems so absurd that I don't know how to answer at first. I stare at her. She's wearing thin, wired glasses, her dark wavy hair falls perfectly to her shoulders. Even her makeup looks flawless, as if she's not real at all. Just an actress on a set.

"I don't want to be here," I say.

"You tried to kill yourself, Sloane."

"Because the handlers were there," I shoot back. "I figured if they were going to take me, they may as well get a show, too."

The doctor nods with a disappointed expression and glances at the pill. "I think you should take this before we begin."

"And if I don't?"

She tilts her head. "Then you don't. This isn't a trick, Sloane. I want to help, but you're really on edge."

"No, I'm pissed. I want my life back. I want to go home."

"And you will," she says, leaning forward. "You will." She sounds so earnest that my first instinct is to believe her. People can't fake caring like that. Or at least they shouldn't be able to. "Please," she adds, motioning to the medication. "It really will make you feel better. All I want to do is talk."

I want to go home. I want my bed. I don't want to give in to the therapy. But if the pill will take away the sadness that is crushing my chest right now, maybe I'll take it this one time. Just to get me through. So I nod, and I pick up the little red pill and swallow it.

Dr. Warren adjusts her glasses and smiles at me. It's been twenty minutes since I took the medication, and I have to say, my body feels pretty good. My legs are over the side of the chair as I rest my head against the back. My muscles that have been clenched for days are finally relaxed and loose.

"I know that missing James is a main source of pain for you right now," Dr. Warren starts. "Maybe it would help if we talk about him."

"And why would I tell you?" I ask dreamily, and look past her to where the sun is shining outside the large windows. "You don't care about us."

"Of course I do. I'm here to help you, Sloane. I've devoted my life to helping stop this epidemic."

"Right."

"I'd love to hear how you and James met," she pressed again.

"He was best friends with"—I pause, a moment of raw emotion capturing me—"with my brother," I finish.

"The brother who committed suicide?"

I nod, and slowly the warmth of the medication seeps back in and washes away my pain. I'm so numb it's almost euphoric.

"Do you blame yourself for Brady's death?"

I flinch when she uses my brother's name. The fact that she even knows his name unsettles me. I don't want to talk about

Brady, and yet I find myself answering anyway. "Of course," I say.

"Why?" Dr. Warren leans her elbows on the desk.

"I was there," I say, trying to explain. "If I knew how to swim . . ."

"Does James feel guilty too?"

"Yes." I remember how many nights I held James's head in my lap, watching him cry. Listening to him tell me that he'd let Brady down. Let me down. I hate the image and I try to push it away, but it's stuck on a continuous loop that I can't stop. Like how I can't stop myself from telling the doctor this, even though I don't want to. I'm compelled to spill my guts—my ravaged, emotional guts.

"So you both took the blame," she says. "Took the loss hard. I bet that built quite a bond between you and James. Is that how you got together?"

"No. We'd started dating before that."

The doctor leans forward. "Tell me about it."

Even though something in my head tells me not to talk about him, my emotions overwhelm me. I miss him, and I want to remember what it was like before. For the first time in so long, I'm allowed to cry. I'm allowed to let it out. So I close my eyes and lean my head back into the chair.

And I tell her about the first time I realized I had feelings for James.

"Let me get this straight," the doctor says when I finish. "James tried to avoid the relationship at first?"

"Passive-aggressively, yes. We both loved my brother and didn't want to piss him off."

"Then how did you go from that to a relationship?"

"It took a while," I say, glancing at her. "Even that first day was confusing. After we'd gotten back to camp, it was awkward. Horrible. I figured it'd pass eventually. Then that night, the three of us got into our tent, Brady on one side of me, James on the other. It was a huge tent, and Brady was curled away from us. But James lay right at my side, his arm nearly, but not quite, touching mine.

"It felt like forever. All I could hear was his breathing, my breathing. I tried to close my eyes, but my body was tingling. I sensed him looking at me, and swallowed hard, wishing I could be asleep already. And just then, his hand brushed mine, so lightly, it was like nothing at all. I hitched in a breath and turned sideways, only to find him staring back." I smile. "His blue eyes were so confused, and I thought he was going to kiss me."

"Did he?" Dr. Warren asks.

I shake my head. "Nope. Instead he swore and then climbed up, grabbing his sleeping bag and his backpack. He unzipped the tent flap and went outside. He ended up sleeping in the car that night."

Dr. Warren pulls her eyebrows together. "Why would he do that? Were you upset?"

"Well, I definitely didn't sleep well. I felt guilty and embarrassed. Later James told me that when he touched me, when I looked at him, he got a hard-on." I laugh.

"So he's a romantic?" Dr. Warren grins.

"That's just James. He actually meant it as a compliment. But he was set on not liking me. So he went to sleep in the car. He was hoping I hadn't noticed—which I didn't. I wish I had, though, because I spent the next few weeks feeling miserable. Like I'd done something wrong."

The timer on her desk goes off, and Dr. Warren smiles at me again. "Fascinating story, Sloane. I hope tomorrow I can hear more."

I nod, feeling decent for the first time in weeks. Talking about James helped, as if he were here with me—the old James. The one I've missed so desperately. Although it might be naive, for a second I think it'll be okay. That maybe Dr. Warren really does want to help me.

"Wait," she says, handing me a Dixie cup. I glance inside and see a yellow pill. "Take this, Sloane."

"But—"

"It'll help the feeling last longer," she says, and smiles. I don't want to go back to the misery I felt when I walked in here, so I swallow it and leave.

As I'm walking down the hallway, heading back to my room, I feel a wave of dizziness. I rest my palm on the cool tile of the wall to balance myself. A streak of fear races through me. *Oh, no. What was in that pill?* I touch my forehead, thinking back on the session. But as I search my memories, I become disoriented and the world seems to tip sideways.

A hand touches my elbow. "Let's get you back to your room, Miss Barstow."

I look over to see the dark-haired handler, a sinister smile on his lips. I yank my arm out of his grip. "Leave me alone."

"Now, now," he says, teasingly. "Let's not be difficult. I can restrain you again."

But I'm not going to let him intimidate me. Threaten me. The Program can't have me. So I swing out my arm, punching the left side of his jaw. He immediately recovers and twists my hand up behind my back, cursing under his breath as he slams me against the wall. When there's a sudden pinch in my arm, the sedative, I laugh. "I don't care how many drugs you and the doctors give me," I say. "I'll never let you take my memories."

The handler leans in, his breath warm on my ear. "You stupid girl," he whispers. "We already have."

And then I sleep.

CHAPTER THREE

I'M IN MY CHAIR BY THE WINDOW AGAIN, THE SAME one I've sat in for three days. The sky is overcast and I'm glad. It's a bitter feeling, something like "if I can't be happy, no one should." I wonder what James is doing, but then I push the thought away, remembering that he doesn't know me anymore.

"I'm guessing another kicked-dog joke would be in bad taste, right?"

I don't turn toward the guy's voice, and instead continue to stare outside. I might even appear catatonic.

"Are you always so mean?" he asks.

"Yes," I answer automatically. I wish he would go away. I wish they all would go away.

"Charming. So anyway, I brought you this and wanted to

invite you to our card game tonight if you're up for it. But leave your horns and pitchfork behind." He sets a large pretzel stick on the table next to me and I look at it, but not at him. "Very exclusive card game, I might add." I can hear the smile in his voice.

I lean over and pick up the pretzel stick, examining it for a second before taking a bite. I say nothing and go back to watching the darkening clouds outside of the window. I hope it rains soon.

"You're welcome," the guy says, sounding defeated. "Maybe I'll see you later."

I wait until he's gone before looking up. He's on the couch with a red-headed girl, laughing hysterically, as if we weren't in The Program. As if this was a party in someone's parents' basement.

The pretzel becomes dry in my mouth and I think I might choke on it. And just then, the guy glances over his shoulder at me, his dark eyes concerned, and I turn away again.

"When did you and James start dating?" Dr. Warren asks. I sit back, looking her over as the medication makes the edges of my vision hazy. The doctor has her hair pulled up into a bun, her makeup and pantsuit paired nicely. She's perfect. She's fake.

I've been in The Program for close to a week now. I take the pills when they're offered, opting to sleep rather than live an actual life. Even though I don't trust Dr. Warren—not even a little—I took the pill sitting on her desk when I walked in. In therapy, it's like my past is more attainable, as if the medication can help me zero in with clarity. And when I'm with James in my head, I'm not so lonely anymore.

"I don't feel like talking today," I say, wanting to keep the thoughts to myself.

She sighs. "That's understandable. But I'm just really curious about you two. He's such a source of anger."

"No, he's not," I say instantly. "He's the only thing I care about anymore."

"But you're angry."

"Because you took him. You changed him."

"*I* didn't do those things. James was at another facility. But I've had a chance to look through his file." She lowers her voice. "It says that James attempted suicide in The Program. Would you rather he was dead?"

Her words cut through me and I touch my chest, startled. *James tried to kill himself?* Oh my God, the thought of it, just the thought makes tears stream from my eyes. "No," I whisper. "I wouldn't want him dead."

"That's good, Sloane," she says, like it answers a question. "That how you're supposed to react when someone wants to kill himself. Now, tell me more about James. It'll make you feel better, I promise."

I sniffle, putting my forearm over my face as I think back on my and James's life together. "I used to avoid him," I start, relaxing into the medication. "He'd be at the house with Brady, and I would duck out of the room, or just pretend he wasn't there. A few times he asked if I was okay, but I couldn't look him in the eyes after the camping thing. Brady told me I was acting weird." I laugh softly and lower my arm, remembering the face my brother would make when he said it.

"After a few weeks," I continue, "James got annoyed. He even paid Brady five bucks to get him to call me into the room with them. I thought he was making fun of me, but when I stormed off, things changed."

"How so?" Dr. Warren asks.

"James followed me upstairs, telling my brother he was coming to apologize. When he knocked on my door, I didn't want to let him in at first. But he said please." I smile, still able to hear his voice in head. Hear the soft, desperate way his words struck my heart. I was helpless to resist him, even then.

I wait before telling Dr. Warren the rest, wait as the drugs course through my veins, enveloping me in calm. I want to tell her everything. But first, I relive the moment for myself, seeking my own safe place in The Program.

When I opened my bedroom door, I found James leaning against the frame, looking utterly miserable.

"You hate me," he said.

"No."

"Then why are you ignoring me?"

I was thrown off, and looked past him into the hall to make sure no one was around. "What do you care?" I asked. "You already told me I wasn't allowed to . . ." I motioned between the two of us, my face burning with embarrassment.

"Yeah, I say a lot of stupid things, Sloane. Why did you listen to that one?"

I stepped back then, confused. Was he . . . ? Did he . . . ?

James pushed my door open wider and walked in, closing it behind him. I stared at him, not sure what he was going to do.

"Here's the thing," he said. "I don't want to like you." My heart sunk. "I don't even want to notice you're pretty. I want to tackle you in the dirt and make fun of your hair. I shouldn't be thinking about putting my arms around you. And I sure as hell shouldn't be thinking about kissing you right now."

I tiny gasp escaped my lips, and my entire body warmed at his confession. But I was terrified of what would happen next, what it would mean. "You can't kiss me," I said, taking another step back. "You'll ruin everything."

"I know!" he agreed. He looked around my room, clearly annoyed, and then back at me. "What have you done?" he asked me.

"Me?"

"God," he said, ignoring my question. "Do you know how many girls I *don't* like? And then the one I do . . . It's my best friend's little sister?"

Butterflies went crazy in my stomach. "You like me?"

His eyes met mine, and then he furrowed his brow like he thought I was stupid. "Yes, Sloane."

"And you're being mean to me because . . ."

Then suddenly, James's face cleared and he laughed. "I don't know exactly. But I've been trying to not like you since you gave me a hard-on in the tent so—"

"What?"

"Don't worry about it. Okay, so listen. We're not going to kiss or anything," he said, as if I'd propositioned him. "Maybe . . . I don't know, maybe if we hang out—just the two of us—we'll realize that we don't really like each other. You could end up hating me. I can be a total shithead."

My mouth twitched with a smile. "James, I've known you since I was in second grade. I'm not sure spending *more* time together is a great idea."

He watched me for a while, thinking it over. "Probably not," he said quietly. "But I want to anyway."

"Oh."

He shrugged. "Come here."

I widened my eyes, startled. *I thought he said we wouldn't kiss.* "No."

James didn't wait and instead moved to wrap his arms around me, pulling me into a hug. He rested his cheek on the top of my head, and I wasn't sure what to do. We didn't move for a long moment, and eventually I slid my hands from my side and put them around his waist. He sighed when I did.

"Freaking hell, Sloane," he breathed into my hair. "We're gonna end up making a mess of things."

"I know."

He squeezed me one more time and then dropped his arms, turning and leaving the room without another look back at me. I was stunned, standing there alone in my room. But after a moment, I put my hand over my heart and smiled.

I startle when the buzzer sounds the minute I'm done talking, signaling the end of therapy. I feel better, the remembered moments with James enough to make me want to live another day. Even if it's just today.

I stand to leave when Dr. Warren calls my name. I turn back and she smiles, sliding the Dixie cup with a yellow pill toward me. "You forgot your medication," she says.

Even though the calming effects of the last pill are still heavy in my system, I get a sudden sense that something is wrong. I look down at the medication, trying to figure out what's really going on.

"What's in the pills?" I ask, narrowing my eyes at Dr. Warren.

"I told you, just something to relax you."

"Then I don't need it," I say. "The last dose is still with me."

Her expression doesn't falter. "Take the pill, Sloane."

My heart kicks up its beats, and I move back a step. "No."

Dr. Warren removes her glasses, setting them beside her before folding her hands on the desk. "This is an important step in your recovery," she says. "You must take it or we'll have to give it to you intravenously. And that's never pleasant."

"You'd force me?" I ask. Even though I knew the situation all along, knew that I was in The Program against my will, the idea of being physically restrained again is enough to make me panic.

"This is treatment," Dr. Warren says. "Think of it as your antibiotic. We need to treat the virus, and then you'll be free of it. Take the pill and go home, Sloane. It's as simple as that."

I consider arguing, fighting my way out. But there's nothing outside this office but the stark white halls of The Program. And so I throw the doctor a hateful glare and lean forward to grab the yellow pill, swallowing it down before walking out.

CHAPTER FOUR

IT'S NEARLY DINNERTIME WHEN NURSE KELL COMES in to get me, saying that Dr. Warren has denied my request to eat in my room. The nurse helps me get dressed because I'm still groggy from my therapy session. I'm not sure I've had one clear moment since coming to The Program.

Nurse Kell holds my arm as we walk to the dining room, and the moving around actually helps me wake up a little. I try to think back on where the day went, but it's all a blur. "Stop drugging me," I mumble. "It's too strong."

Nurse Kell looks concerned. "Oh, dear. Well, I'll certainly mention it to Dr. Francis. Maybe he can change your dose."

"Yeah," I say, pulling my arm from hers now that I can stand on my own. "I'm sure he will." I turn away and head toward the serving line, looking over the different foods set out on trays. I don't want to eat. I don't want to talk. What I want is to take this tray and smash things with it, but I know that won't get me home any faster.

I grab my food and head to a table in the corner and sit down. I want to go home. I just want to go home.

"Are you going to eat or are you a starver?"

I look up to see the guy from the leisure room, the one who gave me a pretzel, standing at the end of my table with a tray.

"A starver?"

He shrugs. "It's pretty common around here."

I glance around, noticing how several patients are just poking at their food with plastic spoons. It makes sense, I guess. With no will to live, why eat?

"How can I resist a menu like this?" I murmur, looking down at my plate. There are chunks of meat and potatoes in gravy, along with a side of broccoli and orange Jell-O.

The guy laughs. "So you're funny? That's refreshing. Mind if I sit?"

I don't really care either way, so I just shrug. The guy pulls out the chair across from me and then exhales heavily. "My name's Realm," he says.

"Realm?" I look at him.

"It's Mike Realm, but everyone just calls me Realm."

"So can I call you Mike?"

"Nope."

My mouth twitches with a smile, but I immediately straighten my expression.

"It's okay sometimes," Realm says, grabbing the roll off his tray and dipping it in the mashed potatoes. "Your face won't break if you smile."

I look him over. His hair is crazy, but now I see it's styled that way. The scar on his neck stands out pink against his skin, and he still has shadows under his eyes like he's been inside too long. But he's cute—I'm sure under normal circumstances he is.

"If I smile they'll think they got to me."

Realm pauses before answering. "And that's a bad thing? You want to stay here?"

"No. But I don't want them to win, either."

"Ah, well, sweetness. You're gonna have to decide which you want more if you plan on going home." He takes a bite, chewing slowly before talking to me again. "What's your name?" he asks. "I tried to steal your chart, but I got busted."

"You were going to steal it?"

He nods as if he's proud.

"My name's Sloane Barstow, but you can call me Sloane."

"Can't call you Barstow?"

"Nope."

"Okay."

Realm doesn't go on, and he finishes his food in silence while I pick at mine. "If you eat more," he says, wiping his mouth with a paper napkin, "the drugs won't hit you as hard. I'm guessing they've got you pretty doped up. Keeping you under control."

"Seeing that I can't remember large chunks of time, you're probably right." I take a bite of my now-cold mashed potatoes.

"What color pills do you take?" he asks, leaning forward on his elbows.

"Red before therapy, yellow after."

He nods and looks away, fidgeting with the hem of his scrubs.

"And then," I continue, "there's what the handler gives me."

Realm looks up suddenly and tilts his head. "What? What do you mean?"

I take a sip of my milk and flip my gaze over to where the dark-haired handler is standing, not looking at me for once. "The one by the door," I say behind my cup. "He injects me with sedatives."

"What?" Realm says loud enough to earn a few stares. "That asshole! What's he giving you?"

"I don't know exactly," I say. "But it pretty much just knocks me out where I stand."

Realm ducks his head as he lowers his voice. "Are you being serious about this?"

I scoff. "Why would I lie to you? To impress you with my tales of Program misadventures? Yes. He injected me the day I came here, and again in the hall after therapy. I haven't seen him today, at least not until now."

"Sloane," Realm whispers, his dark eyes a different shade of worry. "If he does that again, if he hurts you, you need to tell Dr. Warren."

"I tried. But she—"

"Tell her I made you tell. She'll believe me." Realm looks

around then, noticing how others have finished their dinner and are headed out to watch TV or play cards. "I should go," he says like he doesn't want to. "But remember, the card game invitation stands, okay?"

I nod, having forgotten until he mentioned it. I watch as he leaves and notice that he goes out of his way to walk past the handler. When he passes, Realm looks sideways at him with a death stare, and for a second I think he's going to get in a fight. But instead, the dark-haired handler, the one I'm scared of, pushes off from the wall and leaves the room.

It's odd that Realm has that effect on him, but then again, maybe they've gotten into it before. Realm did seem pretty pissed when I mentioned the handler drugging me. I decide then that Realm is someone I should stay close to for a while. At least until I figure out how to navigate The Program on my own.

"You made it," Realm calls the minute I stop at their makeshift card table. The other guys stare up at me with eager eyes, but I pretend not to notice. Realm pushes the kid nearest to him over and grabs a chair for me, sliding it in its place.

"I was sitting there," the other guy says.

"And now you're not." Realm collects all the cards, even though it seemed as if they were mid-hand. He starts reshuffling them. I sit next to him, feeling the stares of everyone at the table on me.

"You let her join and not me?" A girl's voice cuts through

the air. A redhead stands across from me, pointing her finger in my direction. "I thought you said no new members, Realm?"

He tilts his head like he's trying to apologize, but I hear the guy next to me suppress a laugh. "My darling Tabitha," Realm begins, "I've told you that we are very exclusive. But I promise, if Sloane drops out, you can have her spot."

She shoots me a vicious glare. "Oh, I—" I start to say as I stand, but Realm catches my thigh and eases me back down. When I look at Tabitha again, her eyes are angry.

"Whatever. You're a bunch of losers anyway."

"Nice chatting with you, Tabby," one of the guys at the table calls out as she walks away.

"Don't mind her," Realm says as he deals the hand. "She's always bitchy, and no, she's not going to do something horrible to you later. She's going to forget. She always forgets, which is why we don't let her play. She can never remember the rules."

Something about the coldness of this statement hits me, and I'm ready to run away. Realm must notice because he looks at me. "It's a side effect of her suicide attempt. She took QuikDeath and, even though they revived her, she has some brain damage. She's getting better, though, which is why she remembered me saying she can't play. But twenty bucks says she's back here tomorrow asking why you can play and she can't."

"Enough whispering," the guy next to me says. "Deal the cards."

Realm smiles at him, and then grabs a pretzel and balances it between his lips. "Boys, this is Sloane. Hands off."

They all laugh, shooting odd looks at Realm, and I wonder if I've somehow been claimed. But then Realm introduces me to Derek and Shep. They seem all right—although Shep's BO is a little strong next to me. He's fifteen, and Derek is seventeen. They've all been here close to three weeks, hoping to get out in six. From what I can tell they look pretty balanced, other than the fact that Shep is scratching absently at his thigh to the point where I think he's going to draw blood from underneath his scrubs.

Realm offers me a pretzel, but I shake my head. "So what's the game?" I ask as they pick up their cards. Realm smiles, not looking at me.

"What else? Bullshit."

They all start laughing, and I remember the game from junior high. James, Brady, and I would sit around my kitchen table and play when my parents were out. Sometimes Lacey would come by and join us.

James used to be the master at this game. He knew just how to act and would trick us all into calling bullshit, only to prove he was telling the truth. Thinking about that now, my cards shake in my hand.

"You know how to play?" Realm asks.

I nod but can't answer.

"Bullshit, Sloane!" James would yell out, slapping his hand on the table. "You are the worst liar ever!" He and Brady would laugh hysterically, and I wouldn't even bother flipping over my cards. I would just pick up the deck. It got to the point where I wouldn't try to lie because James would always bust me. Every time.

"Your turn," Realm says, nudging my elbow.

I glance at my hand and see that I'm supposed to come up with a ten. I have the ten of clubs, but I pull out a two of diamonds and set it down. "One ten," I say.

There's only the briefest moment of silence before Shep moves next to me. "One jack," he says. Derek goes after him and the game continues, but I stare at my ten.

There's no one to call me on my bullshit anymore.

CHAPTER FIVE

IT'S MONDAY MORNING, A WEEK AND A HALF INTO
The Program, and Dr. Warren is sitting behind her desk, smiling kindly. Before the appointment I tried to eat as much food
as possible, hoping it would weaken the effect of the drugs. But
my body has already begun to feel heavy, making me sag into
the chair.

"Did you and James have a physical relationship?" the doctor asks.

I laugh. "They don't have sports at my school."

"That's not what I mean, Sloane."

Obviously I know what she meant, but it isn't any of her
business. I don't trust Dr. Warren. "What's in the pills?" I ask.

She sighs. "We go over this every time. And the answer is
always the same. They're just something to relax you."

I shake my head slowly. "No," I say. "It's more than that. It makes me talk to you, even if I don't want to."

Dr. Warren watches me for a long moment, her eyes scanning me as if weighing out her answer. "Let's get back to James," she says. "Isn't that what you really want to talk about?"

I wince at his name, reminded again of how much I miss him. The room is becoming transparent, my memories clearer than the world around me. I'd do anything to get back to him. "Yes," I say, giving up on my question. "James and I had a physical relationship. He's the physical type."

"I can gather that much."

I don't like the way she says it, as if without James I'd still be a virgin and at home with my parents right now, baking cookies. "I'm the one who wanted him, if you must know. He would have been fine with waiting"—I pause at this—"well, he would have been fine with waiting a little longer at least."

"Were you careful?"

I curl my lip. "Yes, Mom. We always used a condom because we would never want to bring a kid into this messed-up world."

"Condoms aren't always—"

"Look," I say, "I know the statistics, but I hardly have to worry about it now, do I?" My voice takes on a hard edge, and Dr. Warren glances away. I'm angry at the way she's portraying James, and I want to set her straight. I want to tell her that she could only dream of having someone like him in her life.

"Perhaps we can talk about your first kiss."

Scoffing, I curl up in the chair. The drugs are loosening my clenched muscles, taking away my inhibitions.

"Did you kiss him first?" Dr. Warren asks, like she's my best friend.

"No," I say, my heartbeat loud in my ears. "I would've been too scared. Too shy. James was so hot-and-cold then. I didn't know what to think."

Dr. Warren leans back in her chair, her arms folding over her chest as she starts to smile. "Tell me about it, Sloane. Tell me everything."

I realize that she's right; I do want to talk about James. And the minute I start, I'm ready to stay with him forever. Even if only in my mind.

"He would send me notes," I say. "After he admitted his feelings, he would leave notes under my pillow. Letters that he was writing to me. At first it seemed more like he was yelling at me. He'd comment on how much he hated liking me, but then in the next line explain it was because he spent all of his time missing me. I was never so confused in my whole life. I never wrote back, but his letters kept coming, as if he was arguing with himself. Soon they became less angry. Sweeter. He'd compliment something I wore to school, say how he thought about kissing me." I laugh. "He talked a lot about kissing me. Said that maybe we could sneak off and see a movie, just the two of us."

Dr. Warren writes in the file. "James sounds complicated."

"He's the opposite, actually. He wants things simple, and me and him dating . . . *that* complicated everything."

"How long did the letters go on?"

"Almost every day for about a month. But after a few weeks of them, I started to stay in the same room with him. We would joke and actually make eye contact again. Brady said he was glad that I was done acting weird, and I felt like he knew. That he had to see the way James and I looked at each other.

"The first time James and I kissed," I say, "he told me that from then on he'd *always* have to kiss me. Just me. I felt so special, so loved. I replayed that moment in my head nonstop. But then I started to worry that maybe I'd read too much into the kiss. I was so afraid of losing him, and he wasn't even mine yet.

"A week later James came by to pick up me and Brady for a day at the river, but my brother backed out at the last minute—said he had a date, but that James and I should go ahead. We'd barely waited for him to leave the room before we took off, but I was nervous. James hadn't mentioned the kiss, and I hadn't gotten any more letters.

"James drove us out there, and we didn't speak on the way. I was wearing my bathing suit under a T-shirt and shorts, even though I didn't plan to go in the water. It was like we were pretending to still go through the motions of a normal Saturday. When we got there, James laid out a beach blanket for us, dropped a few snacks from his backpack on it, and then stripped to his suit. He went swimming, leaving me there."

"But why did he act so cold when he'd already kissed you?" Dr. Warren asks.

I meet her eyes. "James . . . as strong as he is, has serious abandonment issues. When he was eight, his mother left him in her car at the train station." I swallow hard, feeling his pain. "She never came back. Instead someone had heard him crying, called the police. After that, I'm not sure he trusts anyone. Only me and Brady." I sniffle. "And Brady failed him too."

Dr. Warren nods as if she understands, but I don't think she does. No one understands James except me.

"And what happened at the river that day?" she asks softly.

"While James was in the water," I start again, "I considered hiding his clothes—a little joke to put us in a good mood, something to break the awkward silence. So I grabbed his shorts and stood, ready to run off with them. But then something fell out of his pocket and landed in the grass."

"What was it?" Dr. Warren asks, looking riveted.

"A ring. A stupid, plastic ring with sparkles. I'd held it in my hands, wondering what he was doing with it. I sat back down on the blanket and examined it, jealous about the girl it must have belonged to. Then I felt a drip of water and saw James standing above me, running a towel over his hair."

I let the memory unfold as Dr. Warren listens, my words tumbling out without my permission. Inside, I can see it all, I can remember every second.

"What do you have?" James asked. When he saw the ring, he tossed his towel aside. "You going through my pockets, Sloane?"

"No, I . . ." But I stopped, feeling jealous. "Whose ring is this?"

James laughed and then sat down next to me, his thigh pressed against mine as he reached to pluck the ring from my hand. "You shouldn't snoop," he murmured.

"You're not going to answer?"

He looked sideways. "It's for you, stupid," he said with a smile. "I got it for you."

I stared at him, trying to decide if he was telling the truth, but then he took the ring from my hand and slid it onto my finger. James leaned forward, pausing when he got really close to me. "Can we kiss now?" he asked. "Is that okay?"

I close my eyes as I sit across from Dr. Warren, remembering how warm James's mouth was on mine, how his tongue touched my lips before I opened them, letting him in. Letting him lay me back on the blanket as his mouth found mine, again and again, always gentle, yet urgent.

I'll never feel that passion from James again. I'll never be that girl again. Tears start to stream down my cheeks as I cry, missing James. Missing myself. I wish everything could just go back to the way it was, but instead I'm slowly losing everything—I'm witnessing my own death.

Dr. Warren doesn't say anything, but she hands me the yellow pill. I take it gratefully, wanting to sleep. Wanting to feel better.

But never wanting to forget.

"Wakey, wakey," a voice whispers in my ear.

My eyelids feel heavy as I try to lift them, and when I turn to the voice I feel warm breath on my face.

"You've been out too long, Miss Barstow. They asked me to come retrieve you."

My eyes fly open, and I see the dark-haired handler leaning over my bed. I reach out to push him away, but he catches my wrists. "Don't fight," he soothes. "I'm not going to hurt you. I only like the willing."

I yank my arm from his, accidently hitting myself in the mouth. I wince and touch at my lip, seeing a bit of blood there.

The handler tsks. "You should be more careful." He walks over to my closet and pulls out a clean pair of scrubs and my robe, laying it over the bed. "Help you get dressed?"

"Hell no," I say, sitting up in the bed. "And I'm pretty sure this is sexual harassment."

He smiles. "How so?"

I'm not sure if making my skin crawl is enough of a reason to file charges, but I won't mind taking the chance. "Get out or I'll call Nurse Kell," I say, motioning to the door.

The handler shrugs. "If you want." He starts walking that way and then stops, looking back at me. "But what if I can offer you something?"

"I don't want anything from you."

"Not even a memory?"

I pause, but then push back the blankets to climb out of the bed. "What do you mean?"

The handler beams under my attention. "If I can save you a memory, something you could take out of here with you, would it be worth it?"

I swallow down the sick feeling in my stomach. "Would what be worth it?"

His eyes narrow deviously then, scanning over my body. I instinctively fold my arms over my chest and step back from him. "Being friends," he says, but the tone is nothing short of sinister.

"Just leave," I snap, pointing behind him.

He nods, not looking fazed in the least. "You think about it, Sloane. If you change your mind, you know where to find me."

"Drop dead."

He opens the door, but as he walks out, he says nonchalantly, "Wonder how much you've lost already." And then he's gone.

I stand there, staring at the closed door. *What I've lost?* I look suddenly to my hand, but the finger is naked. The purple heart ring that I always wear is at home in my mattress. I wouldn't forget that. *James gave it to me when* . . . I stop, thinking. A spike of fear rushes over me. *He gave it when* . . . *Oh, God.*

I cover my mouth, realizing for the first time that a memory is gone. I stumble back against my bed, my mind racing over everything I can think of. The ring. How did I get the ring?

There's a quick knock at the door. I'm sure it's the handler, so I yell out for him to go away. The door opens, and Dr. Francis is standing there, his eyebrows pulled together.

"Sloane," he says carefully, "Roger said he couldn't get you to come out of your room. Is something the matter?"

Yes, there is so much the matter that I wouldn't know where to start. But I can't turn in Roger for being a creep. Not yet. Not in case he can help me. I clear my throat and straighten, putting on a calm exterior. Let's see if Dr. Francis can call bullshit.

"He woke me up and I was cranky," I say. "I think my medication is too strong."

Dr. Francis purses his lips as if thinking this over. "Maybe you just need to get used to the dosage."

"Maybe," I respond, my voice bitter. He nods then, stepping away from the door.

"It's time for lunch, and the staff is concerned that you're not eating enough. Nurse Kell tells me you've lost four pounds since arriving."

"No fast food," I respond. "Bring on the chicken nuggets, and I'll eat the hell out of them."

He laughs then, looking relieved that I can make a lame joke after all. "I'll see what I can do," he says. "And I'll adjust your medication dosage. We want you to feel comfortable. I know this is a difficult transition."

I smile, clenching my teeth so hard I'm afraid they'll break. *A difficult transition?* Yeah, that's a fair assessment. Dr. Francis waits as I go in the bathroom and change into my clean scrubs, wrapping my robe tightly around me. I still try to search my mind for the story of the ring, but I know it's gone. I've lost a piece of James and it's so devastating that I have to stare at my reflection for nearly a minute before I can pull myself together.

As I head out behind the doctor into the hallway, I keep my mind trained on a single thought, holding it close to me. *James, James, James.*

SUZANNE YOUNG

CHAPTER SIX

AFTER TIME IN THE EXAMINATION ROOM WITH DR. Francis—just a basic physical and blood test to make sure I'm taking my meds—I'm sent to lunch, where I sit alone in the corner. I drink some juice and take bites from an apple, but don't bother with anything else. I'm too upset about the ring. When I leave and find myself in the mostly deserted leisure room, I sit again at the window and stare out.

I continually take cautious glances around for Roger, wondering when his slimy self will show up, asking for a trade. Wondering if I could say no when it means keeping a part of myself.

"Psst . . ." I look over my shoulder and see Realm by the door, holding something behind his back. No one else notices him, and I feel myself smile. *Come here,* he mouths.

I'm not sure I should go, but the room is quiet and I'm bored. I get up to find out what he's doing. Realm grins madly when I approach, and I follow him into the hall. "Wait here," he says, poking his head around the corner toward the nurses' station.

"What's behind your back?" I ask, trying to look over his shoulder between him and wall.

"Hey, hey, sweetness," he says, glaring at me. "No peeking." He checks one more time and then does some weird hand signals like we're in the military.

"What?" I ask.

"Run." He rushes ahead of me, and we dash down the hall and through the stairwell door. He eases it shut and I stand there, sort of shocked.

"That was close," he says.

"What are we doing?"

"Hiding out. I have contraband."

"But if they find us—"

"They won't. No rounds for another twenty minutes. Sit." He points to the stairs behind me.

Since I've already broken the rules by coming out here, I sit down on the concrete, crossing my legs as I stare at him. "Now will you show me what you have behind your back?"

He smiles broadly and pulls out a white bag, the logo on the side unmistakable.

"No way."

"A little birdie told me you wanted chicken nuggets."

"Realm! How did you—"

"Shh . . . ," he says, looking toward the door. "This isn't on the menu, so if they see it, they'll take it. Now do you want it or not?"

My brother and I used to beg our parents for McDonald's every Saturday. We'd have to clean our rooms, do the dishes, all sorts of chores that we totally blew off, knowing our parents would get it anyway because my father was hooked on the fries.

And here in this stairwell, I've never been so happy to see greasy food—almost like a little piece of home, which I guess is sad in a way.

Realm comes to sit next to me, reaching in the bag to take out a napkin, which he lays on the stair. He pulls out a box of McNuggets, folding back the cardboard and then dumping some fries in the top.

I immediately dive in, even though I have a ton of questions. "How did you get this?" The food is a little cold but still so good. Better than the mashed and bland starches we've been getting here.

"I have a friend who has a friend." He smiles and puts a fry into his mouth.

"What? Realm, can you get us outside?" I ask, my mind suddenly flooded with dreams of escape. He widens his eyes at my reaction.

"No," he says. "Of course not. My charms go only so far, and sweet-talking my way into some drive-through isn't the same as a jailbreak. I just thought . . ." He looks down. "Shit, Sloane. I thought this would cheer you up."

I feel horrible and ungrateful, and I reach out to touch his hand to get his attention. "Sorry," I say. "This is awesome. And it does cheer me up." I force a wide, overly enthusiastic grin. "See?"

Realm chuckles, a soft smile staying on his lips as we go back to eating.

"So how did you know about the chicken nuggets?" I ask, pulling my leg underneath me and settling in.

"Finally got my hands on your chart. Imagine my surprise when Dr. Francis noted that you were craving them. Did you really tell him that?"

"Yes." I laugh and slap his shoulder. "But you can't read my chart!"

"I can, but I definitely shouldn't. You won't tell on me, will you? Are you a rat, Sloane?" He looks at me suspiciously.

"I'm not going to sell you out, but you have to tell me what you read."

He stiffens at this, and then scratches his chin. "Um . . . not much."

A wave of sickness washes over me. "You're lying."

Realm's eyes meet mine. "Who's James?"

The tender way he asks makes me nearly fall apart. How can I even explain who James is to me? "He was everything," I say. "And now he's nothing." I close my eyes.

"I'm sorry," I hear Realm say, feeling him touch my knee. "I shouldn't have brought it up."

I sniffle and wipe away the tears just as they start to brim over. "It's okay," I say. "I've just had a bad day. And—"

"I reminded you how much life sucks. I really am sorry."

"Don't be," I whisper. "James is my boyfriend, but—" I stop, not wanting to admit that James didn't remember me. As if it proves that I didn't mean that much to him.

"He was in The Program too," Realm says quietly. "It's in your file."

I nod. "They came and got me about a week after he returned."

"Did he know you?" Realm asks, sounding anxious.

"No." Saying it is like a punch in the gut.

Realm doesn't try to say it's okay or offer any hope of James remembering. Instead he points to the last McNugget. "You going to eat that?" he asks.

I stare at him. "You just made me cry and now you want my food?"

He shrugs. "I just asked if you were going to eat it."

I laugh then, pushing the box in his direction. "It's all yours. I think I might puke from eating so fast."

He pauses with the food halfway to his mouth. "Thanks for oversharing, Sloane." He eats the chicken anyway, and then we pick through the fries before cleaning up, the grease clinging to my fingers, but it's not gross. It's almost a relief compared to how scrubbed and antiseptic I feel in this facility.

"Hold up," Realm says, handing me the bag. He pulls the door open and then puts his eye to the crack. "All clear."

He motions me forward, and we sneak back inside, giggling as we run down the hallway. We're almost back to the leisure room when we see Nurse Kell turn the corner and spot us.

Realm instantly grabs the McDonald's bag and tosses it into an empty room, the trash sliding under a bed.

"Where have you two been?" Nurse Kell asks.

"Just giving her the tour," Realm says, putting his arm around me as if we're best friends. It occurs to me that he is my best friend, at least in here. Nurse Kell eyes us for another second longer and then nods toward the leisure room.

"All right then," she says. "The boys are looking for you, Michael. You're late for your card game."

He thanks her, and we start heading off when Nurse Kell calls me back. "For you," she says, holding out a Dixie cup. I peek inside and see a bright-yellow pill.

"Why? I feel fine."

"Doctor's orders, dear." She hands me a cup of water, and I take the pill, anger starting to well up inside me again.

"I thought he was going to lower my dosage," I snap at her. "Guess not, huh?"

"Go back to your friends now, Sloane." She smiles and brushes my hair off my shoulder. But I push her hand away and go into the leisure room.

"Where'd you go?" Realm asks when I sit at the table with him and the guys. They'd already dealt me in, and I pick up my cards.

"Nurse Kell wanted to make sure I stayed obedient," I tell him.

"I like the sound of that," Derek says, and they start laughing. Realm just eyes me with concern.

"Hey!" A voice cuts through the air, and I turn to see Tabitha making her way over, her red hair pulled into a messy knot on top of her head. "Realm, I thought you said you weren't letting anyone else play."

He sighs, but looks up at her sweetly. "Hello, Tabitha. I'm sorry, but the table is full."

"Then why does she get to join? That's not fair, Realm. You promised."

"Next time, okay?" He smiles at her. She shoots a hateful look in my direction, and then nods sadly before stumbling away.

The guys don't joke this time and instead start playing the round. She just had this conversation and yet she comes back, like part of her brain is broken. She took QuikDeath, and I wonder if Miller had survived, if he'd—

A thick, choking grief envelops me at the thought of my friend. My Miller, so lost and alone even though we were right there. I'll never see him again.

There's a soft touch on my wrist. "You're crying," Realm whispers. Startled, I look at him while he takes a cautious glance around at the nurses. He reaches to swipe under my eye with his shirtsleeve and then calls bullshit to no one in particular, just to distract them. They all start laughing and sifting through the cards, but I watch Realm, grateful. We go back to playing, but as the minutes tick by, my reflexes get slower. Soon they're yelling at me to throw down a card, and I have to fold my hand and step out.

Realm stands when I do. "You don't look well," he says.

"Tired. Nurse Kell gave me a pill and—"

"Wait, that's what happened in the hall? Why would she give it now?"

"I don't know."

Realm puts his arm on my mine and steadies me against him. I don't argue. I'm starting to feel disoriented, and the prospect of getting all the way to my room seems impossible.

"I'll be back, guys," Realm says, tossing his cards down. They grumble something I can't hear, and then Realm is easing me away. "Can I walk you home?" he asks, joking.

I don't respond and instead hold on to his elbow as he leads us out. Once we're in the hall, Realm slides his arm over my shoulder. "It's okay," he whispers. "I'll get you back safely."

The hall seems to tilt in front of me, but at the other end I think I see someone. I think I see Roger. I stagger back and grab a handful of Realm's shirt. "Don't let him near me like this," I beg.

"Who?" Realm shoots a glance in Roger's direction and then freezes. "What's wrong? Did something happen?"

Roger looks at us, and I'm suddenly scared that he'll come for me now, when I'm too weak to fight back. I nearly stumble over my own feet. "Just get me out of here," I say.

Realm rushes me in the other direction, but his eyes are dark when he looks back over his shoulder at Roger.

When I'm finally in a private room, it takes a second for me to realize it's not mine. Everything is so foggy. "Where am I?" I ask.

"My room," Realm says. "Hope that's okay." He keeps his head out the door, looking around as if he's keeping watch. I stagger toward his bed.

"I can take you back to yours when you wake up. You look like you're about to crash hard," Realm adds.

I don't argue about being in his room as I climb onto his bed, laying my head on the pillow with a sigh. My eyes are already closed when Realm comes to cover me with his blankets, tucking them carefully around me.

"I'll be back later, okay?" he says.

"Mm . . . hmm."

He chuckles softly and I feel a touch on my forehead—a kiss, I think. And then he leaves to let me sleep off the medication, and I try not to worry about what—or who—will be waiting for me when I get up.

CHAPTER SEVEN

I WAKE UP TO THE SOUND OF SHOUTS COMING FROM the hallway. I sit up suddenly, regretting it the moment I do because it feels like my brain might fall out. Pain pulses in my temples as I try to get my bearings and look around the unfamiliar room.

"Michael!" I hear what sounds like Nurse Kell yell. "Get off him!"

"Stay away from her, or I swear to God, I'll kill you myself!"

I gasp, sure that's Realm's voice. I climb quickly out of the bed and go to the door, opening it just a crack to look out the way Realm does. Halfway down the hall, Realm has got his forearm to Roger's throat, pinning him to the wall. But Roger isn't saying anything. He's just staring back at Realm as if challenging him.

"Michael," Nurse Kell says again, only softer. She touches Realm's arm and he suddenly drops it, making Roger stumble to the floor. For a minute I think Realm might kick him, but instead he steps back with obvious restraint.

I open the door more and it creaks, making all of them look over at me. When Realm turns in my direction, I see that one of his eyes is puffed up. Nurse Kell immediately bristles. "Sloane," she says. "Return to your room." Then she takes Realm roughly by the elbow. "We need to see Dr. Warren now," she hisses.

Realm shrugs at me, almost like an apology, and then lets himself be led down the hall. My heart pounds in my chest as it fills with worry. What if they send him away? Hurt him? Realm is my only friend, and what if they take him from me too?

Just then I notice Roger, still sitting on the floor. When my eyes meet his, he winks, and then gets up to hobble away.

I wait in the dining room, not touching my food as I sit by myself. They haven't brought Realm back yet and I'm completely panicking. I haven't told anyone what I saw, but I heard Derek and the other guys say that Realm punched out a handler and now he's getting shipped off to another facility. My fingers shake as I try to eat a spoonful of Jell-O.

"Can I sit with you?" Tabitha asks, motioning to the empty chair across from me.

"Oh. Sure." It's a chance to see her up close for the first time. She has dyed red hair, but from the roots I imagine it's naturally dark. Her skin is pale and her eyes are a light hazel.

She's pretty in a really emo sort of way. She sort of reminds me of Lacey—or at least, the old Lacey.

"I see your bandage," she says, taking the first bite of her food. "Did you try to slit your wrists?"

"Sort of. But I wasn't trying to kill myself. I was just pissed."

She laughs. "Yeah, right. So where's Realm?" she asks, and I suspect it was her real question from the beginning. "He said I could play cards with him today. Oh"—she pauses, smiling—"maybe he'll let you play too. He's pretty nice. Cute, too, right?"

I stare at her, trying to see if there are any obvious signs of damage. I've never heard of anyone surviving QuikDeath before. Lacey had thought about taking it. She wanted Miller to take it with her.

Wait—Miller. What happened to Miller?

"What's that look? You don't think he's hot?" Tabitha is grinning from ear to ear, but I don't answer her and instead look down toward my tray.

What the hell happened to Miller? In my mind, it's like he's there and then suddenly . . . gone. "Oh my God," I say. "I can't remember."

"Are you okay?" Tabitha asks, sounding frightened. "Should I get the nurse?"

"No," I say quickly. I stretch my hand out and cover hers. "They're taking my memories," I whisper to her. "They're erasing me."

She blinks quickly as if she completely understands, but then her eyes glaze over. "Don't talk like that," she says pleasantly. "Or you're going to get us both thrown into a new facility to start over."

Tabitha abruptly stands, taking her tray with her, and walks away. My hand feels cold on the white table, and I'm shaking. First the ring and now Miller. What else is missing that I can't find? What's happening to me?

And suddenly, I know. I know what I have to do if I plan to make it through this. I leave my tray on the table and walk toward the exit doors. I'm almost there when an older handler stops me.

"Where are you going?" he asks.

"Bathroom."

"There's a bathroom here," he motions toward the back of the room. I try to think fast.

"No tampons in there."

He stares me down, as if he can tell if I'm menstruating just by looking at me, and then he waves me out. "Hurry up," he says before going back to monitoring the room.

I rush out into the hall, not sure where I'll find him. Desperation is making tears sting my eyes, but I blink them back. I need to be stronger. I need to save myself.

It's when I pass the supply closet that I see him and skid to a stop, sliding in my slipper socks. Disgust twists in my stomach as I watch him counting off rolls of toilet paper and then marking the number on a clipboard. When he notices me, he smiles.

"Hello, Miss Barstow. Can I help you with something?"

"Yes, Roger." I nearly choke on his name. "I guess you can."

*   *   *

Roger locks up the supply closet and leads me back to my room, smiling the entire way, even humming a song. I can barely push myself forward, but I have no choice. The Program has given me no choice but to hold on to what I can.

Roger opens my door and steps aside for me to walk in. When I pass him I smell the strong scent of mints, and I know I'll never be able to taste peppermint again without gagging. I pause just inside the room, not looking at the bed.

When Roger shuts the door and locks it, I cross my arms over my chest. "First tell me what's going to happen to Realm."

Roger chuckles. "Oh, I'm sure Michael Realm will be just fine. He has a habit of getting out of things the rest of you are punished for."

I furrow my brow. "What does that mean?"

"It means he'll be back soon. Now I hope this isn't why you took me aside, Sloane." He cocks his head as if truly curious. I'm terrified.

"How do I know you can really give me my memories?"

"I can't give you back your memories," he says, almost apologetically. "What I can do is let you hold on to select memories. Block them from the antigens."

"Antigens?"

"The little yellow pill you take," he says. "It seeks out your memories, the ones that are targeted by Dr. Warren. First you take the red—a sort of truth serum, if you will. And while you talk, it acts like a dye, attaching itself to the thoughts. Then you take the yellow to wipe them all away. It's not exact, but soon you'll have less and less to sort through, and they'll be easier to pinpoint."

The pills—they're eating my memories. Dr. Warren said they were just to relax me, but she lied. What else has she lied about?

"How can you help?" I ask Roger. "What can you do to stop them from erasing me?"

He reaches into his pocket and opens a small container. He pinches out a small purple pill. "This can save one stray thought, one thing you don't want to lose. Of course, it might make you sick, but it could be worth the risk. And if you tell Dr. Warren about this, they'll strip your mind completely. So if you take it, know that this has to stay between us."

I look at the little pill he holds up, not sure if it can be true. If he's just lying to do something horrible to me. "And what do you want in exchange?" I ask, fearing the answer.

He smiles then, the skin crinkling around his eyes. "I'm not a monster, Sloane. Maybe all I want is a kiss." He pauses. "This time."

"Bartering for sex?" I try to sound appalled, but I knew it would come to this. I knew and I still asked him here. I had just been hoping for a different answer.

"Course not," he says. "Like I said, a kiss. A little affection. Affection is good for your therapy, Sloane. Did they not tell you that? In fact, I think you've already found that out yourself."

I know he's talking about Realm, but I don't bother responding. He thinks Realm and I are in a relationship, but that will never happen. I'm going back to James.

I reach out and take the pill from Roger's hands, examining it. "How does it work?"

"You'll have to concentrate on a single memory. Then you swallow the pill and hold the thought. Don't mix the memory with anything else or widen the scope, otherwise it won't be clear in your head."

I look between the pill and the handler, my throat dry and my hands clammy. It's just a kiss, but it's like he's asking me to jump off a bridge. I can't move any closer to him, and I feel my resolve start to fade.

"What's it worth to you, Sloane?" he asks softly. "What's your past worth?"

And with that a few tears leak out. I think of James. Brady and Miller. The part of me that won't survive The Program. Maybe this one pill can change the outcome. Maybe it can save me.

"Just one kiss," I tell him.

Roger laughs. "Yes, but I say how long. And it has to be *good*, Sloane. I want to feel your passion."

I wipe hard at my face, pulling the skin roughly until it hurts. I slip the pill into the pocket of my robe and take an unsteady step forward. I look Roger straight in the eyes. "Make no mistake," I whisper. "I hate you."

He smiles. "I like a challenge." He grabs me roughly, pinching my upper arm as he pulls me against him, his other arm snaking around me. His mouth is on mine, wet and strong. I try to turn away at first, but he just squeezes harder, and I can feel how turned on he is as he presses against me.

I whimper and try to move back as his tongue licks my lips.

"Make me believe it," he breathes. "Or I take the pill back." He kisses me again, and this time I let his tongue inside my mouth. Peppermint coats my lips and I can't stand the taste. I can't stand another second of it.

Tears continue to trickle down my cheeks as his hand touches my ass, holding me tight against him. His other hand grips the back of my neck and tilts it so he can kiss me there. "You taste delicious," he says into my skin.

I try to pretend it's James, but Roger's touch is too aggressive. James would never touch me like this. James would never do this to me. Soon I'm sobbing and Roger comes to kiss me once more, his hand sliding under my shirt. And finally I snap and bring my knee up, missing his balls, but connecting with his thigh. He yelps and jumps back. But as I stand there in front of him, soft cries still escaping my lips, he laughs.

"Oh, come on, Sloane," he says coldly. "It wasn't that bad. Other girls trade much more."

"Get out," I manage to say, and I back against the footboard of my bed. "Get out!" I scream.

He flinches and then looks behind him at the door. "Fine," he says, putting up his hand. "But understand this is between us. If you tell—"

"I know." I can't stop crying. I spit out the taste of him right there on the linoleum tile and he looks at it, surprised that I'm even upset.

"Next dose is for bare skin," he warns. "And I suggest you get ahold of yourself because the crying doesn't really work for me." With that he turns and leaves, shutting the door behind him.

CHAPTER EIGHT

WHEN THE TEARS HAVE DRIED, I'M IN MY BED, LYING under the covers. I know it won't be long before they come looking for me, wondering where I am. But I can't go back to the dining hall because my body won't stop shaking.

I take the pill out of my pocket and stare at it. It might not even work, but I have to try. I have to fight. This is my last chance to keep from losing everything.

I put the pill in my mouth and swallow it dry, coughing once when it gets stuck, but then getting it down. I know what I have to remember. It's not romantic. It's not something cherished. But I hope it'll lead to some answers when I get out. Next pill, I'll capture a perfect memory with James.

For now, I imagine the picture of him and Brady, the ring. The things I hid in my mattress so that I could find them when

I got back. I know now that everything that happened at my house that day will be erased from my memory, so I might never look for the items. This is the only way.

I focus on the picture: James's face, his chest bare, as his arm is carelessly around my brother's shoulders. Brady's laugh and the river rolling through the background. The ring—the purple, sparkly, heart-shaped ring—that James gave me, even if I can't remember when. But I used to wear it all the time, so it must have been special.

They're all in the mattress, these things that will lead us back together. So I hold the memory tightly to me as I close my eyes.

Only a few minutes have passed when I'm suddenly ravaged by pain. I cry out, feeling like a hammer just hit me in the back of the head. I lean forward and vomit over the side of the bed, my stomach twisting and my throat burning. I press my hands to my head as if it can stop the throbbing there.

The room spins, and I lie back against the pillow, my eyes squeezed shut. I try to control my breathing, and once again think of the ring and the picture hidden in my bed. It feels like a lifetime of agony, but it's probably been less than five minutes when I'm finally able to open my eyes again. My stomach is twisted, and I know I'll have to clean up the puke before Nurse Kell comes for me.

Slowly, I slide out of bed, careful to step around the mess and then clean it up with toilet paper, flushing it away. My breath comes out in jagged gasps, like I might get sick again at any moment. There is a sour taste in my mouth, but behind that—is peppermint.

I lean over the toilet and gag again.

When I walk into the now half-empty dining room, I'm sure I look bad. I feel hungover; my eyes are bloodshot, and my greasy hair is pulled back into a ponytail. But people don't seem to notice, and it occurs to me that it's better not to be pretty here. It's better to go unnoticed.

I find where I left my tray and pretend to pick at the roll still on my plate. I drink the apple juice, anything to mask the flavors lingering in my mouth. Tabitha's staring at me from across the room as if she's studying me, but soon she lowers her gaze.

I wonder if Roger has offered her the pill. I want to ask her, but how can I ask something like that? And what if he hasn't? She could turn me in and get me sent away for longer.

I miss Realm. I hope that Roger was telling me the truth when he said that Realm would come back soon. What if they're hurting him? Oh, God. What if they're erasing me from his memory?

Just then I see Nurse Kell walk into the room, and I jump up to go talk to her. She looks alarmed and then pleased that I sought her out.

"Hello, Sloane, honey. Are you feeling better?"

"Yes. But . . . is Realm okay?"

She smiles, reminding me again of a grandmother. "Michael

Realm is just fine. He's cooling off with Dr. Warren right now. He won't be sleeping in the wards tonight, I'm afraid. But I hope he'll rejoin us tomorrow."

I almost burst out crying. "Will he remember me?" I ask in a small voice.

Nurse Kell shakes her head as if it's a silly question. "Of course. Why wouldn't he?"

I let out a held breath, but I still can't stand it. How they all act as if there's nothing wrong going on here. As if they're not erasing our minds. "Thank you" is all I can manage as I head out of the room and into the hallway.

I skip out on the card game, and sit in my room playing solitaire instead, with a pack of cards Nurse Kell lent me. I listen to the hall, hoping to hear Realm's laugh. I dread seeing Roger walk by, or worse, stop in. But the place is quiet.

I fall asleep easily, even without swallowing the pills Nurse Kell brings me. When I wake up, I have an early-morning appointment with Dr. Warren, but I take the long way around and go by Realm's room. He's still not back.

I go inside Dr. Warren's office, and she beams like she's thrilled to see me. "Sloane," she says. "You're looking well today."

I know she's lying because I haven't showered or even bothered checking my reflection. I did take a hot washcloth and wipe my neck to clean everywhere that Roger's mouth touched me. I scrubbed it so raw that it left a rash on my skin. I see Dr. Warren's eyes flick to the spot, but she doesn't mention it.

"Before we start . . ." She slides the cup with the red pill toward me, but I shake my head.

"I don't need it. Thank you."

She smiles. "You will take the pill, Sloane. We've already been over this."

I know from what Roger told me that the pill helps isolate memories, highlights them to be taken later. I don't want to put it in my mouth. I want to crush it under my socked heel.

"Have we?" I say. "Maybe I don't remember."

Dr. Warren's jaw tightens. "Follow procedures if you want to be released."

"I'm not taking it," I shoot back. What should be doctorly advice from her feels more like a threat. My anger starts to bubble over.

"Last chance," she says, leveling her gaze on mine.

I lean toward her. "I'm not taking the fucking pill, okay?"

Dr. Warren doesn't even flinch. She sits back calmly in her leather chair. "Marilyn," she calls behind me. A large woman in a white nurse's uniform stalks in, a needle poised in her hand. I barely have time to register what's going on before I feel it pierce the skin on my upper arm.

"What is this?" I yell, jumping up from the chair.

"Calm down," Dr. Warren soothes, not even looking a little sorry. "It's the same dose. But I told you, you will take the medication one way or another. Voluntarily is just the least painful." Dr. Warren looks at the nurse. "Get the other needle ready for after the session."

I stand there, clutching my arm and feeling helpless. I'm so violated, so angry, that I think I might completely lose it right now.

"Today," Dr. Warren says, ignoring my obvious fury, "I want to talk about you and James after your brother's death. How you became so codependent."

"We're not codependent, you bitch. We love each other."

She looks me over thoughtfully, content to wait until I'm fully compliant. Already I can feel the drug coursing through my veins, and I sway on my feet, knowing it won't be long until I'm at its mercy. Telling her all of my secrets.

When I collapse back into the chair, my limbs light and my head hazy, I start talking.

"James and I dated secretly for two months," I say, my temple resting against the fabric. "It was tough keeping it from Brady. James slept over all the time, and each night he'd slip out of Brady's room at three in the morning and climb into my bed. We'd kiss and whisper, James always making me laugh. I didn't want to hide how I felt about him, but I knew it wouldn't go over well. Not with Brady. Not with our parents. So we spent time like that, lying in each other's arms and talking about leaving Oregon."

"Were you having sex?" Dr. Warren asks, making notes in her file.

"No. I mean, we could have, I guess. But we didn't." I smile to myself. "We just made out a whole lot."

I let my eyes close, feeling distant. "After Brady died, James was torn up with guilt. I was worse. If I'd known how to

SUZANNE YOUNG

swim, maybe I could have saved him. He was my brother and I didn't even see the signs. I wondered if it was because I was too involved with James. If he was too involved with me. For that first week, James and I stayed far away from each other. I couldn't even look at him."

"What changed?"

"After my brother was buried and my house was filled with my mother's sobs and my father's drinking, my parents turned their attention to me. They were worried I was depressed too, but they couldn't see it was just grief. My brother was my best friend and I wanted him back"—I pause then, swallowing hard—"but he was never going to come back. He was never going to take me to the top of the Ferris wheel again. He would never teach me how to swim."

Dr. Warren hands me a tissue, and I wipe my eyes even though I'm not sure if I'm crying. I can't feel anything on my cheeks. I'm numb.

"And then one afternoon," I start again, "I found my mother in Brady's room, trying to pack up his clothes, and I lost it. I couldn't stand the thought of his things in a box—in a box like he was in. I told her I hated her." I lower my head. "I'm not proud of it, but I'd been caught up in my parents' emotional wake, and I needed my own time to grieve. They wouldn't let me grieve! The next day I found a pamphlet for The Program near the phone. And I knew I couldn't ever let them see me cry again. And I knew I had to talk to James because Brady told us to take care of each other.

"At school I was overwhelmed with the interviews, the therapy, the monitoring. I felt so alone I thought that maybe I *was* becoming ill. But later that week, I walked out of class to find James standing at the lockers—as if he'd been waiting there all along. And I realized how much I'd missed him. He didn't hesitate when he saw me. He stomped right across the floor and picked me up in a hug, smashing me to him. I wanted to cry—but I couldn't."

"There are healthy forms of showing emotion," Dr. Warren says. "You could have talked to the counselors."

I stare at her, wondering if she's serious, if she doesn't know the extremes the outside world has gone to in order to try to "protect" us. "Believe what you want," I tell her. "But the handlers were looking for any excuse to flag us. All we could feel was the pressure of it."

I turn away, thinking again about how relieved I was to see that James was okay. "That day he gave me a ride home. And then the next. It started to feel like the only time we were normal was when we were together. We would tuck ourselves away where we could cry and no one else could see us. As the weeks passed, we started to talk about other things. About leaving town again, just me and him. About being together forever."

My chest swells as I remember our first time, how scared I was. We were camping, snuggling on a blanket next to the warm fire. I was so in love with him.

I close my eyes now and think about how James kissed my neck, his mouth hot. His hands gentle on my skin. Soon he was kissing me passionately, seeming to want me more than ever before.

His knee moved between my legs, and I pulled his shirt over his head when he stopped, gasping for breath. "Wait," he said. "We shouldn't."

His blue eyes were heavy lidded, filled with desire. Lust. I pulled him down and kissed him again, working at his belt, even when he told me again that we didn't have to. He'd brought protection, which showed me he'd at least considered it could happen. And we used it, just like we always would after.

I open my eyes and see Dr. Warren waiting for the story. I wish I didn't have to tell her anything, but I just can't stop. I hate that I can't stop because I know what it means. She's going to steal this moment away from me, and the thought is unbearable.

"The night James and I first had sex," I say, "it wasn't about our hormones. It was desperate, sad, even a little painful. And then it was beautiful and hopeful. It was a promise we made to each other, that we would protect each other. Take care of each other.

"James told me he loved me, and that he would never let anything happen to me. I promised the same—" I choke on my words. "But I lied. I didn't protect him. I tried so hard, but I wasn't strong enough. They came and they took him. And now he doesn't love me anymore."

I cover my face and start sobbing, realizing how much it hurts to be alive. How I don't want to live with the loss. "I have nothing," I say through my hands. "I'm all alone now."

"You're not," Dr. Warren asks. "I'm not saying James is a bad guy. Neither is Brady or Miller or Lacey. But they're the reason you're really here. They were infected, Sloane. They infected you. And now you have to get better. Just like a cancer, we have to cut out what's making you sick."

I look at her, still hating her, but with the pain raging in my chest, maybe a little less so.

"Here." She offers the yellow pill. "Take it. Empower yourself, sweetheart. It'll make everything right."

I consider her offer. Then I think of Roger's disgusting mouth on mine. I think of how his purple pill will let me hold on to some of my memories. So instead I look at Dr. Warren and say, "Go to hell."

And then someone grabs me, and I feel a pinch in my arm.

CHAPTER NINE

"SLOANE," A VOICE WHISPERS.

My eyes flip open, and I start to scream as I see a figure next to my bed.

"Shh . . . shh . . . ," Realm says, quickly putting his finger to his lips. He shoots a cautious look at the door, and I force myself to quiet down.

"You scared the hell out of me," I whisper, and then lean closer so that I can see him better in the dim room. The only light comes from the moon outside the sealed window. I pause when he comes into focus. "Your eye."

Realm has a black eye that looks like it might still hurt.

"It's fine," he says, waving me off. "I just wanted to make sure you were okay. Didn't mean to leave so abruptly." He grins, but he's checking me over, making sure I'm all right.

"It was very rude," I offer. Then I sit up and wrap my arms around his neck. He chuckles and holds me gently, almost like he's embarrassed that we're in an embrace. "I was so lonely," I say.

Realm reaches to smooth back my hair. "Sloane . . ." He pauses. "No one hurt you, did they?" His voice is filled with concern, and I think he's talking about Roger, but I can't tell him about the pill. About the kiss.

"No," I lie. "I just didn't think you were coming back." I slowly release him and lie back down in my bed, glad he's here.

"You should sleep," Realm whispers. "Meet you for breakfast?"

I nod, smiling. "Maybe they'll have waffles."

He laughs. "If not, I'll find you some."

I curl up on my side as he fixes my blankets. "You probably would." I watch as he leaves, quietly closing the door behind him. Seeing him again is like a huge weight lifted off my chest. Even though I know I was upset earlier, I can't remember why. I'm just glad my friend is back.

The next morning. Realm is waiting at my table, looking fresh in a pair of new lemon-yellow scrubs. His hair is still wet and brushed back, making him look younger somehow. Paired with his black eye, it's almost adorable.

"It's not waffles," he says, as if expecting me to be disappointed. "But I filled out a suggestion card, so hopefully tomorrow."

I laugh and sit next to him, not bothering to get my food yet. "Did you get that shiner from the handler?" I ask, leaning to look at it. Realm watches me as I examine him, a sad expression on his face.

"Roger got an elbow in," he says quietly. "But I nearly choked him to death, so it's about even."

I tense and turn away, wishing I hadn't let Roger touch me, but knowing that I got to keep a piece of myself in return. Or at least I hope.

"What?" Realm asks.

"Nothing," I murmur. "I'm just hungry." I get up and walk to the food line.

I'm at the end of my third week, and I continue to refuse my pills. I almost wish I didn't know what the medication did to me so I wouldn't have to have this battle every day. But I do know. And I want to fight.

After a therapy session and a fresh injection, I'm halfway back to my room when he walks into the hall.

"Hello, Sloane," Roger says. "Sorry I haven't been around. Been spending a lot of time at your new school."

At the sound of his voice, goose bumps raise on my arms. "Leave me alone," I say, my words slightly slurred.

"Don't you want you know why?"

I turn to look at him as his dark hair falls over his eyes. "No."

"Does the name James Murphy sound familiar?" he asks.

I gasp and stop walking, steadying myself on the wall. James is my boyfriend, or at least he was until he went into The Program.

He'd been friends with Miller—and before that . . . What? Who was James before that?

I press the heel of my hand against my forehead. I can't remember.

"Seems James is being difficult. No wonder you two were together for so long. You're a couple of troublemakers." Roger laughs, and I want to lunge at him and scratch out his eyes.

"Is he okay?" I ask.

Roger nods. "He's fine. Just a pain in the ass. He's always testing his handlers, slipping away. He's lucky he'll be eighteen soon, otherwise he might end up back here."

James is okay. I smile and lean against the wall.

"You know, Sloane," Roger whispers, walking to stand close to me. "After another session or two, James will be gone from your memory altogether."

"Shut up," I say, squeezing my eyes closed when his fingers brush my bare arm.

"I told you the price and I think it's fair. What do you say?" He leans closer, his peppermint breath on my ear. His finger glides up my arm and onto my shirt, grazing the side of my breast.

The room is tilting from my medication, but I'm trying to hold on. I don't want to be this vulnerable around him. I don't want his disgusting hands on me. "No," I snarl.

"Hmm . . . ," he says, and loops his arm around my waist, putting my head against his shoulder. "Maybe I should help you to your room."

I try to pull away and nearly fall when I hear a shout from down the hall. "Hey, Rog," Realm says, his hands in the pockets of his yellow scrubs. "Looks like you might need some help."

Instead of responding, Roger lays me down on the floor, backing away. "Wasn't doing anything wrong, Michael," he responds.

"Is that right?" Realm calls, walking toward us. The coolness of the white tiles feels good against my cheek. Realm's image is sideways as he approaches. "Weren't doing anything wrong with any of the other girls, either?" Realm asks. "What would Dr. Warren say?" Realm's features are clouded as he comes to stand over me. I reach to touch the hem of his pants, fisting the fabric as I try to pull myself up.

"You keep a secret and I will too," Roger says, his eyes narrowed to slits as he backs down the hall.

Realm takes my hand and gently tugs me to my feet. "Sloane, can you walk?" he asks.

I try to say yes as I lean into him, but I can't seem to get my balance. Realm bends and then slips his arms under my knees and scoops me up, my head against his chest. He starts toward my room as Roger gets as far against the wall as he can.

"This isn't over," Realm says to him before kicking open my door. I can feel his body tense around me, and I wonder what Roger would have done to me if Realm hadn't shown up. But I push the thought away, clinging to Realm as he lays me in my bed. I ask him to stay, not letting go of his shirt until his arms are around me. Then I drift, unconscious.

When it's time for dinner, Realm and I don't talk about what happened. At least not at first. He helps me get my food even as Derek and Shep break his balls, saying he's whipped. I'm trembling, alternating between hot and cold flashes like a bad reaction to the medication.

"Can I sit with you?" Tabitha asks, poised at the end of our table. The guys laugh, but Realm moves over.

"Of course, Tabby."

I smile at him, thinking he's kind. He's smart. He reminds me of James in a way, always knowing how to make me feel better. James makes me laugh too, although I can't remember the last time we did that.

"Here," Realm says, putting a piece of corn bread on my tray. "You need to eat, Sloane. You're wasting away."

"Maybe I want to waste away."

"Don't say things like that in here," he whispers fiercely. "You'll get flagged again."

I nod, feeling bad for upsetting him, and I take his hand under the table. "I'm just feeling sorry for myself," I say quietly. "My memories . . . I don't have many left."

Realm squeezes my hand and doesn't let go. He looks at me like he understands, and then we go back to our dinner, listening as the others talk. I nod when Derek tells us that he's going to move out of the country once he's eighteen.

I'm grateful Realm is holding on to me. It doesn't feel romantic. It feels like a lifeline.

CHAPTER TEN

AFTER A SPIRITED GAME OF CARDS, REALM AND I
retreat to the couch to watch a movie with a few others. I'm
curled up next to him, and no one says anything: no nurses tell
us to move apart. We can do what we want and it's nice. It's the
first time in a long while that I feel in control.

When Nurse Kell comes in and tells us all it's time to return
to our rooms, Realm pulls me in the other direction instead.
"Wanna come hang out in my room?" he asks, motioning
down the hall. I shrug, holding on to his arm as we walk.

Opening his door, he allows me to go in first, and then he
checks the hallway before closing it behind us. "It's fun to sneak
around, isn't it?" he asks.

"It is. And I thought nothing could beat being constantly
medicated." I laugh, but a serious expression comes over Realm's

face. He goes to sit on his bed as I sit in the chair facing him. I start to fidget, knowing he wants to talk about Roger.

"Sloane, I have to ask. . . . Did he rape you?"

"What?" I look up, startled. "No."

"Then what happened?" Realm swallows hard and I know there's no use in denying it altogether.

"He offered a trade."

"Oh, God."

"It was for a kiss. Some . . . touching, but I kneed him really hard when that happened. It was just a kiss." I feel sick thinking about it, and lower my head, not wanting Realm to see my face.

"And in return?"

"He gave me a pill. Said it would let me hold on to a memory."

Realm swears under his breath, rubbing roughly at his face. "I'm going to kill him," he says, mostly to himself. "I told him to leave you alone."

"He's done it to others, hasn't he?" I ask.

Realm nods, and then looks over at me, pained. "I think maybe it's been going on for a while."

I cringe thinking about girls here having sex with that freak, and I can't believe I ever let him touch me. I just wanted to keep my life. Keep myself. I feel violated and stupid, and I wrap my arms around myself as I sit back in the chair.

"It doesn't work, you know," Realm says. "The pill to block. With the memory out of context, it'll never come back or make sense. You shouldn't take it."

I flinch as if I've been slapped. I'd let Roger touch me, and now I wasn't getting what I was promised. It was for nothing. I did it for nothing.

"It doesn't work?" I ask, my voice strained. Realm shakes his head. My world practically crumbles around me. My only hope is gone. I'd pinned everything on keeping the memories. I'm truly lost.

"You should give the pill to me," he says.

"I can't," I say quietly. "I already took it."

Realm's face flares with anger. "You idiot," he says. "You could have been killed."

Stunned, I lower my eyes, Realm's harsh words stinging. I move to get up but he reaches quickly for my hand.

"I'm sorry," he whispers. "I didn't mean that. Please don't go. I'm just frustrated, Sloane." He stops talking, and when I finally look up again, he exhales. "Sorry," he repeats, sliding his fingers from mine. "Let's just change the subject, okay?"

I don't have anywhere else to go, so I sit back down. "Whatever," I say. Realm is always so accepting of The Program, so ready to let them take his past. But that's not me. I don't want to change.

Realm scoots over on the bed, patting the blanket. "Will you sit with me?" he asks. I nod, and move to put my knee on the bed, climbing up next to him.

"It's going to be okay," he says softly. "It's almost over."

I stare at him, the air seeming to rush out of me. "Is that all I have to look forward to? The point where I'm empty?"

He smiles sadly. "It won't hurt anymore once you forget. It's the only thing that can save us now." He bends to rest his forehead against mine, whispering. "We can't go on like this. You have a huge hole here." He puts his palm over my heart, and the touch is intimate and almost comforting. It's not butterflies or romantic—I don't have those feelings for him. But it's a touch that makes me feel human. Alive.

"I don't know if I can make it," I say, closing my eyes.

"You can. You've made it this far. And hell, you're not dead, right?" He moves back and takes my chin, making me look at him. "Now I want *you* to hold *me*," he jokes, curling me against him as we lie back against the pillows.

"It's lucky that we were both here," he continues as he begins to play with my hair. "Otherwise I'd have to snuggle with Nurse Kell."

I laugh, putting my hand on his chest, over his heart. I'm surprised by how fast it's beating. "You nervous?" I ask.

"Well, I am in bed with a pretty girl. I think this sort of reaction is beyond my control."

I sit up, and Realm shifts to lie flat on the bed. I get on my elbow and look down at his face. The black under his eye has faded, and his skin looks healthier than it did the first time I met him. The scar around his neck is healed, and I wonder how old it is. I trace my index finger over the raised pink line, and he holds his breath, his dark eyes meeting mine.

"Does it still hurt?" I ask.

Realm licks his lips but is slow to answer. "Every day."

I pause, my finger under his chin. "Me too," I respond.

Realm reaches to draw me closer, and I don't pull away. I'm so lonely, so broken that I don't think I'll ever be fixed. Being with someone could make me forget for a while. Realm's been good to me. He's my friend.

But as he leans forward, something inside of me seizes up. Just when his mouth meets mine, I turn away, making his lips brush my cheek instead. "I can't," I murmur. Realm is not my boyfriend. He's not James.

I close my eyes and lower my head to his chest, hugging him and hoping he won't send me away. I don't want to be alone right now. Realm immediately starts to apologize, but I stop him.

"It's not you. I'm . . . I'm with James," I tell him, not sure if it's cruel to say. "I love him."

Realm adjusts his position, but doesn't push me aside. Instead he wraps me in a hug. "I understand," he whispers.

"I'm going to find him again," I say, mostly to myself. "The Program can't erase James from my heart. I know they can't."

"If it's meant to be . . . ," Realm says, sounding like my mother. But underneath, I hear his hurt. I don't respond and just let him hold me, knowing that I shouldn't be here like this. But no one ever comes in to make me go back to my room. And when I start to fall asleep, I think that my guilt is gone—if only for a moment.

I've become comfortably numb.

CHAPTER ELEVEN

I WAKE UP AND LOOK AROUND AT THE STARK WHITE walls. I'm alone in my bed, alone in my room. After falling asleep at Realm's, I woke up at about three in the morning and made my way back to my own bed, feeling empty.

When I walk into the dining room, Realm is waiting at the table for me, a stupid grin on his face. His friends whistle as I walk up wearing my lemon-yellow scrubs, holding a tray of scrambled eggs. Realm elbows Shep in the chest. "Get out of here, man." But the smile never falters.

"What's going on?" I ask when I'm sitting next to him. I don't care if they're gossiping about me—not really. At least that way they won't try to hit on me. And after Roger, I hope no one ever does again.

Realm shrugs. "They may have noticed a girl going into

my room with me last night. If they figured out it was you, and thought we got it on, it's not my fault."

"You didn't deny it?"

"Nope. And it's still not my fault. You should have worn a disguise if you didn't want to be noticed." Realm reaches over and opens my milk carton for me, and then absently goes back to his eggs. I stare down at the milk, thinking that opening it was a sweet gesture, even if slightly possessive.

"I meant to ask," I say, "how much longer do you have here?"

Realm pauses, but doesn't look up. "Two weeks. And you'll have a week and a half after that."

Panic starts to pull at me, making it hard to breathe. "A week and a half is a long time." My voice cracks, and I'm suddenly terrified of being here alone. Being all alone with nobody but the stranger with my face. And Roger—who is definitely pissed now.

"Sweetness," Realm says. "It's going to be okay."

"No, it's not," I whisper. "I'll forget everything. And then Roger—what about him? What will he do when I can't fight him off?"

Realm's posture changes. "Roger won't mess with you again. I promise. I won't let him."

"You won't be here."

Realm looks sideways at me, his expression deadly serious. "I'm giving you my word that I won't let him. I don't care what I have to do, he'll never touch you again." He sounds like he means it. Although I'm scared something might happen to him, Realm just smiles, making my worry evaporate.

Then he leans forward to put a soft kiss on my cheek, one that smells like breakfast, and goes back to eating.

Dr. Francis examines me again, and says that I've regained a pound. He's pleased as he adjusts my medication dosage, saying that I've made such strides in my recovery that he can finally lower it. I want to believe him, but I don't. Not when he still works for The Program.

After I'm checked over, he ushers me to Dr. Warren's office. She looks happy to see me, her hair pulled into a high, girlish ponytail, her suit replaced with a colorful blouse.

"You look cheerful," I mumble as I walk in. She smiles at this.

"Thought you could use a change. Do we need Marilyn today?" She slides the Dixie cup toward me.

"Yep."

I can see her tense, but she just waves her hand and the nurse comes in, holding me still as she stabs me with the needle. It doesn't take as long this time for my fight to go out. I think that the dose has been increased, and not scaled back like Dr. Francis promised. Either that or I have fewer memories for the medication to attach to.

I sink down in my chair. "What are you going to pick at today?" I ask.

"I'm just listening, Sloane. I've never done anything but listen."

"Liar."

She sighs. "Why do you love James so much?" she asks. "Is it because he reminds you of the time you spent with your brother?"

"No. It's because he's hot." I laugh, resting my head back against the chair. She's the crazy one if she thinks I'm going to tell her.

"Would it hurt if I told you that James didn't love you?"

I glare at her. "What?"

"I've been through James's files, and he told his counselor that he felt obligated to take care of you. That he wanted to save you because you were so unwell, and he didn't want you to die like your brother."

She can't be telling me the truth—James was probably just trying to protect me from them. And yet Dr. Warren's words are like a punch in the heart.

"James loved me," I hiss. "And your twisted lies won't change that."

"How do you know that, Sloane? When did you realize that he truly loved you? That you loved him?"

"Like I'm going to tell you," I scoff.

Dr. Warren nods, and then raises her hand to Marilyn. "Another dose, please."

"Wait, what—"

There's pain in my arm as Marilyn gives me another shot. "You can't do that," I say, scared of overdosing, of dying in this facility.

"Sloane, we will do whatever we have to. We're trying to

save your life and stop the spread of an epidemic. Now please cooperate or we're going to have to take you to an examination room."

The threat of the exam room truly frightens me. What will they do? Cut open my head? I glare at Dr. Warren and rub my arm.

"Okay," I say. "Okay."

Marilyn leaves and Dr. Warren settles in with my file, ready to write down what I say. I consider lying, but then a wave crashes over me that makes me too weak to be dishonest.

"James had dated girls before me, quite a few actually," I start. "So when we became a couple out in the open, some of those girls tried to say it was because my brother was dead. The same crap you're saying now. Of course, they didn't know that we'd been seeing each other before—but I was too ashamed to tell anyone. Not after keeping it a secret from Brady.

"My brother had only been gone a few weeks when my parents sat me down for a talk. They said they were worried about me, but I was doing fine. Far better than they were. Then they told me that they were concerned about me getting involved with James—that two people who suffered a tragedy shouldn't be together because it increases the risk of suicide. I then pointed out that maybe they shouldn't be together."

My mother slapped me that night. I can still feel the sting on my cheek. I felt terrible for what I said, but I never apologized. Now I probably never will because I won't remember.

"I left then," I tell Dr. Warren. "I got in the car and drove straight to James's house. It was after ten when his dad opened the door, clearly pissed."

I remember Mr. Murphy's face, how closed off he was.

"Sorry, Sloane," he said. "No visitors this late." He looked a lot like James, only bigger, heavier. Colder.

Tears had stung my eyes. "But it's important."

He bristled. "Listen, I've talked with James about this. The two of you . . . I'm not in favor of it." Mr. Murphy reached to put his hand on my shoulder. "I think you're a great girl, Sloane," he said. "And I loved your brother. But you and my son can't heal when you're constant reminders of death to each other. Go home, honey," Mr. Murphy said. "I'm sure your parents are worried."

"Obviously my parents had called," I say to Dr. Warren. "They'd given him the heads-up that I was probably on my way." I stop talking then, opting instead to relax into the memory. Recognize the moment when James and I knew we were forever.

"I love your son," I told Mr. Murphy as I backed off the porch. "Not because of Brady or anything else. I'm in love with him."

James's father lowered his eyes, and then he shut the front door, blocking me out. I stood there, stunned for a moment. But when I headed back to my car, I heard a whistle. I turned to see James running toward me, backpack over his shoulder.

"What are you—"

His face was expressionless. "Let's go." He pulled me to my

car, and we got in. I drove away, but James looked like he'd been crying.

"James," I started. "They said that—"

"Sloane," he interrupted, staring at me intently. "They can't keep me from you."

"Then what do we do?" I asked.

He pointed straight ahead. "Just drive."

Dr. Warren shifts behind her desk, and I look at her. She nods her head, encouraging me to remember everything.

"James and I ran away," I tell her. "We went to a campsite with yurts—those tentlike buildings already set up—and James rented it for the rest of the week. No one questioned him because he paid cash and looked older. When we got inside, it was like our own little house. Our own little life."

I lean back in the chair in Dr. Warren's office, my body warm from the drugs. I think about how James and I rearranged the bed and table, making it all our own. We wanted to stay there forever. There was a deck of cards, and somehow James talked me into a game of strip poker, only he lost.

"Are you purposely losing?" I asked him, laughing.

"Sloane, when winning means getting you naked, you better believe I'm going to try my damnedest to win." He ran his eyes over my T-shirt and jeans. "You could at least take off a sock to humor me."

So I did, taking it off slowly and then tossing it across the room. James's face changed then, the playfulness fading.

"Sloane," he whispered, laying down his cards. "I love you. You make me feel right."

James crawled over the cards on the floor and stopped in front of me, his face close to mine, studying me. "I love the way you laugh. Cry. I love to make you smile." He touched my cheek, and I grinned instinctively. "Make you moan."

Butterflies fluttered in my stomach, and I reached to put my arms around his neck.

"Baby," he continued, "I'm going to live the rest of my life with you, or die trying."

"Don't talk about dying," I murmured, kissing softly at his lips.

"You're the only person I can ever trust. You're the only one who'll ever know the real me."

"I know James loved me," I tell Dr. Warren as tears run down my cheeks. "Because I knew him better than anyone ever could. He always acted like nothing was wrong, that he was tough, but inside, Brady's death tortured him. James hated his father for trying to keep us apart. He resented his mother for leaving when he was a kid. When we were alone, James could be vulnerable, and I loved him then most of all." I wipe at my face and glare at Dr. Warren. "We were together because we loved each other. And that's all there ever was."

Dr. Warren nods slowly, not jotting anything down, just looking on as if she understands. Or maybe it's fake like everything else. The room is liquidy around me, dreamlike.

"Take this," she says, sliding me a black pill. It's different from the usual yellow one I take, and all at once I'm seized with hope. She's going to help me after all. A smile twitches my lips, and I lean lazily forward and take the pill, swallowing it gratefully. When I do, she exhales, setting her pen down.

"I'm sorry for all you've been through, Sloane," she says like she means it. "You should take a moment to say good-bye."

I furrow my brow. "Good-bye to who?"

"James."

The floor seems to drop out from under me, and despite the drugs slowing my movements, I jump out of the chair. *No. No. No.* I quickly jam my finger down my throat, gagging as Dr. Warren tells me to stop and calls to the nurse. I have to throw up the pill before they can erase him. *James.*

But the minute I get the pill back up, the relief is short lived. Marilyn walks in with a needle, poised to strip it all away.

CHAPTER TWELVE

I'M SOBBING AS I STUMBLE FROM DR. WARREN'S office. She doesn't bother to help me. Instead she tells me that it's okay for me to cry. I swear at her and run my hand along the wall as I head toward the leisure room.

James. James. James. I know these are my last minutes to remember him, and I stop, letting myself slide down the wall to sit on the floor. I rest my head on my bent knees and hold on to what I can.

I see James, smiling broadly as he rakes his fingers through his wet hair. "Come on, Sloane," he calls from the water. He's shirtless, the sun glistening off his skin as he stands in the river. I sit on the grass and shake my head.

James walks out of the water, dripping, as he approaches me. He collapses on the blanket, the cool skin of his thigh pressed against my shorts. "One day," he says, his eyes squinted against the sun, "I'm going to teach you how to swim. And then we're going to the ocean."

"Never."

"Never?" James repeats, sounding amused. He pulls me down next to him and traps me in his arms. His skin is cold, but hot underneath. "Never?"

I giggle and shake my head.

"And what if I want to get married on the beach?" he asks. "You still say no?" He bites on his lip, leaning closer to me. "You'll refuse to marry me?"

Tingles race over me, and not just because he's close but because I'm overwhelmed with how much I love him. How he's the other half of my heart. "I'll never refuse you," I whisper.

James smiles and then kisses me softly, trailing his mouth to my neck before returning to my lips again. "It's me and you," he says. "Madly in love until the end."

And the words echo in my head as I collapse on my side in the hallway, drowning in my pain.

I feel something next to me, but my body is heavy and I can't move. I try to turn, but my hands are locked at my side. My eyes fly open. A face looms over me, and I start to scream when his hand covers my mouth.

"Shh . . . Miss Barstow," Roger whispers. "We wouldn't want to draw attention to ourselves, would we?"

I twist my hands again and realize he has me in the

restraints. I know I'm not completely helpless. I can bite down on his hand, scream out. But then what? They'll restart me in The Program—making sure I don't remember anything that I'm not supposed to.

I shake his hand off my mouth. "What do you want?"

He smiles, his eyes gliding over my body under the sheets. "I think you'd be a little too feisty to trust with any of my naked parts now," he says. "So I'm not offering a trade anymore."

I furrow my brow. "Then what?"

"I want Michael Realm out of here. But first, I want to watch him squirm."

The vulnerability of my situation crashes down on me. "What are you going to do?"

Roger shrugs. "Michael is inappropriately fond of you, so I think this scene alone will be enough to push him over the edge, don't you?" With a sickening smile, Roger leans over me, placing a kiss on my collarbone, smart enough to avoid getting close to my teeth. He runs his tongue along my skin. "It's too bad," he murmurs, kissing again. "We could have had a lot of fun."

"Yeah," I growl. "I would have enjoyed kneeing you again."

Roger pulls back, examining my expression. "You think you're in control?" he asks, his peppermint breath warm on my face. "Do you think you're beating The Program?" He laughs softly. "Sloane," he whispers. "You used to love someone. Do you remember?"

His words hit me harder than any slap. There's a twist in

my gut, a pain in my heart. Love? I . . . I did love someone, I think. It was . . .

Roger moves away with a satisfied grin. "I should go," he says. "Michael should be out of *therapy* by now." He starts to walk away, but then turns back. "Forgot." Roger pulls a needle out his pocket and stabs me in the thigh. He covers my mouth as I cry out, but it's only minutes before things start to get hazy. He pulls back the blanket to untie the drawstring of my pants and pulls up my shirt to expose my stomach, making it look like I've been struggling.

My head falls back against the pillow as he watches me carefully, waiting for me to pass out. I can feel the tears leak from the corner of my eyes and slide across my temples.

"Sorry I had to strap you down, Sloane," he says. "But you were a danger to yourself." He pats my shoulder consolingly and walks out.

There's a soft slap against my cheek. "Sloane? Sweetness, wake up." There's another quick tap, and I open my eyes. "Oh, thank God," Realm murmurs, moving to undo my restraints. "What happened?" he demands.

"Roger," I choke out, my voice raspy. "He—"

Realm stops dead and stares at me. "Roger did this to you?" His breathing quickens as he covers me with the blanket, a deep flush on his cheeks.

"He didn't," I assure him, knowing he's thinking the worse. "But he's baiting you. He wants you gone." Realm's jaw is clenched so tight it sets his face in sharp, hard angles. He undoes the other strap and then rubs my wrist where it's red as he sits on the edge of my bed.

"Sloane," he begins quietly. "I'm going to be leaving for a few days, but you'll be safe, okay? I will come back for you."

I widen my eyes. "Wait, what?"

"I need you to be strong," he says. "Just be strong until I get back." He stands up, looking at me like he doesn't want to leave. Then he says good-bye and walks out the door, shutting it behind him.

I'm still groggy, but I get out of bed anyway. The tile floor is ice-cold under my bare feet. I fumble with the door handle and just as I get it open, I see Realm stalking toward the nurse's station. Roger's poised there, laughing with the nurse. I'm about to yell for Realm to stop, but before I can, he cocks back his arm and decks Roger, sending him flying over the desk.

"Michael!" the nurse yells out. But Realm jumps over and grabs Roger by the neck, his fist pulled back to hit him again.

"Which arm?" Realm snarls.

Roger looks at him, his cheek already puffing out from where Realm's fist connected. I lean against the door frame, barely able to stand.

"Don't do this, Michael," Roger says. "You'll expose us all."

Realm punches him hard in the face again, and I wince, sure that Roger's nose is broken. The nurse is still screaming for them to stop, but she doesn't dare intervene. Not when Realm looks so crazed.

"Which arm did you touch her with?" Realm demands, his face close to Roger's bloodied one. And when the handler doesn't answer, I watch as Realm grabs Roger's right arm and yanks it so hard behind his back the snap is audible.

I stumble in the doorway and fall to my knees. Roger howls and Realm lets him go, backing away. Roger's arm hangs at an odd angle below the elbow and I try to catch my breath, horrified by the sight. Just then security rounds the hall, and I'm afraid for Realm.

But instead of pulling out their Tasers, the guards skid to a stop in front of him. While one guard helps Roger to stand, the other takes hold of Realm, whispering something to him as he leads him in the other direction. And rather than fight, Realm seems calm—eerily calm even though he just broke a guy's arm and is being hauled off by The Program to God knows where.

"Realm?" I call after him, the start of a cry in my voice. What are they going to do to him?

He looks over his shoulder then and his eyes widen when he sees me. But he doesn't say anything. He just nods as if we have an agreement.

And then he lets security take him away.

I wait for Realm to come back. When I ask Nurse Kell she says she doesn't know what will happen, a disapproving look on her face. I feel exposed and empty with my only friend gone. Roger had been right: I'm not in control of anything.

The first day without Realm, I see Roger in the hall with a

security guard on his left. Roger's right arm is in a cast. He has a bandage over his nose and has a black eye. A twisted satisfaction stretches over me. I watch him carry a box of his things, his career here clearly over. And since I haven't been pulled into a meeting, it looks like my name stayed out of it. Realm really did find a way to get rid of him.

When he passes me, Roger pauses long enough to glance sideways at me. I don't smile because the look in his eyes is pure hatred. It's a look that says, "This isn't over."

I turn away, not acknowledging him, and halfway down the hall I see Tabitha standing in her doorway. When she catches my eyes, she nods—just like Realm did. As if we all have a secret pact I don't know about. Maybe now that Roger's gone, we'll all sleep a little easier.

The day drags after that, and when I finally make it to dinner in the dining room, Derek and Shep are at my table. "Hey," they say when I sit down.

"Hey." I'm not used to talking to them without Realm around, and they look as lost as I feel. "Cards tonight?" I ask, hoping they'll distract me from missing Realm.

"Naw," Shep says, pushing away his hamburger. "I want to wait until Realm comes back." His green eyes are sad, and I want to reach out and touch his hand, but I don't.

I feel strange, as if I'm hollowed out somehow. I feel vulnerable and empty.

"So you know how he kicked the shit out of that handler?" Derek asks me. I nod, nervous about what will come next. "I

heard some of the nurses talking, and they said Roger was deal-
ing medication and Realm busted him. But then the handler
said he'd hurt us if Realm turned him in." He puffs up his
chest. "Now obviously I can take care of myself. So I'm going
to assume the threat was made on you. It explains why Realm
went crazy on him."

I shrug and poke at the salad on my plate.

"Anyway," Derek continues, "Kell seems to think they'll let
Realm come back. But they fired Roger. Made him sign some
confidentiality agreement with The Program. Can you believe
that? He should be in jail."

"They'd never jeopardize The Program," I state. "We're the
cure, remember?"

When I look up they're all staring at me like I've lost my
mind, and I consider that maybe I have. Maybe this emptiness
is where my heart used to be. I stand up, pushing away my tray
and head into the leisure room, taking a seat by the window
and staring out.

CHAPTER THIRTEEN

I'VE BEEN IN THE PROGRAM FOR FOUR WEEKS AND eight hours. Realm still isn't back, but I haven't given up hope. I don't remember much of my past, but there is a sense that I was happy once. And it makes me think I could be again.

Tabitha and I are standing in front of the leisure room as she shows me her fingernails. As a reward for good behavior, they let her have some polish, and although her nails are still short, they're now neon pink. She wiggles them admiringly.

"They look great," I tell her, also noticing how she's started to brush her hair.

"Thanks," Tabitha says. "I leave in two weeks, can you believe it? I think they're going to let me get my hair done, too. Dr. Warren thinks I'd look better with auburn instead of red. What do you think?"

I shrug. "I like it how it is."

She smiles as if my compliment truly means a lot to her. But then she notices something behind me and her grin widens. "Sloane," she says.

"What?"

"Loverboy is back."

I turn quickly and see Realm walking toward us, his lemon-yellow scrubs freshly pressed. A weak sigh escapes from my lips as my whole body releases my fear. I run toward him and he holds out his arms for a hug.

"You're okay," I whisper in his ear the minute he swoops me up, my feet dangling over the floor. He smells like soap and laundry detergent, and I'm so happy I don't think I can let him go.

"I'm okay," he says, hugging me tight. When he sets me down, he waves to Tabitha and she giggles and walks away.

Realm then stares down into my face, his skin looking paler. "Did anything happen while I was gone?" he asks, putting his hands on my shoulders and massaging them softly.

"Roger was fired."

Realm smiles and then hugs me again. "Told you he wouldn't bother you again." He rests his cheek on the top of my head. "You didn't tell anyone about what he offered you, right?" he whispers quietly.

"No."

"Good."

"The boys won't play cards without you," I say, wanting to change the subject. "I think they miss you."

"Did you miss me?"

And even though we're hugging, even though I'm so glad to have him back, I feel strange about his question. "Of course," I answer, because it's the truth. I pull away and notice the bandage on his knuckles. When he sees me looking he holds it up. "Cut it on his tooth," he says. "Two stitches."

"He looked worse, believe me."

Realm seems satisfied with this, takes my hand in his uninjured one, and leads us to the leisure room.

The card game is in full swing, and Realm and I have pretzels dangling from our mouths as we call out bullshit. Everyone is laughing.

"There's no way you have diamonds," Shep yells at Derek. "I have them all, dude. Bullshit."

It's the closest thing you'll ever get to a diamond from him. I blink. The voice in my head is not mine. It's from somewhere else, and I see a purple heart-shaped ring with sparkles in it. I'm stuffing it in a mattress, but I don't know why. *Whose ring is that?*

"Sloane," Realm says, bumping my knee. "You okay?"

I nod, looking back at him, but not really seeing him. Inside I feel a pull—something yanking out my heart. I miss someone. I know it plainly, and yet I can't conjure up a face. An image. It's like an ache, a phantom pain for an appendage that's no longer there. I don't know what I've lost, where I've been. I think on it, and I don't know if I had a boyfriend before The Program, if I'm even a virgin anymore. I'm a stranger to myself.

This thought makes tears spring to my eyes. I want to be me, and yet I'm not sure who I am. I cover my face, sobbing into my hands, and then Realm moves into the chair with me, wrapping his arms around me.

"Whoa," I hear Shep say, sounding nervous. "What's wrong with you, Sloane?"

"She's fine," Realm says quickly, rubbing my upper arm as I cry into his shoulder.

"Doesn't look fine," Shep answers.

I feel Realm tense, but then he sighs. "She just missed me a bunch, right, sweetness?" he says jokingly. "It must have been tragic sitting here with you guys for three days."

They scoff, but I feel the tension leave the table. "Come on," Realm says, helping me stand up. I'm too embarrassed to look at the guys, so I keep my face hidden against his shirt. "Game's done for tonight."

"Ah, man!" Derek yells, and I hear the smack of his cards on the table. Realm doesn't respond, and leads me out into hall and toward his room. By the time we get there the tears have stopped, and I feel a little more in control, although still empty.

"Come hang out with me?" he asks. I nod and he smiles, sneaking me into his room.

I'm sitting in a chair by Realm's bed as he lays out another round of solitaire. It's past eleven, but no one has come to kick me out. It's been three days since Realm came back, and night after night, I've been allowed to stay in here with him. It's strange, and I'm not sure if I should be worried or grateful. It's definitely better than being alone.

"Why don't they bother us?" I ask.

"What's that?" Realm groans and lays the cards aside. "How can I not win? I'm playing myself."

"They never send me back to my room. Why?"

Realm stretches, raising his hands above his head. "Maybe they think we're a cute couple."

"I'm serious."

"And I'm tired." His dark eyes look me over. "Come to bed with me?"

I look at the door, considering going back to my room, but when my feet touch the floor and I feel its coldness even through my slipper socks, I decide to stay.

"I guess," I tell him, pretending like I don't want to. He rolls his eyes and holds up the blanket as I climb in next to him. He puts his arm around me, sighing as I snuggle against him. This is how we've been since he came back. He lets me stay in here, holding me close. It's been nice.

"This isn't so bad, right?" he asks. "There are definitely worse things."

"We're in The Program," I remind him. "I don't think it can get worse than this."

Realm brushes my hair aside, his fingers running down my neck, tickling me. He continues down my spine, a feather light touch over my scrubs, and then back up again. "It can always get worse." His other hand reaches to take my scarred wrist, and he brings it to his mouth, kissing the mark there.

I swallow hard. His gesture is kind. Even sexy. Realm flattens his palm on my lower back, pressing me into him. He kisses my inner forearm, my shoulder. "I could love you, Sloane," he whispers next to my ear. "You don't have to be alone."

You used to love someone, Roger had told me once. What did he mean? *Was* there someone before The Program?

Realm brings his mouth close to mine but pauses to look in my eyes as if asking permission. His feelings are so clear, so sure. I don't know what I feel right now, other than alone. So I lean forward and kiss him.

Realm's lips are soft but unfamiliar. Warm but not hot. My hands hesitate on the sides of his face, and I realize as his tongue touches mine that I don't feel lust or hurt or anger. I don't feel love or disgust. I feel . . . grief.

His hand slides down to pull my thigh over his hip. We could do anything right now; no one is bothering us. He lays me back in the bed, lying between my legs as he trails kisses down my neck and back up again. My eyes close, and I try to feel something other than sadness as Realm knots his fingers in my hair, murmurs how beautiful I am.

His hand is cool as it slips inside my shirt, grazing my stomach before pausing at my bra. And all at once my eyes open, and I'm struck with sudden guilt. A sense of wrong so intense that I push Realm's hand away and roll out from under him.

"No," I say, climbing off the bed. I straighten my scrubs as I catch my breath. "I can't . . . I can't."

"I shouldn't have done that," Realm says quickly, his face reddening as he talks. "I'm so sorry. Don't go, please."

I shake my head, backing away. "I . . . I should sleep in my own bed tonight. I'll see you tomorrow, okay?" And then without waiting for an answer, I hurry out into the hall toward my room. My heart pounds, and I feel so confused, so unsure of myself. I'm racked with guilt and I don't even know why.

I pass the nurses' station, but the young nurse doesn't ask why I'm coming out of Realm's room after hours, or what we were doing in there. She just types something into the computer and watches as I go into my room. Once I'm inside, I crawl into bed and pray for sleep.

CHAPTER FOURTEEN

I SKIP BREAKFAST THE NEXT MORNING AND AVOID Realm. I'm embarrassed that I bailed like that, no explanation. I liked kissing him—he's a good kisser. But something made it feel *wrong*, like I shouldn't be touching him at all.

I pull my legs under me as I sit on my bed, staring at the door and daring myself to leave the room. I have to face him and hope he pretends like nothing happened. He's my best friend, and I might like him as more than that. . . . But I don't know. Maybe I'm just an idiot.

Finally gathering the courage, I walk out into the hall and check the leisure room first. Derek sees me and nods a hello as he and Shep watch TV.

"You guys seen Realm?" I ask.

"Nope," Derek says, not looking away from the screen.

"Think he's got an early session with Dr. Warren today."

I curl my lip. I have therapy this afternoon, and I'm dreading it, although she tells me my progress has been exceptional. Not like I can remember if she was telling the truth.

I head down toward the offices, wondering if I'll catch him coming out. When I get to Dr. Warren's door, it's closed, and I figure Realm might still be in there. I lean against the wall next to it to wait when I hear raised voices.

"Michael," I hear Dr. Warren say, "sexual contact is not permitted. It's against the law, and we will prosecute you to the fullest extent of—"

"We're not sleeping together." I recognize Realm's voice, and I immediately touch my lips, scared he's in trouble. "I told you," he says. "I'm doing what I'm supposed to, and we kissed. That's it."

I stand outside the door, listening and worried. I didn't think they cared that Realm and I hung out, but maybe they do. Maybe they've been watching us this entire time.

"Even that is crossing the line. And after your little dustup with Roger, I don't think we can handle anymore of your liability. I'm sorry, Michael. I'm going to have to send you to another facility."

No! Panic overtakes me, and I almost burst into the room to defend him, but Realm is talking again.

"If you send me away now, you'll jeopardize her recovery," he says. "Sloane already thinks I'm leaving next week. There's no reason to create a situation where she casts you as the bad guy. Her transformation has been remarkable, don't you think?"

Tiny prickles of fear race up my arms. What's he talking about?

"Yes. She's come a long way," Dr. Warren muses. "Fine. You can stay the week, finish this stage of the therapy, but I'm warning you: hands off. They could bring a lawsuit against The Program."

"You know as well as I do that physical contact can do wonders for recovery. For trust building."

"Hands off," Dr. Warren repeats with a finality in her tone. She exhales. "Michael, are you certain she can complete treatment? There are other options—"

"Sloane will return on time," Realm says. "I just need a little more space to make sure the memories are cleared out. She's very fragile right now."

I stand there completely stunned as I try to wrap my mind around what I've just heard. Is Realm even a patient? I . . . I don't know what to think anymore. Did he set me up?

"Fine," Dr. Warren responds. "Then I guess we're done here."

"Almost," Realm says in a quiet voice.

I'm still next to the door when it opens suddenly. I push back against the wall, my heart pounding, as Realm stalks out. He starts to leave and then pauses. I hold my breath.

"Don't get caught standing there," he murmurs, not turning to me. "Or they'll send you away for another six weeks.

Maybe more." He lowers his head and then walks down the hallway.

I want to run after him and ask him what's going on—make him explain. But the realization is just hitting me. Realm is working with them. He's my friend, my only friend, but it's not real. He's part of The Program.

Oh, God. Realm is *part of The Program*! All this time I've confided in him, he's been passing the information to Dr. Warren—things I don't discuss in therapy. My secrets.

Realm. My lip quivers at the same time my hand clenches in a fist. He's . . . he's been messing with my mind. He's no better than any of them.

Realm doesn't sit with me at dinner, and I don't raise my head when he passes me. A few people ask if we're fighting, but I ignore them, picking at the chicken on my tray. Realm is a plant, a fake. I could out him in front of everyone here, and this entire place would explode. But what happens after? Will they send us all through The Program again? Are Derek and Shep a part of it?

Anger is fighting its way past the meds in my system. I look over to where Realm is sitting with his friends, and I stand, my hands shaking. I start over, and Realm looks at me just before I reach him and jumps up.

"Hey, sweetness," he says, and I can see how forced his smile is as he grabs my arm hard, turning me in the other direction.

"Don't touch me," I hiss, yanking away from him.

Realm fixes me with a warning glare and then turns back to his table. "Looks like I've moved from the doghouse to the porta-potty," he says, making them laugh. "I'll catch up with you guys later." They chuckle, but I'm backing toward the door, tears gathering in my eyes. When he notices, Realm grabs me quickly into a hug, pushing my cheek against his shirt as I struggle to pull away.

"Don't let them see you cry," he says quietly. "I'll tell you whatever you want to know, but if they think you're breaking down, they'll keep you. I know you want to go home, Sloane."

I put my hand on his forearm, digging my nails in as hard as I can. He flinches, but he doesn't pull away. I stop, knowing that I'm hurting him, and thinking that even now . . . I don't want to. What I want is for him to tell me that I'm wrong. That he's real and hasn't betrayed me. I sniffle and wipe my tears on his shirt before straightening up.

"My man is smooth," Derek says with a laugh from behind us.

Realm looks down at me, his expression miserable. His dark eyes are so sorry, but his jaw is tight, and I don't know if I can believe any of the emotions he shows me. I'm suddenly struck with the idea that I don't know what's true anymore. Maybe I've finally snapped.

Realm takes my hand and leads me toward the doorway, saying nothing. When we get there, Nurse Kell shoots Realm a worried glance.

"It's fine," he says. Then quieter, "Can you please send the meds directly to her room? Now."

SUZANNE YOUNG

She nods, and then Realm pulls me into the hall. But instead of going to my room, he takes the turn toward his. He keeps his eyes straight ahead, his grip tight on my wrist.

"What are we doing?" I ask, wondering if I should be scared of him. That maybe he could be as dangerous as Roger.

"They can't listen here," he mumbles, and brings us inside. Realm backs me against the door as he closes it, standing with his head bent by my ear. "I know you heard," he whispers, "and please believe me, I really am your friend."

"I don't believe you."

He puts his hands against the door on either side of my head. If anyone were to look in on us, they might think we were in some romantic against-the-door moment. "I'm a special sort of handler," he continues. "I'm embedded with the other patients but was assigned specifically to you because you're . . . difficult."

A pain rips across my chest as he confirms my worst fear: that my only friend in the world, the only one I can remember, isn't real. I've been manipulated, and I feel violated and ravaged. Realm moves closer, sliding one arm behind me as if in an embrace.

"I'm so sorry, Sloane," he says, his mouth touching my ear. "But I promise you, I'm only trying to help. If I didn't intervene, they were going to dig deeper. Do you know what that means?" he asks. "You could have been lobotomized."

I start to feel weak in his arms and I want to lie down, but he holds me fast. "You can't fall apart now," he soothes. "They're going to know something is wrong."

I look up at him then, at the scar on his neck. "I don't understand," I say, my chest aching. "You're one of us."

He nods. "I was in The Program last year"—he motions to his neck—"for an unfortunate incident with a serrated knife. But then I got here, got better. About halfway through, Dr. Warren pulled me aside and asked what I planned to do when I got out.

"I had nothing to go back for. My parents died a long time ago, and I couldn't remember any of my friends. I had *nothing*. So Dr. Warren offered me a job—a future within The Program to rehabilitate patients. I signed a contract."

"What do you do to us?"

He cringes, as if knowing I won't like the answer. "Form healthy relationships; reestablish connections so that subjects aren't shell-shocked when they leave. We were having relapses and meltdowns, and they determined it was from the trauma of reassimilating. Emotions are like raw nerve endings, and without some sort of preparation, it's like sending back an exposed wire."

"So you weren't just pretending to be my friend?" I challenge. "You didn't betray me and tell them the things we talked about? Things I can't even remember anymore."

"Of course I had to tell them," he says. "I had to make sure the therapy was taking. And believe me, sweetness, you wouldn't want to walk around with half memories anyway. You could go crazy."

I yank my hands from his and push him back. "And kissing me? Was that part of my rehabilitation?" I'm embarrassed saying it, feeling cheated somehow. Used.

Realm shakes his head. "No, it wasn't. I shouldn't have done that."

"Then why did you?"

Realm lowers his eyes. "I care about you. I'm lonely too. Just because I'm not a patient doesn't mean that I don't feel the same isolation you guys do. I've been here five weeks, Sloane. I want to leave. And I want to take you with me."

I push him again, backing him to the bed. He doesn't try and protect himself. The thought that Realm could have left at any point while I was held against my will makes me hate him. "Roger?" I ask suddenly. "Was he a part of this too?"

"No," Realm says. "I mean, he used to be. But not anymore. He had no right to do the things he did. I didn't know, I swear—"

"Yes, because your word means so much now."

"I didn't, Sloane. I would have done anything to protect you."

"Is that before or after you helped them erase my life? Do you think I can forgive that? Do you think I can *ever* get over that?"

"I hope so," he says. "I . . ." He stops, and his pale skin is even more white than usual—like he might get sick. "I have nothing. And this is the first time I thought I might be able to build a life again. When I leave here, I'll have six weeks off before returning to The Program at a different facility. I'm under contract for two years—a contract I can't break or they'll erase everything about me. I'm trying to save both of us, and I thought that once you were released, we could be together."

I laugh. I know it's cruel, but I don't care. I'm so hurt that I want to be mean. I want him to know what he's done to me.

"Well," I say, "that's never going to happen. Your contract might end sooner than you think because it doesn't look like my therapy is going to take, *Michael*." I growl his name.

Realm grabs my wrists hard then, pulling me toward him. "Don't say that. You're getting out of here. But you don't leave by fighting. They'll never let you out that way."

I scoff. "What do I have to do then? Kiss you until I'm released?"

He drops his arms. "No, and I understand if you don't want to talk to me anymore. Please believe me when I say that wasn't part of this. I kissed you because I wanted to. You're strong and smart, and you make me want to *live*, Sloane." He looks in my eyes. "But you can't tell anyone about this. You'll compromise me."

There's a loud knock at the door, and we both jump. I wipe again quickly at my face as Realm's eyes flick between me and the door. The handle turns, and Nurse Kell pops her head in. "I have your medication, dears," she says, her voice sickly sweet. Her shoulders are rigid, and I think that she's been looking for us for a while.

"Take it," Realm murmurs to me as he grabs the cup the nurse is holding out to him. He dips his chin to her in appreciation, and I reach for the other cup on the tray.

My hands are shaking so badly, I'm sure Nurse Kell has to notice. I stare down into the Dixie cup but don't take the white pill. Instead I look back at Realm defiantly. His expression weakens, as if begging me.

"No," I tell Nurse Kell. "I'm fine without it tonight." I put the cup back on the tray and turn, walking across the room to stand by Realm's side table. My entire body is pulsing with anger and hatred. I'm going to tear this fucking place apart.

I hear Realm whisper something to her, but I don't turn to look. They can both go to hell. Dr. Warren can go to hell. I don't even want to get out anymore. I just want to take them down.

"Okay, then," Nurse Kell says with a forced cheerfulness. "Everyone else is in the leisure room if you care to join them."

"We'll be out in a second," Realm answers. I look over then and see him watching me, his brow creased with concern. Nurse Kell bites her lip and then backs out, leaving us alone again.

"What was in the medication?" I ask.

He looks defeated. "Something to relax you."

"And what was in yours, Michael?"

"Same as always. Sugar pill."

I cross the room and slap him. My palm stings as it connects with his cheek. He flinches from the pain and then turns fiercely and grabs me by my shoulders, backing me hard against the wall as I gasp. A red handprint is obvious on his face and he's exhaling quickly, like he's about to lose it on me.

"Hit me," I snarl. "I dare you to throw me down and report me. Because there is no way in hell I'll let you get away with this." I lean close to his face. "I'll tell everyone."

The anger in Realm's expression fades, his grip loosens. We're against each other, breathing heavily. But instead of turning me in, Realm puts his mouth over mine and kisses me hard. I try to yank away at first, but in his lips is intensity and passion. It's a sort of comfort that I've missed. Despite everything that's happened, this feels real. And I need something to *be* real after all the lies. I stop fighting.

And just as I let his tongue touch mine, something pierces my thigh. I cry out and push Realm back. He's holding a needle, fluid still dripping from the tip.

His eyes start watering. "I'm so sorry," he whispers. "I can't let them erase me."

"What did you do?" I cry out, completely stunned and horrified. "Realm, what did you just do?"

"I had to, Sloane." He holds out his hand to me, but I slap it away and rush past him.

"Don't touch me!" I scream, pulling open his door. I'm scared he's going to follow me, so I try to hurry to my room. But I'm only halfway down the hall when I feel the first wave of medication crash over me. I stumble forward, not sure how I'm going to make it to my bed.

This is like the effect of the yellow pill that Dr. Warren gives me, only stronger. I suddenly think that The Program is going to kill me for finding out about Realm. That Realm is going to kill me. I stagger in my doorway and then fall, my knee hitting the white floor hard.

I'm on my hands and knees, the room tipping from side to side in front of me as I crawl toward the safety of my bed.

"Sloane," I hear, and then arms are around my waist, helping me up. I turn my head lazily to the side and see Realm.

"No," I say, trying to fight him off. "Leave me alone." But the words are slurred on my lips as he leads me to the bed.

"I'm sorry. It's the only way. I swear, it's the only way."

"What have you done?" I ask, although I'm not sure if he can understand me as sleep starts to drown me like rushing river water.

"I can't let you remember," he murmurs, helping me into bed and then climbing in next to me, holding me protectively in his arms even as I struggle weakly. He's still talking, but his voice is fading out, fading over me. ". . . or I'll never get out."

"I'll tell everyone," I try to say, but I can't keep my eyes open. "I'll tell everyone." And then Realm's gone. And so am I.

CHAPTER FIFTEEN

MY EYES FLUTTER OPEN, AND I COVER MY FACE with my forearm, blocking out the light from the overhead fluorescents. My head is pounding, feeling thick with sleep.

When the fog starts to clear, I look to my side table, and the clock reads almost ten. The room smells like toast, and I find the cart on the other side with a covered tray. The food is probably long cold by now. Why didn't anyone wake me?

I slip on my robe, wondering where everyone is. I pause at my door, before going out into the hall. There's a young nurse at the station typing on her computer, and from the leisure room I can hear the TV. Everything seems normal, and yet . . . I'm confused.

"Ah. You're awake."

I jump and turn to see Nurse Kell walking toward me from

the other direction, smiling broadly. "You weren't feeling well today, so we let you sleep in. Did you want me to get you a snack, honey?"

"Not feeling well?" I look down the hallway as Derek walks by, saluting me in greeting. "I'm . . ." Pushing my hair away from my face, I think back to yesterday. But I can't find anything there. "What day is it?" I ask.

Nurse Kell smiles like the question isn't even odd. "It's Saturday. And the sun is finally out if you'd like to go out to the garden."

"What?" I'm stunned by her statement, never having been let outside before. *Saturday?* "It's Friday, isn't it?" I'm sure it's Friday.

"No, honey. But you were running a fever yesterday, and we had to medicate you. So I'm not surprised you don't remember."

My mind starts to race then, and I know that they've done something to my memory. I keep my face calm, but Nurse Kell can see what I'm thinking. I want to scream. I want to punch her. I want them out of my head. What did they erase this time? Whatever it is, it wasn't theirs to take.

"Where's Realm?" I ask.

"He's playing cards in the other room." She brushes my hair off my shoulder, her face a portrait of concern. "You go see him, and I'll get you some clean clothes for your shower. You should really take it easy today."

I want to slap her hand away from me, but instead I just

turn and hurry toward the leisure room. When I get inside, Realm immediately looks up, smiling around the pretzel cigar in his mouth. "Hey, sweetness. Didn't think you'd ever get up."

"I need to talk to you," I say, shifting uneasily from foot to foot. Realm's face drops, and he yanks out the pretzel and tosses down his cards.

"Hey!" Shep calls, but Realm is stalking toward me. He takes my arm, lowering his head.

"What is it? Are you okay?" he whispers, studying my eyes.

I cling to Realm, pressing my face against his chest. "They did something to me," I say. His body is stiff at first, but then he relaxes around me, gently stroking my hair.

"How so?"

"I can't remember yesterday. A whole day! They won't leave me alone," I tell him, and I feel the tears wet on my cheek, on his shirt.

"Sloane, you were sick. Why do you think they did something to you?"

"I just know." I knot my hands in the back of Realm's shirt, keeping him there, not caring as his friends call out to us—telling us to get a room. Not caring that I can feel the stares of the nurses. Nobody breaks us up, though, and Realm wipes my tears with his thumbs.

"Want to go outside?" he asks, a small smile on his face. "They told me you earned some garden time."

"Why?"

"For being a good girl." He grins. "Kidding. You're getting close to release time. Everyone gets to go out when that happens."

"Not you."

Realm looks away.

"Wait," I say. "You could go outside all this time?"

He nods, and I scoff. "Well, why haven't you?" I ask. "You should be getting fresh air, not be trapped in here."

"I was waiting for you," he says with a shrug.

A smile pulls at my lips as I think Realm's entirely sweet. That he cares about me. "You're an idiot," I say. "But that's what I like about you." The thought of actual sunlight fills me with so much hope that I jog toward my room to get into fresh scrubs. I'm going outside.

"This is really beautiful," I say as we walk down the rows of flowers. The gravel pathway crunches under my sneakers, and in the light, true sunlight, Realm's black hair is a sharp contrast to his skin. I think he'd look better as a blond.

"Hold hands?" he asks.

"No, I like my freedom," I say absently, looking over the expansive lawn. I wonder if I could escape, but I see a tall iron fence just beyond the neat row of trees. My heart sinks just a little.

Realm is kicking at the rocks as we walk, and he seems down. "What's wrong?" I ask.

He looks at me, startled. "Oh, nothing. I was just thinking about when I'm out."

"Soon."

He nods. "Yep." He turns to me then, stopping me in the path. "What are you going to do when you're out, Sloane? Who's the first person you want to see?" He smiles then, that adorable smile that makes me feel like we're sharing secrets. Only out here it doesn't seem so infectious.

I'm not sure how to answer because when I think of home, all I can see are my parents. A few random faces pop up, but they're just classmates, none of them my friends. The loneliness once again overwhelms me, and I stagger back. Realm catches my arm and straightens me.

"Hey," he says. "You okay? Did you remember something?"

"No," I whisper. "And that's the problem. I don't remember anything anymore."

Realm meets my eyes. "Do you remember me?"

"Of course. But I don't know if they're going to take you, too."

"They won't."

I watch as he lowers his head, the black hair dye too dark—fake. "How do you know?" I ask. His throat clicks as he swallows, but then he glances up, smiling.

"Because you couldn't forget me, Sloane. I'm way too awesome."

I laugh, but it's out of obligation. His joke doesn't cheer me up or set me at ease. I don't like the way he looks in the light. Everything around me is too sharply focused. I motion back toward the building.

"I want to go inside," I say, turning and heading back. Realm runs to catch up with me, surprised, I'm sure.

"Sloane," he asks carefully. "Are you mad at me?"

I furrow my brow. "No. Why do you ask?"

"You just don't seem to like me anymore."

I consider taking his hand then, but I don't. I keep walking, and he falls behind a little. I have no idea how to explain to Realm that, in the light, he's not what I thought he was. That I do feel different today. About him. About everything. I'm not quite sure why, but more than ever I'm desperate to go home. I'm going to play this game, beat The Program. I'm going to get out of here.

Realm is practically glued to my side at lunch. Under the harsh fluorescents, he looks more himself. And yet, I sense that something is off. Every time he touches my arm, or tries to take my hand, I shrink away. He doesn't ask again if I like him, but I see the question in his eyes.

I leave him and decide to take a long shower, the nurses allowing it although one of them stays in the bathroom with me. I must be in there almost a half hour because my skin is pruned and I'm exhausted from the heat. Everything about today is wrong, my new freedom, my changed feelings. I almost skip dinner, but I'm hungry so I go downstairs.

At the last minute I decide to sit with Tabitha, ignoring Realm as he waits at our table. I can't make sense of my emotions, of how I want to stay away from my only real friend.

"So are you and Realm, like, broken up?" Tabitha asks, poking her spork into her cube steak. Her hair is a shiny brunette, the red long gone. She hardly looks like the same person, but she seems healthier. Even her short-term memory seems restored.

"We weren't dating," I say, not glancing up.

"Yeah, right. He follows you around like a puppy, and you don't seem to mind." She pauses and smiles. "So can I take a shot at him?"

There's a turn in my stomach, and I'm not sure if it's jealousy or some sort of worry. "Go ahead, but he leaves in less than a week. Quick romance."

"I'm just looking to have sex."

I laugh and look up at her, but she just grins at me. "I knew that would get your attention."

"I hope you're kidding." I'm still smiling as I put a green bean in my mouth. Tabitha stares past me at Realm, making kissy faces to his back as he faces away. Something about this moment is authentic, and I like it. "Hey," I ask her. "Want to play cards with us later?"

Tabitha beams. "Seriously? You're inviting me to hang with the cool kids?" She's trying to sound sarcastic, but her expression tells me she's thrilled to be included.

"You are hereby inducted into the club," I say. And then just to make it official we cheers our cartons of milk.

CHAPTER SIXTEEN

"BULLSHIT, SLOANE," REALM CALLS AS I SIT ACROSS from him.

My mouth twitches with a smile. "No way."

"Show the cards." Realm narrows his eyes like he thinks I'll cheat. I look around the table at Tabitha, who's giggling behind her hand, and Shep and Derek as they yell for me to flip my hand. I roll my eyes and turn them over.

Realm crosses his arms over his chest, looking impressed. "Three queens," I say.

"Can't believe you really had it," Shep says, laughing as he slides the cards toward Realm. When Realm picks them up, he looks me over, studying my expression.

"Guess I can't tell when you're lying," he says quietly.

"Guess you can't." I smile.

"I knew she was telling the truth," Tabitha says, looking proud.

"Did not," Shep argues.

I continue to grin as we start the next hand, and I feel normal. Maybe the most normal I've felt since coming to The Program. My medications have been cut down and my weight has stabilized. The fog that's been with me since the beginning is gone.

This is real. When I look up, I see Realm watching me, his head tilted to the side. Just like in the garden, he seems a little sad, but I don't know why. You'd think he'd be happy to be leaving The Program. He should be happy to be almost home.

Over the next few days, Tabitha wins every hand of Bullshit, even catches me lying once. I can't help but think that none of us should be in here. We're normal. No one's talking about suicide, or crying. When I see the new patients come in, they're a mess—sobbing and fighting. We're a world apart from them now, and I can't imagine that I was ever like that.

I'm sitting in my room reading a magazine when there's a knock at my door. It opens slowly and Realm pops his head in. "Hey," he says quietly.

I smile. "Hey."

Realm enters, shutting the door behind him before taking a seat next to my bed, chewing on his lip. "I'm . . ." He clears his throat. "I'm leaving tomorrow, Sloane."

There's a heavy pain in my chest. "Oh." We stare at each for a long minute, and then I hold up my arms and Realm climbs onto the bed to hug me. We stay like that for a long time before he sniffles and wipes his face.

"This is the first time I've seen you cry," I say, my own voice choked up.

"Can I ask you something, Sloane?" Realm's voice is low like he's not sure he should.

"Of course."

He pauses. "Can we see each other again—after all of this is over?"

I furrow my brow, thinking it's a strange question to ask. That of course I would see him again. But inside, I feel doubt— that maybe I didn't intend to find Realm. Like there's something holding me back from him. When I don't answer right away, he nods, a tear sliding down the side of his nose.

"I should go," he says. "I've got to get back to the boys. They're having a going-away party for me."

"And I wasn't invited?" I ask, not wanting Realm to leave. I feel terrible, like I'm a bad friend to him.

"Sorry, sweetness," he says. "Guys only."

Realm stands but I reach out to take his arm, stopping him from walking away. He pauses, looking down at the floor as if he's afraid to turn to me. I climb out of bed and pull him into a hug, resting my cheek against his chest.

"I'll miss you," I say. "I'll miss you madly."

Realm squeezes me tightly then, his arm clasped around me. "I'll miss you, too."

And when he pulls back, I give him a soft peck on the lips, hoping it's enough. Hoping it shows how much I care. But by the sad smile on his face, I know it's not. So I let him leave.

The nurse gives me permission to take one last walk with Realm, so we go out to the garden. It's sunny and bright, and I think again how beautiful the flowers look. Realm's ride will be here in less than a half hour, and then he'll be gone.

I reach out to take his hand, surprised by how cool it is. He bumps his shoulder into mine, and we walk a little longer.

"Tabitha is leaving on Monday," I tell him. "She's got her new haircut, some new clothes. Shep's getting a new style too—and hopefully some deodorant." I look sideways at Realm and drop his hand. "How come they didn't make you over?"

"Maybe there isn't anything to improve on."

I laugh. "Well, Dr. Warren says that the return is easier if we freshen up our looks. I think she might be right. I'm thinking of straightening my hair."

Realm reaches up suddenly, holding a handful of my curls. "No," he says. "Your hair's beautiful." He shrugs. "You're beautiful."

I blush, but then back away, letting my hair fall from his palm.

Realm kicks at some pebbles on the path. "Sloane, if things were different, if we weren't in The Program . . . do you think we could be together?"

Prickles race up my skin, and I'm sure that I don't know the answer. Realm steps closer and puts his hands on my bare upper arms. "I could take care of you if you want," he says. "And when you get out of here, I'd be there."

"I don't want anyone to take care of me," I say. "I want to figure out how to take care of myself. I don't even know who I am anymore."

"I know you," he says, sounding somber. "And I'd do anything for you, even if you can't understand why right now." He watches me for a long moment, no doubt trying to see if I feel something for him other than friendship.

I wonder then how I'll know when I'm in love, especially if I don't know what it feels like. Have I ever been in love before? Did anyone love me back?

"If you look for me, Sloane," Realm says, "I'll be waiting."

I'm suddenly choked up, and I lean into a hug, closing my eyes tightly. "Thank you for everything, Realm. Thank you for—"

"Michael," a voice calls out. We separate. Nurse Kell is waving to him from across the lawn, a blond woman in dark sunglasses beside her. Realm stiffens next to me, and his hands fall away. He meets my eyes one more time and kisses my forehead. Then he moves to pause by my ear.

"They'll still watch you," he whispers. "They'll look for signs."

"Signs of what?" Fear streaks through me.

"I'll help you any way I can," he continues. "Don't forget that."

I think it's a crazy thing to tell someone in The Program—
don't forget. That's what we're here for. Forgetting is how we've
all gotten better. Tears fall down my cheeks as Realm backs
away, looking helplessly at me as he does. When he turns
around, his sneakers crunch the gravel. I watch him walk out of
The Program. And out of my life.

It's a little over a week later when I'm sitting in Dr. Warren's
office, my hair newly cut and straightened. The mess of dark
curls are now smooth and reach just below my chin. She smiles
the minute she sees me.

"You look fantastic, Sloane," she says. "You have truly been
a model patient."

I nod as if I'm thanking her, but in truth I don't remember any of our sessions beyond the final few. We spent our last
meetings piecing together my memories. She reminds me of
the sequence of events because it occasionally gets jumbled in
my head. She fills in the things I can't remember, like about my
family.

"You'll be happy to know that The Program has a one hundred percent survival rate, and that very few of our subjects
ever relapse. But there are some precautions you'll have to take.
There will be weekly doctor visits for the first month, then
bimonthly until the final evaluation in three months. You'll
have access to therapy and medication if you need it, but it
won't be forced unless you start to exhibit symptoms again.
For the first week, we ask that you take the supplied relaxant,

just to help with the transition to your new school.

"You are not allowed to fraternize in any serious way with nonreturners. Although you're cured, you are still considered high-risk pending your final evaluation. After that you're free to talk to whomever you want." Her mouth twitches and for a second I don't think that she means it. But I'm so close to going home now, I don't mention it. I just nod.

Dr. Warren purses her lips and puts her elbows on her desk, leaning forward. "We want you to live, Sloane," she says. "We want you to have a full, happy life. We've given you the best chance possible by removing the infected memories. Now it's up to you. But know, if you get sick again, you will be flagged. And then you'll be required to stay in The Program until you're eighteen."

I swallow hard, thinking that my birthday is still seven months away. That would be a long time to be stuck here, especially without Realm. "I understand," I tell her.

"Good." She looks relieved as she straightens. "You'll have a handler assigned to you for the first few weeks, helping you out at school and accompanying you outside of your house. This is a precaution because of your fragile state. Take it easy, Sloane. Don't push yourself too hard."

"I'll try my best," I say, looking at the clock on the wall and knowing that my parents will be here any minute. I'm leaving. I'm really leaving.

Dr. Warren stands then, walking around her desk to embrace me. We hug awkwardly, and when she lets me go, she rests her hand on my shoulder. "At first," she says almost in a whisper, "you may be a little distant—a little numb. But that will eventually go away. You will feel again."

I meet her eyes, doing a quick evaluation of my emotions. I'm complacent and calm, but I wonder how I should really feel.

There's a quick knock at the door, and Dr. Warren says to come in. Nurse Kell stands there, her cheeks rosy. "Your parents are here, Sloane." She beams, looking proud. "And the boys wanted me to give you this." She holds out a small wrapped package, and my eyes water.

"Why didn't they give it to me themselves?" I ask, walking over to take it from her hands. Both Derek and Shep are still here, but Dr. Warren promised me they'd be going home soon.

She laughs. "Because they said you would probably cry."

I unwrap the paper and smile at what's inside. It's a deck of cards, but the back design says BULLSHIT. I reach out to hug Nurse Kell. "Tell them thank you for me."

It's all so surreal. I stand for a moment looking around the office, the time I spent in here a complete fog. I don't know what I was like before, but I feel okay now. I guess The Program works.

I say good-bye to Dr. Warren and follow Nurse Kell out, a handler trailing us with a small duffel bag. I don't remember what I wore when I came into the facility, but The Program has provided me with a few outfits—ones I didn't pick out—to send me home with. Right now I'm wearing a yellow polo shirt, the collar stiff and itchy.

The halls are empty, but I hear a spirited game of cards being played in the leisure room, new members taking our places. When we get out onto the lawn, I see my dad's Volvo parked near the gate. He steps out, my mother scrambling to get to his side. I pause, looking at them from afar.

"Good luck, Sloane," Nurse Kell says, brushing my hair behind my ear. "Stay healthy."

I nod to her, and look at the handler who tells me to go ahead. And then I run across the grass. When I get close enough my father rushes forward, swooping me up into his arms, tears streaming down his face. Soon my mother is hugging both of us and we're all crying.

I've missed them. Missed my dad's smile and my mom's laugh. "Dad," I say when I can finally pry myself away from him. "First things first—let's get ice cream," I say. "I haven't had any since I've been here."

He laughs, a painful sort of sound, as if he's been waiting to do it for a long time. "Anything, sweetheart. We're just so happy to have you home."

My mother touches adoringly at my hair. "I love this," she says earnestly, as if she hasn't seen me in years. "You look just beautiful."

"Thanks, Mom." I hug her again. My father takes my bags from the handler and puts them in the trunk as I have one last look back the building—back at The Program.

Something catches my eye, and my smile fades. There's a girl in the window, sitting on a chair with her arms wrapped around her knees. She's pretty and blond, but she looks lonely. Desperate. And I can't help thinking that she reminds me of someone.

"Here we go," my father says, opening the back door for me. I tear my eyes away from the window and climb into the car, the smell of it bringing me back to the times when Brady and I used to argue over who got to pick the radio station. My brother's gone now, but we've made peace with that. Our family got through it and now we're all better. I'm better.

My parents climb into the car, glancing back at me as if they expect me to disappear at any moment, and I smile. I'm going home.

PART III
WISH YOU WEREN'T HERE

CHAPTER ONE

I HAD TROUBLE SLEEPING THE FIRST NIGHT HOME.
The house was too quiet, the sounds in my head too loud. I
missed Realm, missed playing cards with the boys. I missed the
freedom and the restrictions of the facility. In a weird way, I'd
been on my own.

After we'd stopped for ice cream, my mother came home and
cooked a big dinner, chatting away about what I'd missed. Apparently The Program has been picked up in three more states, and
France and Germany are adapting their own versions. I wasn't
quite sure how to feel about that so I stayed silent.

The minute I wake up the next morning, my mother is
waiting with the tiny white pill that Dr. Warren prescribed to
help me get through my day—to relax me. As I sit at the kitchen
table, my mother flips pancakes, humming a song I can't quite

place. My father has left for work. I sit at the small, round table and stare at the empty seat my brother used to claim. I almost feel that at any second he'll come bounding into the kitchen asking for Lucky Charms.

But Brady's dead. Dr. Warren told me that his accidental death was traumatic for me, so they had to erase it. Now, I don't even know what happened to my brother. In my head it's like he was here, and then he was gone with nothing in between.

At the end of my therapy at The Program, Dr. Warren tried to help me line up my memories sequentially, filling in some of the blanks. She said my family was devastated by my brother's death, but that now that I'm cured, we're all okay. I don't remember a time when we weren't okay, so I'm glad. I hate the idea of not having my family.

When my mother—still smiling—puts food in front of me, I thank her. But the thought of eating is far from my mind. Dr. Warren had said that I wouldn't know anyone at Sumpter High—that they would have been erased even if I *had* known them because they were infected too.

So I'm starting over. It's like a new life. It's like a new me.

When Kevin, my handler, shows up, he's polite, and almost kind, on my front porch. I have a sense that I should be uncomfortable around him, but he takes my backpack from me and holds the door. So I chalk it up to the confused feelings that Dr. Warren predicted.

Kevin looks to be just a little older than I am, but we don't say much as he drives us to Sumpter. But then again, my head feels too foggy to ask anything relevant. I think it's the medication.

When we get there, I see that Sumpter is a large, white building—sort of intimidating. Kevin parks in the back lot, taking a minute to radio in that I've arrived. Several students walk past us toward the entrance, some laughing, some alone— and I wonder if I've met them before. A feeling of déjà vu creeps over me, and I look away, feeling unsettled.

"Are you okay?" Kevin asks, startling me. I glance sideways at him and see that his light eyebrows are pulled together in concern. I'm not sure who to confide in, what's even real, but he's the only one here.

"Anxious," I say. "Like I'm . . . unglued. Is that normal?"

Kevin's expression doesn't change. "It is normal for you, yes. But that feeling will fade in a couple of weeks. Right now, your mind is repairing itself. You'll have echoes—a space between memories that will make you feel hollow. But they will fill in. Medication can help with the transition."

His words don't comfort me, and instead I feel a tiny twinge of sadness. But just as soon as it's there, it's like warm water is splashed inside my chest. "Whoa," I say, putting my hand over my heart.

"That's the inhibitor," Kevin says. "It relieves the panic. You should probably take another before going to class." He gets a pillbox from the center console and pinches out a white pill before extending it to me. I take it from him, staring down at it while he hands me a bottle of water.

"So this feeling will go away?" I ask, just to make sure. There are competing emotions, and it's hard to tell which are mine and which belong to the medication.

"Yes," Kevin says. "You will regulate. Eventually."

I look again at the other students out the window. I feel empty, but they look normal. Happy, even. And someday, I'll be like them. Once this damn fog clears. So without another thought, I swallow the pill and let Kevin take me inside.

"Here's your schedule," Kevin says. "It might be tough to pick up in your subjects where you left off, but your teachers have all modified their lesson plans to catch you up. I'll walk you to and from classes and attend them with you." Kevin's gray eyes look me over.

"I'm a little confused," I say. I take a deep breath, and the white pill works its way through my system. My muscles loosen, and an overall feeling of well-being comes over me.

"You're doing great," Kevin says, patting my shoulder.

I smile. Kevin seems genuinely invested in my recovery, and it's encouraging. I might really need the support.

I walk into my first class, and the room is mostly empty. There's a girl with blond hair near the front, and she says hi to me as I walk by. I smile in response, the small interaction confirming that I at least look normal, even if I can't remember parts of my life.

"I'll be in the back if you need me," Kevin says after I'm settled in my chair.

He goes to stand by the bookcase, and I glance around the room, noticing the colorful posters on the walls. I can still remember my old school, how washed in white everything was. This place smells like vanilla—like aromatherapy. Are they trying to keep us calm?

On my desk is a paper—just like on every other desk in the room. As students walk in, they drop their bags on the floor and fill out the forms, delivering them to a tray on the teacher's desk. I take a sharpened pencil from my bag and stare down at the questions on the daily assessment. They seem vaguely familiar.

In the past day have you felt lonely or overwhelmed?

NO.

I fill in the rest of the ovals, pausing when I get to the last question. *Has anyone close to you ever committed suicide?*

NO.

I pick up my paper but wait a beat, feeling like I did something wrong. I look over the questions again but can't find a mistake. At that moment, my teacher walks in, nodding politely at us as she does. When she sees me, she smiles.

"Sloane," she says. "I'm so happy to finally meet you."

The entire class turns to stare at me, curious expressions on their faces. The day has taken on a dreamlike quality as I float to the front to put my paper on the pile. But unlike the other student's assessments, my teacher stops to look over my answers. When she's done, she smiles.

"Good girl," she says. And then she turns to write on the board.

Kevin leads me to lunch and decides to pick out my food for me. He says that I need to keep my weight stable, even though a side effect of the medication is loss of appetite. As he tells me this, I realize that he's right. I can't remember the last time I was hungry.

I sit at a table, alone, and peek out at the cafeteria. Kevin is leaning against the wall, silently taking in the room. There are three other handlers in here, watching their charges. Dr. Warren told me that a handler would shadow me for a few weeks after I'm released, and then monitor me for six after that. I'm on day two.

"Can I sit?"

I jump and see a girl standing there. She's pretty and blond, and I recognize her as the girl from my first-period class who said hi to me. "Sure," I say, although she's already sat down across from me.

"I'm Lacey," she says, her voice deep and raspy like an old-time movie star. In front of her, she unrolls a brown paper bag and pulls out a package of orange cupcakes. I look down again at my lunch tray and the slab of meat on it.

"You're Sloane, right?" she asks.

I must look surprised that she remembers, because she shrugs. "New-kid thing," she says. "We notice all of the returners as they enter. Sort of like . . . will they or won't they?"

"'Will they or won't they' what?" I ask.

"Remember. I'm convinced that eventually one of us will

remember something, and then the entire system will break down. What can I say? I'm an anarchist." She smiles broadly, and I like her already. She's alive. I can feel her vitality oozing off her.

Lacey shoots a glance at my handler. "They'll stop following you soon," she offers, tilting her head toward Kevin. "As long as you don't mess up."

"Mess up?" It hadn't really occurred to me that I would mess up, or even what messing up would entail. I'm cured. But I lean forward to listen because Lacey's been in The Program, has been successful at returning. Maybe she knows something I don't.

"I've been back for fifteen weeks." She lowers her voice and brushes a strand of her blond hair behind her ear. "I'm still missing the pieces that The Program took away. At first I didn't care, right? I was just glad to have survived. But now . . . Now I'm wondering about things. Did you know that they said I wanted to kill myself?" she whispers, as if she's been dying to talk to someone about it. "That doesn't even seem possible. I'm like . . . the most well-balanced person I know. Did they say you tried to kill yourself, too?"

I hold up my wrist, the faint outline of a scar still there. "They say I did this."

"Wow."

We're both quiet for a minute, absorbing our shared mystery. But then Lacey slides one of the cupcakes toward me. "Hint number one," she says as she takes a bite of cupcake. "Pack your own lunch. I'm pretty sure they put sedatives in the food."

My sense of well-being has been interrupted by Lacey's suspicions, and I wish that I hadn't taken the white pills today. I'd like to be lucid enough to figure out if she's being paranoid. But for now I take the orange cupcake and break it in half to lick out the white cream first. And then we enjoy the rest of the period, passing the time with safe conversations about teachers and music.

The bell rings, and Lacey gathers all her wrappers, stuffing them back into the bag. I haven't touched the food on my tray, but I feel satisfied enough. When Kevin begins to make his way over from wall, Lacey grins at me.

"Make him take you to the Wellness Center tonight," she whispers. "I can meet up with you there if you want."

"Really?" I can't help but smile. I've made a friend, and somehow that makes me feel better about myself. It's such a normal thing to do.

"Seven o'clock."

"Excuse me," Kevin states when he gets to our table. "We need to go, Sloane." He takes the tray from in front of me, giving me a disapproving glance when he sees all of the food still on it. With one hand on my elbow, he gently guides me out of my seat. "Miss Klamath," he says to Lacey in greeting.

She waves suggestively at him, and Kevin shakes his head with a smirk as if he's used to her antics. Before I can even say good-bye, Lacey is gliding across the cafeteria and out of my line of vision. When she's gone, Kevin drops his hand from my arm.

"I'm glad you're making friends," he says. "It's good for your recovery."

"What's the deal with the Wellness Center?" I ask. "Can I go there tonight?"

"The Wellness Center was developed by The Program as part of the aftercare, a way for you to interact with others—including nonreturners—in a safe, monitored environment. If you'd like to check it out, I think that would be okay. Let's just be sure you're not overdoing it. Too much stimulus can disrupt the healing process. In fact . . ." Kevin slips a pill box out his pocket, taking out the white pill. "Here. You haven't had a dose since this morning. You might start feeling on edge if you don't."

I consider it. What happens if I don't do exactly as I'm told? Would refusing be considered *messing up*—especially on the second day? I glance around the room, wondering if the other returners felt this lost when they first came back. But I learn nothing, as they all grab their backpacks and dump their trash, heading for their classes.

And so I swallow the pill.

CHAPTER TWO

WHEN MY HANDLER DROPS ME OFF AT HOME, SAYing he'll be back at six thirty, I immediately start on my homework. Although I feel as if I know the answers, some of the questions get muddled in my head. Especially when it comes to math. It's as if certain rules were erased, leaving me with partial answers. Eventually I get frustrated and slam my book shut before turning on the television.

I'm not surprised to see a *Dateline* special about The Program—it seems to dominate every channel. Even on MTV, what used to be ruled by trashy reality shows is now filled with inspirational stories of teens being saved by The Program. I half wonder if The Program is sponsoring the network now.

Just then the interviewer from *Dateline* walks into the facility, the same facility that I was in. I sit up straighter, my heart pounding. I think I see Nurse Kell dash out of the corner of the screen and then the view is filled with security guards.

"You can't be here," the security guard says, pushing the camera away with his hand. "You have to leave."

The interviewer continues arguing until the sound is promptly shut off. The screen is black and I wait, wondering what happened. Instead the interviewer is behind a desk, shaking his head. "When asked to comment, the president of The Program, Arthur Pritchard, released this statement: 'The effectiveness of the treatment—which is still at one hundred percent—is dependent on the privacy of our patients. Any interference could jeopardize the life of the minors, and therefore we cannot comment on the treatment or allow common access to our facilities at this time.'"

I click off the television, wondering what it was like when those reporters tried to get into The Program. Were Shep and Derek around? It had seemed so isolated when I was there. Maybe things are changing.

And for a second I'm afraid. If they stop The Program, leaving us as the only ones changed, what will happen? Will we be discriminated against forever? Does that mean there's something wrong with us? I start to panic when, all of a sudden, the warm water is splashed over me again, and I take a deep breath. The fear is gone, and instead I just close my eyes and lean my head back against the couch cushion.

Something about sitting here in my familiar living room is comforting, and yet I can't help but think I should be doing something different. As if this is real, and at the same time . . . not. I'm relieved when my mom gets home with groceries, and I help her unpack them, thankful for the distraction.

"So how was the first day back?" my father asks from across the dinner table. His eyes are bright, and he's smiling as he takes a bite of steak. The way my parents watch me is like I'm a miracle returned from the grave. They hang on my every word.

"It was good," I tell him. "A little scary at first, but I made a friend."

My mother beams, and she sets down her silverware. "You made a friend already?" She and my father exchange an eager glance. It makes me feel like a huge loser that my parents could be so happy about me making *one* friend.

"Her name is Lacey," I say. "She sat with me at lunch."

My mother pauses, then puts a large cut of steak into her mouth. I wait for her to ask questions, but she doesn't. I stare down at my plate, and near my glass is another white pill. I decide that I don't like this fog anymore. I decide I'm not going to take it.

"I'm meeting Lacey tonight at the Wellness Center," I add quietly, taking a sip from my water. "The handler said it was healthy for me to socialize."

"I agree," my father says, sounding a little too upbeat. I'm struck with a sensation, an . . . outsideness. My parents are acting weird. Or maybe I'm the one who's weird now.

I want to excuse myself to my room, but my mother starts

talking about The Program again. She tells me that in the UK, they had their first class of patients released. She seems so proud of that fact—as if returners are elite somehow. I nod along, my mind racing. I try to remember my life just before The Program, but all I get are repeats of old memories: my father taking me and Brady for ice cream. My mother sewing a Halloween costume. The repeating starts to make my temples pulse, and I stop trying to think back, worried I might be doing damage.

Dr. Warren had been adamant about *maintaining*. She warned me that too much stimulus could affect the reconstruction they'd done on my mind. She said it could result in a break in reality, cause permanent psychosis.

But what if she was lying.

"Sloane." My mother interrupts my train of thought. "You haven't touched your food."

I meet her concerned stare and then apologize, cutting a piece of meat. I can barely choke it down, especially when I notice a chalky aftertaste. Something Lacey said pops in my head—*I think they put sedatives in the food.*

When my mother starts talking again, I wipe my mouth with my napkin, careful to spit out the food. Maybe I'm being paranoid. Maybe I'm losing it altogether. But instead of mentioning it, I ask if I can be excused to get ready for tonight.

My parents look disappointed, but then my mother reminds me to clear my place. "And don't forget your pill," she adds when I start toward the kitchen. I grab it quickly and toss it into my mouth.

But the minute I get into the kitchen, I spit it in the sink and scrape my food into the disposal. And then I grind it all to bits.

I pose in front of the mirror, turning from side to side to evaluate myself. My closet had been emptied and replaced with new clothing, the tags still on them. It seems strange to me that they'd get rid of all of my things, my entire wardrobe. Did they think an old T-shirt could send me into an emotional tailspin? Did I dress in all black and overline my eyes? I don't remember. So right now I'm wearing a pink button down shirt that feels too stiff, paired with a khaki skirt. I look . . . painfully average.

Taking the brush from my dresser, I run it through my hair, sliding one side behind my ears when I'm done. It's nearly six thirty, and Kevin will be here soon to take me to the Wellness Center, but worry has started to work its way into my consciousness. What goes on at the Wellness Center? And what will the people who haven't gone through The Program think of me?

I'm different than them.

I take a deep breath and sit on the edge of my bed, trying to calm myself. I think that I should have taken the pill because right now an inhibitor would come in handy. But then I remind myself that I want to know what's going on around me. And I'm not sure I can do that if I'm medicated to the point of numbness all the time.

Downstairs, the doorbell rings, and I cast one more glance at my reflection. "Who are you?" I murmur, waiting a minute for my mind to answer. But it doesn't.

I don't know what I expected from the Wellness Center, but I certainly didn't expect this. I thought it would be more like The Program facility—sterile and cold. But this place is crowded, people chatting and laughing. I try to relax into it, but I don't see Lacey right away. My anxiety spikes, but I try not to react. I don't want Kevin to know I didn't take my pill tonight.

"So where do you want to start?" he asks, motioning ahead. "There might be some seats near the foosball table."

"Sure," I say, lowering my eyes. Some of the people in the room have noticed me, and it makes me incredibly self-conscious. I'm not sure I'm ready for this.

We start zigzagging our way through the crowd, Kevin's hand protectively on my arm. A few people say hi. When we get close to the table, I hear a loud laugh and look over to the couch, catching the back of a blond ponytail.

"I should be okay," I tell Kevin then, gently tugging my arm free. "I'm heading that way." I point toward the couch, and he nods. To my relief, he goes to lean against the wall near another handler, giving me a little privacy.

"There you are!" Lacey calls out, standing up to meet me as I cross to her. On the couch are two guys—strangers—and I nod politely at them. *God, why am I so nervous?*

"Hey," I say as Lacey pauses to look me over. She immediately undoes the second button on my shirt before she smiles.

"Sloane, this is Evan," she points to a dark-haired guy, "And this is Liam. Actually," she says, leaning close to whisper to me, "Liam isn't even a returner. But he's not depressed so no worries."

I glance at Liam then, taking in his reddish-blond hair, his dark brown eyes. He's watching me with a smirk on his lips, something about it a little unsettling. "Come and sit down, Sloane," he says, patting the spot next to him. "It's so great to . . . meet you."

I dart a glance at Lacey, but she's already back on Evan's lap, chatting away as if this is completely normal and we've all hung out before. I turn and look back over the room.

The Wellness Center is small, although lively. Bright colors, spirited games with laughing. Most of the people here are dressed like me—preppy and stiff. Then there are a few others, some with wide eyes as they search the room. By their comfortable clothes I think that they're not returners. When my gaze lands on Kevin, he nods to me, as if saying it's okay to be confused. It actually makes me feel a little better.

I sit on the couch, but flinch as Liam's thigh touches mine. My mind swirls through different memories, repeating some and reverberating them back to me. I remember camping with my brother, just the two of us. I can feel there's something else, but I don't have time to think about it when Liam leans his shoulder into mine.

"So how long were you in The Program?" he asks.

I'm almost offended by the question, as if it's too personal for someone I just met to ask me. But I'm probably being overly sensitive. "Six weeks."

"And they did something to you, right? Like messed with your head or something?"

Okay, now I am offended. Liam must notice because he quickly apologizes and shoots a cautious glance at my handler.

"I didn't mean it like that," he says. "It's just that I'm friends with Evan, but I didn't know him before The Program. I'm just curious as to how it changes people. How it changed you."

"I wouldn't really know, now would I, Liam?" I ask. The fact that he's *curious* about me makes me feel like a zoo exhibit. I stand up and back away.

"Wait," Lacey says. "Where are you going?"

I don't have anywhere to go. I'm overwhelmed and confused. I shoot a glance in Kevin's direction and see him chatting with another handler. I take it as my cue.

"It's hot in here," I say. "I'm going to get some air." And then before she can argue, I walk away, careful to blend into the crowd so that Kevin won't try to stop me. I don't want him to see me this frazzled—he'll be able to tell I'm not medicated. I want a second to gather myself, and then I'll have Kevin take me home. I just want to think.

I slip out the back door and onto the wooden patio. When I don't see anyone, I walk to the railing and exhale, closing my eyes. For the first time since arriving home, my emotions threaten to drown me. Dr. Warren had warned me about this—I'm overstimulated. It's like my body is revolting against me, and I press the heel of my palm to my forehead, willing myself to calm down. There is no threat. My feelings are just screwed up—resetting. I should have taken that white pill.

Just then I hear the sound of the door and I spin around, expecting Kevin. But I still when I see that it's Liam.

"I'm sorry," he says, shrugging. "Lacey said you were mad and that I needed to come out and apologize."

I stare back at him, wondering if he knows that admitting someone *made* you apologize takes the sincerity out of it. "It's fine," I say, more out of politeness that really meaning it.

A crooked smile crosses his lips. "You know, I was worried you'd come back as some kind of zombie."

My stomach lurches, and I steady myself on the porch railing. "What do you mean by that?" I ask. *Did Liam know me? Had we been friends before and now I'm standing here, like an idiot, not remembering?*

Liam shakes his head. "Don't get upset," he says. "You're going to get me in trouble." He looks around before stepping back from me. A tear streaks down my cheek.

"Stop it," he says, pointing at me. "What the hell is wrong with you? If they see you like this, they'll send us both to The Program."

"But I don't understand," I say, wiping hard at my face. "Do you know me?"

"No, you freak!" he snaps, backing toward the doorway.

"And don't tell anyone that I do. Just stay away from me. I told Evan I didn't want to come here again."

My chest heaves with the start of a cry when someone walks over from the farside of the patio. I hadn't seen him sitting there. He leans his shoulder against the wall, not far from the door. "I'm sure you don't mean to be so rude," he tells Liam, looking him over. "Unless, of course, you're depressed or something."

"Stay out of this, James," Liam says, looking unsure of his path to the door now that the other guy is so close.

The guy raises his eyebrow at the mention of his name but doesn't say anything about it. Instead he takes out his phone, scrolling through it. "I could send an anonymous note," he says. "Alerting them to your condition."

Liam's face pales. "Don't do that, man. I'm not sick. You can't—"

"I can't what?" James asks with a smile. "I'm pretty sure I can."

"Look," Liam says, sounding authentically sorry for the first time. "I don't want to do this again with you. And I don't want any trouble. She's all yours." Liam holds out his hands as if he's offering me to this stranger.

I scoff, letting him know that I'm not his to give.

"I didn't say I wanted her," James says from the wall. "I was just making an observation."

Liam studies him for a second, as if checking to see if he's telling the truth, but then he slowly turns his head from side to side. "That's right," he says mostly to himself. "You don't remember either." Liam looks alarmed and darts for the door.

James swallows hard, but doesn't outwardly seem thrown off by Liam's words. And then before another threat can be given, Liam hurries inside, not even looking back at us.

My heart is still racing in my chest, and when I turn to thank James for sticking up for me, he pushes off the wall and heads for the door.

"Thank you," I call after him. He pauses for a second, his hand on the doorknob. But he doesn't turn to me.

"You shouldn't let yourself cry," he murmurs quietly. "Once you start . . ." He doesn't finish his words and instead sighs heavily. And then he goes back inside, leaving me alone in the darkening night.

CHAPTER THREE

WHEN I FINALLY PULL MYSELF TOGETHER, I GO BACK inside the Wellness Center. It seems too loud, too alive, and I find the couch empty, both Liam and Evan now gone. Kevin is at the wall, talking with Lacey. When I approach, he quickly straightens and walks toward me.

I tell Kevin I'm ready to leave, and then say good-bye to Lacey before turning and heading toward the exit. The crowd in the room is suffocating me as I try not to think about what happened on the patio. Try not to think that Liam might have known me before. He called me a freak.

I notice the guy from outside, James, but he doesn't acknowledge me when I pass. I want to thank him again, but Kevin appears at my side, leading me away.

As we reach the parking lot, Kevin stops me next to his van.

"Sloane," he says quietly, his face showing concern. "Are you feeling all right?"

My lips part to answer. I don't want to lie, but I'm scared of telling the truth. When I pause, Kevin furrows his brow. "Look," he says. "I'm not supposed to tell you this, but I think if I do it'll help you to trust me more." He waits a beat as if trying to decide if he should. "I was assigned to you for a reason," he whispers.

I lift my gaze to meet his. "What reason?"

Kevin looks me over and then shakes his head. "Wait, you didn't take your pill, did you? I can see the panic in your expression."

"What reason?" I ask again.

"Michael Realm," he finally answers. "He's asked me to look out for you."

I rock back on my heels. "Realm? But . . . why would you do that? He's a patient and—"

"I've known Michael for a while," Kevin says quickly. "And he asked this as a favor. He's hoping that once you're well, I can take you to see him. Off the grid." Kevin looks around once, as if he's worried about being overheard. It occurs to me then that he's breaking the rules, that he can be arrested for what he's doing.

And I think that he's right. I do trust him more now.

"Thank you for telling me," I say quietly. "And I'd like to see Realm again. But he told me I'd have to wait."

"You do," Kevin confirms, starting for the door of his van.

"But in a few weeks, you should be okay. Just don't . . ." He stops to look around again. "Just don't do anything stupid. And whatever you do, don't tell anyone about this. You'll compromise us all."

"I'll try." The nerves in my stomach calm. The fact that Realm is looking out for me makes me feel safer. And it makes me miss him. I don't want to screw up my chances of seeing him again.

Kevin and I both climb inside the van, and he starts the engine, glancing over his shoulder to back out. "Kevin," I say. "Let's never come back here again, okay? This place gives me the creeps."

He smiles and agrees, and then we leave the Wellness Center behind.

Lacey is waiting for me outside of class the next morning. Kevin stands off to the side of the door while I stop to talk to her, and Lacey shrugs apologetically.

"I don't know what happened last night," she says, quietly enough so that Kevin won't hear. "But the way Liam tore out of there, I'm guessing he was a dick and you told him off. He can be that way sometimes."

"It wasn't your fault," I say. "He probably didn't even think he was doing anything wrong."

Lacey nods at this, and moves over as several students file past us into class. "It's harder for returners," she murmurs. "People know more about us than we do. There's no one to trust anymore. It's enough to make me . . ." She stops and looks to where Kevin is standing. "Never mind," she says, waving her hand. "We should go in."

I agree and follow behind her. Kevin enters after us, taking his place at the back of the room. I look around again, thinking that everyone seems content, easygoing. But I didn't take my pill again today, and the fog of treatment is slowly clearing. Just then Lacey looks back over her shoulder at me and presses her lips into a smile. She's not medicated, not like the rest. I wonder if we're the only two lucid students in this room right now.

I begin filling out the daily assessment on my desk, lying on the first question. Because I do feel anxious and overwhelmed. But I'd never tell them that.

As I walk into my third-period math class, I see a list of problems on the board. I take out my notebook after I sit, and jot them down, hoping to be able to figure out at least one. Math is becoming a huge source of frustration for me. I'm lost in a calculation when a chair squeaks next to me.

I look over, noticing him—James. He looks a little different in daylight, or maybe it's the fact that my medication has worked its way out of my system, letting images sharpen again.

He has blond hair, cut close to his scalp. He's wearing a short-sleeved button-down plaid shirt that doesn't seem to be his, something about it wrong on him. It also doesn't hide the white scars on his bicep. I see him look at me from the corners of his eyes, but he doesn't turn. In fact, he just leans forward and then takes out his phone to text, or play a game. I'm not sure.

There's a strange mix of anxiety in my stomach as I watch him. I'm about to whisper a thank-you, even though I've already told him. I feel like I should say *something*, but just then our teacher walks in and tells us to take out our books.

I abandon the math problems from the board, and open to the correct page. I sneak a look sideways to see James continuing to type on his phone.

"Mr. Murphy," our teacher calls from the front. "If you wouldn't mind . . ." She raises one eyebrow at him.

James doesn't immediately react, and I shoot a look back to Kevin. My heart rate spikes, afraid that this guy is going to get himself thrown out of class. But before anything else happens, James slips his phone back into his pocket and opens his book, never making a sound.

When that's settled, Mrs. Cavalier starts in on the lesson, and I try not to look next to me. When class comes to an end, James is the first one out the door.

Lacey waves me over to her table when I get to lunch. Kevin tells me to go ahead. He doesn't offer me the white pill anymore, which tells me that maybe I never really needed it in the first place. Maybe they were just to keep me complacent. At home my doses go into the disposal.

I sit across from Lacey, opening my brown bag. Now that I'm not taking anything, my appetite has returned. I bite into my sandwich as Lacey takes out her cupcakes, sliding one over to me.

"Evan broke up with me today," she says conversationally. "He said my rebel ways make him nervous. Which I think is funny considering that he's the one who's best friends with a non-returner. That alone is asking for trouble—they're paranoid and dangerous. Hell, they spread suicide. And truly, Liam is scared shitless of us. I bet he's the one that told him to end things."

"Liam's not scared of me," I say, taking the cupcake from the plastic to break it open. "But that other guy might have worried him just a little." I lick the cream, and Lacey tilts her head questioningly.

"What other guy?"

I glance around then, trying to find him. When I see him sitting alone at a table, I don't mention it at first. Instead I look him over. He's really cute, in an intimidating sort of way. His light-blue eyes gaze out the window as he drinks from a carton of milk. I wonder why he helped me last night, yet he won't look at me otherwise. At just that moment, he turns to meet my stare and I freeze.

Across from me Lacey laughs. "James Murphy," she says.

"What?" Startled, I turn back to her.

She smiles. "That's James Murphy who you're currently eye-humping. He's in my science class, but he doesn't say much. And when he does, it's usually obnoxious or combative."

I can feel my cheeks redden. "I wasn't . . ." I stop to laugh.

"Okay, not the point. So are you friends with him?"

"Nope." She bites into her cupcake. "I'm pretty sure that he hates everyone here. He's been in and out of the office since transferring. I would have recruited him to my 'Lacey Against the World' plan, but he's too unpredictable. He ended up assigned two handlers because he kept going off the grid. Can't believe they didn't send him back. Trying to keep up appearances, I guess."

She crumples up her wrapper, and I pick through the rest of my lunch, careful not to look at James again. If *Lacey* thinks he's trouble, that has to be saying something. But I might ask Kevin about him later.

"Wait," Lacey says, looking up. "Is he the one that scared Liam yesterday?"

"Uh-huh." I don't go into details, but I'm not sure why. It's like I'm suddenly protective of James's reputation, even though I barely know him. Still, I owe him for sticking up for me. So I don't mention that he threatened to turn a non-sick person into The Program. That could get him arrested, I bet.

Something tickles the back of my mind, but I can't put it into words, this odd feeling I have. A feeling that has no meaning because I can't remember what it relates to. It's like I'm about to discover it when a memory of my brother sitting alone at the table calling out fractions on flash cards echoes in my mind. I blink quickly and try to clear it away.

"Well, who knows then," Lacey says, not noticing my temporary distraction. "Maybe he's not a total tool. So . . . do you remember having any boyfriends or anything? Evan is the first that I can remember. How sad is that? He uses way too much tongue."

"Ew." I pop the tab on my Diet Coke. "Not sure I needed to know that."

Lacey leans her elbows on the table, the smile fading from her lips. "They watch you, you know. They monitor us all the time, even when we don't realize."

A chill runs over me as I stare back at her. Her dark eyes are painted with blue shadow, the liner dramatically cat-eyed. Her blond hair is flipped up at the ends, very preppy—almost comically so. It occurs to me suddenly that this is not how she wants to dress. That this is fake.

"Are they watching right now?" I whisper, suddenly paranoid as I lean closer to her.

"The place isn't bugged or anything, but they take note of who we interact with. Where we go. They're looking for signs of failure."

"And if they find it?"

Lacey straightens then. "We don't know. No one has failed. Yet."

I lower my eyes, thinking that I don't want to be the first person to get sent back to The Program. I don't think I could bear being locked up there alone. I feel fine—a little confused, but not depressed. Although to be honest, I'm not even sure what depressed would feel like.

"Anyway." Lacey sighs as if wanting to go back to the easy

conversation. "If you want me to introduce you to James, I can."

I shake my head, trying to relax the tension that is now squeezing my shoulders. "That's okay," I say. "I doubt he's my type."

Lacey snorts. "How would you know? I'm sure they've wiped out your dating history, too."

She's right. I don't know anything about myself anymore. I don't even know if I've had a boyfriend before.

"Maybe you like dudes on motorcycles." Lacey grins. "Or supernerdy guys." She giggles, but it's deep and throaty. "I'll tell you one thing, now that I'm free to date, I'm going to try all thirty-one flavors. It's like I have a clean slate. I'm a born-again virgin."

"Just remember that some of those thirty-one flavors will be disgusting," I say. "Like, who would be the pistachio cream?"

Lacey smiles. "Already had him."

I laugh again, shaking my head. "Have you ever asked anyone about your past? About who you dated before?"

Lacey seems to freeze at this. "I did actually, and my parents nearly died when I brought it up. They wouldn't tell me a thing. Everyone else ignored the question because they didn't want to get flagged. You know that, right? If anyone tells you about who you were, what you did before The Program, they can get flagged or arrested for messing with a returner."

I lower my eyes, the thought troubling me. The fact that The Program has such complete control of what and who we're exposed to.

Lacey continues. "After all the strained glances between my parents, I finally just went to search my room, looking for anything—a picture, a birthday card. But it's all gone. Probably a good thing, though. I mean, how healthy could my past relationships have been if I was suicidal?"

She has a valid point. "Still," I say, "I'd like to know. Just seems weird that other people can know and not tell me."

Lacey pushes her lunch bag away and levels her stare at me. "It is weird. And trust me, it doesn't get any less weird. But there are a lot sick people out there. You and me, we're not like them anymore. Sure, I get a little irritated when I can't remember something, but I'm not trying to slash my wrists, either. The Program worked. For better or for worse. Truly," she says, looking down. "I'm not sure which it is."

The expression that crosses her features is one of regret with a touch of sadness. I glance over at Kevin, hoping he hasn't noticed Lacey's change, but he's watching us. He's clearly seen.

"I did meet a guy while I was at The Program," I offer, completely downplaying how complicated my and Realm's relationship was to make it sound like gossip. With that, Lacey's lips twitch with a smile.

"Really, now? That is scandalous, Sloane. A boyfriend?"

"No. Just a friend." Lacey crinkles her nose as if I've disappointed her. "But," I add, "he was the type of friend I'd sometimes kiss."

The bell rings overhead, and I straighten, glad I snapped

her out of whatever she was thinking about. She smiles broadly at me.

"I have to go," she says, standing. "My chem teacher is giving me a hell of a time about not catching up. Maybe she'll eventually take the hint that I hate science and have no plans to *ever* catch up." She sighs and then waves before turning to leave.

I wait a minute, still taking in what Lacey had told me about being monitored, about nobody telling us who we used to be. I thought being clearheaded would help me figure stuff out, but instead it's only made it more confusing. Just then Kevin appears at the end of the table.

"Do you monitor me when I don't know?" I ask quietly.

"Yes."

Tiny pinpricks of realization slide over my skin, and I nod, acknowledging that I heard him. It's a helpless feeling.

"But . . . ," he continues, "I try not to notice when you break the rules—like slipping out of the Wellness Center when you think I'm not looking."

"Oh." I feel exposed, but it also affirms to me that Kevin isn't the bad guy. At least not that I can tell. And if Realm sent him, I should trust that. I should trust Realm.

CHAPTER FOUR

THE MINUTE I GET HOME FROM SCHOOL, I RUN TO my bedroom and begin searching. The place still looks mostly the same as I remember it, except maybe a little cleaner. Although I can tell that things are missing, I have no idea what they could be. I open drawers, push aside the new clothes in my closet, but there are no hints that I ever had a social life. Either I was a nobody, or I had to have the people around me erased.

"Damn it," I say as I slam the drawer closed. I just wanted something—anything—to give me a clue to what I was like before. I take a minute to look around, see if I missed anything, when I hear my mother call me from downstairs.

"Sloane," she says. "Dinner."

I head for the door, disturbed that I didn't find anything—not even a picture. It's like someone came in here and swept it all away. What worries me most is the idea that I was ever sick enough to be sent away in the first place. It doesn't seem possible.

My father is working late, so it's just my mother and me. I poke at the fried potatoes on my plate. I want to ask her about my past, but I'm afraid that she won't tell me . . . and that she will. What if knowing really will make me sick again?

"So how was school?" she asks. "Settling in okay?"

"Pretty good, I guess." I chew slowly. "Mom, what happened to all my clothes?"

"We got you new ones. Do you not like them?"

"No, they're fine. I just wonder what my old clothes looked like."

"Pretty much the same. But Dr. Warren suggested that we get you a new wardrobe to give you a fresh start. If you don't like them, we can go shopping after school." She smiles. "That might be fun."

A fresh start. My heart rate begins to speed up. "Great," I say halfheartedly. "But I was wondering . . ." I swallow hard. "Would you tell me if I asked if I ever had a boyfriend?"

My mother doesn't noticeably react as she cuts into her chicken. "Sure, honey," she says, not looking up. "You did date a little, but nothing serious."

"Oh." I can't explain why, but that answer makes me feel bad. "Friends?" I ask. My mother bristles then.

"What's this about, Sloane? You should be worried about the present, not the past."

"You're right," I say, just to get rid of the crease between her eyebrows. We start eating again, and after a minute, I smile. "Do you know anything about a James Murphy?" I ask, cutting into my meat.

My mother looks up at me. "No. Is he a classmate of yours?"

"We have math together, and my friend said that he'd been in The Program just before me. He sounds kind of bad." I laugh.

My mother nods, smiling kindly. "Then that should be a real sign to steer clear of him, don't you think? The last thing you need so soon after returning is more problems. You have to remember that you were unwell, and now you're cured. You're not supposed to dwell on the past. You're supposed to be focused on now."

"I'm not dwelling," I say, my face stinging from her scolding me. "I don't have a past. Can you understand how confusing that is?"

"I'm sure it is. But they took the memories that were corrupted. And if you keep digging around in your head, reality is going to slip away. The doctor told us—"

"How do you know they only took the bad memories?" I challenge. "I can't remember anything. I don't even know what happened to Brady, only that he's dead. What happened to him?"

"He drowned," my mother answers simply, as if that in itself is an explanation. I knew this already. Dr. Warren had told me in a therapy session. But there were never any details.

"How?"

"Sloane," my mother says in a warning voice.

"Who's to say they only erased what they were supposed to?" I ask. "My life has so many holes in it and—"

"This discussion is over," my mother says quickly. I meet her eyes over the table, and I can see she is in full panic mode. "You tried to kill yourself, Sloane. They told us you were resistant in The Program, too. We could have lost you, just like we lost your brother. The Program kept you alive, and for that I'm blessed. Any inconvenience you may feel now will fade soon enough. And if you just can't bear it, maybe we should call the doctor and see if there is another treatment available. I can't go through this again." She starts to cry. "I just can't."

My mother pushes back from the table, leaving her barely touched food behind as she heads toward her bedroom. I feel guilty, as if I'm just a problem that continues to repeat itself.

And so with that, I toss my napkin down and retreat upstairs.

It's an hour later when my mother knocks at my door, asking if she can talk to me. I let her in, still hating that I upset her. She looks older than she does in my memories, making me think the way I remember things isn't accurate at all.

"About your brother," she says, coming to sit next to me on the bed. "It was a very tragic loss, Sloane. One we'd all prefer to forget."

"What happened to him?" Chills spread over my body. "Brady was a great swimmer. How could he drown?"

"It was a rafting accident. And your doctors had to take

the memory because it was very traumatic for you. They felt it contributed to your illness."

I hadn't considered that my brother might have hurt himself. Brady wouldn't do something that selfish. He loved us. We were happy.

"I miss him," I tell my mother, looking at her.

She blinks back her tears and smiles sadly. "I miss him too. But we had to move on as a family. Your brother drowned in that river and it devastated us. Still, we've found our peace again. Please don't make us relive the pain. Do you promise?"

There's a tightness in my chest, and I think what she's asking is unfair, especially because I can't remember losing my brother. I need a little more closure, a chance to grieve now that I'm home. But instead, I just nod, and she pats my thigh.

"Now," she says as if everything is cleared up. "Tell me again about all these friends you're making."

"Oh . . ." I furrow my brow, surprised by the subject change. "Well, it's only one friend. The girl Lacey I told you about? She's really nice. I think you'll like her." I'm not sure that's true, but I'm hoping it'll make my mother less cautious with me. "I was hoping that maybe she could come over for dinner one night."

My mother presses her lips together, thinking. "Maybe in a few weeks—when things settle down."

I don't like her answer but I don't tell her.

"And the boy?" she asks offhandedly.

I laugh. "There's no boy. I was just wondering about someone in my math class. It's no big deal."

My mother smiles, but it looks forced, and I feel my heart sink. She's not going to let Lacey come here, and she certainly isn't going to let me date anyone—possibly ever. I'm starting to think that I need to find Realm. I'm not sure there is anyone else I can confide in. He'd told me to wait to find him, but I can't. I need someone to talk to, someone who will understand. I wonder if Kevin will take me to him now.

My mother reaches out to brush my hair behind my ear. "I'm glad we had this talk," she says, gazing at me lovingly. "We're so happy to have you home, honey. You have no idea how much we've missed you."

I tell her I missed her, too, but really I'm thinking about the ache that has started deep in my chest, a pain that I can't place and I can't understand. It's like longing, whether for myself or someone else, I don't know. There is a part of me missing and no matter what I do, I'm not sure I'll ever fill it.

It's nearly a week later, and I'm in math class again. Kevin told me that I wasn't ready to see Realm because I haven't healed yet, and it's imperative for my brain to do so. He reminded me that although he's looking out for me as a favor for Realm, he really is concerned for my health and that it is his first priority.

James Murphy sits in the desk next to me, paying attention as our teacher continues to talk. I lower my head, letting my hair fall forward, blocking the right side of my face enough so that I can stare at James through my dark hair.

The scars on his bicep are white, but they've got a weird

crisscrossing pattern. I can't figure out what could have caused that sort of injury, but it's not angry and pink like a normal scar. Is it a burn?

James glances sideways, catching me looking at his arm. His face is expressionless, and he turns back to the front, as if he didn't notice me at all. I swallow hard.

I go back to my notebook and copy down a few problems from the board. I look at Kevin, who's staring out the window, daydreaming. I peek at James again, the thought that he refuses to acknowledge me making me that much more curious about him. And although I'm not checking him out, I do notice how attractive he is—I mean, I can't really miss it. He isn't overly styled: in fact, his chin is unshaven, the stubble there a little darker than his hair. When I look at his mouth, there's a ghost of a smile there, even though he's staring straight ahead. James leans forward and turns the page of his notebook, jotting something down quickly.

I watch as he turns the spiral-bound notebook sideways, continuing to stare ahead. I'm not sure what he's doing when he silently taps his finger on the page.

I realize suddenly that he wants me to read it. I lean over slightly.

Why are you staring at me?

He darts a glance in my direction, and I can feel the heat in my cheeks, my embarrassment getting the best of me. I shrug.

James nods and goes back to his notebook, scribbling something else before turning it toward me.

It's giving me a complex.

A laugh escapes from my lips, and I quickly cover my mouth. Nearly half the class turns toward the sound, but James is the picture of innocence as he flips back to his original page and folds his hands in front of him.

"Is there a problem, Sloane?" the teacher asks. Within seconds Kevin is standing at my side, looking concerned.

"No," I say. "I'm sorry. I choked on a piece of gum."

"Perhaps that's why we don't allow gum in the classroom," the teacher responds, sounding annoyed at the interruption.

"Are you not feeling well?" Kevin whispers. "Maybe we should go out into the hall for some air."

"No," I say instantly. "I'm fine. Really."

Kevin shoots a nervous look at James, and then walks to the front and interrupts our teacher midsentence. I don't dare turn to James, but I can feel him watching me.

"Of course," the teacher says to my handler. "Sloane, can you come sit in the front, please?"

I gather my things quickly and take an empty desk directly to the side of the teacher. I sit there for the rest of class, feeling kind of humiliated. But maybe just a little bit charmed.

After class Kevin pulls me aside and levels his stare on mine. "What was that about in there?" he asks.

"I laughed. It's not a huge deal." I don't appreciate him being so nosy, but then I think that a regular handler might be a lot more intrusive than Kevin's being right now.

"Do you know James Murphy?" he asks.

"No."

Kevin exhales as he straightens. "Then let's keep it that way. James isn't the sort you want to get to know, Sloane. I can't protect you if you're going to go down that path."

"And what path is that?"

"A self-destructive one. Just promise me you'll stay away from him. Please."

I don't like being told who I can and can't associate with. But Kevin's eyes are pleading with me, so I nod, even though it's going to be a hard promise to keep.

CHAPTER FIVE

LACEY HAS TAKEN UP PERMANENT RESIDENCE ACROSS from me at the lunch table, always sharing her cupcakes, always entertaining me with her stories about guys. I haven't been back to the Wellness Center since that first time, and Lacey hasn't mentioned meeting her there again. I just hope my mother will eventually let her come over to our house.

"Oh," Lacey says, biting into the orange frosting. "I ended up having coffee with a new guy last night." She beams.

"Really?" I have to admit, I'm a little jealous. The thought of going out on a date sounds so exciting, so free. Even if I were allowed to date, I'd have to take Kevin along. How creepy would that be?

"He's cute," Lacey starts. "He has a car, and best of all, he's over eighteen."

"So no Program?"

"Right. He's so freaking normal I'd say he was boring, but right now I don't mind. He knows how to kiss."

I laugh. "I think that may be the real reason you like him."

"It's not funny," she says, tossing a rolled-up straw wrapper at me. "Overusage of tongue is a serious problem. I think that's the real epidemic here."

I'm cracking up. Kevin stands more alert from the side of the room as he watches us, but I can't stop.

"And yes, part of why I like him is his technique. But I have plenty of other reasons, too." She grins. "He's really nice to look at."

"Wow," I say. "With so much in common, I think you may be soul mates."

"Oh, shut up." She laughs. "I'll tell you one thing," she says, getting more serious. "The minute I graduate, I'm out of this town. Out of this state. I hear that back east they've contained the outbreak without The Program. Think of all the normal people who'll be walking around there."

I widen my eyes. "They've contained it? I didn't hear that."

"It's not mainstream news," she says, sipping from her drink. "Total underground, but it's for real." She smiles. "Maybe you'll come with me."

"I'd have to take Kevin with me," I say, motioning toward my handler.

Lacey seems to consider this. "He can come," she murmurs, running her gaze over him. "I like blonds."

Kevin notices us eying him. Lacey laughs and turns back to her cupcake.

"So," I ask a few minutes later. "Did you keep any friends from The Program?"

Lacey shakes her head. "Nope. They were all pretty lame." She glances up at me mischievously. "Are you thinking of finding your friend—the one with benefits?"

"He didn't have those kind of benefits, and yes, I'm thinking about it. Do you think I should? Do you think it could make me sick again?"

Lacey's expression darkens. "I wish I knew what makes us sick, Sloane. But we don't know. And neither do they. I say you go find him. You deserve to live the life you want." There's a hint of tragedy in her voice, as if she's wondered about getting sick again before.

Over Lacey's shoulder I notice James Murphy watching us, and there's a twist in my stomach, both anxious and excited. Lacey must read it because she turns around and sees him, and then looks back to me.

"I knew you liked him."

"No, I don't," I answer quickly. "It's just that he doesn't seem to want to talk to me, and to be honest, it makes him that much hotter." We both laugh.

"Well, trust me," she says, crumpling her wrappers, "James may be hot, but he's a troublemaker. Someone like him could get you flagged again. So make sure you enjoy him for what he is: eye candy." She winks and then walks away.

* * *

At the end of the day I'm at my locker, but Kevin is nowhere in sight. I consider waiting for him, but then I realize I'm happy to be on my own. I hurry outside. It's my handler's responsibility to find me, not vice versa.

It's a nice day out. The sun is warm in a cloudless sky and I actually enjoy the walk. A few people look at me, as if realizing I shouldn't be unescorted, but they still say hi to me. It isn't until I'm a few blocks away that I realize how truly far my house is. Maybe I should call my mother for a ride.

"Hey. It's Sloane, right?"

I'm startled by the voice and turn to the street as a car slows next to me. I duck to look in the passenger window and abruptly stop on the sidewalk. "Yeah."

"I'm James," he says. "You know, the one you stare at in class."

My cheeks warm, but I try to play it off. "I don't stare at you."

He smiles to himself, clearly knowing that I do. "So can I give you a ride somewhere?"

I'm embarrassed and not sure this is a good idea at all. Kevin had said to stay away from James, that he was on a self-destructive path. "We're not supposed to talk to each other," I say.

"Really? Well, if you'd like we can drive in complete silence."

I laugh, adjusting the strap of my backpack on my shoulder. "This your car?" I ask.

"Nope. Does that mean you'll get in?"

"I shouldn't take rides from strangers," I say. James lowers his eyes, his playfulness fading. "But . . . ," I continue. "You seem harmless enough."

He looks surprised. "I do?"

"No. You look like you're going to cause me a lot of problems. But it's a long walk home." I step off the curb and open the passenger door. He doesn't say anything as we pull away, and when we pass the turn for my house, I don't tell him. I clear my throat.

"Do you think they follow us?" I ask.

"Who?"

"The handlers."

James taps his thumb on the steering wheel as he takes a left onto the main road, passing all the car dealerships and restaurants. "Yes. But not today. They all rushed off to the high school, some big incident they're trying to keep quiet."

"Is that where my handler went? I thought he just got tired of me."

"He definitely could have." James smiles. "You seem like the pain-in-the-ass sort—a twinkle in your eye. But more likely he was Tasing someone in the hallway. He'll probably drive by your house later. They still drive by mine sometimes."

"Oh." I honestly didn't know that Kevin drove by my house, and it makes me a bit uneasy. "So what do you think they'll do if they see us together?"

"Nothing. What are they going to do—spank us?" He chuckles.

"They could put us back in—"

"Sloane," James interrupts. "Are you hungry? Maybe we could hit Denny's or something. I like pancakes."

"People will see us at Denny's," I answer quietly.

"Right, good point." He turns to smile at me, but it seems strained, as if his confidence is just an act. "McDonald's drive-through?"

"Why did you really offer me a ride home?" I ask, my curiosity too much. James has ignored me since standing up for me at the Wellness Center, and now he's talking to me. Driving me around.

He shrugs. "I don't know."

"Then why did you—"

"I *really* don't know. I don't want friends, Sloane. I just want to graduate and get the hell out of here." He exhales, staring out the windshield. "And then you show up, watching me with your big brown eyes. Looking at me like you know me."

"I don't know you."

"And I don't know you. So why did I care that that asshole was being mean to you outside on the patio that night? Why have I worried about you since? Can you explain it?" He sounds frustrated, and I realize that he has the same conflicting feelings that I do. Emotions that are there, but without cause. Feelings that aren't attached to memories and therefore meaningless. I'm suddenly scared and think about James being high-risk.

"I'm on Hillsdale Drive," I murmur. "You passed my street a while back."

James makes a sound like he's about to say something, but

instead he makes a hard U-turn and drives us back in the direction of my house. He doesn't talk, and the tension grows. A pain starts to work through my body, a dread. An ache. I want to get far away from James Murphy because I think he may be the cause of it. I feel . . . sick.

When he stops in front of my driveway, I move quickly to get out. I toss back a thank-you and hurry toward my front door, glad my parents aren't home to see me so flustered. When I get on the porch, I glance over my shoulder. The car is still there, James is talking to himself and looking pissed. I pause right where I am as I watch him wipe roughly at his cheek and pull away.

CHAPTER SIX

"SO I KNOW YOU AND JAMES AREN'T AT ALL INTO each other," Lacey says, biting into her cupcake as she sits across from me in the cafeteria. "But he's been watching you this entire time. I might start feeling bad for him if you don't at least acknowledge him."

I don't, keeping my back to his end of the cafeteria as I eat my lunch. James makes me self-conscious. His shifts between flirting and avoiding me are stirring up emotions I don't understand. And I don't want to get sick again.

"Okay," Lacey says when I don't answer. "I'm just saying the more you ignore him, the more I'm convinced you're in love with the guy. And he looks positively pathetic today."

"He does not. And I don't even know him, so how can I love him?"

Lacey smiles as if I just told her that I want to marry him and have his blond-headed babies. "Well, whatever you're doing," she says, "you're messing him up hardcore."

I worry suddenly that she's right. What if by talking to him I started some chain reaction of events? What if we get infected again because of me?

I put my chin on my shoulder and look back at James. When I do, he straightens. He holds my stare in a way that pins me in place until I hear Lacey calling my name, making me turn around.

"Oh, Lord," she mumbles. "This is not going to end well."

"Let's just drop it."

"Fine." She holds up her hands as if I'm a lost cause. "I do have something for you though."

This peaks my interest. "Yeah?"

"It's a little trick I learned a few weeks into my return." With a cautious glance at Kevin, she reaches down to take something from her backpack. She taps my knee as she passes it to me under the table.

"What is it?" I ask, bringing it onto my lap to look it over. It's a small pad of paper with the name of the school psychologist at the top. The entire pad has been filled out with his signature, requiring only the date and time. I look across the table at Lacey, my eyes wide.

"If you need some time off," she whispers. "Just fill it in and give it to your teacher. They never check. They expect us to be in therapy—they definitely don't expect us to skip. We're the good ones, remember? Sorry that I've used up half the passes already." When I look at her questioningly, she shrugs. "What? How did you think I found the time to sample so many flavors?"

I laugh, thinking about Lacey sneaking around school, making out with guys behind the building or in the custodian's closet. And then, completely not meaning to, I take another look back at James. And he smiles.

"Not interested at all," Lacey says offhandedly. "So sure."

I don't waste any time using the pass. It's like having the key to an intricate lock right there in your pocket. Before my final class, I fill one out and then pause at the entryway, trying not to give myself away. After a deep breath, I turn to Kevin.

"I actually have a session with Mr. Andrews," I say, motioning back toward the office. "It'll probably last through the end of the day."

Kevin glances at his watch and then nods. "I'll walk you there."

I smile as my heart explodes with panic in my chest. "Oh. Sure. Okay." Kevin waits as I show my teacher the fake pass, letting him mark me as present in the roster. Then he dismisses me.

I don't talk as Kevin and I head down the empty hall toward the office. I don't know what I was thinking. My handler is going to see that I don't have a session, and then he's going to check the pass. I'm going to get so busted. I don't think he'll be able to ignore this, no matter what sort of favor he's doing for Realm.

And where will I tell him I got it from? I won't turn Lacey in. They can put me back in The Program if they have to.

The Program. An acute sense of dread slips over me, and I consider confessing to Kevin that I don't have a session; asking him not to turn me in. But that would just be stupid. I have to ride this out, and if that fails, deny, deny, deny.

"You've done well," Kevin tells me as we walk. "I'm honestly impressed with the progress you've made so far. Not all returners are so cooperative."

"Thanks," I say, the pass burning a hole in my hand, proving that his trust is misplaced. "I appreciate you saying that."

"Realm told me you were remarkable in The Program, and now I see it." He pauses. "You know, I was at your house that day. I was one of the handlers who brought you to the facility," he says softly. "And you were . . . really sick. I'm so glad to see you healthy now. I've really been pulling for you."

I can feel the color drain from my face when he says this. "You were there?" is all I can mumble. *Oh, God. They took me from my own house?*

Kevin nods and puts his hand on my shoulder. "I was. And when Realm contacted me about your release, I was hesitant. I didn't think you'd be a good candidate, but now I see it. You're very clever."

"Candidate for what?"

Kevin motions toward the office door as if reminding me

that I have therapy. As he holds it open, he smiles. "I'll have Realm get in touch with you soon," he says. "I think that'd make you both pretty happy."

"I would love to see him."

"I'll see what I can do."

He leaves, but I'm stunned, standing in the middle of the front office. Kevin has seen a side of me that I can't remember. He said I'd been really sick. I can't even picture it.

"Can I help you?" the secretary asks, startling me.

I look at her and then check back over my shoulder to make sure Kevin is gone. When I'm sure he is, I smile. "Hi," I say. "Mr. Bellis wanted copy paper?"

I hurry through the empty halls and stash the ream of paper in my locker. My heart is racing with the worry of getting caught, but I feel alive right now—as if I'm escaping more than just fifty minutes of class. I start toward the back door, hoping to sneak through it toward the far lot.

When I get outside, I remember about the football field. "Damn it," I murmur. Even though sports aren't played anymore, they've kept the lawn intact, even mowing it short. But it rained heavily last night and the field looks half-flooded. It's the only way to the far lot unless I walk around the building, possibly getting seen by the front office. I sigh and move closer to the field to check it out.

The air around me is warm from the sun. It smells new and clean, and I'm suddenly reminded of the times I spent camping with Brady. Sometimes it would pour rain, and we'd be stuck in the tent, playing cards and eating beef jerky. It was still fun, though. We always had fun.

As my sneaker squishes in the wet earth, I think about how much I miss Brady. It's like my memories of him end with us happy. Just happiness and then he's gone, a quietness in its place. I wonder how I handled losing him. My mother said it was tough on me, but I wonder if I was brave. Or I wonder if his dying was what finally broke me.

"Sloane!"

I jump and spin around, nearly wiping out on the field as I see James jogging up, his cheeks pink from running. The sun reflects off his hair, casting him in gold. I hate how gorgeous he is.

"Are you trying to get me in trouble?" I ask the minute he's in front of me, breathing hard. I look behind him to make sure no one's watching, but he just smiles.

"Define trouble."

I shake my head and turn, starting across the field, even though my sneakers are getting sucked into the mud. "Freaking hell," I say, trying to jump from grass patch to grass patch.

"So you skip class too?" James asks.

"Obviously. But I don't try to get caught by yelling people's name across the field."

"Are you pissed because I had a minibreakdown in the car?"

I stop, and James bumps into the back of me, nearly sending me headlong into the mud. I grab for his shirt and he grabs for my hand and soon we're both off balance. When we're finally standing straight, our feet are practically on top of each other's, James holding me by the wrist. I worry that someone will see us like this. He shouldn't be this close. And he definitely shouldn't be looking at me like that.

"I have to go," I say, yanking away. Only when I do, James's foot slides in the mud and then he's falling back, landing faceup in a pile of mud.

"I am so sorry!" I say, putting my hand over my mouth. But instead of jumping up and trying to clean himself off, James starts laughing hysterically.

"You did that on purpose," he says. "You're so dead." He gets up, trying to grab for me, but his knee slides, and he ends up sprawling out on his stomach, covered in mud from head to toe. "Oh my God," he says. He rolls over and lands with a splat right next to my feet, and I can't stop myself from bursting out laughing.

"You laughing at me?" he asks, still staring up at the sky.

"Yes," I say immediately. "I absolutely am."

He lifts his head, mud smeared on his ear, and grabs my pant leg. "Oh, yeah?"

"Don't you dare."

He knots the jean fabric in his fist, yanking on it playfully. "Do you like getting dirty?"

"I will beat you senseless." I see where he's smeared mud on my clothing already. I'm afraid he might actually drag me down with him. "I have no problem kicking your balls," I add.

He chuckles and pulls me again, making me stumble, but I correct myself before I fall. Around us the world smells like earth and life. I try to pull from his grasp without letting my other sneaker slip in the mud.

"James," I say calmly, "let me go or I swear I'll scream."

"Really? You would get me thrown back into The Program?"

And when I think about it, I know I wouldn't. I kick his hand and yank back, but my other sneaker flips out from under me and I fall.

James swears and moves quickly, trying to catch me, but I'm faceup in the mud before he can. The cool, mushy earth surrounds me as I catch my breath.

"Sloane?" James is kneeling next to me, looking concerned. "I wasn't really going to pull you into the mud."

I stare back at him, my fingers digging into a clump of mud at my side. James actually looks worried. He's such an idiot. With a fierce right hook, I smash a handful of mud on the side of his face, catching him completely off guard as he falls to his side. The minute he's down I start taking clumps of mud and grass and throwing them at him, burying him.

He's laughing, bits of dirt on his teeth before he sits up and lunges, tackling me. "You're nuts," he says. "Oh, and I think you're hungry." He's got me pinned, my ears half-buried in the mud, blocking out the sound of his threats.

He holds up a huge handful of mud, his own face covered nearly completely. He looks ridiculous, his blue eyes standing out against the dark dirt. He holds the mud over my face, little bits of dirty water dripping on my cheek. "You're going to eat this," he says.

"Don't!" I'm half laughing, half begging, trying to turn my face so he won't stuff the dirt into my mouth.

James takes both my hands in one of his, pining them over my head as he moves to straddle me, wiping the mud on my neck, smearing it with his fingers.

"Ew!" he says dramatically. "This must feel so disgusting." He shoves it down the front of my shirt.

The mud is cold and slimy, and I turn from left to right trying to get away from it, giggling the entire time.

"You pushed me in the mud," he says, grabbing another big handful from next to my face. "Then you threatened my balls. I think you should pay, don't you?"

"No!"

James lets my hands go, but doesn't get up. He's so proud of himself, having pinned a girl half his size, but I don't point this out. He exhales and throws the clump of mud off to the side, looking down at me as if he doesn't know what to do with me now.

"You're a vicious little thing," James says as he finally crawls off me. "You would have really hurt me if I let you." His sneakers make a sucking noise as he stands up. When he holds out his hand to me, I look at it doubtfully.

"Truce?" he asks.

"Whatever." I take his hand and let me him help me up,

even let him hold my arm as we make it across the muddy field, heading toward the back end of the parking lot.

"You're filthy," he says, like it's a surprise, pausing at his car. "You should let me drive you home."

"And what about our clothes?" I ask, when I stop outside the passenger door.

"If it were my car, you'd have to ride home naked." He smiles at the idea. "But since it's my dad's, I don't care if it gets dirty."

I decide to at least take off my cardigan, leaving the muddy tank top underneath. James takes off his shirt altogether, and I try not to notice. I have to try pretty hard. When we sit in the car and turn to each other, we both crack up.

"Maybe you could spray me down with your hose before I head home?" James asks, starting the car.

"Like a dog."

"You can scratch my belly if you want."

"Gross."

When we get to my house, my parents are just climbing out of their car. I forgot it was their support group day and they'd be home early. As we stop at the curb, James laughs. "Good thing you didn't really ride home naked."

"Not sure this is much of an improvement." I flip down the mirror and see my mud-covered skin and then glare at James. "I think you're a bad influence," I tell him.

He grins. "I hope so."

I shake my head and start to open the door. "It might be

weird if I spray you down on my front lawn while my parents watch," I say. "Although you strike me as an exhibitionist."

"Oh, I am. But that's fine. I'll wash up at home."

I get out, but before I close the door, James calls my name. "What?" I ask, a smile teasing my lips.

"It was a good day," he says simply. "Thanks."

I agree, then close his door, watching as he drives off. I almost wish I'd stayed in the car. That was . . . nice. In a really strange and dirty way.

"Sloane?" my mother calls, her voice tight. When I turn, the looks on my parents' faces are almost comical in their confusion.

"Sorry," I say, although I don't sound it. "I fell in the mud, and James brought me home."

"James?" my mother says, exchanging a concerned glance with my father. It stops me cold.

"What?" I ask.

"It's just . . ." My mother pauses as if debating something. "Sloane, you're not supposed to date after—"

"Oh, we're not," I say quickly. "It's not like that."

My mother lets out a held breath. "That's good. We just want to keep you safe, honey."

Her tone is tense, but rather than press her, I go inside to clean up. I don't want to ruin my first fun day in what seems like forever. Or at least, the first one I can remember.

CHAPTER SEVEN

I'M SURPRISED WHEN I WAKE UP THE NEXT MORN-
ing to find Kevin waiting at my front door. I thought we'd gotten past the escorting me to school stage of our relationship.
"What's going on?" I ask.

"We just want to make sure you're not doing anything to
jeopardize your health, Sloane," my mother says calmly. "So
I've asked Kevin to watch you a little more closely." I step back
from her as if I've been slapped in the face.

"You called the handler on me?" I turn to Kevin. "And what
did she say? That I was smiling too much?"

Kevin bristles. "She said you were riding around with James
Murphy. Is that true?"

My first instinct is to deny it, but I know there's no use. "So?
We're friends." My mother tsks next to me as if I'm confirming

her fears. Kevin tilts his head like he's disappointed.

"This is your warning, Sloane," he says firmly. "You're not to have contact with Mr. Murphy anymore. Do you understand?" Kevin looks completely serious, and I think that I've killed whatever bond we had. He doesn't trust me anymore, and like he'd told me before, his main objective is to keep me well, not to help me break the rules.

"Yes," I say to Kevin, the bitterness clear in my voice. I look over at my mother then, anger rolling over me. "I just got home and already you're trying to get rid of me?" The minute the words are out, I regret them as her face falls.

But instead of apologizing, I straighten my back and walk out, leaving Kevin to trail behind me.

My handler takes the seat next to me in math class, blocking my view of James. I'm so surprised by Kevin's change in demeanor that I don't bother talking to him. He's like a real handler now.

I wonder if James has been warned as well, especially with how severe a reaction Kevin is having. Then again, if they'd ordered James to stay at least fifty feet away from me, it'd probably make him want to talk to me more, so I smile. I'd thought that maybe he was a jerk, or difficult. But after yesterday, I feel light. As if James reminded me what it was like to have fun again.

After class, I walk down the hallway with Kevin carrying my books like I'm helpless, when my phone vibrates in my pocket. I'm not sure who would text me other than my mother, and I definitely don't want to talk to her. But then I see James down the hall, leaning against the lockers. He's got a phone in his hand, twisting it between his fingers as if he's waiting for something.

"I have to run to the bathroom," I say to Kevin, catching him by surprise.

"But—"

"Does The Program limit how many times I can relieve my bladder now?" I ask.

Kevin smiles. "No," he says. "That still belongs to you. I'll wait for you though." He stands at my locker and I cross the hall, rushing into the girl's bathroom. Once inside a stall, I take out my phone.

I THINK YOU HAVE AN ADMIRER. HE LOOKS GOOD IN WHITE.

I don't recognize the number, but I know it's James. I lean against the wall and respond: WELL, APPARENTLY YOU'RE BAD NEWS. NOT SUPPOSED TO TALK YOU AGAIN. EVER.

I bite my lip, wondering how he'll answer. If he'll say that maybe they're right, that we shouldn't be around each other. But my phone vibrates instantly.

YEAH. THAT'S PROBABLY NOT GOING TO HAPPEN. WANT TO SKIP OUT?

I laugh, thrilled at how quickly he dismissed the idea. HOW?

I'LL DISTRACT YOUR BOYFRIEND. MEET AT MY CAR IN TEN?

God, James is going to get me flagged. But at the same time, I can't help it. I really, really want to leave with him right now. And my mother . . . How dare she turn me in. I'm so mad at her I almost want to get caught just to spite her.

But I push that idea away, knowing that I don't want to go back to The Program. I couldn't do it again, especially without Realm. I close my eyes, my heart racing in my chest. I want to go with James. But it's too early to use another pass. They'll be suspicious.

I CAN'T RIGHT NOW, I type back. ANOTHER TIME?

James doesn't answer right away, and I worry that he's annoyed or that he's already started some elaborate plan to get us out. I wonder how much longer I should wait when a message pops up.

ANOTHER TIME.

"Your handler looks like he's got a stick up his ass today," Lacey says. She reaches into her lunch bag, but instead of taking out cupcakes, she holds a shiny red apple. When she sees me notice, she bites into it. "Need to watch my figure."

"You look great," I tell her, but she waves me away.

"Don't try to change the subject," she says. "What did you get busted for? I've seen him crowding you today."

I sigh. "It *might* have been because I was with James Murphy yesterday. And when he dropped me off he was shirtless and covered in mud. But nothing happened."

"Clearly."

I smile, but soon it fades as I think about how Kevin found out. "My mother betrayed me," I say quietly. "She called the handler on me."

"Whoa," Lacey says. "That's pretty harsh." We don't talk

for a while as I pick at my food and Lacey polishes off her apple. When we're both done, she meets my eyes from across the table. "I'm sorry," she says. "I don't know what I'd do if my parents did something like that to me. It's . . ." She exhales. "I'm just sorry."

I smile gratefully and let the conversation ease back into normal things. Lacey is going out of town this weekend with her new, older boyfriend. I'm a little envious, but I'm glad she seems happy. I run my eyes over the cafeteria until I find the spot where James always sits, but today the seat is empty.

James is nowhere in sight.

My mother doesn't speak to me at dinner, which is just as well because I don't want to talk to her. My father looks between us helplessly, but neither me nor my mother bother to explain. When I'm done, I dump my plate in the sink and go to hide out in my room.

I read over James's texts a dozen times, thinking that he's definitely flirting. He made it sound like they couldn't keep him away from me, and that in itself is incredibly romantic. Unless I'm reading too much into it, which is entirely possible. Maybe he just likes the challenge of getting around The Program. Or maybe he just wants to piss them off.

I wonder how he got my number. Like Realm, he might break into things, steal files. I definitely wouldn't put it past him. James is bad. And that makes him sort of good.

There's a noise from downstairs, like a plate breaking. It

startles me, and I turn toward my door. My father's voice is loud, carrying up the stairs as he tells my mother to stop. That she's causing it. I hold my breath when he says that it's her fault.

Are they talking about me?

I've never heard my parents argue before, but it feels familiar somehow. Tears begin to well up in my eyes as emotions flood me, emotions I can't remember and yet they hurt. They sting. My mother's voice is barely audible from here, so I ease to the door to listen more closely. Then it hits me—a sudden pain in my head.

I moan against it, staggering back. It's like a screwdriver to my frontal lobe, and I nearly collapse. Am I having an aneurysm? Am I dying?

I don't know what's happening, and I'm terrified as I try to get to my door, to call for help. Then an image fills my mind—a brightly colored memory among all the foggy ones. I see myself holding something in my hands, lifting my mattress and stuffing objects in a slit there. There's a slit in my mattress?

The pain fades to a dull ache, and I collapse against my closed door, trying to catch my breath. Is it possible that I remembered something? I slowly climb to my feet and walk around the side of bed. I get down on the floor.

I lift the heavy mattress. I feel around underneath it, disappointed when I find nothing. I'm about to drop the mattress when I brush a bulge under the fabric. My heart leaps with anxiety and excitement. I duck my head down to look,

SUZANNE YOUNG

my arms starting to shake with the weight. And I see it, a small slit cut in the fabric.

It's real. I rest the corner of the mattress on my shoulder and pull out the objects. *What the hell?*

There's a plastic purple ring and the white backing of a picture. Why are these in my bed? And why do I remember hiding them?

I drop the mattress and then sit on it, setting the ring aside as I flip the picture over. When I do, shock floods my body.

It's a picture of Brady—possibly just before he died, but I don't remember. And next to him . . . Next to him with his arm around him is James. James from my math class is standing with my dead brother. Smiling.

CHAPTER EIGHT

FROM THE DOORWAY OF OUR NEAR-EMPTY CLASS-
room I see James sitting at his desk, his notebook open as he
appears to be drawing. I turn and look at my handler. "I forgot
my book," I say, having left it in my locker on purpose. "Any
chance you could grab it for me? I don't want to be late."

I walk purposely toward my seat in the front, pausing there
as if reminding Kevin that he's already taken care of my problem
of oversocialization. He nods and says he'll be right back. But the
minute he's through the door, I stomp over to James's desk. He
doesn't look up, just continues to shade in the picture of a figure
with long, curly hair that he's been drawing in his notebook.

I pull the picture of him and Brady from my pocket and
slam it down on his open page, startling him.

He sits back in his chair, staring up at me. "What the hell?"

"How did you know my brother?" I ask, poking hard at his image on the picture. James's blue eyes are confused, and when he looks down at the picture of him and Brady, he pales considerably.

James pulls the picture from under my hand and examines it. "I've never seen this before," he says.

"And my brother?"

James swallows hard. "I don't know him."

"Then why are you at the river together? Why is your arm over his shoulder? My God, were you friends with him?"

James continues to study the picture and then hands it to me, rubbing roughly at his face. "Go back to your seat before the handler comes in," he says, no emotion in his voice.

"I need to know if you—"

"Later," he snaps. "Now go." James's face is hard, and I know he's not going to tell me anything more right now. Our teacher enters the room, and I stuff the picture into my pocket and hurry toward the front, angry that I'll have to wait for answers.

Just as I slide into my chair, Kevin walks back in and lays the book on my desk. He goes to the back to stand watch, making sure no one interferes with me. But I feel like I've already started to unravel.

I haven't told Lacey about the picture, intent on confronting James first. Could that be why he's really been talking to me? Did he have something to do with my brother's death? I feel deceived, and I'm not even completely convinced I should—

not if James doesn't know the answer either. But more than anything, it's almost like I can get part of my brother back. I just need James to fill in the gaps in my memory.

I barely pick at my food and nod at Lacey at all the right times. I wait for James to sit at his table, but he doesn't come to lunch again. I want to scream and run out looking for him. Glancing over at Kevin, I see him chatting with a teacher, and I take out my phone. I scroll through to find James's last message and hit reply.

I WANT TO TALK. NOW.

I hold my breath, setting my phone on the table as I wait for him to respond. I glance at the clock and see there are only ten minutes left of lunch. My fingers are actually trembling. The phone vibrates, and I nearly knock over my Diet Coke trying to get to it.

"Holy hell, Sloane," Lacey says. "You doing okay?"

"Fine," I tell her, and pull up the message.

BASEMENT. NEAR STORAGE ROOM.

Oh, yeah. That sounds like a fantastic idea. I wonder if he wants to get caught. I take another cautious look at Kevin.

"What's going on?" Lacey asks seriously, leaning toward me. "You're doing something devious. I can see it in your eyes."

"I need to get out of here," I whisper.

"Tell me about it."

"No, I mean, I need to get out right now. Do you think I can?"

"Oh!" She peeks over her shoulder, finding my handler still

talking with the teacher. Lacey nods her chin to the back stair-well. "There," she says. "If you move quickly he won't notice the door open."

I bite my lip, not sure if I can get away with this. Wondering how long it'll take Kevin to find me. But then I decide that I have to take the chance. "Hey," I tell her, smiling weakly. "If I get dragged away, try and remember me okay?"

"You got it. Now go."

I back out of my chair, walking slowly and calmly toward the exit. When I'm close, I look at Kevin. His back is to me. My heart racing, I escape the cafeteria.

The storage room door is heavy, and it creaks when it opens. It's freaky, and I debate whether I should be in here at all. It's dark.

"Over here." James's voice comes from the corner, desks and old boxes stacked around him. I can't see him well, but I keep moving. When his hands touch my upper arms, I jump, making a soft sound. "Sorry," he says. "I can't find the light."

I stare until his outline starts to come into focus; the place so dark it's like we're the only people in the world. God, I'm an idiot for being here. I cross my arms over my chest, even though he can't see me. Just then the room fills with light, and I find James near the wall with his hand on the switch. When he looks at me, my expression is deadly serious.

"How do you know Brady?" I ask.

"I told you that I don't. I've never seen him before. Did you ask him?"

His words sting, and I step back, the air pushed from my lungs.

"Well, did you?" he asks.

"James," I say, the tears thick in my voice. "My brother is dead." And the fact that he doesn't know him—that my brother is gone from his memory—makes me break down. Seeing the picture has stirred up the pain, the grief I must have felt but don't remember. I put my face in my hands, and then suddenly James pulls me to him as I quietly sob into his shirt.

"I'm so sorry," he says. "I had no idea. I'm an asshole, okay?"

"You are," I agree, but don't move away. I'd wanted James to know Brady. I wanted him to tell me about him. And now it's like I've lost my brother all over again.

"Stop crying," James says softly. "You can't go back to class like that."

"I'm not going back," I say, straightening from his arms. "I hate this place. I hate everything."

"Believe me, Sloane," he says. "I can relate. But I don't want you to do anything stupid. How do you plan on getting out?" James tucks my hair behind my ears. I let him, but lower my eyes.

"Not sure."

"I can help," he offers. "I've made skipping class into a fine art. I have the clearance code of a Program doctor. The office won't know it's expired unless they check into it and see he's retired."

"Really?" I sniffle and wipe at my cheeks.

"I'm not an amateur," he says. "Technically I'm at therapy

right now. But if I sneak you out, do you want to grab lunch or something? I'm starving."

I wait, still wanting to be mad at him for not knowing my brother, but realistically knowing it's not his fault. "It depends," I murmur.

"On what?"

"Do you think . . . Do you think we can get our memories back?" I ask.

"No," he says sadly. "I've asked everyone. Researched it. And from what I can tell . . . No." His voice takes on a hard edge, and I like it. I like the anger there.

"But do you want to try?" I ask. "You can come by my house, look at Brady's stuff and see if you remember anything?"

"Will you make me a sandwich?"

I smile. "Yeah. I guess."

James is quiet, and I think he's going to refuse, but then he takes out his phone and dials, dissolving into the voice of an old man—pretty expertly, I must admit. And when he's done he looks nervous, as if coming with me might start something he's not sure of. But we leave anyway. Together.

"Your parents coming home anytime soon?" James asks as we pause on my back porch.

There is a tiny burst of butterflies, even though I try not to notice them. "No, not for a little while."

Kevin had rushed off campus after James called in an emergency at the other high school, so luckily I didn't have to lie to his face. The office bought the phony call without question. I'm almost scared at how good James is at getting around the rules.

"Will they be able to tell if we go through their stuff?" James asks, as we step inside my cluttered kitchen. The pots from last night's dinner are still on the stove, dishes next to the sink.

"I hope not." I push the door closed behind us, and lock it. James looks around the room, taking it in and then glances back at me.

"Familiar?" I ask.

He shakes his head. "Sorry. No."

I'm definitely disappointed as I lead James upstairs, wishing he could tell me what he knows about Brady. I want to find out if he has any details about how my brother died. How I survived it. But he's nothing short of confused as he follows behind me. We pause at a door.

"This was my brother's room," I say quietly. Tears start to itch behind my eyes, but I blink them away.

James passes me and walks inside, looking over the room as if he's hoping it'll just hit him. But as the minutes tick by, it seems less and less likely. When his blue eyes finally meet mine, the apology is in them. I turn and walk out into the hallway.

It doesn't seem real, how part of our lives can just be wiped out. How James and I can share a connection and yet not even know what it is. He knew Brady. How could he forget him? I'm starting down the hall, James behind me, when I hear him stop.

"Your bedroom?"

I turn and see him standing at my door. "Yep."

"Can I see it?"

"Why?"

"Just curious."

I should say no and lead him out before my parents get home, but it's nice having him around. It's nice knowing I'm not the only person feeling helpless. James walks into my room and wanders around, looking though the pile of junk on my dresser, testing the softness of my bed. When he sees me watching him, he smiles.

"I know I'm loathsome. You don't have to say it."

"I'll try not to."

He laughs then and gets up. "Can I see the picture again?" he asks. I'm leaning against the doorframe when I take the photo out of my jeans, and then James is right in front of me. Close.

He takes the picture from my hand, studying my face as he does. My breath catches and I don't say anything. "He looks like you," James murmurs, glancing again at the image.

"We were related." But my heart isn't into the sarcasm, and it just comes out sad. James seems to notice.

"I'm sorry he's gone," he whispers, examining me once again. "And I'm sorry I don't remember."

It breaks my heart to hear him say that. I don't even know if he and Brady were that close, but the ache that I have tells me that they had to be.

Without thinking, I lean forward and hug James, making him stagger backward against the other side of the doorway. At first his hands are awkwardly at my hips as I rest my head on his chest. His arms wrap around me protectively, the shock of his touch almost jarring in its comfort.

"I'm sorry," I say suddenly, and straighten up. I back away, not sure there is anything I can tell him to make the impromptu affection less awkward. But James grabs my wrists and pulls me to him again, this time hugging me tightly like he's the one who needs it.

We stand like that, his heart pounding against mine. James rests his hand under my hair at the back of my neck. "I like this," he says. "And it's weird because we don't really know each other, but . . ." He trails off and I don't try to fill in the words for him because I know what he means.

Me and him, together like this. It's the strangest feeling, full of things I don't understand, both comfort and agony. But the one thing I am sure of is that I feel is safe.

"James," I say.

"Sloane."

"I think we've done this before." I'm so certain, and yet, I'm not sure what to think about it. How can I feel so close to someone I don't know?

A long silence passes and then James moves me back, his hand still on my neck. "I should go," he says. "I'll . . . I'll talk to you tomorrow." His face is a mask of uncertainty, and I wish I hadn't said anything, hadn't insinuated that we'd been more than friends. He looks completely freaked out.

"I'm sorry—" I start to say, but he shakes his head.

"You have absolutely nothing to be sorry about," he answers, sounding kind. Polite. He turns then, walking out into the hall, and all I can do is follow him. My eyes are stinging with the start of tears. I don't want him to leave.

When he gets to the back door, he pauses, holding it open, but not looking back. "I really am sorry about your brother, Sloane," he says.

And I don't have time to answer before he leaves me standing alone in my kitchen.

CHAPTER NINE

I LIE IN MY BED, THE PURPLE RING ON MY FINGER.
Why would I save something like this? It's just a cheap plastic
ring. I bring my hand closer, praying for some clarity. But it
doesn't come.

Turning on my side, I examine the picture again. It makes
my heart ache to see how happy Brady looks, and to know I'll
never see that expression again. And next to him is James, just
as carefree.

I'm confused and hurt by how James treated me today. I
don't understand if I said something wrong, pushed him too
far. I thought he was having the same feelings, but I guess not.
I can't wrap my brain around his behavior, and more than that,
I feel rejected.

I'm just looking for what I lost.

I avoid James when I go back to school, which is just as well since Kevin seems to be constantly at my side. I half expect to find him in the bathroom with me when I brush my teeth at night. But when I hit week two of recovery, he pulls me aside in the hallway after math class.

"Here," he says, handing me a small piece of paper. I look down at the address on it, and then at him.

"Michael will be waiting for you." Kevin nods toward the paper. "But Sloane," he says cautiously, "they've pulled me off your case. I'm not sure if you'll get a new handler or . . . what is going on. That's why I'm giving you Michael's contact info." He exhales then, as if he's truly sad to leave me here. And although I'm glad to not have him watching me anymore, I hope they don't give me another handler.

"Be careful," Kevin whispers as he backs away, watching me until he turns to leave.

I wait a beat. Kevin seemed nervous about something, but Realm will know what's going on. He always seems to know everything.

"Sloane?"

I'm staring blankly into my locker when he says my name. James is next to me, and I immediately roll my eyes. "Go away," I say. "I'm not in the mood for your hot and cold affection today."

"You're saying you want my affection?" He grins, but I don't return it.

"Look," I tell him. "Just because I said that I thought we'd"—I lower my voice—"comforted each other before, doesn't mean I was propositioning you. You didn't have to run off and make me feel stupid like that."

His smile fades. "I know."

I wait, but he doesn't expand. "*You know?* Wow, thanks for the apology. Nice talking with you, James." I move to walk away, but he reaches out to take my elbow.

"Wait," he says quietly. "Don't be mad. I have my reasons."

"And you don't care to share them?"

"Not really. But maybe I'm not as tough as you think." I'd say he was repeating some cheesy line he'd heard in a movie except for the fact that he looks miserable when he says it. I gently take my arm from his grasp before people notice.

"So what do you want now?" I ask him seriously.

"I wish I knew, Sloane. But I am interested in finding out more about your brother. About . . . you. I mean, we could have all been friends."

I nod. "You looked pretty happy in the picture."

"I just wish we could get our memories back."

It occurs to me then that Realm might know what to do. He's always been one step ahead, always known more about The Program than anybody.

"There is someone," I say. "He was my friend in The Program, and he's really smart. He might know what to do."

James looks me over as if trying to decipher some secret code, but then he shrugs. "Okay, who is he?"

"His name is Realm, and I have his address. I'm going to show up and see if he can help."

"Sounds like a terrible plan."

"Got a better one?"

James laughs. "Sloane, I never have a plan. Tell you what, how about you sneak out of your house tonight and meet me on the corner of Barron and Elm. I'll drive you to your boyfriend's house."

Realm's not my boyfriend, but I decide not to deny or acknowledge it. I agree to meet James at the corner at six, but I can see the uncertainty in his eyes, as if he's still trying to figure out who Realm is to me. And I leave him like that, glad to let him wonder about me for once.

The house is set back from the street, hidden down a long gravel driveway behind large trees. As we pull up, the rocks crunch under the tires, and I take in how isolated it looks. A small wood-shingled house surrounded by a forest, a few dead flowers in the beds.

"You sure you know this guy?" James asks. "This looks like a place where unsuspecting teenagers come to have sex and get murdered."

I laugh and look sideways at him. "Don't embarrass me in front of my friend. Realm's a good guy."

"Was he more than a friend? Not that it's any of my business." He lowers his eyes. A sudden rush of guilt spreads over me.

"No, it's okay to ask. He, um . . . It was complicated, I guess."

James doesn't say anything but I can feel a heavy silence fill the car. Not sure what else to do, I open the door and get out, waiting for James to follow me up to the house. On the front porch, I'm overwhelmed with nervousness and excitement. I'm about to see Realm again. It's been over a month. Will he look different? I know I do.

The door opens just a crack as he peers out, reminding me of how he would do that in The Program when we were sneaking around. My smile spreads, and then the door flies open and Realm steps forward, swinging me into a big hug before I can even get a look at him.

"Hey, sweetness," he says, crushing me against him. "I can't believe you're here."

Realm smells good, not like detergent and soap, but of clean skin. A hint of cologne. I pull back to look at him. His hair is shorter, his complexion less ghostly. It's then that he notices James leaning against the porch railing.

"Oh, hi," Realm says, sounding surprised. He offers his hand and James takes it. "Michael Realm," Realm says.

"James Murphy."

The smile abruptly falls from Realm's face, and I see the color that was just there drain away. "Nice to meet you," he practically whispers, and takes a step back. He shoots a dark look at me.

"Come in." He pushes the door open and motions for us to enter. James thanks him, and I can't help but see the small bit of satisfaction in his expression at Realm's discomfort.

We stand around the entry as Realm follows us in and then bolts the door. The house is more like a cabin with exposed wooden beams and a rustic decor. It doesn't strike me as something Realm would be into, but then I don't really know what he was like before The Program. Neither does he.

"So how've you been, Sloane?" he asks, checking me over.

"Weird," I say. "Everything has been a little weird for me. You?"

"Oh, I'm just peachy."

Realm leads us into the living room, and I sit on the couch while James takes a chair near the fireplace. Realm collapses next to me, wrapping me in a hug once again. "God, I've missed you," he says. "And I like the hair."

"You said not to change it."

"Well, I was wrong. You look great. Healthy, too." He glances at James, who is pretending to be fascinated by a painting of eagles on the wall. "So," Realm says, dropping his arms in front of him and settling into the cushions. "How do you two know each other?"

"We're not dating, if that's what you're really asking," James says evenly.

Realm smiles. "I'm not asking that."

James nods. "Fair enough."

There's a small sting to my self-esteem as James quickly dismisses our relationship, but I ignore it and touch Realm's arm to draw his attention. "We're here because I need your help," I say.

"I'd do anything for you."

At that second, an odd sensation comes over me and I

pause, trying to place it. It's not romantic, almost cautious . . .
But it's gone before I can finish the thought. Like an emotional
déjà vu.

I reach into my back pocket and take out the picture, giving it to Realm. When he sees it he sucks in a harsh breath.
"Where did you get this?" he asks immediately.

"I found it. It was strange. I was home, and then all of a
sudden I had this flash of a memory, a memory from before. I
saw myself putting this picture into a slit in my mattress. That's
my brother," I say, pointing to Brady's face. "And that's him." I
jerk my thumb over my shoulder and hear James chuckle.

Realm's jaw is tightly clenched, and he hands me back the
photo. "And what are you asking me?" His voice is cold.

"I don't remember her brother," James interrupts. "I want
to know how to get my memories back."

Realm eyes him. "You can't."

"I don't believe you," James says, as if sensing something in
Realm's voice. James had said that he didn't think we could get
our memories back, but he must have changed his mind.

"Realm," I say, trying to diffuse the tension building
between him and James. "You told me in The Program that if
I needed you, you'd help me. What did you mean? How did I
have that memory?"

Realm intertwines his fingers with mine as he stares down
at them, his hand cool. "Remember Roger?"

My stomach twists at the name. Although it's foggy, I do
remember the creepy handler. "Yeah."

"The purple pill?"

I pause. There's the hint of a memory, an overpowering taste of peppermint. I shiver, my thoughts jumbled as if they've been manipulated somehow. But there had been a pill, and I took it. "He said I could save a memory," I murmur.

"Wait," James speaks up. "You got to save a memory? How did that work?"

"Later," I tell him. He scoffs, looking like he's about to walk out.

"I told you then, Sloane." Realm takes his hand from mine. "The memory would show up out of context, confusing you more. You shouldn't have taken it."

"Well, I did. Now how do I get more?"

Realm's brown eyes look at me sadly. "You really can't. The memories are gone. Permanently."

"But I want to know who I was," I say. "I want to know what happened to Brady. What happened to me."

"You should just move on. Start over. It's the best—"

"What is your deal?" James calls out. "Do you work for The Program or something? Who would tell someone to forget their past? We want to know, shithead. I want to know how I knew her brother."

Realm shakes his head but doesn't lose his cool. Instead he gets up and walks to the fridge to grab a beer. He doesn't offer us one. After a long sip, he stares at James. "You're kind of a dick," Realms says.

James shrugs. "Tell me something I don't know. And

besides, you're really not all that different from us, are you? You've got a real pretty scar on your neck. Do you remember how you got it?"

"I don't want to."

"Wouldn't you want to know so that you don't make the same mistakes again?"

Realm laughs, sounding bitter. "That's the great thing, James Murphy. Some mistakes are destined to repeat themselves." He looks at me then, and then takes another long sip of beer. "Right, Sloane?"

I'm completely thrown off by Realm's behavior. "I have no idea what you're talking about," I say. "I'm here to find out about my brother, about my past. And I don't know why you're acting like this. You sent Kevin to watch over me. You offered to help."

"To help you move on," he says softly, his eyes weak. "Not . . . *this*."

"Ah," James says from the fireplace. "Now it makes sense. Sloane, let's go. He's not interested in helping. He just wanted to get in your pants."

"Why don't *you* just leave?" Realm snaps. "I don't recall inviting you."

James grins. "Maybe you did and don't remember."

Realm seems to tire of the back and forth with James, and finishes his beer before leaning against the counter and rubbing hard at his face. I can see that something is tearing him up. Something beyond James and me.

"You know, don't you?" I say, suddenly sure. I cross the room to stop in front of him. "You know something about my past."

He grabs another beer out of the fridge, starting in on it before leveling his stare on mine. "Maybe. But I wish I didn't. I don't want to hurt you."

"Dude," James says likes he's ready to fight. "I swear—"

Realm reaches out then, running his fingers lovingly through my hair. His look is far away, and I'm suddenly embarrassed, like we're sharing an intimate moment. Realm and I were never together. Not like that. But the familiarity of his movement shuts James up.

"You talked in The Program," Realm says. "We would talk about our lives sometimes when we were in bed."

It's like a slap in the face, the way Realm makes it sound like there was something going on between us. The coldness with which he says it.

"And you said I'm a dick?" James asks, laughing. "Not really an appropriate topic for company, do you think, Michael?"

"It's Realm."

"Yeah, well. I'll call you what I want. And I think you should apologize because Sloane doesn't strike me as the kiss-and-tell type." He straightens. "Or maybe I should just beat your ass right now."

"No," I say, swallowing hard. "I don't want any fighting." I look at James. "It's fine. I promise it's fine."

James nods and sits back down, his arms crossed over his chest.

"I didn't mean that," Realm says. "And we weren't sleeping together," he tosses to James, although it's obvious that he doesn't want to clear that part up. "We were . . . just friends."

"Who share a bed," James mutters. "I'm sure."

"Realm," I say, ignoring James's comment. "What did I tell you? And how do you remember? I don't recall anything personal about anybody."

Realm leans against the counter and drains at least half of his beer as I wait. "You have to understand something, sweetness. Your head"—he taps lightly at my temple—"is a very delicate place right now. The pieces were fit back together like fine china. One crack, like that picture, can shatter the whole thing. I don't want to hurt you. I really don't. If we just give it some time . . ."

I lean into him, putting my hands on his chest as I stare up at him. *"Please."*

Realm looks defeated, and finally nods. "Your brother didn't die in a rafting accident, Sloane. That was something The Program made up. Brady killed himself. And you—both you and his best friend, James—were there when he did."

I gasp, Brady's image filling my mind. "No," I say, staggering back. "My brother didn't . . . My parents said it was an accident. Why would they lie? Why would . . . ?" I feel like I might hyperventilate, and then there's an arm over my shoulder. James walks me to the couch, helping me sit down. "No," I say again.

The room is quiet for a while as I try to gather myself.

I search my memory, looking for anything about Brady that could have led to this. But all I can see is my brother happy and smiling. What could have happened to him?

James uses his thumbs to swipe under my eyes. "It's going to be okay, Sloane," he says firmly. And the way he says it, so absolute, fills me with a sort of security. I turn back to Realm.

"You shouldn't have kept that from me," I tell him, feeling betrayed.

Realm sets his empty bottle on the counter, looking at the fridge like he means to get another. "This can make you sick again. I'm risking your life telling you this and . . . God. What am I doing? It's too soon. Please, Sloane, this doesn't change anything. You have to move on. You're safe. I need you to be safe."

I feel James tense next to me.

"What else?" I ask, my voice barely a whisper. "What else do you know, Realm? You have to tell me."

Realm stares at me, his face pained. And then he shakes his head. "That's all I have. I'm sorry."

"Realm—"

"I think you should go now." He pushes away from the counter and strides over to the door. He unlocks it and pulls it open, not looking back at us.

"What?" I say. "No, you—"

"Sloane." His tone is final as he glances at me. "I want you to leave."

"This is bullshit," James says, getting up. He takes my

hand. I watch Realm's eyes flash as James holds my fingers in his, but he looks away.

Knowing I can't leave like this, I pull my hand from James's. "I'll meet you outside in a sec," I say. James narrows his blue gaze on mine, a look so full of suspicion that I almost step away from it. Then he nods and leaves, shoulder-bumping Realm on the way.

Realm laughs bitterly. "Lovely meeting you, Mr. Murphy."

When we're alone, I walk over to Realm. He stares at me, his jaw set in a challenge, but his eyes are almost desperate. And suddenly, I hug him. He chokes out what sounds like a cry as he holds me tight to him.

"I've missed you so much," he whispers. "I've tried to keep you safe, Sloane. And then I'm the one who hurt you. I shouldn't have told you about Brady."

I pull back. "I want to know all of it," I say. "You have to tell me everything. I don't understand why my brother would kill himself." The tears threaten to come again, and Realm puts his palm on my cheek.

"He was just sick. It wasn't your fault."

"Then why did they take the memory?"

Realm closes his eyes. "I can't talk about this right now, sweetness. I've messed up huge. I need . . . I need to think. You shouldn't have found that picture."

"Yes," I tell him. "I should have."

"I want you to be happy," he says. "I swear it's all I want." He throws a cautious glance toward the car where James has his

head against the steering wheel as if he's tired of waiting. Realm exhales. "You should go for now, okay?" Then he leans forward and kisses my cheek, pausing there for a long moment.

"What if I don't want to go?" I ask, hoping he'll tell me more about my brother, my past.

Realm seems to consider my question. "There are so many things you can't understand right now," he says. "But I need you to know that all I've ever wanted was for you to get better. Do you believe that?"

I nod. "I do."

"I just . . . I love you," he whispers, not able to look at me.

"I know." And I don't have anything else to say back. Right now I'm completely grief-stricken, feeling like I've just lost Brady, even though he's been gone for years. But here's Realm, so ready to love me. Take care of me. Fill up the empty spaces in my heart.

I get on my tiptoes and press my lips firmly to his. Realm responds immediately, surprising me by backing me against the wall, his tongue eagerly finding mine as if he's been waiting to do this since I got here.

My heart pounds, but the emotion is guilt, as if I'm being completely unfair. To him. To myself. I turn away then, breaking the kiss to hug him instead. Realm lets out a soft laugh, clinging to me tightly.

"You don't love me back," he says.

"Not like that. But maybe—"

"Maybe someday?" he finishes for me. Realm looks tired.

Maybe a little buzzed. "You should go," he says again, and walks me onto the porch, keeping his eyes trained on the floorboards there. Then, without another word, he goes back into the house and bolts his door shut.

I stand there, still stunned by the revelation about my brother. I look at the car, and James is watching me. He nods his chin as if asking if I'm okay, but I don't respond. I'm not okay.

I'm so not okay.

CHAPTER TEN

WE'RE HALFWAY BACK TO TOWN, PASSING DARKENED fields, when James looks sideways at me. "That was some kiss," he says.

A blush rises on my cheeks. "I was saying good-bye."

"With your tongue."

"What do you care?" I ask, ashamed that he saw, even though I'm not entirely sure why. "You couldn't even stand to hug me in my room that day."

"I took that hug like a trooper," he says with a smirk. "And I don't care who you make out with. I just think he's hiding something, so I'm surprised you'd be so naive. Thought you were smarter than that."

"And I thought you weren't going to be obnoxious."

"Never said I wouldn't be obnoxious," James says. "I try not to make promises I can't keep."

We're silent for a few miles, and I start thinking again about my brother. Brady had an accident—that's what my mother told me. She said he'd been rafting, but she never said I was there. She never said he killed himself.

I sniffle, and it's then that I realize I'm crying. "Hey," James says softly. "I'm sorry. I don't mean to be—"

"It's not you," I say, waving off his concern. James glides the car to the side of the road and parks. "I'm thinking about my brother," I tell him. "I don't remember him dying. But we were there, James. Me and you. What if we helped him kill himself?"

"Maybe we did." His voice is empty. Sad. He looks away, as if he's searching his own memories. When he lowers his head, I know he's found nothing. We have nothing.

"What if he said good-bye?" I whisper. "What if he said good-bye and I don't remember it?" Something inside of me breaks then, and I start to sob, picturing Brady's smile, hearing his laugh. We were so close. How long had he been sick? And how could I not have noticed?

James puts his hand on my shoulder, and I lean into him. He's stiff at first but then rearranges himself in the seat to let me rest against his chest.

"You know," he says softly, brushing back my hair as he talks, "I can't remember what happened to my mother. I know that one day she was there, and then she was gone. I don't know if my parents fought, if she had a reason for leaving. When I asked my father, he told me that she had moved away for a job and then decided to stay. But that we were fine on our own." He pauses. "Ten bucks says his hand is bullshit."

I stop and wipe at my face, sitting up, but staying close to him. He looks at me wide-eyed. "What?" he asks.

"We played Bullshit in The Program. Did you?"

He laughs. "Uh, no. I was in isolation most of the time, or at least, that's what they told me. Seriously? You got to play cards?"

"James," I say. "I used to play Bullshit all the time with my brother."

His face clouds over, and he reaches absently, tugging at a string hanging down from the bottom of my collared shirt. "Really?"

I nod. "I bet . . . I bet you played with us."

James doesn't meet my eyes, but pulls slowly on the string, unraveling the hem as if he's lost in a thought. "I can't remember who taught me," he says.

"My brother did."

"Possibly."

When the string finally breaks, James seems startled by the now uneven hem of my shirt. "Damn, I'm sorry." But when he looks up, I don't respond. I can feel the puffiness of my face, and I'm sure that, up close, still half-leaning on him, I don't look great. But I'm trying to find something in his eyes— a feeling that I can identify. There are so many emotions raging inside of me: guilt, sadness, attraction.

"Why are you staring at me again?" he asks, although this time he doesn't sound like he's teasing me.

"Realm said something to me before I left."

James rolls his eyes. "Oh, yeah? What was that?"

"He said . . ." I pause, not sure I should even tell him. But it seems wrong to keep it from him. To keep anything from him. "He said that he loved me," I say.

James lowers his head, twirling the piece of string around his finger. "And how do you feel?" he asks.

"Not the same."

"Probably shouldn't lead him on by kissing him then, huh?" His tone is harsh, judgmental. I'm frozen for a second. I'd confided in him only to have him throw it back in my face.

I move away from James then, pulling my seat belt on and making it lock a few times in the process. "Just forget it," I say. "You wouldn't understand."

"You're right." He switches the car into gear. "I don't understand. And you don't owe me an explanation."

"Thanks," I say bitterly. "Glad you cleared that up." We don't speak again, and I wonder how James can confess to me about his mother, only to turn cold in the next second. I wonder if he used to do this to Brady when they were friends. To me.

I wonder if it was always this difficult to be around him.

When I get home, I slip through the back door, hoping my parents didn't notice that I was gone for the last hour. I can hear the sound of the TV in the living room as I climb the stairs, pausing at Brady's room.

I go inside and lie across my brother's bed, staring up at the ceiling and hoping it will reveal secrets. Stolen memories.

"What happened to you?" I ask, meaning it for both my brother and for myself. I'd searched my room, hoping to find something else, but there was nothing there. Hardly any pictures outside of family ones. There was no obituary for Brady, cut out and laminated with a prayer on the back. No newspaper article immortalized in a scrapbook.

I know better than to ask my mother, her lies seeming to mount. I'm not sure what happened to me and her, but I don't trust her anymore. She called Kevin to report me. I bet she had something to do with me getting sent to The Program in the first place.

In my pocket, my cell phone vibrates, and I quickly take it out, hoping it's Realm, even though we didn't exchange numbers. I pause when I see James's name flashing on the screen.

I click it off and put the phone back in my pocket. Being around him is so confusing. We share a past, but every time we get closer to finding out what it is, he backs away. He hurts me. I don't think I can take any more hurt right now.

I curl up on my side, thinking things over, when a knock on the door startles me. I look up to see my father. "Hey, honey," he says. "I was just coming up to say good night, but you weren't in your room. What are you doing in here?"

Blinking quickly, I sit up. "I miss Brady," I say, trying to gauge his reaction. His face falters, his brown eyes weary as he rubs at them.

"Me too," he answers. His khakis are wrinkled, and the faint smell of alcohol clings to him. I wonder when he started drinking.

We're quiet for a long moment, and I bite my lip, trying to decide if I should ask. "Dad," I start, "did Brady commit suicide?"

My father takes in a harsh breath. He doesn't respond right away as he lowers himself onto the bed next to me. And then, to my absolute horror, he covers his eyes with his hand; his shoulders are shaking.

"Yes," he chokes out. "Brady killed himself."

My body stills as my emotions click together, even though there are no memories attached. But it's like my feelings—my grief—finally make sense. As my father tries to pull himself together, I try not to fall apart. Realm told me the truth. What else does he know?

"And what about us?" I ask my father. "Were we okay after? Me, you, and Mom?"

My dad looks at me, his dark eyes unfocused and red-rimmed. "No, sweetheart," he whispers. "We really weren't."

I nod, knowing somewhere inside that it's true. That this idea of our family moving on so easily after losing Brady was absurd. "I hate that I can't remember what happened to him," I say.

"Why?" he asks seriously. "It's a gift. I would give anything to take away the pain. The time when he was sick . . . that

SUZANNE YOUNG

wasn't the real Brady. Not the real us. We've gotten the chance to reset, Sloane. We've gotten the chance to be happy again."

"Dad," I say softly, tears beginning to stream from my eyes. "None of us are happy."

He doesn't deny it, doesn't even try to pretend that our family is pulling through. Instead, he stands up, touching the top of my head as he leaves the room.

When he's gone, I curl up on the bed with my misery, alone and heartbroken. I want to know what happened to my brother, and I want to know what I used to be like. But most of all, I just want to be happy. After a short pity party, I go back to my room and find Lacey's number where she scribbled it into my notebook. A headache has begun pulsing in my head, so I take a large dose of Advil before picking up my phone.

Lacey is grinning from ear to ear when she pulls up to the corner at nine. "You're becoming such a rebel," she says, as I climb into her neon-green Bug. Fast-food bags are crumpled at my feet, all of the drink holders full. Lacey's wearing a plain, yellow blouse, but her makeup is dramatic—very nonreturner-like. It's awesome.

"Are you sure you want to go to the Wellness Center?" she asks. "I thought you hated that place."

"I do," I say. "But my handler is gone, and no one's watching me anymore. Maybe I'll enjoy the experience this time."

"Sloane," Lacey says in low voice. "They're always watching. Never forget that."

After a long pause, Lacey turns on the radio, filling the car with a pop song about love, its lyrics sickeningly sweet. I have to clasp my hands in front of me to stop from shutting it off and telling her all about James, about my brother. But I don't want to depress her.

In my pocket, my phone buzzes with another text message, but I reach to turn up the volume of the radio instead of checking it.

The Wellness Center is crowded when we walk in. With the popularity of The Program growing worldwide, there has been a new push for assimilation—I saw it on MTV. Handlers line the walls, but between them, people are laughing, playing games. There's a new section with computer stations; a group of guys are crowded around one of them. They're all dressed in preppy clothes, and I glance down at myself and see that we match. It's like the uniform of the returners. I unbutton my shirt to the line of my bra, and then follow behind Lacey as she makes her way to the couch.

I can't believe I came back here, especially after vowing not to. But I needed to get out of my house, and this is the only place where people my age hang out anymore. At least, the only place where people like me, who have no other friends, hang out. Lacey collapses into the cushions, scanning the room as if looking for someone.

"Who is he?" I ask, nudging her with my elbow.

She widens her eyes innocently. "No idea what you mean. I swear I'm not searching for the guy who promised he'd be here tonight."

"Oh," I say, smiling. "So I finally get to meet your mystery boyfriend?"

Lacey turns to me. "I think it's about time." Her expression is more serious than I expect, but before I can ask for more details, I catch a black shirt out of the corner of my eye, the color shocking within this room. It's Liam.

"I'll be right back," I say quickly, jumping up.

Liam weaves through the crowd before slipping out the door to the back patio. When I get outside, the night air is crisp around me. Liam's facing away as he stands at the railing, looking toward the parking lot. We're alone out here, but I want to ask him about that first night I came back. How he knew me and James.

"Hey," I say, drawing his attention. When he turns, I'm startled. Dark circles ring his eyes, and his hair is matted. Unwashed. It strikes me then that he's sick. Oh, God. He's sick.

"Sloane." His mouth pulls into a sneer, anger and hatred painting his features. "Did they send you to collect me? Are they recruiting returners now?"

My heart begins to thud in my chest, the idea that Liam's dangerous backing me slowly toward the door. "No one sent me," I say. "I just wanted to ask you something, but never mind. It's not that important."

Liam lunges, his shoulder banging against the door to stop me from opening it. I gasp and step back.

"I'd love to hear your question," he says, his eyes wild and unfocused.

"I just want to go inside," I say softly. "Move and I won't—"

"Won't what? Report me? Of course you will."

He's right. I will report him the first chance I get. He's infected. He can infect others. "Let me through, Liam," I say.

He stares at me, and then leans closer as if whispering a secret. "Do you remember me?" he asks.

"I remember you calling me a freak."

He smiles. "Before that."

There's a twist in my gut. "No." Just then the handle of the door turns, but Liam keeps his weight on it, preventing it from opening. I think about calling for help, or running, but at the same time, I don't want to draw that kind of attention to myself.

"We dated," he says, a bit of satisfaction in his voice. "Nothing serious, but they took that memory anyway. What else did they take? Don't you see what you are? You're empty. You're nothing. And I'd rather be dead than be like you."

My lip begins to quiver as I'm filled with shame and humiliation, but mostly anger. I reach out to push him, only succeeding in making him stagger a step. He laughs, and then coughs, bringing his hand to his mouth. When he pulls it away, there's blood smeared across his fingers.

"What's wrong with you?" I ask, stepping back.

"QuikDeath," he says. "Because there's no point. We'll never be free of The Program, and even when we are, who's to say they don't change the rules? That they don't come after us as adults? My cousin?" Liam says, tears beginning to gather in his eyes. "He killed himself yesterday. He was twenty-one, Sloane. That means the epidemic is evolving."

"Or maybe he just committed suicide," I say, my stomach in knots. Fists pound on the other side of the door, shaking it.

Liam coughs again, spitting blood onto the patio. Red streaks his lips. He's going to die. He's going to die if I do nothing to stop it. I reach to take out my phone, but Liam slaps it from my hand, sending it across the wooden planks.

His eyes momentarily roll back in his head before he focuses on me again. His body convulses. And then he collapses against the door, sliding to the ground, his eyes locked on mine. "You're no one," he whispers before he goes still altogether.

I pause only a second, my breaths coming out in quick gasps like I might hyperventilate. The door shakes again, and I decide that I can't be here when they find him. I can't be involved in this. So I run, grabbing my phone on the way, and scramble down the stairs into the parking lot of the Wellness Center. I text Lacey and tell her that I'm at the car. We have to leave. Now.

As I wait there, hiding, people flood the patio. Handlers move people aside, the Wellness staff clearly horrified that someone would commit suicide in such a safe place. I block out all the things that Liam told me. I block out his theories. Because an ache in my forehead is pulsing, worse than it was earlier.

When Lacey reaches me, she looks frazzled. She doesn't say a word as we speed away, leaving the Wellness Center behind us. When we're a safe distance away, she finally turns to me.

"Who was it?" she asks. "Who terminated?" Her face is pale with fear.

"Liam."

Her eyes widen. Then she turns back to the road, pressing her lips together. "Did you see it?"

"Yeah."

"You were smart to get out of there. Things are getting crazy. You feel it too, right?"

And I do. But I'm not sure I can handle any more talk of the epidemic tonight, not when my head is killing me. "Yes, but I have to get home," I say. "I don't want my parents to worry." But really, I have something else in mind. I need to talk about tonight, both about my dad and about Liam. I need to talk to someone who'll understand. I need James.

"Your parents?" Lacey sounds surprised. Then she tightens her grip on the steering wheel. "Maybe you're not as rebellious as I thought." She pulls up to the corner before my house. "Better get out here," she says. "Wouldn't want my car to give you away."

Her voice is tense, and I think she's shaken by the suicide. I just hope it's not enough to make her sick again. To make any of us sick.

CHAPTER ELEVEN

LATER THAT NIGHT, AS MY PARENTS SLEEP, I TAKE A massive amount of Advil, get into my mother's car, and drive to see James.

At the curb, I exhale and gaze at his large white house, wondering where his room is. I want to tell him that my father confirmed that Brady killed himself. And I want to tell him about what Liam said about the epidemic, and how I had to watch him die from QuikDeath.

In my hand, my phone vibrates. I hope my parents haven't realized that I'm missing. I check the screen.

WHY ARE YOU SITTING OUTSIDE OF MY HOUSE, STALKER?

I close my eyes. I'm just about to shove my phone back into my pocket and peel out, when it vibrates again. I shouldn't even read it.

STAY THERE.

Yeah, right. I can't face him now. I turn the ignition, but a figure streaks across the lawn toward my car. I swear under my breath and wait.

A second later the door opens, flooding me with uncomfortable light as James gets in. When we're immersed in dark again, I feel him staring at me. "Well?" he asks.

My heart races in my chest. I'm worried that he doesn't care about what I have to say. I shouldn't be here. "Forget it," I tell him, sounding exhausted. "This is dumb."

"Where were you tonight? I texted."

I meet his eyes. "I know. I went to the Wellness Center with Lacey. And something . . . happened." His shoulders tense, and I go on. "That guy Liam? He killed himself. He took QuikDeath, but not before saying that he and I used to date, calling me empty for not remembering. He said that his cousin committed suicide yesterday at the age of twenty-one. Liam says the epidemic is evolving—"

"You saw Liam die?" James asks, ignoring the rest.

I nod. "And I talked to my dad earlier," I say. "He's drinking; he and my mother are fighting. Everything's falling apart at home, but I finally asked him about my brother." Tears trickle over my cheeks. "Realm was telling the truth. Brady did kill himself." I'm consumed with grief, absolutely consumed.

"I'm sorry," James says.

I shake my head. "And I don't even know why I'm telling

you all this. You made it pretty clear that you're not interested in finding out about the past. I—"

"No," James says coolly. "I'm not interested in your love life. I am, however, interested in finding out what happened to your brother, and how I fit into it."

My face stings, and I turn fiercely toward him. "Why do you do that?" I ask. "Why do you say things that you know will hurt my feelings?"

He flinches, but then fixes me with an annoyed look. "Hurt your feelings? Sloane, I'm not your boyfriend. I don't even remember how we know each other. So whatever fantasy you've built up in your imagination, it's not real. Things weren't pretty before The Program, so let's not start pretending they were. Don't make this more complicated than it needs to be."

The pain in my head suddenly explodes, and I cry out, leaning forward against the steering wheel. It's as if a hammer has just been smashed into my forehead.

"Are you okay?" James touches my shoulder, sounding scared.

"Just get out." I close my eyes against the pain. I'm not sure what's happening to me, but it's intense. When I can straighten, James is trying to talk, but I don't listen. "Get out of the God-damn car, James!"

He waits long enough for me to wonder if he will. When the interior lights come on, I know he's leaving. The door slams, but I can't move for a minute, waiting for the pain in my head to pass. It doesn't. And now a cracking sensation rips inside my chest.

Your brain is like fine china.

I open my eyes, squinting as I look out the windshield. I have to find Realm. Something is wrong with me. I think I'm breaking.

It's dark as I drive up Realm's long driveway, my headache finally resolving into a bearable throbbing. It started raining the minute I pulled away from James's house—a sign of things to come, I guess. Now the pattering on my windshield comes harder. I hope Realm's home. He has to be.

I knock impatiently on the door, soaked from the walk to his porch. My shirt clings to me, and my pulse is loud in my ears as the headache continues, making me weak all over. When I hear the locks click, I practically push my way in.

"Sloane?" Realm stands there, rubbing at his hair, wearing just pajama pants and a terrified expression. "What are you doing here? What's wrong?"

"I'm falling apart," I tell him, sounding desperate. "I'm completely falling apart."

"Sweetness." Realm hugs me, and I put my cheek against the warm skin of his chest. "Sit down," he says, leading me to the couch. Outside, thunder booms in the sky, but Realm's living room is warm with the remains of a fire burning out. He sits next to me as I continue to shake, my wet clothes uncomfortable. "What's going on?" he asks.

"Headache," I say. "And pain in my chest as if my heart is being torn out. It's overwhelming. I don't think I can survive it."

"Shh . . . ," Realm says. "Of course you can. You survived

The Program, didn't you?" He pauses, letting out a harsh breath. "Is this because of what I told you about Brady? Did I cause this?"

"No. It's not your fault. I asked my dad, and he confirmed that my brother killed himself." I close my eyes, hating saying the words out loud. "And then I went to the Wellness Center, and this guy said I was nothing without my memories." I look up to meet Realm's gaze. "Am I nothing?"

"No. You've just been cured."

Cured. There was a time when I felt lucky to have been spared from the epidemic. But now it's left me a bundled mess, lost in my own life. "That guy from the center," I say. "He died in front of me tonight—QuikDeath. Afterward I went to tell James, but he was so cruel. Distant. And I don't know why, but it crushes me, the way James acts sometimes." I pause. "That's when the headache got worse, and the pain in my chest started. God, Realm. It's like I'm losing my mind."

Realm stares into his lap, his brow furrowed as if he's thinking. When he doesn't say anything, I take his hand. "Why do I hurt so badly?" I ask. "I haven't seen this in any other returners. I think I need my memories back."

"You don't," he says. "Sometimes it's better not to know."

I look at his downcast dark eyes, his scarred neck. I think about how he loves me, how he saved me in The Program too many times to count. My head pounds, my body aches, but I think that in this moment, maybe what I need is for someone to care about me.

So I lean forward and kiss him, ignoring the sharp guilt that attacks my conscience. I push it away and let my mouth capture Realm's. It takes a second for him to react, and then he's kissing me, his hand around my waist as he pulls me onto his lap, peeling off my wet shirt.

I want to forget about everything. I want to forget about James.

My chest fills again with jagged pain, but then Realm rolls me off the couch, getting on top of me as we lie on the carpet. He's kissing my neck, his hands searching my body as I try to feel him. Feel what it would be like to be with him.

But I'm a million miles away, and all I feel is lost and abandoned. I'm alone.

Realm's mouth stops at my ear, panting wildly. I realize that I'm on my back, staring at the ceiling as tears leak from the corners of my eyes. Realm's hand slides away from my breast, and he turns me toward him.

"You don't want this," he says, sadness in his voice. "You still love him."

His words startle me, but I don't argue. He's put a name to the emotion raging inside of me. I know suddenly that I do love someone. Someone else.

Realm tries to laugh it away, shaking his head. "God," he says. "He's such a dick, too." Realm lies next to me, shoulder to shoulder, as we both gaze up at the wooden-beamed ceiling.

"It's James, isn't it?" I ask softly, not sure what to do now.

"Yep," Realm answers. "You love him. Always have. And

not being with him is confusing. You may not remember him, but your heart does." Realm turns his face toward me. "I wanted to be the one to make you happy, but you'll always be his."

I swallow hard, not disbelieving it, but not understanding it either. Loneliness crawls over me. "No," I say. "That part of my life is over. I don't think he feels that way about me. At least not anymore."

"He does." Realm sighs. "He definitely does."

"Was it because of Brady?" I ask, thinking it's the clear explanation. "Is that why James was with me, because my brother died?"

"No. You loved each other. I believe the word you used was 'madly.'" He pauses. "You've always loved each other. You always will."

I lie next to Realm, half-naked on his floor, as he tells me that I love someone else—something I can't remember, but something I can feel. The frustration I came in with eases, although the headache is still there.

"And my headache?" I ask.

"Your brain is repairing itself. That one memory you had cracked the smooth sequence of events they placed in therapy. Your mind knows something is wrong. Now it's slowly binding back together. Let's just be glad it was one memory, and not all of them."

I look sideways at him, wondering if he truly believes that I'm better this way. "Why don't you want me to remember everything?" I ask. "What could I have told you that was so awful that it's worth living like this?"

Realm smiles sadly. "Some things are better left in the past. For all our sakes." Tears run from his eyes then, and I think about what I've done to him tonight, how I've wronged him.

"So if I have these feelings about James, where does it leave you?"

"In love with a girl who loves another. Very Shakespearean, if you ask me."

I lean into him, putting my hand over his heart and wishing I could care about him in the same way. But even now, even when James is still so far away from me, I know that I can't love Realm. He's not mine.

We settle in next to each other, the coals in the fireplace burning out. "The guy that died," I say quietly. "He said the epidemic is spreading to adults." Realm tenses. "What happens if that's true?" I ask.

"You shouldn't worry about things like this so soon after treatment," he says. "You should be focusing on recovery, listening to your handler when he warns you of—"

It occurs to me that I haven't told him about Kevin. "Realm," I say. "They pulled Kevin off my recovery."

He looks over at me immediately. "When did that happen?"

"Yesterday."

Realm swears under his breath but then apologizes. "Don't worry," he says. "I'll check into it. I'm sure you're just too damn healthy to need a handler or something."

He lies back, but I notice a crease between his eyebrows as he stares away. I trust him to find out what happened. I think then that I should get up, put my shirt on at least, but instead we stay like this for a long time, not saying anything else.

It's nearly three a.m. when I get back out to the car, my headache little more than a dull throbbing now. I'd thought Realm would ask me to stay the night, but then he reminded me that my parents would probably report it if they woke up to find me missing. I didn't want to leave, though. I liked the freedom of being off the grid, if even for a few hours. No one watching me—dissecting my movements. Tomorrow I might have a new handler to face, or at the very least, I'll have to face my parents. I'll have to face James.

Just then my phone vibrates in my pocket, and I smile, thinking it's Realm, who wouldn't give me his number but took mine. But when I look at the message, my heart skips a beat. It's James.

"Don't read it, Sloane," I tell myself, dropping it onto the passenger seat before turning up the radio. I'm finally feeling decent for the first time in a while, and I don't need him screwing it up. I make it through one light before picking the phone back up and checking it.

ARE YOU OKAY? ☺ FOR YES, ☹ FOR NO.

Idiot. I ignore him, continuing to drive home, thinking about what Realm said. That sometimes it's better not to know. Maybe I should believe him. He has no reason to lie to me.

In my lap my phone buzzes with another message.

I'm in front of your house. Come outside.

What is he doing at my house? I pull to the side of the road to type back a reply. A bitchy one. NOT HOME. JUST LEAVING REALM'S.

The minute I write it I want to take it back, the spike of guilt slamming me hard. Realm said that I'd loved James. Not just that he was my boyfriend, but that I loved him "madly." I look at my phone, but it's silent. I hate myself right now.

ON A ROMANTIC STORMY NIGHT? I'M SURE THAT DIDN'T GIVE HIM THE WRONG IDEA.

I groan. THOUGHT YOU DIDN'T CARE? First he pushes me away, and then has the nerve to—

I DON'T. NIGHT.

It's like the bottom drops out, leaving me sick to my stomach. But I know what it is now—the emotion. Should I tell James about our past? Does he even deserve to know that we'd had a relationship?

I glance at the clock. It's late, and I decide to shut off my phone, blocking James out of my life. I have to stay away from him. He's toxic to me. And I don't want to go back to The Program. I could never get through it again. So I pull back out onto the wet streets and find my way home, sneaking in without my parents ever hearing a thing.

I'm exhausted as I pull into Sumpter's parking lot before school. There was no handler waiting on my porch when I left, so my mother let me borrow her car. I thanked her, even though it took all my restraint to not call her out on her lies about my brother. Either way, I assume I'm free from monitoring now—although I've gotten no confirmation from Realm or The Program.

When I get out, James is standing next to his father's car, texting on his phone. Mine vibrates in my pocket, but I don't even look at it. When I turned it on this morning, I had five missed messages. But even now, I don't read them and just go inside the school.

In the past day have you felt lonely or overwhelmed?

NO. I scan the rest of the questions as I sit in first period and realize that I'm going to have to lie on this entire questionnaire. Filling in the rest, I stop at the last question, taking a breath.

Has anyone close to you ever committed suicide?

Yes. My brother—maybe others, too. But what do I fill in? The Program doesn't think I know. They think they've stolen the memories away. I nearly break off the tip of my pencil filling in NO.

"Are you ignoring me?" James whispers as he walks past my desk in math class. He doesn't wait for me to respond as he goes to sit in his seat, but his tone is clear. He's annoyed. Well, he can go to hell because I'm not taking the bait this time.

I stare down at my desk, pretending he didn't ask, and open my notebook. The class drags on, and I hear someone clear their throat repeatedly from the back. At one point, I sigh heavily and turn around to see James staring at me. I roll my eyes and go back to my math problems.

My phone buzzes, and I think that I shouldn't look. That I shouldn't give in to his tantrums. Discreetly, while the teacher is reading aloud from the textbook about a formula I can't quite remember, I check my phone.

YOU LOOK NICE TODAY. OH, AND I'M AN ASSHOLE. SORRY.

I press my lips together, trying not to smile. I will not let him make me smile.

NOT ACCEPTED. Way to take the high road, Sloane.

DID YOUR TONGUE SAY GOOD-BYE TO YOUR FRIEND AGAIN LAST NIGHT? I BET HE LIKED THAT.

YOU SAID YOU DIDN'T CARE. GET OVER IT.

MAYBE I'M CONCERNED ABOUT YOUR REPUTATION.

I stifle a laugh. REALLY?

NO. I'M JEALOUS.

I glance over my shoulder at him again, and meet James's blue eyes. He shrugs, looking a bit pathetic. Like maybe he is actually sorry. I turn back around and put my phone in my pocket, trying to think things over. I know I don't want to be with Realm, not like that. But honestly, James is a little much for me to handle, especially when he seems to like and then dislike me on a daily basis.

God, if I just had my memories, I'd understand everything so much more. I'd know what happened to my brother, to me and James. I'd know who my friends are. I'd know what happened with my parents. There's so much that is just out of my reach, but if I could only—

The bell rings, startling me. I get up slowly, trying to decide

SUZANNE YOUNG

my next move. Just then I see James walk by, a small smile on his lips as he passes. "See you around, Sloane," he says, too quietly for anyone else to hear.

And I know from the way my body reacts that Realm was right. I loved James. But maybe we're better off this way.

At the end of the day I wander around the halls for a bit, examining everyone as I pass them, trying to discern if I had possibly known them. I'm still getting headaches, but nothing like the one I had last night. I wonder if my brain has nearly finished repairing itself.

"Took you long enough."

I stop a few feet from my locker to see James standing there, looking bored in the now deserted hallway. "What are you doing?" I ask.

"I'm sneaking around with you. Let's go." He motions toward the back door.

"Um, no. You were pretty quick to dismiss my feelings last night. Something about not pretending that things were ever good . . ."

He smiles. "I say stupid things, Sloane. All the time. But maybe the thought of not talking to you again made me crazy. Maybe I couldn't even sleep. And maybe I'm trying to make it up to you."

"By possibly getting me in more trouble?"

"That's the idea."

And I can't help it, I laugh. The devious spark in James's eyes makes me think that trouble from The Program is exactly what he wants. Is that what I'd liked about him before? His defiance?

"If anyone sees us together, they're going to call my mom. And then she'll call The Program," I say.

"Then we should hurry up and get out of sight. You ready?"

I debate whether I want to purposely break the rules even more. Realm told me to stay alive, to stay safe. This could jeopardize both.

"You will have so much fun with me," James whispers.

"Yeah?"

"I'll try like hell."

I sigh, taking one more cautious look around the hallway, and then before anyone can notice, I grab my stuff and follow James out of the school.

CHAPTER TWELVE

"SEE YOU HAVE YOUR DAD'S CAR AGAIN," I SAY AS we drive.

"Stole it. He doesn't like me to take it anymore. Something tells me that he never did, but he was trying to be nice after I got back from The Program."

I twist my hands in my lap, not sure if I should bring up our past relationship. I notice as he drives that James has the string from my shirt still around his pinky. "Where are we going?" I ask.

"There's this spot I found the other day. It's . . . beautiful. I wanted to show someone, but, well. I don't really have any friends."

"Maybe it's your sparkling personality."

He laughs. "Come on, Sloane. I'm not that bad, am I?"

"You're awful."

His smile fades as he seems to think, taking us past fields and pastures. "I don't like getting hurt," he says. "I remember that, even from being a kid. I think it has to do with my mother leaving—even if I don't know why or how—but I like to keep everything at a distance. That way it can't destroy me."

"You must have let Brady in," I say quietly. He must have let me in once too.

James nods. "And now that relationship is gone and it kind of hurts. Knowing that I had something that isn't there anymore. It's like a hole in my chest. Sometimes I think that pain might kill me."

I understand what he means. This emptiness that doesn't seem to have a reason. Something that can't be filled in. I know now what Realm meant when he said keeping one or two memories could drive you mad.

James exhales heavily and then goes to turn on the radio. "You're ruining the fun, Sloane. This was supposed to cheer us up."

"You're right." I settle back in the seat and watch him for a minute, liking the easy, calm expression on his face, especially when I know there's something darker underneath. And that maybe the other side of that darkness is fierce love.

A love he had for me.

James turns onto a two-lane street, and I notice his arm again, the white scars that are there. Absently I reach out and run my index finger over them, and he takes in a quick breath.

"Sorry," I say, dropping my hand. "I'm just wondering what they're from."

"It's okay," he says. "When I got back I asked my dad about them. He said I had had an ugly tattoo, and The Program removed it. Strange, right? That they'd just take ink off my body. If I'd known they were going to do that, I might have gotten a special message for them tattooed on my ass."

"Graphic."

He laughs. "Sorry." James looks at me, his eyes traveling over me like he's trying to figure me out. "It felt nice," he says quietly. "When you touched me like that."

Butterflies flutter in my stomach, but James goes back to watching the road. I reach out again, my fingers trembling slightly as I run them carefully over his scars. Tracing the patterns there.

I watch as his shoulders relax and his mouth softens into a smile. His skin is so warm, and I think that I must have liked touching him before. I lean forward and press a gentle kiss onto his scars. And then I straighten and look out the passenger window, desire filling my entire body.

"I kissed it and made it all better," I say.

And it's quiet until James responds, "Yes, you did."

My pulse has mostly calmed when James pulls up next to a grassy hill. He shuts off his car and then reaches into the back to grab a blanket.

"This is it," he says, sounding pleased. I stare out the

window, my heart in my throat. "What's wrong?" he asks.

"It's . . ." I try to catch my breath, push away the sadness. "We're at the river," I say.

"I know it's a little cold out, but this place is gorgeous," he tells me, as if I need convincing. As if this is the first time I've been here.

I look over at him, tears in my eyes. "I know," I say. "Brady used to take me here all the time."

James's face falters, and he glances down at the towel in his hands. I can see him searching for the memories and I know the minute he can't find them. "Sorry," he murmurs. "We should—"

"No," I say. "I love this place. Honestly." And I mean it. If I was ever going to feel close to my brother, it would be here. James seems comforted by this as he climbs out of the car. He waits for me before walking over the grass.

The river is breathtaking. The sun glitters off the surface as tiny ripples wrap around the bigger rocks on the side. "This is even better than I remember," I say.

"I was hoping you'd like it."

I look sideways at him. "You thought of me?"

He shrugs and I wonder if he didn't mean to admit that out loud. We face the slow-moving water, birds chirping above us as the trees close us in, making the area intimate. Private.

I'd spent years in this spot, years watching my brother jump into the river. He loved it here, and the fact that James does too only confirms that they were close. That we'd all spent a lot of time together.

James spreads out the blanket, and then when I'm next to him, we sit quietly, arms resting on our bent knees as we watch the water.

And for a minute, I feel like I'm home. Not my actual house, which is currently strangling me with the lies that I've been told. But my true home, here at the river with James, with the memories of Brady. I have the urge to rest my head on James's shoulder, but I don't think I should.

James shifts and his body bumps mine, knocking me sideways. He mumbles a halfhearted apology and then lies back, putting his hands behind his head as he stares up at the clouds.

I settle next to him, looking around us, the cool breeze sending goose bumps over my skin. It's so peaceful here that I don't think I ever want to leave.

After some time passes, James yawns dramatically. "Hey," he says. "You want to go swimming?" He looks over at me, squinting his blue eyes against the sun.

"It's cold. And besides, I don't know how to swim."

"Seriously?"

I nod.

James sits up, curling his leg underneath him, an expression of disbelief on his face. "Well that's just goddamn sad, Sloane. What are you, five? Get undressed. I'm teaching you right now."

I laugh. "First, no. I'm afraid of water. And second, why am I getting undressed again?"

His lips curve up. "You don't have to be scared. I won't let you drown."

My heart is pounding at the thought of getting in the water, but James isn't helping to calm me down. "And the clothing option?" I ask.

"That would just be for fun. I promised fun, remember?"

I shove him then, laughing as I do. James stands, towering over me as I lie on my side, staring up at him. "Come on," he says, seriously. "Come in the water with me. I'll take my clothes off too."

"Something tells me you just really want me to see you naked."

"Maybe you'll be impressed."

"Oh my God." James has a talent for making me forget the world around us, for making it all feel normal. I'm sure that's why I loved him. Or at least part of why.

Even though it's barely sixty degrees outside, James pulls his shirt over his head, the muscles corded and strong over his body. He pulls down his shorts and stands in just his boxer briefs, windmilling his arms as he stretches. He glances over at me. "See. You look impressed."

I smile. "Maybe a little."

"Do you need help with your shirt?"

"No, I think I'll keep it on. But I will enjoy watching you freeze your ass off."

"So impressed," he says over his shoulder as he walks to the water. He swims out to a small boat dock on the other side of the bank, waving to me once he's on it. Then he does a flip before splashing into the river below, reminding me of my brother when he does.

His clothes lie in the grass, crumpled up. I consider hiding them, leaving him to drive home in a pair of wet boxer briefs. James is splashing, yelling in a shaky voice that he's not even cold. I pick up his jeans and fold them over my arm, looking toward the path. But when I start to walk, something falls out of his pocket.

At first I worry that I lost his house key or something important, but then I spy an object a few feet away. When I recognize it, tingles race over my skin. I get down on my knees and crawl over to it. I drop James's pants and pick up what I'd so nearly lost.

It's a ring. A pink plastic heart similar to the one I'd found in my mattress. James must have given me the other one, and it must have meant something for me to save it. For a second there's a hint of a memory, just a flash of me stuffing it into my bed, but I can't hold on to it. Instead I start to cry. I clutch the ring to my chest and then fold over, my cheek on the grass.

I'm not complete. I'm missing a huge piece of my heart, memories of things I must have said and done, things I can't have back. I want them, all of them. I want to be myself again.

"Sloane?" James's voice is frantic. Drips of river water hit me before he kneels down on the grass beside me. His arms wrap around me, his skin cold against mine.

"This ring," I say, holding it up to him. "Where did you get it?"

"After we texted last night, I went to Denny's to sulk. I saw it in a gum ball machine there." He reaches to take it from me, possessive of it. "I felt bad for the things I said to you, and when I saw it . . . I don't know. I had to get it for you." He studies my expression. "Is that dumb?"

I shake my head. "No. You've . . . I think you've given it to me before. A different ring." I smile, wiping at my cheeks. "But just as cheesy."

James's eyebrows pull together as he thinks, looking down at the ring in his hand. Then he takes my finger and slides the ring on. We both sit there, staring at it, trying to decide if it belongs there or not. When James and I look at each other again, we're both confused, unable to remember why this ring is so important to us.

"Can I do something?" James asks, still holding my hand.

"What?"

"Can . . ." He pauses. "Can I kiss you, Sloane?"

That was so not what I was expecting him to say. I don't answer at first, and James drops my hand and crawls closer to me, his face near mine as he's poised almost over me. My heart races as I stare back at him. He's so beautiful.

"Please?" he whispers. "I really want to."

Something about the way he watches me—a knowing look that seems to see into my heart. "I don't know," I say, my chest tightening as I let my feelings for him spread over me, leaving me unprotected and vulnerable. His expression grows serious, as if I'm refusing him. But then I put my hand on his cheek. The hand that wears his ring.

"Okay, yes," I say.

James smiles quickly, and then leans forward to press his mouth to mine, laying me back in the grass as he kisses me passionately. His lips are hot, and I dig my fingers into the bare skin of his back, kissing him like I've missed him my whole life. They way he moves, tastes—it's all so familiar, and yet . . . not.

The sun lowers in the sky, the temperature dropping further. But it doesn't make us stop. Every second lasting both forever and not long enough. And when we're thoroughly exhausted, still dressed, James collapses next to me, laughing out loud.

"This is the first time in almost three months that I've felt anything at all," he says.

"Was it good?"

"Oh, yes. That was all sorts of good."

I slap his chest. "I meant the feelings. Were they good?"

James moves then, rolling so that I'm under him. He brushes my hair away from my face. He's tender and defenseless, as if every part of him is exposed. He's not the asshole I thought he was, not even close. What I see is someone broken and fierce. Someone loyal and hardened. Someone who could belong to me completely, and me to him.

James smiles as he traces his finger over my mouth. "I think . . ." He stops and looks into my eyes, his stare arresting, pinning me in place. "I think I'm in love with you," he whispers. "Is that crazy?"

His words strike my heart, and the ache that's been a constant in my chest goes away completely. I lick my lips and smile. "So crazy."

"Then I guess I love you madly." And then he leans down and kisses me again.

CHAPTER THIRTEEN

AS WE HEAD BACK TO TOWN WE'RE QUIET, BUT NOT
uncomfortably so. James keeps my hand in his lap, playing with
my fingers. His every touch is gentle, yet possessive. I'm sure he
feels the same way I do. As if we've done this before.

I think about telling him about our past, but decide against
it. I'm not sure how to say it without sounding like I made this
happen somehow. Manipulated him. I don't want him to think
that. I want this all to be real.

"What do we do now?" I ask him, because I know one of
us has to ruin the moment. "My parents will never let me date,
and definitely not you. And then there's The Program. I may
not have a handler anymore, but Kevin was pretty adamant
that I stay away from—"

James's jaw tightens, but then he shakes his head. "I don't

care what they think. I don't care what anyone thinks."

"They can send you away again."

"I'm not scared."

Worry pulses though me, and I lean over, putting my chin on his shoulder. "What if I'm scared for you?"

James looks sideways at me. "Aw . . . look at you being all sweet. Told you you'd be impressed." He kisses me quickly and then goes back to the road, as if that's the end of the conversation.

"James," I say, feeling tension starting to settle in my shoulders. We've been gone most of the day. It was reckless. I'd pushed the idea away until now, enjoying the freedom of being with James instead. But now I know how stupid it was.

I check my phone and see that I've missed four calls from my house and one from a private number. "My parents have been looking for me," I say.

Something in the tone of my voice makes him turn. I watch as his sun-kissed skin pales, his fingers tightening on the steering wheel. "What do you think they'll do?" he asks.

And then I know it, feel it inside. "James," I say, choking up as the realization slides over me. "My parents are the ones who sent me to The Program in the first place. I think . . ." And the idea is horrible. The fact that they betrayed me like that. "I think my mother is the one who did this to me."

I can still see her face when I'd told her off the morning Kevin was waiting at the front door. And I know I've seen it before, that look of stubborn love that makes her think she's doing the right thing. Kevin took me to The Program from my own house, which means my parents had to be in on it.

James's expression is pained and he chews on his lip. "Call home," he says. "Call home and put it on speaker."

"What? Why?"

"So I can listen."

I'm terrified of what will happen. I check the clock and see that it's nearly six. My fingers shake as I dial. James glides the car into the empty lot of an abandoned farm, and parks.

I blow out an unsteady breath, clicking on the speaker just as it starts to ring. My mother answers immediately, and I almost hang up.

"Hi," I say.

"Sloane! Where are you? We've been so worried." In the background there is a rustling, making me think she's covering up the receiver. I swallow hard.

"I'm okay," I tell my mother. "It was such a beautiful day; I thought I'd go swimming."

"I need you to come home, honey," my mother says calmly. She doesn't acknowledge the fact that I can't swim. My breath is caught in my throat.

"Hang up," James says then. "Hang up the phone."

"Who is that?" my mother shouts quickly. "Sloane, who are you with?"

I click END, and then lower the phone to my lap. "She wasn't alone, was she?" I ask, too devastated to look up.

SUZANNE YOUNG

"No. I don't think so."

I let the realization hit me. I know my mother loves me; I'm sure I've always know that. And in her heart, she believes in The Program. And because of that . . . I can never trust her again.

"Sloane," James says. "It's going to be okay. I won't let anything happen to you."

I meet his eyes. "Promise."

"Yes."

"Do you think you promised that before?" I want to tell him then, tell him about us. But he seems hurt that I asked him about before, like I've accused him of something.

"If I'd promised you, Sloane, then they wouldn't have taken you to The Program. I would have died trying to protect you. I wouldn't have let you down. I'd hate myself if I did." He shakes his head as if he can get rid of the thought. "No, I'm promising it now—even if it means running away. Hiding out for the rest of our lives. I promise I won't let anything happen to you. Can you trust that?" James's face is scared.

And I don't know what happened to land us in The Program, but the truth is, we did let each other down one way or another. We didn't make it. But I have James back, here and now, as mine.

I grab him by the collar of his shirt, letting the phone fall to the floor. I pull James to me, kissing him hard. His hand is in my hair as he kisses me back. The sky is darkening from the setting sun, but we climb into the backseat, yanking at each other's clothes, tongues tangling in a heat that I know I could never have with anyone else. This could be the last time I see him. This could be the end.

"I think I broke my femur," James says, as he lies underneath me. "On the console when you were attacking me? I think I broke it."

I laugh. "Shut up."

"I didn't mind, though," he says conversationally. "Like when you bit my shoulder. It was—"

I reach up and put my hand over his mouth, not moving it even after he licks my fingers. "Shut. Up." As if agreeing, he pulls me closer, resting his cheek on the top of my head. When it's quiet, I move my palm and rest it on his chest.

"It was nice," he whispers, but not jokingly. "It wasn't weird, either. And that's . . . kind of weird."

I close my eyes. "It's like we've been here before," I say quietly, wondering if he knows the truth.

He doesn't answer and I put my elbow in the corner of the seat, rising up to stare down at him. He smiles when I do, looking completely and utterly in love with me. "You brought protection," I say. "Expecting this?"

"No," he says. "But it's good to be prepared."

"You expected this."

"I hoped, maybe."

"James!"

"What? I got you a ring!"

I'm still laughing as I lower my head to his neck, resting it there and letting the night fall around us. We've probably set off every red flag there is, and yet, I'm not sure I'd change any of it. Being here with James is just—

"You're right, you know," he says. "You're just right for me. And I'd bet my life that we've done this before. Because I can't imagine I wouldn't have fallen in love with you the first time."

I smile, looking at the pink ring on my finger, at the fading scar on my wrist, and I think that we've been through a lot to get here. And I'm never going back.

Once we're dressed and driving again, James stops at the gas station to get us snacks, our improvised dinner. I called Lacey, but when she didn't pick up I tried her house. Her mother said she was out on a date. I'm just hanging up when James returns with a paper bag filled with beef jerky and a map of local campsites.

This is dangerous. We've screwed up pretty big, and yet we're not trying to change course. Clearly we've both lost our minds. My thoughts turn to my parents. Even though I'm angry, I can imagine my father sitting on my bed, staring out my window and wondering if I'm okay, or if I've killed myself. My mother is probably on the phone with The Program, begging for them to save me.

I've let them down, and obviously not for the first time. After all, they had thought the only course of action was The Program. They let them change me.

"Hey," James says quietly. I look at him and see the way he

watches me, filled with worry. "You're wasting perfectly good protein." He motions to the Slim Jim in my hand and smiles, but it's forced. It's his way of calming me, I think.

My phone buzzes in my pocket, and I jump, startled. "It's from a private number," I say when I look at it. "Maybe it's Realm?"

"That would be awesome," James murmurs, and opens his PowerBar to take a bite as we sit in the parking lot of the gas station.

I don't respond, feeling guilty for not telling James about what happened, or almost happened, at Realm's house. I open the message.

I NEED TO SEE YOU IMMEDIATELY.

When I repeat it to James, he scoffs. "Of course he does."

Realm knows about me and James—our past—so I don't think this is a social call. He must know that my parents are looking for me. Or The Program found out that he helped me and tracked him down. I'm suddenly scared for him.

"I have to go to Realm's house," I tell James quickly, moving to snap on my seat belt.

He tenses. "Why? I didn't kiss you good enough?"

"Hey!"

James winces. "Sorry. That was uncalled for. What I mean to say is, do you think he'll taste me on your lips?"

"Hey!"

James closes his eyes, then looks at me apologetically. "I'm not normally a jealous guy, I swear," he offers as explanation. "At least as far as I can remember. But when it comes to Michael Realm, I might be a little murderous. But just a little." He pinches his fingers together.

"I'm not going to Realm's house to hook up. He needs to see me, James. He might be in trouble for helping me."

"A real nice guy to drag you into his mess."

"He's my friend. Can you not be a jerk about it?"

James doesn't answer at first, just turns over the engine and pulls out into the street. "Fine," he says, like he doesn't care either way. "But if he kisses you, I'm going to fight. I'm completely immature like that."

"I know."

James exhales, checking his rearview to make sure no one is following us. Our time is running out. I'm not sure we can escape The Program. Especially when I know that we couldn't before.

CHAPTER FOURTEEN

MY HEART SKIPS A BEAT WHEN I SEE A BLACK ESCALADE near Realm's house, the windows tinted too dark to see in. As James parks and turns off the engine, I wonder if I should be scared. What if this is a setup? Would Realm do that to me?

"I don't like this, Sloane," James says, meeting my eyes. "Whose car is that?"

I shrug, but my hands are starting to shake. "He wouldn't turn me in," I say, but I sound like I'm trying to convince myself. "He knows a lot of stuff, and that message . . ." I look down at my lap, my throat beginning to constrict with fear. "It has to be important."

James puts his hand over mine. "Let's just leave. I'll take care of us." When I look up, James's expression is desperate.

"I know, but—"

Just then the front door of the house opens, and a woman walks out onto the porch as if she's been waiting for me. I recognize her immediately, even though she's not wearing sunglasses this time. She was there the day Realm was released from The Program. The sight of her brings a sick feeling to my stomach, confirming that something *is* wrong. Where's Realm?

"Is she from The Program?" James asks, putting his fingers on the key in the ignition, ready to turn it on.

"No," I say. "She picked Realm up from The Program." The woman puts her hands on her hips as if impatient, and I look at James. "I should talk to her," I say.

James groans. "If I see anything strange, I'm getting us out of here. I'll throw you over my shoulder if I have to."

"Like some crazed Neanderthal?"

"Total caveman."

I smile and lean forward to kiss his lips softly, nervously. And then I get out.

The wind blows my hair around my face as I slowly approach the house, my heart thudding wildly in my chest. I half expect a handler to jump out from the bushes to grab me, inject me with a sedative. I take a nervous glance back at James, who is watching intently from the car.

"Michael's not here," the woman calls as she waits for me to get to the porch. "And he's not coming back."

I take in a startled breath, stopping at the bottom of the steps. "He's not coming back? My God, is he okay?"

The woman tilts her head, looking me over. "He's fine. But like I said, he won't be back."

I look around, devastated that he'd just leave without telling me first. Without saying good-bye. I was just here yesterday. "Who are you?" I ask the woman.

"I'm Anna, Michael's sister. I take care of things when he's away." She smiles at me then, sizing me up. "He said you were very pretty."

I'm staring at her, confused. Upset. "I don't understand," I say. "He just sent me a text. Why would he—"

Anna holds up her hand to stop me. "I sent the text, Sloane. Michael left this morning. But he wanted me to speak with you. He said you'd need him."

"I do," I say. "I'm in trouble, and I need him right now. So call him and tell him to come back!"

"Sloane," she says kindly. "There's a lot you don't know about Michael, and his reasons for leaving—I promise—were out of his control. But he cares about you. He wants me to help you."

Realm always wanted to help me. He was all I had in The Program. He was good. Safe. "How are you going to help me?"

"There are things that Michael didn't tell you—things he doesn't think you could forgive. But he wants you to know that he loves you. That he wants you to be happy." She pauses and meets my eyes. "But more than anything, he wants you to run."

"*Run?*" Fear streaks down my back. I'm frozen in place, unsure of how to respond.

Anna looks past me, toward the car. "Is that James?" she asks, nodding toward him.

"Yeah." I search my memories, wondering if there will be a hidden clue to what's going on, but there's nothing. I'm completely lost.

"My brother doesn't like him much." Anna smiles at this. "But he understands."

"Understands? I'm freaking out right now. What's going on?"

Anna must hear in my voice that I'm done with the cryptic messages because she sighs, as if dreading this part. "They've been monitoring you, Sloane. Texts, phone calls. Midnight drives? They came and saw Michael today, knowing that you were here last night. The minute they left, he called me to come by. Said he was leaving, that he had no choice but to . . . fulfill an obligation, let's say. But he knew you were in danger, you and James, so he left you some provisions. Even made me promise to give up my car." She laughs at this, but she doesn't seem bitter. "My little brother can be fairly convincing when he needs to be. Then again, he's all I have left. And vice versa."

I can understand that she would do this for her brother, knowing that no matter how crazy the request, I would have done anything for Brady. Realm had said that he didn't have anything outside The Program. I wonder why he never told me he had a sister.

"Kevin is a friend of ours," she continues. "And when he got pulled off your case, Michael knew something was up. Obviously he was right. I'm sure you're aware that there is an

Amber Alert out for the two of you right now." She motions to James.

"What? No. I . . ." And now I know that I can't go home. That the flag has been thrown and nothing can be the same again, or at least, the same as it was a few weeks ago. I want to panic, but I'm trying to keep it together. I'm trying to be strong.

"The epidemic is spreading," she says. "Michael wants you to go east—says there's a group there that can help hide you. Kevin will help. He's been conspiring with your friend Lacey for some time. They know about the rebels."

"Rebels? Against The Program?"

"You don't have to be part of it. Michael never was. He honestly believed in The Program, maybe even still does a little. But things are changing. He thought that your James might take up the cause. He says he's quite the troublemaker."

We both look back at James then. He's behind the wheel, the phone to his ear as he argues with whoever is on the other end. His father? It's clear by the expression on his face that it's done, the life we had here. When he sees me watching, James's mouth stops moving and he lowers his phone. He knows they're looking for us too.

"You should go," Anna says. "The car has a few supplies, a little bit of money and directions. Kevin will be waiting with Lacey at the rest stop on the Idaho border. Pick them up and leave the state. Michael will find you," she says. "When he can, he'll find you."

I stare at her, seeing a small resemblance between her and

Realm. I'm about to wonder if I should trust her when I realize that I don't have any other options. This is our only hand to play.

Anna gives me the keys to the car before starting to walk into the house. She pauses suddenly, and turns to me. "Michael wanted me to give you one last thing," she says. She removes a small plastic bag from her coat pocket and holds it out to me. I take it and peek inside. There is one bright-orange pill.

"It's meant to bring back the lost memories," she says. "Some more quickly than others. Michael got his hands on it when he was in The Program. He'd been saving it for when it was all over." She swallows hard. "But he wants you to have it instead. He has a warning, though." Anna takes a step closer to me, her eyes deadly serious. "He said that some things are better left in the past. And true things are destined to repeat themselves."

I touch the small pill, wondering if it could have all that power, all the power to make me whole again. "He only gave me one?" I ask, thinking of James.

"There is only one," she whispers. "And now it's yours. Michael is giving you the choice that The Program didn't. But he was very clear that if you take this pill, you might never forgive him. You might hate him."

And suddenly I wonder what secrets Realm has been keeping from me. "I could never hate him," I say, even though now I'm not so sure.

"Easy to say when you don't remember." She walks away then, pulling open the front door, but stopping to look back at me. "You'll be the only one who remembers, Sloane, and that in itself could be a curse. I hope you choose wisely. I'd hate to hear that you couldn't handle it, and terminated." She presses her lips into a sympathetic smile. "I think that sometimes the only real thing is now."

I don't answer, and watch as she goes inside, leaving me on the darkened porch of my lost friend's house. I gaze down at the bag, my back to James as I reach inside to take out the pill. I stare at it so long that my vision starts to tunnel—the color just a streak across my mental picture.

I blink quickly and look at it again, wondering how it would change me—getting my life back. I'd remember Brady's death—feel that pain all over again. And then there's the life I had with James. I could take this pill and remember *everything*, but James still wouldn't. Can I really handle loving him completely when he's still so new to accepting us? Or what if we never really loved each other at all? What if Realm was wrong about that?

I could give James the pill, but what if he finds some horrible truth about Brady or me or his mother? He could realize that there really isn't anyone to trust. Maybe we all betrayed each other.

It's like I hold a lifetime in my fingers. I'd be complete, but at the same time . . . what if I don't like who I was?

I look to the sky where the sun has set, leaving the clouds streaked in the same shade of orange as the pill. Realm has given me a gift—a choice. He's given me his friendship, his love, and in my way, I love him back. But he said I wouldn't forgive him for the things I'd find lost in my head. Do I believe that? Do I believe him?

Tears race down my cheeks, and I stare down, one small object so full of information. Life. Loss. Right now, I have what I need. I have James. A way out of here. But this could all be a lie, a hanging string to be pulled, unraveling everything.

Can I stand knowing what happened to my brother that day? James and I were there, but we hadn't stopped it. There's the slash on my wrist. The way my mother looks at me, filled with concern and knowledge. God, what if I was a horrible person? Maybe . . . maybe that's why I wanted to die. Maybe I was the reason James wanted to die.

A small whimper escapes my lips as I let the pill drop back into the bag. I want to crush it under the heel of my shoe, but I'm terrified that I'll change my mind later. So I fold the bag into a small plastic square and stuff it into the back pocket of my jeans. I won't take it, but I won't destroy it, either. At least not yet.

And with that choice, my heart breaks. I'm saying good-bye to who I used to be. Who I can never really be again. The people I once knew are different. Some are changed like me, others are dead. Knowing that can only bring me more pain. More agony.

I miss Realm, and I'm glad I won't know what he doesn't want me to remember. This way, I'll forever keep him as my friend and hero. There's nothing wrong with that.

This is the only choice.

I straighten my posture as I glance down the driveway to where James is parked, loving me madly. Loving me for who I am now.

We'll meet Lacey and Kevin and sneak away, start over somewhere else. We'll leave our parents, our lives. But most of all, we'll leave the reach of The Program.

And as I walk back to the car, the pill safely tucked away in my pocket, I think that maybe Realm is wrong. That James isn't the only troublemaker, the only one willing to take up the cause. He's not the only one who wants to fight.

So with that thought, I begin again—thinking to myself that sometimes . . . the only real thing is now.

EPILOGUE—TWO WEEKS LATER

AT THE DOOR OF THE LEISURE ROOM, THE GIRL pauses. Her body hums from the latest round of medication and she looks wearily at the handler near the door. The Roseburg facility is crowded and loud, and the girl swallows hard and turns to the nurse next to her.

"I want to stay in my room," she mumbles.

Nurse Kell smiles, her face filled with compassion as she brushes the girl's strawberry-blond hair off her shoulder. "Why don't you try and make friends, Allison? It's good for your recovery."

Ally scoffs. "What's good for my recovery is going home!" Her voice is loud, and several patients and handlers look over. Ally notices a guy at the table, a pretzel stick dangling from his lips like a cigar, staring at her.

"William," Nurse Kell says softly. "I think I may need assistance." Her voice is curt, and when Ally notices that she's motioned to the handler, she backs away.

"No," Ally says quickly. "I'm sorry. I—"

"There you are, sweetness," a voice says. Ally turns around just as the guy takes the pretzel from his mouth, looping his arm in hers. "I thought we were playing cards today?" He widens his eyes as if telling her to go along with it. Ally shoots a look at Nurse Kell, and then the guy next to her clears his throat. He glares daggers at the handler, and William backs away, raising his hands almost apologetically.

"Right," Ally says, nodding quickly, tightening her grip on the guy's arm. "Sorry I'm late."

"It's okay." He grins. "But now you owe me." He nods at the nurse and she rolls her eyes at him, as if he's always doing things like this. Then the guy pulls Ally toward the table where two others sit, holding cards.

"Aw, come on!" one of the boys yells, slapping down his hand. "You're always trying to bring in girls, Realm."

"Yeah, yeah," he responds. "But look how nice this one looks." He turns and winks at Ally, pulling out a chair for her. She sits down, her heart racing at the thought of being thrown into isolation again. She wants to go home, but there doesn't seem to be a way. This guy, though. He seems to have it figured out. He's probably a good person to know in here.

Ally looks him over then. His hair is bleached blond, washing out his pale skin just a little. His eyes are a deep brown and very kind. He's cute—not that she should really notice in a place like this. And on his neck she sees a jagged pink scar, healed, but still dramatic. She feels a pang of sympathy for him.

"What's the game?" she asks quietly.

"Bullshit," Realm answers. "You know it?"

"No." Ally shakes her head.

"Hmm . . ." He looks around at the guys. "How about Asshole?"

Ally smiles, remembering how she'd taught her best friend's little sister to play last summer. The summer before her best friend killed herself. "Yeah," she says, lowering her head. "I know that one pretty well."

"Realm!" A voice cuts through the leisure room, and Ally looks up, startled, to see a girl walking toward them. Her hair is a bright orange, and she seems unsteady. Ally wonders how much medication she's on.

"Hello, Tabby," Realm mumbles.

"You said I could play!" The girl's voice is angry, and then she notices Ally sitting there. "How come she's here?"

"Sorry," Realm says, touching Tabitha's arm. "Table's full. Next time, okay?"

Ally considers leaving, feeling bad for shutting out this girl who clearly needs the game more than she does. When she goes to stand, she feels Realm's hand touch hers. "Stay," he says. His steady eyes meet hers, and she sits back down.

After the other girl is gone, Ally gnaws on her lip, feeling bad. "It's okay," Realm says, as if reading her thoughts. "Tabby always asks to play, but we don't let her. She won't mess with you, though. In fact, tomorrow she'll be here asking all over again." He lowers his voice, leaning his head toward hers. "QuikDeath," he whispers. "It gave her short-term memory loss."

"Oh." Ally fidgets uncomfortably as Realm shuffles the cards, introducing her to Shep and Derek—saying they've been here two weeks and will be out in four. Same with Realm. But they look comfortable with each other, as if they've done this a million times.

Outside, a storm is blowing wind and rain against the windows, sounding as if the world around her is washing away. Ally has felt this way before, just today, even. Dr. Warren told her she was being difficult, that measures would have to be taken if she didn't start cooperating. But now, watching these boys play with a sort of calmness, normalness to them, Ally wonders if maybe she can make it. If she can beat The Program.

"Your play, Sloane," Realm says, putting another pretzel between his lips.

"Ally." She looks sideways at him. "My name is Allison." She notices the pained look that crosses Realm's features, breaking his controlled expression. But then he looks at her, all smiles again.

"Sorry," he says. "My medication cocktail must have been a little too strong today. Allison," he continues. "Your play."

Ally nods and puts down her next card, noticing the warning glances the other guys give Realm. Shep mouths "shut up," but Realm doesn't say anything back. He stares through the window at the storm outside, a faint smile on his lips.

But by the time the game is over, Ally half thinks she imagined all the tension, because the boys are laughing and calling each other assholes. Everyone is content, almost dreamlike. Or maybe it was the pill Nurse Kell made Ally take. She can't be sure.

And later, when Realm asks Ally if he can walk her "home," she laughs, feeling the first bit of hope in a long time.